GOTH GIRL, QUEEN OF THE UNIVERSE

LINDSAY S. ZRULL

GOTH GIRL, QUEEN OF THE UNIVERSE

LINDSAY S. ZRULL

flux
®
Mendota Heights, Minnesota

First Edition
First Printing, 2022

Book design by Sarah Taplin
Cover design by Sarah Taplin
Cover illustration by Jordan Kincaid

Flux, an imprint of North Star Editions, Inc.

Library of Congress Cataloging-in-Publication Data
Names: Zrull, Lindsay S., author.
Title: Goth Girl, queen of the universe / Lindsay S. Zrull.
Description: First edition. | Mendota Heights, Minnesota : Flux, 2022. |
  Audience: Grades 10–12.
Identifiers: LCCN 2022008193 (print) | LCCN 2022008194 (ebook) | ISBN
  9781635830781 (paperback) | ISBN 9781635830798 (ebook)
Subjects: CYAC: Cosplay--Fiction. | Foster home care--Fiction. |
  Contests--Fiction. | Overweight persons--Fiction. | Mental
  illness--Fiction. | Detroit (Mich.)--Fiction. | LCGFT: Novels.
Classification: LCC PZ7.1.Z73 Go 2022 (print) | LCC PZ7.1.Z73 (ebook) |
  DDC [Fic]--dc23
LC record available at https://lccn.loc.gov/2022008193
LC ebook record available at https://lccn.loc.gov/2022008194

Flux
North Star Editions, Inc.
2297 Waters Drive
Mendota Heights, MN 55120
www.fluxnow.com

Printed in the United States of America

This book is for the foster kids who are still looking for their forever families.

And for Dixie and Kim, who found me when I was lost.

CHAPTER 1

ALL THAT WE SEE OR SEEM
IS BUT A DREAM WITHIN A DREAM.
EDGAR ALLAN POE, "A DREAM WITHIN A DREAM"

I'd be safer if I tried to blend in, but I've never been the kind of person who hides.

My black lace-up boots announce my arrival at Detroit River High. I own the corridor like I'm a model on an ironic linoleum runway in New York City. To my left, a group of band nerds snicker and stare at my glossy black lipstick. It doesn't matter. You learn a lot of rules as a foster kid who transfers between schools every few months. Want to know what the most important one is? Foster Care Pro-tip number one: The new girl is always a freak. Just embrace it.

"Hey, new girl!" someone yells. I pause, then turn to face a tiny blonde with the build of a ballerina. She's holding a plastic Starbucks cup in her hands. Her posse stands a few feet back, watching with obvious excitement. I smell a dare.

"Can I help you?"

"I think I saw you in *The Wizard of Oz*," she says through a fit of giggles.

I roll my smoky eyes and start to turn back around, but not before I get a face full of ice water. The shock of the cold makes me gasp. Everyone screams in laughter.

"Look! She's melting," someone yells.

There goes a perfect mascara application.

The hordes always think their jokes are clever. They're not. I've heard them all before.

Keeping my pride intact, I walk confidently in the direction of the nearest bathroom. The bell rings. Everyone rushes toward their nearest classroom, like cockroaches running for cracks in the walls. After slamming the bathroom door behind me, I cram the rubber stopper into the floor gap. I'm going to need some semblance of privacy to fix this disaster. When I finally get a glimpse of myself in the mirror, I groan. Mascara runs down my face in long, dark rivers. My lipstick is smudged, and the contouring I carefully applied to my round cheeks is patchy now. It took me two hours to perfect my look this morning. Thankfully, I took a dozen selfies before I left my new foster house, so I can still upload my masterpiece on Insta.

Now, I don't mean to sound like I'm some self-obsessed caricature. I worked hard for my confidence. I plan on keeping it intact, thank you. This look is my armor. I am an ethereal warrior, painted for daily combat. Besides, when you've spent your entire life bouncing from foster homes to group homes and back again, the fans start to feel like the only constant in life. They are the only real family I have.

But what to do now?

A good goth queen is like a good Girl Scout. We are always prepared. I take the emergency makeup bag out of my satchel and get to work. Prioritizing the disaster-relief tactics makes handling stressful situations like this easier. Step one: wipe off the drippy mascara. Step two: touch up the contouring. Step three: select a different lipstick. Now I'm in the mood for Goddess Green, with its earthy tones and tiny green sparkles. Let's see how the mindless hordes like that. Those witches won't get the best of me today.

When I finish my new look, I admire it in the greasy school bathroom mirror. Not bad. I reach into my satchel and dig around for my decade-old phone. It's the most I could afford on the monthly allowance I get from my social worker. The Edgar Allan Poe case I found for it is one of my prized possessions, however. The patron saint of goths stares up at me with his perplexed eyes, accented by his pinched tortured-poet brows.

I take a few selfies and upload them onto my Instagram, @GothQueen_13. I have followers from all across the goth spectrum. While I'd categorize my look as Nu Goth, since almost everything I own comes from thrift stores, I try to incorporate Victorian Goth aesthetics whenever I can—without the price tag. Hey, not every goth queen can afford ball gowns and corsets. A little second-hand velvet here, a nice vintage choker there, and I can look like the modern version of any classic gothic literature heroine.

On Insta, I add a caption about not letting the bullies win. My fans love it when I post about being myself in the face of ignorant buttheads, even if they don't know what my real adversity looks like. Aka: the foster care sob story.

When I'm done, I scroll through comments from this morning's look.

LiZZ13: "OMG you're like a dark LOTR elf!"

BloodFeud29: "What shade of lipstick is that? It would go perfect with my fae aesthetic. ☺"

LizardsRQT: "Seriously, how do you pull off masterpieces EVERY SINGLE DAY?!"

Reigna_NYC: "DM me. I'm your mother."

. . .

Wait. What?

My hands grip the cool white basin of the sink, grounding me where I stand, while my mind soars backward. Back to the last time I saw my birth mother.

I was seven. We lived in a small, dingy apartment that smelled of cat urine from years of tenants before us. We'd only lived there for a month when my mother started acting strange. New rules emerged without explanation. (1) No leaving the house. (2) No turning on the lights. (3) Keep the blinds closed. (4) Never speak louder than a whisper.

At first, the new rules were a game. Bumping around in the dark was a challenge I was happy to accept as a seven-year-old. But as time went on, I saw warning signs I'd witnessed in my mother many times before. These always led toward horrific events, like morbid bread crumbs of premonition. My mother began staying up all night, peering through the window blinds in the darkness. She paced in the living room for hours on end. She held conversations with herself, which were difficult to follow. She grew angry when floorboards creaked beneath my feet. At some point I realized we were in hiding. From who or what, I never knew.

I was vaguely aware that other kids my age were going to school. I watched through the blinds as they left the apartment building in the mornings and played outside in the late afternoons. The silence—the invisibility—began to eat me up inside. Have you ever wondered if you are *real*? I was a ghost, trapped between four cigarette smoke–painted walls.

One early evening, my mother fell asleep for the first time in days. I dared to turn on a lamp, keeping one trembling hand braced on the light switch while I watched my mother where she slept on the couch.

Bang! Bang! Bang!

Someone pounded on the front door, startling my mother from sleep. I fumbled for the light switch, but it was too late.

"What have you done?" my mother whisper-hissed at me, her eyes wide.

I loved my mother, but I was terrified of her when her eyes grew wild. I'd seen her like this before, many times.

The banging continued.

"I know you're in there!" someone yelled. "Open the door or I'll call the police!"

My mother grabbed my hand and dragged me into the bedroom. "Get under the bed."

I dropped to my stomach and shimmied under the bed frame, pushing aside long-forgotten socks covered in dust bunnies.

"Don't make a sound," she whispered as she pulled the bed sheets low so their seams brushed the floor in front of my face. I watched the pads of her feet walk out of the bedroom, disappearing back into the living room.

The lock chain on the front door rattled as my mother opened it. I can't remember what was said. All I remember was the unnatural calm of my mother's voice in the presence of screaming anger. I remember forgetting to breathe until my lungs felt like they would burst. But what I remember most from my hours under the bed was how I held my body perfectly rigid while I watched a family of spiders crawl around my frozen hands.

Sometime late in the night I must have fallen asleep. I woke up sore and groggy. Sunlight striped the floor from between the blinds. I held my breath to listen. The voices were gone. I dragged my body out from under the bed as quietly as I could, then I paused to listen again.

No sound.

The bedroom door creaked when I pushed it open. The echo reverberated in my bones.

Still nothing.

My hands instinctively covered my mouth, to muffle the sound of my heavy breathing as I tiptoed out of the bedroom and into the living room.

No one was there, not even my mother, who hadn't left the apartment in weeks. I checked every room. I was alone.

My mother never returned.

CHAPTER 2

OF MY COUNTRY AND OF MY FAMILY I HAVE LITTLE TO SAY.
EDGAR ALLAN POE, "MS. FOUND IN A BOTTLE"

I manage to make it to Spanish class, eventually. The teacher, Ms. Eva, lets me off with a warning for my extreme tardiness, given that it's my first day. I take an empty seat at one of the desks arranged U-shape style, encircling the teacher like she's a Shakespearean actor.

"Gracias, señorita," I say to her with a cheeky grin.

That's pretty much all the Spanish I know. Unfortunately, my head is far too chaotic to focus on verbs at the moment.

What. The. Hell.

Is someone trolling me? How would anyone even guess that I don't know my birth mom already? Online, I keep my private life *private*. I learned that the hard way when I was a kid. Tell the mindless hordes that you're a pathetic foster kid and they'll pounce like lions at the scent of blood. They'll tear your self-esteem to shreds and make you feel more worthless than you already do. Or worse, they'll pity you. Like I said, I had to work hard for my confidence. Which is why I never tell *anyone* about my background. Not even my beloved Insta fans. I don't want to ruin the one good thing I have going in my life.

Which is why I'm suspicious about this comment, very suspicious indeed. I clicked on the comment maker's profile. They appear to be a new user. Not a single photo upload yet, no bio, nothing. Smells like a rat. So I didn't respond. It only takes one infectious rodent to start a plague. See? History class taught me something useful after all.

I scratch my pencil into the edge of my Spanish worksheet until a tiny hole appears.

Ms. Eva walks up behind me. "Jess, less doodling and more conjugating, please."

I salute her and she walks away. What do homely Spanish teachers do when they get off work? Salsa dance in dimly lit clubs with men wearing tight pants? Take evening courses on Mexican cuisine with their gaggle of teacher girlfriends? I eye her from across the room. She has the face shape for a perfect Madonna. Along the edge of my worksheet, I make a bullet point list for her imaginary makeover. If I had her frame I would accentuate those killer cheekbones, dye my hair a richer shade of gold, manicure the brows just a tiny bit, but keep them thick and fierce like a goddess of art pop . . .

Someone is staring at me. I can feel it.

When I look up, there's a guy with round cheeks and giant puppy dog eyes staring back at me from a desk facing my direction. He glances away the second I make eye contact. I watch as his face grows bright red. His shaggy black hair covers his face as he leans over his Spanish worksheet, like that's what he's been doing all along. His T-shirt is a little too big, but he does have a specific aesthetic going on. I have to admire a guy who's brave enough to wear a howling wolf graphic from the early 2000s. Ironically? Unironically? Not sure yet.

I return to my work page, back to Ms. Eva's makeover. Perhaps I'd give her a rockabilly style with a kerchief tied in her hair and open-toed, chunky heels. Hey, I may be goth, but that doesn't mean I can't admire other fashion genres. My voluptuous frame straight up rocks my preferred dark aesthetic, but I can design the hell out of a badass skinny model just as well. I sketch out a new look for Ms. Eva, complete with high ponytail and a polka-dotted skirt.

The back of my neck starts to prickle again. I glance up at Geeky Guy. Unsurprisingly, he's staring. He visibly jumps, then looks back down at his desk, his face flashing crimson a second time. What's his deal? I can't be the first goth girl he's ever seen in this city. This time, I wait him out. My eyes drill holes through his skull and into his mushy, mushy brain. Eventually, he peeks up from behind the curtain of dark hair. I meet his gaze with one eyebrow raised, along with both of my middle fingers.

He doesn't gawk at me again for the rest of the hour.

When the class bell rings, everyone scrambles for the door. I don't *do* rushing, so I stuff my papers into my satchel at a leisurely pace. There's no point in running just to get to the next torture chamber. When I emerge into the hallway, normies run in all directions, complaining about teachers and hollering at their friends. I glide past them all, on my way to my locker to swap out my Spanish book for geometry. When I slam the locker door closed, Geeky Guy is standing next to me, his round cheeks the color of a fire-roasted tomato. He's not very tall, and his slouchy shoulders make him appear even shorter. A platinum-blonde Asian girl with a pixie cut leans against the lockers behind him, looking amused.

"Um, hi," Geeky Guy says as he fidgets with a thick paperback novel. "I'm Oscar."

I place one hand on my hip and wait. He obviously has more to say than hi.

"Sorry, it's just, I think we got off on the wrong foot." He looks back at Pixie Girl, who crosses her arms in front of her chest in an expectant stance.

Oscar tries again. "I just wanted to say sorry, I guess."

"You already did," I say.

"Yeah, you're right. Sorry . . ." He shakes his head, flustered.

So, the wolf T-shirt = not ironic. Just a guess.

"You apologize a lot, Oscar," I say.

"Yeah, sss . . . yeah." He stands in front of me for an awkward second.

"I'm not going to apologize back or anything."

"No, I wasn't expecting you to," he stammers. "I wanted to explain. I like your look."

Is this a setup? Coming from a guy who likely hasn't had a good haircut in, well, maybe forever, this seems like an odd comment. I glance at Pixie Girl. She's clearly enjoying this display. It makes me suspicious.

"My 'look.'" I stand up to my full height so I can stare down my nose at him. "Are you mocking me?"

"I'm serious!" he says, mild panic flashing across his eyes. He grips his novel to his chest like he's swearing on a Bible. There's an elaborate crown on the cover, bejeweled and dripping with crimson blood. It's surrounding a cold, pockmarked moon.

If I had a dollar for every time some kid pretended to like my "look" only to publicly humiliate me about it later . . . well, I wouldn't have to worry about paying my phone's data plan. I could buy a better phone, for that matter. And a car.

"Go away," I say, turning toward what I assume is the direction of the math hallway.

"Wait, I . . ."

"Listen"—I turn toward him menacingly—"if you think you

can set me up for another Wicked Witch of the West moment, you can go ahead and tell your little friends I'm not going to fall for it again." I point my chin toward Pixie Girl, who doesn't look afraid in the least.

Oscar just stares at me. "Who? Emily? She doesn't have anything to do with . . ."

I turn around again.

He follows me, reaching out for my shoulder. "Wait."

Before his hand can touch the fabric of my artfully ripped black T-shirt, I react. My arm reaches out, taking him by surprise as I elbow check him into a locker. Everyone in the hallway turns in our direction at the sound of his soft body hitting metal. Oscar looks up at me with a mixture of alarm and confusion. His book falls to the ground, the worn pages splayed out like a paper fan. The metallic title gleams under the corridor lights: *Prince of Moons*. Oh god, he's one of *those* people. Mega fans of the Prince of Moons series gobble up all the books, video games, and TV episodes from the infamous Prince of Moons universe. They're super geeks, one and all.

Pixie Girl—Emily—bends forward in laughter, her hands braced against her knees. I'm fairly certain there are tears from extreme amusement in her eyes.

I release Oscar and turn toward the math corridor, growling over my shoulder.

"Do not touch me. Ever."

People duck out of my way as I stomp past them. They give the weird new girl incredulous glares, like I've proved myself to be some kind of monster. Honestly, maybe I have.

Somewhere behind me, I hear someone whisper, "I knew she was crazy."

Is it just me, or is the air in this building getting thicker? Breathing is becoming a challenge in this humid hallway. Sweat prickles my forehead while my guts clench tight, like I'm unintentionally bracing for a hit.

My feet veer left toward the exit. Screw math class. I need fresh air to wrap my head around this bombshell that's already shaking up the carefully constructed walls of my composure.

No one notices as I slip out a back door during the between-class hustle. The cold January air hits my hot cheeks like a caress. I lean against the brick exterior of the building, watching as haggard Detroit city people hustle by on the sidewalk. Around here, it's not unusual to see kids skipping class. I don't intend to stay outside long. The school security guards will find me soon enough. I just need five minutes of calm.

With my eyes closed, I listen to the rattle of trucks on the street, horns honking with road rage, and the soles of shoes clacking along the sidewalk at a brisk pace. It's cold in Detroit. No one is wasting time walking at a leisurely pace in midwinter.

Then the sound of a raised voice shatters my ill-found peace. Someone is swearing at the top of his lungs, ranting in the cadence of someone lost to reason.

"I need a woman who's a *real* woman! Not some Nazi, bimbo, Redcoat bullshit bitch who doesn't like my music! Women don't like me because I'm a motherfucking genius!"

The logic is hard to follow, but the signs are not. Psychotic episodes aren't a rarity in a city where people can't afford health care to treat their mental illness.

When I open my eyes, I see him. He's pacing in circles on the sidewalk a block away. His sneakers are worn and he isn't wearing a coat, despite the freezing air. He's clearly agitated. He isn't talking to anyone in particular, just yelling into the abyss. His words float up above him in foggy bursts, lingering there like cartoonish speech bubbles of profanity.

"Do you know who invented the internet? I did! Those fuckers stole my idea and made billions off of it. What do I get? Nothing! I'm too smart for you all. You low-class idiots with nothing but a skanky-ass skirt to your names!"

People on the sidewalk are giving him a wide berth, crossing the street to avoid him. No one tries to talk him down. I suppose it's hard to blame them. You never know what a stranger in a rage could do to you. He is a modern-day leper. Rendered invisible by illness.

"FUCK YOU, MOTOR CITY!" he shouts. "AND FUCK YOU, BITCH!"

A woman in a long wool coat ventured too close. She entered his cage of misty January breath. She scurries away, visibly shaken.

Out of the corner of my eye, I can see the school security guards hustling toward him. For them, it's just another day on the job. Thank the Goddess, they don't notice me where I stand, huddled against the brick. They're distracted by the thunderously ranting man on the street, the poltergeist that walks among the living.

My hands are shaking, but not from the cold. Silent as a midwinter night, I duck back inside the school's heavy doors. They are meant to be a barrier between that world and the realm of scholarly achievements. Adults think school is a safe haven from the outside world. It doesn't feel that way to me. The bedlam is everywhere. It just takes different forms.

Something familiar is stirring inside me. Worries I thought I'd long ago forgotten. I know, without a doubt, that my old nightmares have come back to haunt me.

CHAPTER 3

THERE ARE SOME SECRETS WHICH DO NOT
PERMIT THEMSELVES TO BE TOLD.
EDGAR ALLAN POE, "THE MAN OF THE CROWD"

That afternoon, I sit alone on the school bus back to my new foster home. It's not the classiest ride in town, but it's free. I pull my janky phone out of my pocket and pop headphones into my ears so I can tune everyone out with the moody, orchestral sounds of Dark Sanctuary. Then I settle in to check my Insta comments. Whenever I start to feel lost in the world, all I need to do is look online. Yeah, there're a lot of jerks lurking on the interwebs, but Insta gives me one superpower: blocking. I use it liberally.

My Insta followers shower me with good vibes.

VicTORY33: "You're such an inspiration. Don't let anyone tear you down."

WightGrrl: "When life gives you sour limes, you pull an Elphaba."

Forest0Doom: "Bad Ass! You come back stronger every time."

Then, "DM me." From the same user who said she was my birth mom, @Reigna_NYC.

I chew on the corner of my lip, ruining my lipstick, for sure.

If this person is messing with me, they are crueler than any troll who called me hideous or shallow. My finger hovers over the block button. I can't make myself press it. Instead, I shove my phone back into my pocket and turn to stare out the window at the concrete landscape of Detroit. In the span of one block, we pass a colorful mural painted along the wall of an abandoned warehouse and a pile of dirty clothes, discarded from Goddess knows where. This city has been coming back from the brink of extinction ever since the hipsters moved in to "save" it, but that came with a whole different layer of problems. Sure, there are fewer abandoned houses and more community gardens. That means the rents are rising and the locals are getting pushed out of their communities because they can't afford to live here anymore. Detroit has a complicated history. Kinda like me.

I don't remember my father. Or even know his name, for that matter. All I know about my own family is that the State of Michigan took me away from my mother when I was a baby. Then again at five years. Then again at six. Then, the last time, when I was seven. Like I said, it's complicated. Each time my mom got her life together again, the state gave her another chance. But when your mom struggles with mental health, she doesn't always make the best decisions.

My social workers (of whom I've had several throughout my many years in the system) tell me that my mother was institutionalized after a breakdown of some kind when I was seven. She was released and given an opportunity to get me back as long as she did three things: (1) secure stable housing, (2) find a job, and—most importantly—(3) take her medications and keep seeing her doctors. Those things never happened, so I stayed in the system, wondering why I wasn't worth fighting for.

It hurt. A lot.

Thus, I've jumped from one living situation to the next, every few months. I've never been firmly rooted anywhere. I've never felt like part of a family or lived anywhere that I could honestly call home.

With squealing breaks, the bus stops at my street corner. The door folds open and I jump down onto the sidewalk. I kick city garbage down the block as I walk toward the brick bungalow I now live inside. Weeds grow between the cracks in the concrete front steps and there's a warm glow coming from the windows. After a few deep breaths, I push the door open. Inside the house, the air smells like caramelizing onions. The sizzle from the kitchen greets me at the front entrance.

"Is that you, Jess?" my new foster mom, Barbra, calls over the sound of pots banging.

All I want to do is run upstairs to my room, where I can exist in peace. Instead, I do what I'm supposed to do with every new foster placement: I make an effort to be likable. Even if that effort always fails in the end.

I pop my head around the corner and see Barbra laying a tortilla out on a hot pan. She reaches for shredded cheese, then applies a hearty amount to the top.

"I thought we could celebrate your first day at Detroit River High with a quesadilla." She smiles at me. She's making an effort too.

"Oh, um, thanks," I say as she piles cooked peppers and onions on top, then sandwiches the creation with another tortilla. The melting cheese oozes out the side. I fight the urge to retreat into the safety of my bedroom. I didn't eat today, since crowded cafeterias make me feel vulnerable, so I'm actually really hungry.

"I know you're vegetarian," Barbra says as she flips the quesadilla to toast the other side. "So I stocked the fridge with veggies for you. I want you to feel comfortable here. You can eat whatever you find in the kitchen."

Usually foster parents just scoff when I tell them I don't eat meat. So this unexpected gesture takes me by surprise.

"Don't you eat meat?" I ask.

Barbra cuts the quesadilla into triangles, then sets the plate down in front of me. "Yeah, I do. But I've been thinking I need to start eating healthier anyway, so you've given me a good excuse." She smiles brightly. "Besides, I've heard plant-based diets are better for the planet."

I decide not to point out that melted cheese is hardly healthy or plant-based. I don't want to give her any anti-cheese ideas, after all. On the table, I notice she's set up a selection of salsas, hot sauces, and a side of sour cream. I put a dab of salsa verde on one triangle and take a bite. Oh my Goddess. So good. For the last three years since I went veggie, I've mostly only eaten side dishes like mashed potatoes and salads, since foster parents usually refuse to make meat-free meals. I could get used to this.

Barbra watches me with a smile on her face. "How was your day?"

I shrug. "Fine." I don't make a habit of telling fosters details about my life. It's easier that way.

"Did you make any friends?"

I shrug again, then reach for the last slice of quesadilla. "Uh, not exactly."

"How about your classes? If you feel like you might be behind in anything, I'm happy to help you catch up."

Her earnestness makes me slightly uneasy. There's a proper order of things in the foster world: adults give me a place to sleep and food to eat. There's no obligation to be friends. I take the empty plate over to the sink and wash it.

"Thanks," I say. "I'll be sure to let you know."

Foster Care Pro-tip number two: Never admit if you need help. Fosters will hold that over your head forever, using your failings as a reason to punish you or give you up. Anything aside from the essentials for survival is extra, like guacamole. Additional services come with hefty fees.

"Is that a different shade of lipstick than you were wearing this morning?" she asks.

Warning! Warning!

I put the plate in the drying rack. "I have homework," I say.

"Oh, of course." Barbra moves to clear the table of its mosaic of spicy sauces. "Would you like to do it down here?"

"No, that's okay," I say quickly. "I'll concentrate better in my room."

I jump up the stairs, two steps at a time, and breathe a sigh of relief when I close the bedroom door. Solitude, at last. I pull my phone out of my satchel. After opening the Insta app, I open my DMs, then type in the profile name of the mysterious Reigna_NYC.

"How could you possibly know you're my mother?"

I hit send.

The memories I have of my biological mother are fogged with the perception of a child, like mist covering a scenic landscape. There is no doubt in my mind that my mother loved me before she disappeared, even if it was a confusing type of love.

I remember weeks of eating nothing except ice cream for breakfast, lunch, and dinner because my mother knew it was my favorite food. Then there were the days when she wouldn't leave the safety of her bed. She'd sleep the hours away as if she'd forgotten about me altogether. As a five-year-old, I'd stand on chairs to fill heavy pots at the sink, then lug them to the stove, sloshing water all over the kitchen floor. I knew how to boil noodles until they turned into an edible mash that I'd savor until my mother emerged from her darkened room, bleary-eyed like from a dream.

For months I'd go to school with my mother championing my every achievement. Then she'd start to shift into blurry lines, unrecognizable in her own transformation. One day she'd be a glorious visage, dressed impeccably in silk. The next day she'd forget to change out of her pajamas or put on jackets in the February cold. She'd cut the cord to the television, then sit watching its blank screen for hours. I'd find raw meat in the oven, covered in maggots, the stench making me gag when I threw it down the garbage chute. My teachers would call home to ask about my absences. My mother would turn off the phone.

Most of my memories make little sense to me now. They show my biological mother in conflicting lights. I've never been able to make sense of her two sides—the one that cared about me and the one that didn't. There *is* one thing that I'm sure of though: my biomom loved me once.

And I love her still.

CHAPTER 4

I CALL TO MIND FLATNESS AND DAMPNESS; AND THEN
ALL IS MADNESS—THE MADNESS OF A MEMORY WHICH
BUSIES ITSELF AMONG FORBIDDEN THINGS.
EDGAR ALLAN POE, "THE PIT AND THE PENDULUM"

When I wake up the next morning, there's no response from the mysterious Reigna_NYC. I try to put it out of my mind as I go through the best part of the day: my morning makeup routine.

Today, I've chosen hot-pink lipstick to complement smoky eye makeup lined with just a touch of fluorescent pink liner alongside the black. It takes practice to make smoky eyes look good, instead of like you fell asleep with too much eyeliner on after a long night of partying. I add a small stick-on crystal below my left eye, just for fun. It adds a pop of glamour to counteract the ripped fishnet tights I'm wearing underneath some black cutoff shorts. A scoop-neck T-shirt shows off a bit of shoulder. I'd enhanced it by tearing out the collar and embroidering some tiny skulls all along the back. Tasteful. I like it. My long hair is wrapped in a slick bun on top of my head. No elaborate braids today. I'm keeping it tight.

I run down the stairs two at a time. When I get to the kitchen, Barbra holds out a Pop-Tart and an open travel mug filled with steaming coffee.

"I figured you didn't have time to sit down for breakfast," she says.

My plan was to simply leave. I don't do family breakfasts, but the roasty smell of coffee makes my hands reach out for the mug in spite of myself. After one heavenly sniff, I screw the spill-proof lid on.

"Thanks," I say as I stuff the Pop-Tart into my satchel.

"I was wondering if you might want to go shopping this weekend?" Barbra asks.

I freeze. Not this again.

"What's wrong with my clothes?" I ask.

Every time I move to a new foster placement, I get this lecture. My clothes are too dark and my makeup too scary. No one will ever take me seriously if I look like a morbid clown. Fosters say I'll never get a job after high school. I'll fall in with a rough crowd. Blah. Blah. Blah. Every new foster parent tries their best to turn me into a "nice girl," like it's their good service to the world. Why do I have to look a certain way to be considered "nice"? Or—how about this —why should I want to be considered "nice" at all?

"There's nothing wrong with your clothes," Barbra says. "Actually, I like them very much."

Sure she does. I eye her cardigan and Midwest mom jeans.

She notices my skepticism. "I do! I figured it might be nice to get some new things to go with your new life. You know . . . new school, new house. You can pick out whatever style you like." She smiles. "And it might be fun."

I highly doubt that, but I shrug anyway. "Sure. Maybe."

"Okay," she says as I open the door. "Have a good day!"

Have I found myself in a '90s family sitcom? I run down the street just in time to jump on the bus where it waits at the corner.

"I won't wait next time," the grumpy bus driver warns.

"I won't ask you to," I say. My gut catches the back of a seat when the bus driver abruptly puts pedal to the metal. A full face-plant is narrowly avoided, thanks to my girth. There are some benefits to being a larger human.

"*Ow*," I mouth to myself. I won't give the bus driver the benefit of a full display of indignation.

After I sit down, I take a hesitant sip of coffee. Damn, that's good. Thank the Goddess for spill-proof travel mugs. If there's one great thing about Detroit, it's that its artisanal coffee–roasting game is on point. Well, there're a lot of great things about Detroit, but right now I'm worshiping the gods of caffeine, so that's where my prayer goes this morning.

My phone buzzes in my back pocket. I nearly drop it as I pull it out to check my Insta notifications. Nothing from Reigna_NYC. It's ridiculous, but my heart sinks a little. Okay, I'm getting way too invested in this mystery person. They're probably a troll. I distract myself by scrolling through my fan comments from this morning's look. As expected, many hands-raised emojis. Yeah, I know I'm rocking it today.

I stuff my phone into my satchel, then sip my coffee while Detroit whizzes by.

When I get off the bus at school, I hear someone calling my name. I'm sure they're yelling at a different Jess, so I keep on walking.

"Jess!"

God, there're a lot of people in this school. I turn sideways to squeeze past two separate groups of excited girls.

"Jess, wait up!"

I turn around. A few yards behind me, a hand waves up above the crowd of teens all filing toward the front doors. I pause and wait hesitantly for Oscar to catch up. Today his oversized shirt proudly displays a romantic scene of a knight on a rocky planet slaying a space dragon to save some damsel in the background. It has to be from *Prince of Moons*.

"Hi," he says, out of breath from his short run.

I give him my best What Do You Want stare.

"I just wanted to say I'm sorry again." He swipes his stringy hair away from his eyes.

"Like I said yesterday, you apologize a lot."

His lips literally squeeze shut momentarily to stanch the flow of apologies that I'm sure were about to spill out.

He tries again. "It's just, I wanted to ask you something, and I didn't get to because, you know." He kind of mimes pushing someone.

I stare at him.

He waits.

"What do you want, Oscar?"

"Right." He shakes his head as if to clear it. He's gripping that stupid book in his hands again, running his thumb over the pages like it's a good-luck charm. "I have a proposition for you."

"Propose it then."

"Well, it's . . ." He looks down at his book like it might tell him what to say next.

I snatch the book out of his hands and hold it out of his reach. "Focus, please. I don't have all day."

"Okay. Okay." He shivers. I'm not sure if it's from the January cold or from nerd-book withdrawals. "It's just that I can't really explain it here."

I look at him sidelong. "What does that mean?" What could this guy possibly want to propose that can't be explained in a busy school parking lot?

"I mean, I need to show it to you. At my house. After school."

"In private?"

"Yeah! Exactly. In private."

I toss his book back at his chest.

He fumbles for it.

I start to walk away.

"Hey, wait!" Oscar runs after me.

I whirl on him. "If you think I'm going to just go to your house and give you a little 'private time,' you gotta be out of your mind, weirdo. I may dress up, but I'm nobody's plaything."

I've seen this before. Some people get the wrong idea when they look at me in my low-cut shirts and fishnet tights. Refusing to hide my body doesn't mean I take my fantastic boobs out for anyone who asks.

"No!" Oscar's face looks genuinely horrified, so I instantly know I'm sniffing up the wrong tree. "It's nothing like that. I swear."

I cross my arms in front of me. "Try to explain then."

He tries, like *really* tries. He opens his mouth and everything. "You're . . . I mean, I saw how good you are at makeup, and . . . I wondered if you could. There's this competition thing." His face grows red.

My eyes widen. Goddess, I'm an asshole. "Are you saying you want me to teach you how to apply makeup?" Suddenly his longish hair makes sense. Maybe he's growing it out intentionally.

"Kind of," he says. "More like I thought you could just do it for this competition thing."

"On you?"

"What? No! I mean, maybe a little, but it's not what you're thinking."

"Are you sure? Because I'm thinking drag, and there's no shame in that. Actually, it sounds pretty awesome."

"No, it's not drag. Just, please. I have to show you." His eyes dart around the emptying parking lot. He hands over his phone number on a little piece of paper. "Text me. I'll give you my address. Please?"

Oscar is a strange creature. Still, something tells me this might be very interesting. I nod at him, then head off to class.

After school, I take the public bus toward Oscar's house. The lawns in this neighborhood are green, and the sidewalk isn't even cracked like it is on my side of town. Going to this weird guy's house alone is sooo not SSDGM. I could get murdered. For all I know, Oscar literally wants to wear my face as a mask. I wonder how long I could be gone before Barbra calls the cops to report me missing. Some foster parents I've had would wait weeks so they could keep collecting the foster parent checks. Or, at least, they'd wait until the social workers decided to make a routine house call.

I look at the address on my phone. His house is the low brick ranch-style so popular in the suburbs around Detroit. This could be a giant mistake. I knock on the front door anyways.

A tiny old woman opens the door. "¿Hola?" she says.

"Hi, er, ma'am. I'm looking for Oscar."

"I'm coming, Abuelita!" Oscar scuttles into view.

The older woman smiles at him and says something in Spanish. Oscar's face grows beet red. I'm beginning to think he blushes more than not.

"¡No, Abuelita! *¡Ella no es mi novia!*" Oscar waves his hand for me to enter as his grandmother talks excitedly. He shakes his head furiously at her.

"Wait." I stare from Oscar to the tiny woman and back again. "You already speak Spanish? Why are you in my Spanish class?"

Oscar turns back to me briefly. "My abuela thinks I'll learn about Mexico in that class."

"Do you?" I ask, curious.

"No." He turns back to his grandmother, who is gesticulating excitedly while she speaks.

I shrug. "Too bad." Looking around the living room, you'd never guess Oscar lives here. There isn't a single shred of *Prince of Moons* paraphernalia in sight.

He turns back to me again, exasperated. "Um, would you mind going into the basement? I'll meet you down there in a sec."

Well, that sounds like something a serial killer would say. I hesitate, but Oscar and his grandmother are in the midst of a heated discussion in Spanish. His grandmother's eyes are sparkling while Oscar's face grows pinker and pinker. I decide I'd rather die in a basement than get into the middle of whatever this is.

I open the door Oscar keeps pointing to. The steps are dark, but there's a light at the bottom. When I step off the last stair, I stop dead in my tracks.

The entire basement is covered, floor to ceiling, with weapons of such ridiculous proportions they can only have been inspired by *Prince of Moons*. There are workbenches draped in chain mail and tools. There's a collection of metal-tipped arrows scattered across the floor. The window is lined with daggers displaying bejeweled handles that gleam in the sunlight. All along one wall, there are enormous battle-axes with golden comets engraved along the blades.

Yep. I'm going to be killed in a basement.

Along the far wall there are several dress forms, like from

Project Runway. Only, instead of displaying gowns, they're showing off ornate metal breastplates in various stages of completion. Most of them are designed to fit Oscar, short and husky as he is, but one of them is clearly for a woman, with a ring-encircled planet over the spot where her heart would be. What the hell is this?

I jump when I hear Oscar running down the stairs.

"Whew, I'm really sorry about that," he says.

I'm pretty sure I'm frozen in place.

He stands, hands on pudgy hips, beaming. His shoulders aren't even slouched like they usually are at school.

My voice sounds about as freaked out as I feel. "Why did you invite me into your kinky sex dungeon?"

Oscar throws his hands into the air. "It's not a kinky sex dungeon! God, you sound like Emily."

I look from one corner of the room to the next. Assessing the situation. "Then what, pray tell, are you doing with chain mail and whips?" I ask, pointing to an ornately handled cord with multiple fringed tails that look like tiny shooting stars.

"That's a near exact replica of the Queen of Thieves' Whip of Nightmares!" He gathers the whip up into his arms and cradles it, like I've somehow hurt its feelings. "This got over thirteen hundred up votes on ReadMe."

"It got you what on what?"

"*Up votes* on *ReadMe.*" He says this slowly, like I'm somehow the weirdo in this situation. "It's an online forum where cosplayers can share their newest creations."

I'm really starting to feel like I've fallen into some sort of wormhole and landed in an alternate dimension.

"I'm going to need you to put the weapon down and start from the beginning." I take the whip out of his death grasp and set it on a workbench. "Or I'm going to take my cute butt out of this dungeon and run home. I'm not kink shaming you or anything. This just isn't my jam."

Oscar nods, like I'm finally making sense. "Right. This," he says, gesturing to the room, "is my workspace. I make cosplay weapons and armor."

"You *made* all of these?" I'm stunned. And here I was thinking he spent all his grandma's money at online fantasy-supply stores.

"Yeah!" He grabs a sword off a wall mount and does a ridiculous-looking move that can only be described as nerd choreography. He whaps my arm.

I literally scream. This is the end. I knew it was coming. But when I look down at my arm, I don't see any blood. As if it's an afterthought, I realize it didn't hurt at all.

"What the hell?"

"It's foam!" Oscar grins. It turns out he has tiny dimples in his cheeks. I guess I haven't seen him smile before now.

I stare at him blankly.

He points over his shoulder. "That one over there is almost entirely 3D printed. I took an art class at the community college last year so I could learn how to paint the metal and the gems realistically. And I make them look worn with sandpaper. There are a million little tricks you can learn on YouTube." He runs a hand over one of his elaborate suits of armor. "Like how a Dremel tool can make holes for rivets, which adds to the realistic illusion. All the details hide seams and make the pieces look more badass."

"But," I try, "if this were real life, no one would add pounds of extra metal to their armor. It's meant to keep them safe and agile in battle."

"Er, yeah. It's a fantasy." He rolls his doe eyes at me like I'm an insufferably slow student. "It's not meant to be used in *real* battle."

I'm starting to think there's a lot in Oscar's life that's based in fantasy, but it's hard to knock him for it when he sounds so proud. I'm looking at his life's work right now.

"You mean to tell me," I say as I look from battle-ax to giant hammer to bow, "that you made all of these weapons out of craft material?"

"Well, special craft material, yeah."

"Of course it's special. What, is it magic or something?"

"I'm not a child, Jess." He puts his sword down with the tenderness of a parent laying their toddler down for a nap. "I know *Prince of Moons* is fake. I also know I live in the real world."

"Do you though?" I ask, genuinely not sure.

"Look," Oscar says with a stern expression. "I didn't ask you to come here so you could make fun of me like everybody else does. This is my space. I'd appreciate some respect."

Okay, he's right. I'm being a jerk. "Touché," I say. "Apologies, milord."

He smiles. Just like that, Oscar is giddily excited again.

"So," I ask, running my fingers over the detailing on one of the suits of armor. Dang. It really is made out of painted foam. I'm actually pretty impressed. "Why exactly did you ask me to visit your dungeon?"

"It's not a . . ." Oscar sighs. "I wanted to ask if you'd join our cosplay team."

"Your what?"

"Cosplay. Costume play."

I raise my eyebrow at him. "I thought this wasn't a kink thing."

"It's not. It's a legitimate hobby. Think of it as art competitions for people who want to role-play their favorite video games and movies."

"Role-play?" This still sounds like a kink thing to me, but I let him continue.

"Yeah, there are conventions where we all get together, wearing our creations. Then we compete for who made the best costume."

"I didn't know nerds could literally compete at being a nerd."

"It's a skill, like any other."

"Okay," I say. "I think I get it. I like to sew. It's like that, but . . . more fantastical."

"Exactly."

"So why do you need me?" I pick up a huge hammer and test its weight, or lack thereof. "Looks like you've got this cosplay business down to a science."

"Well, kind of," he says. "I've spent years mastering the art of foam armor making. And I've experimented with plenty of different methods for weapons crafting. But that can only get me so far in a competition."

I put the hammer back on its wall mount. "I know nothing about armor. So I really don't think I'll be able to help you."

"That's okay." He holds up his hands in reassurance. "Because what I don't know is how to sew, or do makeup or hair." Oscar points to my face and I feel weirdly exposed. He continues, enthusiastically. "Video game characters don't just wear armor. And many of the hairstyles are so far beyond my capabilities that our team can't compete in the big leagues."

Uh-oh. I heard a word I don't usually like.

"Team?" I confirm. "So it wouldn't just be me and you?"

"Nope. Some of the biggest competitions are for groups. We'd have to make a skit from our favorite movie, TV series, or game, then show off the costumes we made by acting them out."

"So . . . it's theater."

"Kind of. It focuses more on the costumes than our acting skills."

"Well, that's good, because I'm not an actor."

"Me neither," he admits. "So far, Emily has agreed to join, and so has my friend Gerrit. You wouldn't know him. He doesn't go to our school."

"I should tell you that I'm not really a go-team kinda gal," I say with hesitation. "But I'm listening. For the moment."

My eyes travel to the adjustable dress forms in the back of the room. I'd kill for a good dress form, but considering how often I have to pack up and move, I don't need the extra baggage. Foster Care Pro-tip number three: Never own big or heavy items. Besides, dragging around something that looks like a human body might give fosters the wrong impression.

"I promise it will be fun." Oscar clasps his hands in front of his chest like a kid asking for ice cream. "We really need your skills to make it to the big one."

"And what, exactly, is the big one?"

"The World Cosplay Expo in New York City." He says this quietly, like it's the name of a god. "There are many regional competitions where we can qualify for the WCE. We just need to try out different cosplay looks until we win an invitation to compete in New York." He nods toward his cluttered workbench. "There's even some serious prize money involved at that level. More importantly, that's where we can get recognition to start a business."

My warning flashers are on again. "Whoa, hold up. I never said I'd start a business." If I were the space dragon from Oscar's

T-shirt, I'd be sprouting some serious smoke jets from my nostrils right now.

"Of course not." He holds his hands out, placating me. "That's *my* dream. I'd split the money with you fifty-fifty, since you'll have to do half the work by making us look good. My portion will go toward turning this into a full-time career."

So there's money to win in this wacky dress-up game. That could be interesting.

"What about the other, um, players?" I can't make myself say the word "team" just yet. Feels too much like a commitment.

Oscar shrugs. "Emily and Gerrit have their own reasons for joining. They already agreed the winnings would go to the makers. You and me."

"I don't get it. Why wouldn't they want the money?"

"Oh, I'm sure they'd *like* the money, but they won't be putting in the same amount of time and skill we are."

I lower my eyes at him.

"Would! Same amount of skill we *would* be putting in. If you agree, that is."

I'm not sure I'd call this team *promising*, but it might benefit me. I could post my looks on Insta, work on my own brand, learn some new makeup and sewing skills. Buy a new phone with a better camera. Still, this is a lot to take in.

"I'm not sure," I say. Do I really want to dress up like a *Prince of Moons* character, even if I could win something out of it?

Oscar nods enthusiastically, his hair falling into his face again. "Just so you know, I would pay for all the supplies. And the travel money for going to the competitions."

"So there's traveling involved in this thing."

That might be a problem depending on how far Oscar wants

us to go. One of the many downsides of foster care is the fact that the state needs to be involved if I cross any borders. It's a ton of paperwork. Not to mention hoops to jump through and chaperones to convince. *If* I agree to this, I'm not super excited about telling social workers or fosters that I want to dress up for money.

"Yeah," Oscar smiles. "The upcoming conventions are in Kalamazoo, Chicago, and a few other local-ish places. Plus, the WCE in New York. It'll take some coin, but I've got us covered."

"You mean your grandma has us covered," I point out.

"No." His eyes dart away for the briefest of seconds. "I mean, I have money from my mom. Instead of using it for college, I'm using it to start my business. This would be a business expense."

Hm. I didn't peg Oscar as being a rich boy, but whatevs.

"Are you sure your mom is okay with us using her hard-earned cash to go play dress-up?"

Oscar shrugs. "Well, if she's not, there isn't much she can say about it." He reaches out toward some chain mail and runs his fingers over it.

"She's not going to sue me for using her money for fabric or makeup or anything?"

"She's dead."

Oh Goddess. I suck.

"Sorry," I say, chastened.

"It's okay," Oscar says. "It was a long time ago. And, for the record, my dad lives in Mexico. That's why I live with my abuela."

Now I avoid *his* gaze. I'm used to being the sob story, not the other way around. Maybe I could try just a little bit harder to be less of an ass to Oscar. If anyone knows how hard it is to not have parents around, it's me. Maybe this *would* be a mutually beneficial situation. Maybe I can give up my solo act and try working as a team for once. That's a lot of maybes. And there are a lot of deadly weapons in this game, even if they are made of foam.

"How about I touch base with you on Monday?" I ask. "I need to think about it over the weekend."

"Of course."

My phone buzzes in my butt pocket. Oscar scurries backward as I scramble for it.

"I'm not going to push you again," I say with a smirk.

"Just, you know"—he bites his lip—"I'm a bit jumpy around unpredictable people."

When I open my phone's screen, there's a notification saying a DM's waiting for me. I don't wait a second longer to read it.

Reigna_NYC: "If I wasn't your mother, how would I know you have a birthmark on your upper left thigh? Also, you look exactly like me."

There's a blurry photo attached. My hands shake as I stare at the image of my birth mother. In my mind all the memories I have of her snap into place, like a puzzle that was missing the most important piece. She's me, but with about twenty more years and a million more worries on her face. Reigna has dark hair, round cheeks, and small eyes surrounded by crow's feet. My ears hum. My breath gets lost in my throat.

"Are you okay?" Oscar asks.

I jump, completely forgetting where I was. Quicker than the Prince of Moons can swing a lightning sword, I stuff my phone back into my pocket.

"I gotta go," I say by way of explanation. Then I walk back up the stairs.

In fact, I don't stop walking until I find myself on my own

side of town. I'm filled with rage, hope, and excitement. I have so many questions, but something's eating at the back of my mind.

There's always a reason foster kids are put into state custody. From what I've seen, it can be a pretty grisly one. Kids who are put into state custody because of poverty or family illness can generally request unsupervised contact without much of a problem. But for others ... let's just say that abuse and neglect can leave lasting scars. That's why foster kids aren't allowed to have unsupervised contact with bioparents without the state's permission. It's supposed to keep them safe. That includes me, since my biomom's mental illness resulted in a dangerous living situation when I was little.

If my biomom wanted to follow the rules, she would have contacted my social worker first. Clearly, she's reaching out through different channels for a reason. Given the fact that she has a seriously tumultuous relationship with the state—from being forced into psychiatric hospitals to having her daughter taken away—I can't risk getting my social worker involved. If my biomom says or does the wrong thing, the state could cut off contact before it even gets started. After nine years of wondering what happened, I won't ruin my one chance to find out.

No one can know my biomom is back in my life.

CHAPTER 5

THIS HAIR IS MOST UNUSUAL—THIS IS NO *HUMAN* HAIR.
EDGAR ALLAN POE, "THE MURDERS IN THE RUE MORGUE"

A knock on my bedroom door drags me from the depths of sleep. I poke my head out from under the blankets. Sunlight streams through my windows. Oh Goddess, what unholy hour is this? On the nightstand my alarm clock reads 11:04. That's what I get for staying up until 3:00 a.m. stressing about Reigna_NYC. Not to mention the old nightmares that woke me up every hour since.

"Jess?" Barbra knocks on the door again.

"Come in," I grumble. Goddess, I can smell my own poisonous morning breath. I'm a ghoul.

The door creaks open a few inches as Barbra peeks through the crack. "I thought maybe we could go on that shopping trip today. What do you think?"

She looks ridiculous, barely peeping through the crack in the door. I know she's trying to be respectful of my privacy, so I guess I dig that. Most fosters just barge in whenever they please. Probably hoping to catch me in some illicit act. Foster Care Pro-tip number four: Never assume your room is private. Do nothing in your fosters' house that you wouldn't do in front of your social worker.

"You can open the door the whole way," I say.

She does, but she doesn't step in. She keeps her eyes pointedly on my face, avoiding looking at anything I might have lying out.

Her aggressive politeness makes me smile, in spite of myself. I hide it under the duvet.

"Do you think today might be an okay day?" she asks. She's holding her '90s-style sneakers in her hands like she isn't sure if she'll need them or not. "Or we could go later this week?"

"It's still morning," I say with a yawn. "Why are you so bubbly?"

She smiles. "I've been up since five. I went to sunrise yoga, then a meditation class." She doesn't say it to rub it in or anything, but her energy levels make me feel even more tired.

"So," she asks. "Want to go?"

She's clearly set on this shopping thing. Better to get it over with now rather than drag out the foster kid/parent bonding tension. Foster Care Pro-tip number five: Remember the foster honeymoon phase is temporary. Put on a good show of effort in the beginning and it can buy you a few extra weeks before they realize they don't like you.

"Yeah, sure." I sit up in bed, then catch a glimpse of my haggard face in the mirror. Holy Queen of Thieves. I look like fresh hell. And grave dirt. Since when do I forget to take off my makeup before bed?

Oh yeah, since I started freaking out about the fact that I might possibly have reconnected with my birth mom.

"I might need a few minutes to freshen up," I say.

Barbra's face brightens. "Sure! How many? I'll make sure I'm ready." She starts slipping on a sneaker, like somehow I will be ready faster than her.

"Um." I glance in the mirror again. "How about sixty?"

"Oh." Barbra pauses tying her laces. "Okay." She takes the shoe off. "I'll make us some lunch." She trots off down the stairs, whistling like she's in a musical from the 1940s.

Once she's gone, reality smacks me hard. I reach for my phone, but I'm still not sure how to respond to Reigna_NYC now that I'm quite possibly convinced she's my real mother. I throw my phone onto the duvet.

An hour and twenty minutes later, I'm freshly made up with foundation two shades lighter than my natural skin tone topped off with green eye shadow and black lipstick. My lace-up boots clunk on the steps as I walk downstairs to find Barbra reading a newspaper at the kitchen table. There's a veggie hummus wrap on the table for me. She's eaten hers already, evidenced by the empty plate sitting next to her. Barbra looks up from the paper.

"Ready?"

I nod and take the wrap to go.

"So, where to?" She asks as we buckle into her rusty car. "I'm happy to drive to the bigger mall in the suburbs if you'd like. Or even the outlets."

I barely restrain a shiver. Few things scare me as much as mall people with their boring outfits and venti whipped-cream-topped mocha lattes.

"Actually I was thinking of somewhere else. I can direct you," I say, pointing left at the next intersection.

Fifteen minutes later, we're walking into Goodwill. I take a deep breath and inhale the scent of my favorite store. It smells of mothballs, sweat, and the potential for something great.

Barbra looks at the racks of used clothes with one raised eyebrow. "You know, you don't have to get things secondhand today. I'm happy to buy you some new clothes."

"These are new," I say. "New to me. Besides, the fashion industry is one of the biggest perpetrators of pollution. I can be fashionable without buying new things one hundred percent of the time."

"Well," Barbra says, grinning as she pulls a voluminous blouse off a rack, "it's a good thing I don't know much about fashion."

I eye her dirty sneakers and mom jeans. Somehow, without realizing it, she's managed to wear a normcore outfit. A very brave fashion choice . . . if only it were a fashion *choice* in the first place, instead of just one of the many items in her closet that have survived three decades.

"You're not so bad," I say.

She takes this as encouragement, digging through the racks of shirts with vigor. She squints at a poster on the wall indicating the prices. Her eyes go wide.

"You can get a ton more for your money here." She holds up a large sweater with cats all over it. "Thoughts?"

I can't ignore the thinly veiled joy in her eyes. "Tolerable," I say. "Goofy cat items are kind of always in."

Barbra snags an abandoned cart and tosses the sweater inside along with a few pairs of faded stretch pants. "How have I never shopped here before?"

"Most people find used items to be mildly disgusting," I say, trying to ignore the fact that "most people" consider foster kids to be the human version of thrift clothes.

"I don't," Barbra says. "They have character. Too bad they can't tell us their stories." She uses her thumbnail to scrape at a stain on the front of a pair of slacks. When it doesn't come off, she hangs the slacks back on the rack.

A lump forms in my throat. I need some space, so I shuffle away.

As I scan the store, I see so much potential here. There's a multitude of ways to turn discarded pieces of trash into beloved wardrobe highlights. My mind travels back to Oscar's offer. As I look around the store, there are so many items that could be flipped into cool costume pieces. Creativity butterflies flutter in my stomach. Am I actually getting excited about this cosplay idea?

I mosey over to a promising shelf filled with black jackets. Most are torn or stained, but one blazer with massive shoulder pads catches my eye. Instantly, I can see possibilities for turning it into a gothic dream coat. Alteration ideas flood my brain. I could cut the sleeves for a 1980s rebel-with-a-cause look. Or I could embroider a quote on the back, maybe something from Edgar Allan Poe, the patron saint of goths. Add some black lace for a vaguely Victorian-in-mourning feel. This blazer is a maker's dream come true. I could amplify this sucker to the max. My Insta followers will flip when they see what I do with this!

Then reality smacks me. I'd need to get more sewing supplies to do any of this, and I'm out of cash. There's no way I'm asking Barbra for more charity.

I put the jacket back on the shelf.

Across the store I see Barbra walk out of a dressing room. She places several hangers on the discard rack, except for the cat sweater and a pair of pleated pants that are definitely too long for her. When she sees me, she heads in my direction. I pretend to sift through the rack in front of me.

"Look what I found," Barbra says when she reaches me. "I thought you might like them, if they're your size." When I look up, I see she's holding up a pair of black Converse. I check the tag. Yep, they're my size. I'm so surprised she's actually encouraging my goth look that I don't protest when she throws them into the cart.

"Oh, that's cool!" Barbra reaches around me and picks the blazer back up off the rack. "I remember when shoulder pads were in. Haven't seen anyone wear them in decades." She holds it up to me. I take a step away. "Don't you like it?" she asks, confused.

Her chipper tone irritates me, which I know is unfair. I can't forget that she's a foster. She's not a friend. That's a strict line I will not cross. I've learned that lesson too many times.

"Yeah, I like it," I say, turning away to another shelf. I flip through pants without really looking at them.

"Then let's get it." Barbra throws it into the cart.

I reach in to pull it out again.

"No, I don't want it. I was just thinking of doing some alterations on it, but I can't."

Barbra looks at the blazer, then back at me. "Why not?"

"It requires special supplies that I don't have right now."

"Like what?"

"Like . . . I don't know yet. Patches or rhinestones or something."

"Like from the craft store?"

"Yeah."

She throws the blazer back into the cart again. "Well, considering you're such a cheap date, I think we can splurge on a trip to Michaels. Can you believe this cat sweater is only four dollars?"

I can, but I don't say anything. I'm torn. I want the blazer, but I don't want to take Barbra's charity.

"How about we make a deal?" I say. "I'll hem those pants you're getting in exchange for the shoes, blazer, and some supplies from the craft store."

"I already offered to buy you some new clothes," she says. "You don't need to do anything for me in return."

"I just really need to make this as even an exchange as we can," I say, holding up my hands to emphasize that this is important to me. There's a panic inside of me that I need to squash down. I can't owe Barbra anything for any reason. Not even if it's just a stupid $6 jacket.

Barbra looks at me for a few seconds longer than I like. Then she nods. "If that's what you want to do, then okay."

I appreciate that she doesn't fight me on this, but I only feel mildly better. This bonding excursion was a terrible idea. We don't speak much during checkout or on the way to the craft store. Not that this seems to bother Barbra, who hums lightheartedly to herself during the entire drive across town.

A trip to Michaels is something akin to a journey to the Holy Land for me. My fingers literally tingle when we walk past the aisles of stickers, yarn, holiday decorating supplies, and bead-storage containers. I could spend hours here, soaking up the creative energy and drafting new ideas for bigger and better looks. This is my happy place. Well, this and Sephora. Anywhere I can find new ways to decorate myself. I pick out black thread, ribbon, fringe, appliques, and filigree trim. Anything that could help me experiment with different design ideas.

I literally stop in my tracks when I see it. The Singer Stylist 7258 computerized sewing machine sits on a glorious pedestal in the sewing section. It practically glows with an aura of awesome. The specs say it has an automatic needle threader and can do seventy-six different types of decorative stitches. Basically, there's nothing this mechanical dream machine can't do. If I were a cartoon, I'd be drooling right now.

"In the market for a sewing machine?" Barbra asks. In my crafting wonder, I completely forgot she was here.

"No," I say.

"How exactly are you planning to hem my pants then?" I hear the teasing in her voice.

"The old-fashioned way, by hand. It's tried and true."

Barbra looks at the price tag and lets out a low whistle. "Yikes, that's a lot of money."

"Yeah, like I said, I'm not in the market."

"Fooled me with that goofy grin on your face." She eyeballs all the supplies in my arms. "Do you want to be a designer after school?"

I don't give much thought to "after school." I'm usually a little too busy trying to keep my head above water in the present. The future isn't something I like to think about.

All I say is, "Not likely."

What I don't mention is that being a professional designer would require a college degree. Very few foster alumni ever reach that life goal. There are too many obstacles in the way. After we're emancipated from the foster care system, we're on our own. We don't have the luxury of a family to fall back on if we need help, or a cosigner for student loans, or a place to crash when the dorms are closed.

Like I said, foster teens don't usually have the luxury of thinking about the Future in grand terms.

My phone buzzes. I walk down the sewing machine aisle, away from where Barbra crouches, reading the information on the box of the Singer dream machine. When I read the message on my phone screen, it's exactly what I need to hear right now.

Reigna_NYC: "I love you."

No one has said those three words to me since I was seven years old. My hands tremble as Barbra putters away, admiring ribbons of all shades.

Then three little dots appear on my screen.

Reigna_NYC: "I gave you up because I believed we had to go into hiding for your protection. Back then, I thought we were royalty in line for the throne. I'm better now. I'm getting healthy again. For you."

Like my life couldn't get more complicated than it already is.

CHAPTER 6

MEN HAVE CALLED ME MAD; BUT THE QUESTION IS NOT YET SETTLED,
WHETHER MADNESS IS OR IS NOT THE LOFTIEST INTELLIGENCE.
EDGAR ALLAN POE, "ELEONORA"

Maybe I should explain a little something about my biomom. She has schizophrenia. Now, don't start *Beautiful Mind*-ing me. I didn't even know my mom was sick until social workers told me she'd been institutionalized multiple times. Before then, I just thought the things we did were normal. Doesn't every kid have to hide in the back of her car so kidnappers can't see her during trips to the grocery store? Doesn't every family move three times a year to avoid stalkers? It wasn't until I was seven that I learned, no. No, they do not.

Up in my room I tap my pencil on my geometry homework. Math is not happening for me tonight. Instead of thinking about shapes and equations, my brain keeps wondering, "Why?" Why couldn't my mother keep her shit together when I was a kid? Why is she contacting me after nine years of radio silence? In the back of my mind, I know I should report this to my social workers. At the very least, I should tell Barbra. For some reason, even the thought of doing that feels like a betrayal.

Social Services would insist on getting involved, supervising every word we share. Or worse. They could keep me from speaking to her altogether until she jumps through a million hoops to prove she's not a threat to me anymore. For unsupervised contact, she needs to have a job and a stable place to live, and she has to attend all of her doctor appointments and take her meds. My biomom says she's better now. She understands that she was sick. To me, that's enough, but it might not be for the state. I should give her a chance to be in my life again without all the added complications. Right?

Honestly, I don't know what to do.

My fingers absently pick at the shredded hem of my raven-patterned pajama bottoms. I need a serious distraction, not right angles or protractors. I'm talking chain mail and giant foam blasters. What a strange turn my week has taken.

A few years ago, my social workers used some grant money to buy me a cheap laptop, since it's a requirement for high school. Now my computer stares me down from the other end of the room. I close my notebook. Perhaps a little research will help.

What was the cosplay forum Oscar mentioned? ReadMe? I type that into Google. Yep, it's a thing. Not that I doubted Oscar, but given that guy's obsession with fantasy you just never know.

In the ReadMe search bar I type "cosplay." Here goes nothing.

The first eye-catching result I get is "Hot Babes of Cosplay." Tagline: "Showing off the hottest babes of cosplay."

Alert! Alert!

My spidey senses are telling me to back away slowly. I click on a seemingly innocuous thread right under the first one: "Cosplay." Simple. Straightforward.

Wrong.

There are hundreds of threads that start off with photographs of sexy models showing off boobs and butts in tiny, skintight renditions of Hollywood's biggest female action stars. Alongside those are gaming's girl sidekicks in revealing "armor." Those breastplates can*not* be comfortable. Or helpful in the face of a battle. In what world would an exposed belly button be considered appropriate safety wear?

Is Oscar seriously inviting me to join a soft-core porn group? I knew that room looked kinky as hell.

The ReadMe photos are followed by hundreds of comments. My biggest mistake: reading those comments. I will not repeat the inappropriate jokes and sexist critiques that follow each image. Suffice it to say I'm disappointed in humanity.

Now, don't get me wrong. I'm a feminist. I love a good low-cut dress and some booty shorts. Some of us were born with a little extra, and I am in full support of rocking what we've got, but this feels different. It's . . . limiting. I certainly don't look like Kendall Jenner or Gisele Bündchen. Is this seriously what women in this community are expected to be?

As I scroll down, I only see one big girl on this thread, and she's dressed as an ogre. AN OGRE! Where would I even fit into this universe? Would I be expected to play the role of the ugly creature, like one of Cosplay Cinderella's ugly stepsisters? Hell no! I am more than that. I may not fit Hollywood's stereotypical ideas of what a woman should be, but I deserve better than this.

Anger boils up inside of me. Without thinking, I pick up a pencil and throw it across the room. It makes a mark on the lavender-painted wall. I spin in my computer chair until I have the willpower to look back at the screen again.

Then I click on gold.

My jaw literally drops when a photo of a woman dressed as the Queen of Hearts pops up on my screen. She's classic fairy-tale feminine, only she's distorted. Her hands are long and mangled, dripping in fake blood in a gruesome interpretation of the monarch of Alice's Wonderland. Her face is contorted in pain or madness, maybe both. It's a far cry from the bright and sexy images I clicked past earlier in the thread. The photo caption reads: "Yaya Han as the Queen of Hearts in her famous 'Alice skit.'"

This character resonates in my bones. It's unexpected. It's challenging. It's ... goth. This badass reigns over an underworld that few people can understand. In a strange way, this character reminds me of my biomom. She's fantastical, yet horribly misunderstood. She represents both the beautiful and the twisted. Who is the real Queen of Hearts without her bloodlust? Who is my biomom without her schizophrenia? I wish I knew.

Maybe I could find out.

She is more than schizophrenia; she's my mother. More importantly, she still loves me, even after all these years of separation. We might have a real shot at discovering who we are without this terrible disease hanging over both of our heads.

Then I remember something. I jump up from my chair as if I'd been electrocuted, like Frankenstein's monster brought back from the dead.

Oscar said the cosplay finals are in New York City.

I glance back to the computer screen. I no longer notice the long-legged beauties in bodysuits. I'm staring at the Mad Queen of Wonderland with newfound respect. This strange little hobby of Oscar's might turn out to be more than a competition for me. It could be a way to reunite with my biomom in person without the state getting involved. I could go to New York City and find her.

This wild idea is starting to smell of opportunity.

Maybe I should murder Oscar for one of his dress forms ...

On Monday morning I wake up less than fresh. My stress dreams are in full swing again, like when I was a kid. They're always the same. I'll try to speak, but nothing makes sense. There's urgency in my tone. Whatever I'm trying to communicate is incredibly important, but shadowy figures give me worried glances. I'm incomprehensible to them. One by one they leave. No matter how hard I try to speak, the dreams end with frustrating solitude and excruciating words that are never expressed.

I don't want today to be tainted by my subconscious acting a fool. In the mirror, I force myself to stand up straighter. Mind over matter, my friends. Just shake off the gloom.

I strut down the stairs wearing the black Goodwill jacket I spent all of Sunday altering. My fingers are raw from hand sewing through thick fabric, but it was worth it. I've added fringe and filigree trim off the shoulder pads and wound braided cords across my chest. Elaborate iron-on appliques dance across the jacket in a regal pattern. I've also altered the black Converse, cut them into a ballet flat shape, then laced black ribbon through eyelet holes that I punched into the thick canvas. The ribbon crisscrosses up my leggings before tying in a bow at my knees. In honor of my beau Edgar Allan Poe, I drew tiny black ravens on the white toes of the shoes.

I'm ready to command my destiny, no matter what weird places it may take me.

In the kitchen, Barbra looks up from her paper, then sets her coffee cup down in surprise. She grins widely.

"Oh, your coat!"

In spite of myself, I give an uncharacteristic little spin.

She claps her hands together. "Your shoes! You're like Cinderella and Prince Charming all rolled into one."

I'm thrilled that she of all people understood the aesthetic I was going for, but I keep my cool.

"I'm sure I'll get interesting reactions."

"You're so creative." She takes a sip of her coffee, then nods to the pot. There's still plenty for me. She's set the travel mug out next to it, ready for me to take as much as I want. My heart squeezes just a little. I'm not sure if it's a good thing or not.

When I get off the bus at Detroit River High, I run through the halls, looking for Oscar. I find him talking to Emily near the gym. They make a funny pair, him in his faded fantasy T-shirt and her in a bold-patterned button-down that's so chic she could be on the cover of *Vogue*.

"Hey." I walk up to them with the determination of a warrior. Oscar actually flinches.

"I'm not going to hit you again."

"Okay, just, you know, wasn't sure."

I turn to Emily. "Hi, I'm Jess. We were never formally introduced. Also, I'm in, but I have a few conditions."

Emily raises one thin eyebrow. "Okay..."

"First"—I turn back to Oscar—"I will not be the big girl who is relegated to playing the ogres or other such hideous fantasy creatures."

"I never intended for you to..."

I cut him off. "Second, I will only play royal characters."

Emily laughs.

I stare at her.

"Wait, you're serious?" she asks. She tilts her bleached, pixie-cut-rocking head skeptically.

"Very."

"Um." She looks from me to Oscar. "I guess I just wouldn't have pegged you as the princess sort."

"And what sort did you expect me to be?"

"Any other kind?" She eyeballs my long black hair, which is slicked back in an early 2000s Victoria Beckham–Posh Spice style. "But fine. I already told Oscar I refuse to be the stereotypical cute Asian girl who only wears frilly Lolita dresses or sexy anime costumes." She folds her arms in front of her chest. "That's fine for other girls who like that, but I'm not them."

"Great," I say with a firm nod. "I totally get that. And I will only play royalty."

Oscar looks from me to Emily, his eyes wide. I think I see tiny pinpricks of sweat forming at his temples.

"Hey," he says, his voice cracking. "Let's tone it down a notch."

Emily and I both turn on him.

"Excuse me?" I say.

"Hell no," Emily says at exactly the same time.

We look at each other. A tiny smile turns up at the corner of her mouth. I think I may actually like this chick.

Oscar holds up his hands in surrender. "Sorry! I just meant, I think we can work under these conditions."

"How, exactly?" Emily asks.

"Geekdom is a vast community. There's plenty to work with."

"If you say so," Emily says.

I'm not buying it.

"The internet would suggest otherwise," I add. "Do you know how many soft-core porn sites I had to sift through to find any girls who looked like me?"

"Right?" Emily says, her brown eyes wide. "I'm a gamer. I am one hundred percent disappointed in the lack of diversity in the video game world. That's why my masterful life plan is to learn how to code so I can make the rules. I'm getting tired of playing sexy babes and white dudes with unrealistic rippling muscles." She gags for effect.

"Someone needs to tell that to the comic book and Hollywood realms too," I say.

Emily nods her head in approval.

I turn back to Oscar. "Which brings me to my second condition."

Oscar looks a little worried despite his assurance that the fandoms have so much variety. He picks at the hem of his baggy T-shirt anxiously.

"I will not exist as a sex symbol. If you want me to be a part of your team, I'm going to need more depth of character than just 'hot cosplay chick.'"

Emily holds up a hand and I high-five her like a dork.

"Okay," Oscar says. "That sounds oddly specific."

"You'd be surprised."

Emily makes a sound of agreement.

All three of us stare at each other for a moment, sizing each other up.

"Okay." Oscar holds out his hand for me to shake it. "We're business partners then."

I shake Emily's hand too for good measure. Her grip is strong where Oscar's is flimsy.

"I hope you both know what you're getting yourselves into," I add. It's possible I'm playing up the melodrama just a tad. What can I say? My life has been hugely influenced by gothic literature.

I strut my stuff down the corridor, mentally flipping off every wide-eyed normie who snickers in my path. At my locker, I take out my phone to message Reigna_NYC. Over the weekend, I thought a long time about how I should reply to her. I could tell her that I don't trust crazy people. I could say she abandoned me and I never want to hear from her again. But the truth is, deep down, I still love her in spite of everything she did to me.

I'm not really sure what the correct response is, but I know what the kind one feels like.

GothQueen_13: "I've missed you."

CHAPTER 7

THEY WHO DREAM BY DAY ARE COGNIZANT OF MANY
THINGS WHICH ESCAPE THOSE WHO DREAM ONLY BY NIGHT.
EDGAR ALLAN POE, "ELEONORA"

We meet up after school to go over the game plan. As I walk up the block to Oscar's house, I can hardly believe I'm doing this again. The last time I saw all those gleaming cosplay swords I felt like a lamb walking into a slaughterhouse. Hmmm ... maybe this is why I'm vegetarian.

I knock on the door. This time Oscar answers.

"Um, I'm here," I say.

"Great!" His face is alight again like it was the first time I saw him pick up a foam battle-ax. "Emily and Gerrit are downstairs." He leads the way.

In the basement, I spot Emily sitting on a workbench, draped in chain mail. She's lazily wielding a sci-fi blaster. Across the room, there's a skinny black guy I've never seen before. I can only assume he's Oscar's friend Gerrit. He's so engrossed in a game he's playing on his Nintendo Switch that he doesn't even look up when we walk in.

"The gang's all here!" Oscar announces like a nerdy dad co-ordinating a playdate.

I follow him toward the table Emily's sitting on and notice it's covered in notepads. Lots of them. They're full of scribbles and drawings. They'd look a little like my fashion sketches if you replaced my goth queens wearing dark veils with his medieval space heroes slaying monsters.

"Alright," Oscar begins. "We have until the end of May to qualify for the World Cosplay Expo. That doesn't give us a lot of time to climb the ranks from amateur to professional level."

"And how exactly do we 'climb the ranks'?" Emily asks.

"By competing. As much as possible. We start small, then work our way up to the bigger competitions. The winners of the big city cons get invitations to World Cosplay Expo." He rubs the back of his neck. "That only gives us four months to perfect our craft."

"Um, excuse me," I interject. "You never said anything about there being a deadline. I don't do well with time limits." My morning makeup routine can attest to that.

Oscar holds up his hands as if to appease me before I run my big beautiful booty right back up those basement stairs.

"It's okay!" he says. "We can totally do this. We just need to work smart."

"And what if we don't win a qualifying competition before May?" I ask.

Oscar's face betrays just the tiniest hint of doubt. "Then we have to wait until next year to try again."

"An entire year?" Who knows where I could be one year from now. With the number of foster homes I have a habit of blowing through, I could be in a group home across the state by then. Would Reigna even still be in contact with me? She does have a horrible track record of disappearing. I chew on the inside of my cheek as I think. No, I can't wait a whole extra year to see her. This is my one shot. We have to make it to New York in May.

I nod in agreement and Oscar relaxes his shoulders, which

had been inching up toward his ears ever since he dropped the deadline bomb on us. He looks to Emily, who shrugs.

"Great!" he gasps. "If we have any hope of killing this competition, we're going to need some kick-ass costume ideas. Given our, er, restraints." He glances up at me nervously. "We're going to need to do some team brainstorming."

"What about him?" Emily nods over to Gerrit. "Any chance he'd be willing to pause his game to grace us with his attention?"

Oscar shakes his head. "Don't worry about him. We made a deal. He's along for the ride. He really doesn't care what we design."

Emily turns around to squint over at Gerrit. His brow is furrowed under his baseball cap, which still has a shiny NBA sticker along the brim.

"Hey! Gerrit! Excuse me for interrupting," she says. "But we'd like your brain over here for storming."

"I'm good," Gerrit says as the faint sound of zombie hordes floats out from the speaker of his Switch.

Oscar clears his throat. "He's really only here at his mom's insistence. This isn't really his thing."

"Oh, you mean like how it's not *my* thing?" I say.

"Or mine?" Emily adds.

"Emily," Oscar sighs. "I never forced you into this."

Emily brushes her sideswept bangs out of her eyes. "Yeah, well, I can't have a blank coding bootcamp application. Gotta prove I'm serious about changing the geek world." She glances over at Gerrit. "Hey, Gerrit, are there any queer characters in that game you're playing?"

"Nope," he says without looking up.

"How about people of color?"

"Or fat girls?" I add.

Gerrit doesn't even pause his game. "Only in zombie form."

We look back at Oscar pointedly.

Oscar pinches the space between his eyes. "Look, can we just try to start this off on the right foot here?" The pleading in Oscar's voice makes me cave.

"Fine," I say. Then I yell back over to Gerrit, "What if I design you into a frilly dress?"

"Cool," he says without looking up.

"Or make you wear three-inch high heels?"

"Whatever."

I look back to Oscar and Emily. Emily nods slowly, clearly warming up to the guy.

"I can work with this arrangement," I say, pleasantly surprised by the free rein.

"Fantastic," Oscar says, grabbing his notes. "Now that we've got that settled." He pulls out a drawing of the full cast of *Prince of Moons*. I guess it'd be pretty good if it wasn't so goddamn geeky.

"I'm not doing that," I say flatly.

"Me neither." Emily puts the blaster down so she can cross her arms in defiance.

"What? Why not?" Oscar protests. "There are several royal characters here, and Emily could easily play the part of the Duke of Shadows." He holds the drawing up to her. "Look, he's the most badass character. He even has a giant mace!"

Emily pretends to barf.

"Fine then, what are your great ideas?" He lowers his eyes at her.

I jump in before there's real blood spilled in the fake-weapon dungeon.

"Let's just think for a minute." On the table next to me, there's list of conventions with dates and locations. I pick it up for proper examination. The first con starts in two weeks' time. The rest are every few weeks after that, leading up to the biggie in May: World Cosplay Expo. A funny feeling tingles in my stomach as I remember it's in New York City. This paper in my hand feels like a sign. A renewed determination focuses my mind.

I slam the schedule back on the worktable. Oscar and Emily look up from their bickering.

"If we're really going to try to win this thing, we need to think smart."

Oscar squints at me like I've suddenly grown two heads.

"I'm listening," he says. He crosses his short arms in front of him like he's settling in for a long lecture.

"The first couple competitions are small, right?"

He nods.

"Then we need to start simple. Learn from each one. Use that experience to work up to the bigger, more difficult costumes." My finger traces elaborate pleats on kilts and seamless spandex leggings worn by the cast of *Prince of Moons*. "This stuff is way too advanced for me to make in two just weeks. You may have been doing this for years, Oscar, but don't forget this would be my first competition."

He nods along with my logic.

"I'm up against a huge learning curve here."

Oscar reaches under the table and pulls a box out from under it. When he opens the lid, my jaw drops. There are hundreds of different designs in there.

I let out a low whistle.

Emily lies back on the workbench and says, "Draw me like one of your elf girls, Oscar." She cracks up.

Oscar dumps the contents of the box onto an adjacent workbench.

"I'm going to get my laptop," he says. "There are a lot of movie clips we need to watch if I'm expected to teach you all there is to know about geek culture in just two weeks."

Emily takes out her phone. "I'm going to order a pizza."

Across the room, Gerrit yells out "Yes!" and I'm not entirely sure if it's for the game he's still playing or the promise of food.

I grab a handful of pages and get to work sorting out the looks I could conceivably sew for us in the next two weeks. There are alien creatures holding giant pokey sticks, tiny elven women with golden bows lined with multiple arrows, humanoid robots sporting light-up gadgets with lasers. This is going to be challenging, but who ever said finding your destiny was easy? If I'm going to sneak my way to New York to meet my biomom, I'm going to need all the magic in the Prince of Moons universe. And pizza. Lots and lots of pizza.

We work late into the night with Oscar explaining the relevance of different iconic films and TV series to geek culture. Some competitors prefer to stick to the original canon for their creations, while others like to put their own artistic flair on character designs. We decide to stick with something canon to start.

Oscar takes a giant bite of pizza with one hand while he sifts through a sketch-filled portfolio with the other.

"Jess, if you're really going to insist on portraying royalty, then I think we need to start this space opera by paying homage to the queen of science fiction."

Emily and I share a quick, worried glance.

"Go on," I say.

Oscar gives us a brief synopsis of the most iconic sci-fi film of all time. He takes out a drawing of someone so influential to pop culture, even I know who she is. The long, white draped dress, the black blaster, and of course, the famous cinnamon bun hair. She is Princess Leia, the ultimate intergalactic princess who just so happens to be a foster care alumna.

Oscar grins when he sees my recognition.

"We gotta go *Star Wars*."

CHAPTER 8

YOU KNOW, SOMETIMES I AMAZE EVEN MYSELF.
HAN SOLO, *STAR WARS: EPISODE IV, A NEW HOPE*

One thing has become abundantly clear during this geek journey so far. There's no way I'm going to be able to hand sew costumes for four people in two weeks. After school on Monday, I make my way down the arts hallway, then poke my head into the home economics room.

The tiny old teacher, Mrs. Heavers, is across the room, grading piles of pickled vegetables that her students jarred that week during class. Someday, maybe I'll have a decrepit mansion where I tin vegetables and mix witchy tinctures. A goth queen can dream.

I clear my throat. "Excuse me," I say.

When Mrs. Heavers looks up, she nearly drops a jar of carrots suspended in liquid. Her watery eyes grow wide for a second. I swear I witness her wispy, white hair blow back. I'm used to that reaction when old people see me for the first time, so it doesn't faze me.

"I was wondering," I say, "if you have any sewing machines I could use?"

Mrs. Heavers collects herself. "Is this for a school project?" she asks.

"Sort of." I pull my Princess Leia sketches out of my satchel. "I'd like to make this."

I set my drawings out on the table and she wanders over to inspect them.

Last night, I shared them with Reigna via Insta. She hasn't responded yet, which is mildly frustrating. We've been separated for nine years, shouldn't she be as excited as I am to talk? It seems to take her hours, if not days, to reply after I send her a message. I'm trying not to let it get to me.

Mrs. Heavers runs a finger over the draped silhouette in my sketch. "Oh my," she says in a low voice. "These are really quite good. What did you say these are for? A student play?"

"Erm, something like that," I say.

Mrs. Heavers's old lady fingers shake as she picks up one of my drawings. "It's been years since anyone asked me to use the sewing machines for extracurriculars."

Something in her voice makes it seem like she's remembering fonder times. Back when students actually wanted to learn how to sew their own clothes or jar their own tomato sauce.

Mrs. Heavers turns back to me with a thin-lipped smile. "You do look like a theater girl. I was a theater girl once, you know."

"You don't say."

"I played Guinevere. I actually kissed Lancelot onstage. Oh, it was scandalous!"

This makes me think Mrs. Heavers and I are going to get along just fine.

"So, do you think you could show me how to use one of those?" I point toward a wall lined with yellowed machines with fake wood paneling near the dials. My guess is they're relics from the '70s.

"I'll be here until six o'clock every school night. You're welcome to join me."

Success!

"Now." She looks at my drawings again. "Do you have a pattern to work from?"

I give Mrs. Heavers a tiny notebook with the measurements I made for myself. From inside my satchel I take out a white bed-sheet that I plan to use for Leia's dress. Fabric is expensive, so I paid homage to the gods of Goodwill. Once bleached, this sucker was as good as new.

"This is what I have."

Mrs. Heavers nods sagely. "Well, let's start at the beginning." I follow her as she shuffles over to a large cabinet. She pulls out some chalk pencils, pins, and giant fabric scissors. "This is fun!" Her old lady smile is infectious.

My phone buzzes, so I take a second to check it while Mrs. Heavers looks over the sewing machines to decide which one I should use.

Reigna_NYC: "These are GORGEOUS! I knew you'd grow up to be talented."

My chest fills with elation. My biomom likes my drawings. She thinks I'm talented. I never realized how much I craved her approval until this exact moment. I want to make her proud of me. It makes me work extra hard to master the sewing machine basics Mrs. Heavers teaches me for the next three hours. Her pickle-grading project is abandoned for the remainder of the afternoon as she shows me how to measure, cut, and pin fabric for sewing. She even lends me some of her own books about pattern design and draping. Who knew old ladies could be so cool?

When I get home around 6:45, Barbra is in the kitchen making dinner. I'm still not used to this. Normally I'd scarf down a salad or something after my foster family went to bed. I used to try to stay out of the way like that. Family dinners often went sour when I attended them, so I learned to eat in the middle of the night to avoid conflict.

Foster Care Pro-tip number six: Do whatever it takes to keep the peace. Wars are costly, especially for the underdog. And you, dear foster kid, are *always* the underdog.

"Honey, you're home!" Barbra calls from the kitchen when she hears the front door close.

Such. A. Dork.

"Hey," I say before I run upstairs to deposit my bag in my room. Mrs. Heavers gave me pins, fabric scissors, and chalk to use tonight so I can get the rest of my fabric pieces ready to start sewing after school tomorrow. I'm extremely glad the team chose something easy for our first competition. I have so much to learn.

So as not to seem like a total asshole, I go back downstairs to humor Barbra. She's stirring a bubbling pot of what looks like thick gruel with mushrooms in it. The counter is littered with tiny grains of rice, parmesan cheese slivers, chopped chives, and a small cardboard box of white wine. I suddenly realize I've never seen Barbra with alcohol before. That strikes me as odd. Most of my foster parents poured themselves a hefty glass of something to imbibe the second I walked through the door, like they needed it to survive my presence.

"I didn't know you drank wine," I say by way of conversation.

She looks at the tiny box of pinot grigio. "Oh, I don't." She points a wooden spoon at the pot. "It's for cooking."

"Fancy."

She seems pleased. "Well, I'm trying."

This makes me feel instantly guilty. I hate feeling like a burden.

"You know, you don't have to cook dinner for me. I'm fully capable of feeding myself."

She doesn't catch the reproachful tone in my voice.

"I just thought it would give us a nice opportunity to hang out," she says. "Would you mind grabbing a couple of bowls from the cupboard?"

I hand them over to her. She plops a sticky glob of the gloopy stuff into each. When I make a turn to put them on the table, she stops me.

"Not yet! I have some garnish." She tops them off with grated parmesan and chives. "There! Doesn't that look delicious?"

I stare at the gray mass in the bowls. "Yes," I say definitively. "What is it?"

"Mushroom risotto. It's vegetarian!"

It doesn't really look like any risotto I've seen, but I'll take her word for it.

We both sit down at the tiny table, our knees nearly bumping from the tight squeeze. I'm surprised to discover that even though the mass looks like something from a horror movie about a glob monster, it's actually pretty good.

"So," Barbra asks. "You were at school pretty late. Are you working on a project?"

"Yep." I stuff a huge mouthful of sticky rice into my mouth so I can't say more. I'm not ready to tell Barbra about the cosplay team. I love that this is something I'm sharing with my biomom. I don't want to taint that with outsider opinions yet.

"What's it about?"

I point to my full mouth.

"Oh, sorry." There are a few moments of blessed silence before she tries a different line of attack. "Your social worker tells me your birthday is coming up."

I shrug. Fosters never celebrate my birthday.

"I got us some tickets to take a vegan cooking class downtown. I thought maybe you'd like that."

My limbs freeze. Actually, that sounds awesome, but therein lies a dilemma. Barbra is forcing that bonding thing again, right when I have my real mom back in my life. This maternal relationship still feels so fragile, like a glass slipper. Too much pressure and it's bound to break. Besides, I can't let my guard down, even if Barbra *is* proving to be a lovable dork.

When I was fourteen, I had a foster family who seemed very nice at first. Until one of their biological kids left his vape pen in the back seat of the car and blamed its sudden appearance on me. It didn't matter that I insisted I was innocent. I even offered to take a drug test. Within two weeks, my social workers showed up to transfer me again. The foster parents said I was corrupting their biological children. When you're a foster kid, no one trusts you. You can't trust anyone either.

Barbra eats her risotto in silence, waiting for my reply.

"When is the class?" I ask hesitantly.

"This Saturday afternoon. Your birthday." She winks at me like it's a secret.

"Can't," I say as I shovel the last glob of risotto into my mouth.

"Oh." Barbra's face falls. "I didn't know you'd have plans since you just moved to a new school. I should have asked first." She scoots her food around her bowl with her fork. "I'm sorry. That was silly of me to assume."

She looks crestfallen, but I can't cave in. I've been here before.

I learned the hard way. Someday she'll see it's better this way. For both of us.

"It's just that I have this school project," I explain hurriedly. "I need to do it with some classmates. It's going to take us all weekend."

"On your birthday?" Barbra's eyes are so big, she reminds me of a toddler. "Is there any chance you could reschedule? I could talk to your teachers if you'd like . . ."

"No." I stand up, nearly knocking the chair over behind me. I take my bowl to the sink to rinse out the sticky rice remains. "I don't want to get off on the wrong foot, you know? New kid already asking for exceptions. It doesn't look good."

I'm surprised by how easily the lie forms. I never lie.

Barbra nods her head. "Yes, of course. I'm sorry I didn't ask. Maybe we can do something that evening instead. Just the two of us."

There's still a bit of risotto in the pot. I scoop it into a glass container for the fridge while I work on my evasion game.

"Maybe," I say with a doubtful tone. "I just don't know when we'll finish for the day. It might be best if you don't wait around for me. Okay?"

Her voice is small behind me as I walk out of the kitchen. "Okay," she says from her seat at the dining room table.

I am a jerk. I know this. But self-preservation comes first, foster kids. Always remember that.

CHAPTER 9

DO OR DO NOT. THERE IS NO TRY.
YODA, *STAR WARS: EPISODE V, THE EMPIRE STRIKES BACK*

I show up at Oscar's house at 9:00 a.m. on Saturday wearing my hair tied back in a black bandana to indicate that I'm ready to work. Oscar answers the door, his eyes bleary from sleep. He's wearing a crumpled sci-fi T-shirt that's a little too short and a lot too tight, so his pudgy belly peeks out along the hem.

"Hi," I say too brightly. "We're working on costumes today." I hold up the massive sewing machine Mrs. Heavers let me borrow for the weekend. It has a case with a handle for traveling.

He looks down at the watch on his wrist. It's designed to look like a droid of some kind. "It's so early . . ."

"Winners never sleep." I push my way in through the front door.

"I really don't think that's true," he mumbles with a yawn. His shaggy hair is matted on one side of his head.

Abuela walks into the room looking like she's been awake for hours. A flour-coated apron covers her vividly colored dress. She smiles brightly and throws her hands up when she sees me.

"¡Mi favorita de las novias de Oscar!"

"No, no, Abuelita." Oscar runs his hands over his face. "We've been through this before. Ella no es mi novia. ¿Cuántas amigas crees que tengo?"

Abuela brushes past him to take me by the hand. I practically throw the sewing machine at Oscar. He grabs it less than gracefully. They made things heavy in the '70s.

Abuela leads me into the kitchen. I allow myself one moment of pettiness as I turn back toward the bewildered Oscar to stick my tongue out at him. I win.

After Abuela feeds me a full breakfast—all the while chatting excitedly in Spanish that I don't understand—I insist I have to follow Oscar into the Costume Lair to work on our project. When I get down there, Oscar has changed out of his pajamas and tidied up a bit. He's also set my sewing machine up on one of his long workbenches. I drag a dress form over to my new workspace.

"So, how's it going?" he asks. His shaggy hair is still wet from a shower. It's dripping water all over the shoulders of his mercifully clean T-shirt.

I don't look at him as I adjust the dress frame to my measurements. "I'm concentrating."

He shrugs, then turns toward his own project: large strips of foam he's cut and painted to look like metallic droid limbs.

We work in the Costume Lair all day. I've nearly finished Leia's dress and started on Han Solo's fancy pants when the basement door opens, interrupting my concentration.

Abuela calls down the stairs. "¿Todavía están trabajando? ¿No tienen hambre?"

"¡Sí, Abuelita!"

"Dale, les haré la cena prontito."

"Gracias, Abuelita."

When she closes the door, Oscar says, "So, it's six p.m. You've officially been working for nine hours. Would you like to stay for dinner or are you planning on going home soon?"

I brush hair out of my eyes as I turn around. Oscar's been busy too, it seems. He's wearing goggles and his hands are covered in foam dust from the Dremel tool. C-3PO's golden legs lie out on his worktable in all their glory. Next to him, there's a trash can covered in foam that's been glued together in the shape of R2-D2.

"Are you trying to kick me out?"

"No. I'm just saying, I don't think you've taken a single break since you got here. Not even to pee and that's kind of impressive, though mildly alarming. Do you always work this hard?" He turns on his Dremel tool and sands down one of R2-D2's seams. It disappears like he's wielding a magic wand.

"Yes."

What I don't say is I have to. I always do. In this world, foster kids need to work twice as hard as everyone else, at *least*. We don't have anyone to fall back on when things don't work out. I change the subject.

"So, um, it's my birthday."

Oscar freezes, mid-sanding. He turns off his Dremel tool, pulls his goggles up to his forehead, and stares at me. "What did you say?"

"You heard me."

"Why the hell have we spent the day in my basement then?"

"Because we have a deadline, dork. The first competition is in seven days."

"Um, yeah, but it's your birthday."

"And?" I wish I hadn't brought it up. I turn back toward my workstation to attack the sleeves on Han Solo's jacket with a seam ripper. I found a basic black coat at Goodwill yesterday. It just needs a bit of adjusting to turn it into the perfect vest for everyone's favorite space smuggler.

Oscar isn't giving up.

"We should have at least gone out for cake or something."

"Working suits me just fine. I don't celebrate birthdays."

"Why not? Birthdays are fun!"

"Not for foster kids."

It slips out before I have a chance to even think about what I'm saying. Now I've made everything extremely awkward. I brace myself for the onslaught of pity that always follows a foster care confession.

"Well," Oscar says, shrugging. "I'm going to go ask Abuela if we have any dessert."

My hand freezes mid–seam rip. That's it? No sympathetic glance or uncomfortable silence? No "I'm so sorry!" or "I gotta go"?

"You do like dessert, right?" he asks.

I lower my eyes at him. "Why wouldn't I like dessert?"

He grins. "I dunno, it's just starting to sound like you don't like fun things."

I throw a piece of balled-up paper at him. He deflects it with his Dremel tool.

"I'm just saying, you're the one who likes to work on your birthday."

"I like dessert!" I insist, fighting a smile.

He sets his tool down and runs up the stairs before I can throw anything else at him. He's still wearing his goggles on his forehead, the nerd.

When I get home around 9:00 p.m., the house is dark except for a single lamp in the living room. I walk in to find Barbra has fallen asleep on the couch. There's a magazine on the floor by her side. *The Vegan Chef.* Guilt threatens to make me second-guess my decision to reject her birthday surprise, even though it was for the best. When I set the magazine down on the side table, she wakes up.

"Oh, you're home," she says. "Happy birthday!"

"Thanks." I turn to leave.

"Wait! Don't you want to see what I got you?"

I hate obligatory gifts. They make my stomach turn.

"You didn't need to get anything for me. Really. We kind of just met." I pull my black sweater tighter around me, like it's a protective shield.

She waves her hand like she's shooing that idea away.

"It's in the kitchen." She gets up to lead me. Doom fills my soul. Will it be some not-so-subtle suggestion to change myself? I've been presented with gift cards for mall stores that sell "more appropriate" clothes, gym memberships to "work away those extra pounds," and even a surprise trip to the beauty salon to get a make-over so I could see "how pretty" I am underneath the makeup I wear.

When we walk into the kitchen, I'm surprised to find a stack of magazines on the table. There's *Threads*, *VegNews*, *Goth Beauty*, and a few others. They're all titles about alternative makeup styles, living a plant-based life, and sewing my own clothes. These are gifts that reflect who I am, not who others think I should be.

"I got you subscriptions to each," Barbra says excitedly. "I thought you could celebrate your birthday all year."

It's so unbelievably sweet that I don't know what to say. As I look at the magazines on the table, Barbra starts pulling things out of the fridge.

My voice unexpectedly cracks when I ask, "What are you doing?"

"I went to that vegan cooking class today."

"You went alone?"

"Yeah, but that's okay." She shrugs. "You had work to do. I get it. School comes first."

The guilt threatens to eat me alive like flesh-eating bacteria.

Barbra sets broccoli, a lemon, and some garlic on the counter. "They taught me how to make a bunch of tasty things. So I went to the store and got the ingredients. I figured we could make some together tonight. That way you won't have missed out completely." She holds up a jar of sesame tahini. "Have you ever had this stuff? It's amazing! I had no idea it existed before today."

I'm so unbelievably touched that I throw all of my hard-won foster care wisdom out the window. I don't even tell her that I already had a full dinner and a huge slice of Abuela's tres leches cake.

"I'd really love that," I say.

Unexpectedly, this might be the best birthday of my life so far.

CHAPTER 10

From my bedroom, I hear someone honk the horn maniacally as they pull into the driveway. It's 8:00 a.m. Commence phase one of Oscar's master plan for geek costume stardom.

I've been packed and ready for the Kalamazoo Fan Fest for at least two hours already. I'm so nervous I didn't sleep at all last night. I've dressed in leggings and my favorite oversized black T-shirt with Edgar Allan Poe's grizzled face on it. I send a silent plea to the patron saint of goths. Please, let this whole harebrained idea work out okay.

Seeing as Poe never responds to me from beyond the grave, I distract myself with makeup, as per usual. I take way too much time creating a makeup look inspired by Darth Maul: black lipstick paired with sparkly red eye shadow and thick black liner. I know I'll have to take it off as soon as we get there (Leia isn't an aesthetically dramatic princess), but I got a few good Insta comments on the science-fiction look already. None from Reigna_NYC yet.

When I poke my head into the kitchen, Barbra is sifting through the vitamin cabinet. She sets several bottles on the countertop.

"Bye," I say hurriedly as the horn honks again.

"Where are you off to?" Barbra asks. She pours one pill from an orange bottle into her palm, then swallows it with a sip of coffee. She grimaces.

"Group project. I'll be kinda late."

She waves. I could get used to this kind of trust. Too bad the guilt demon keeps whispering admonishments in my ear.

I wave back, then head out the door, my Leia dress hidden in a black garbage bag.

When I close the front door, Emily gives me an evil grin from the driver's seat of a white minivan. She revs the engine.

From somewhere inside, Oscar yells, "Cool your jets. My abuela's van is not the Millennium Falcon!"

With zero grace, I cram myself into the vehicle with my makeup bag in tow. Oscar is in the front passenger seat and Gerrit is in the far back, playing a game on his phone. They're both wearing black T-shirts and sweatpants. They can't exactly fit in the car wearing their droid costumes. Oscar's masterpieces are peeking out from behind the back row of seats.

"Why aren't you dressed yet?" Emily demands to know. She's in full Han Solo mode, and she dyed her short hair a rich brown for the occasion. She even has her blaster holster tied around her waist.

"Not everyone is excited to drive through town looking like a space pirate," I say.

"I don't see why the hell not," she grumbles as she reverses out of the driveway.

Oscar struggles with his seat belt as he turns toward her. "I thought you didn't even want to do this cosplay competition thing in the first place?" There's a noticeable tone of glee in his voice. His hair is tied back into the teeniest, tiniest man bun. I suspect Emily had something to do with that.

"Well, that was before Jess joined the team and agreed to turn me into the sexiest man in outer space."

"Touché." Oscar tries to bow to her like a medieval lord, but the seat belt threatens to choke him.

Nerd alert.

"I'm glad you've taken to your role as a cocky rogue," I say.

"Maybe a little too well," Gerrit mumbles from behind me.

"You hush!" Emily gives him a mom-glare through the rearview mirror.

I raise one eyebrow at her. Oscar explains, "I practically had to wrestle a light saber out of her hands this morning when she showed up at my house waving it around like a third grader."

"It's not real, Oscar!"

"That's not the point," he says. "It's staying in the back. Han Solo doesn't get a light saber. He carries a blaster."

"It's called taking artistic license!"

"It's called not sticking to canon."

"Calm down, children," Gerrit says.

When I turn around to agree with him, his eyes are still glued to his phone game.

Oscar pulls a long checklist out from his backpack. "What's our ETA?" he asks Emily.

"Relax. The competition doesn't even start for four more hours."

"Yes, but the Fan Fest doors open in two. We need to find parking, finish getting ready in the bathrooms, and work the floor for a minimum of one full hour for ultimate exposure time."

"Work the floor?" I ask.

"Yes. Show off our wares," Oscar says.

"Ha! Wares. Wears," Emily chuckles. "Get it?"

Oscar rolls his eyes. "We need exposure."

"I wouldn't tell people you need to expose yourself, if I were you," Gerrit pipes in.

"Come on, you guys. This is serious!" Oscar's face is growing pink. "I have to read our audience. We need feedback so we know how to improve for next time."

This geek has his eyes on the strategy game. Now I'm starting to stress.

A two-hour car ride has never felt so long.

By the time we arrive at the convention center, our nerves are frizzled. All except Gerrit, who looked perfectly happy playing video games in the back seat the entire time.

The parking lot is packed with people. Clouds of warm breath float above the vehicles as people step into the winter chill. Several groups of cosplayers sprint toward the entrance, visibly shivering in their flimsy costumes.

"How many nerds are there in central Michigan?" Emily asks, her jaw dropped open like a goon.

I use the sleeve of my jacket to wipe away the condensation on my window. The scene I see outside is intimidating, but there's nothing to do now except go into the convention center. We already drove all this way, after all. I pull open the van's back door and step onto the asphalt.

"I think the correct term here is 'geek,'" Gerrit says as he unbuckles his seat belt to join me.

Oscar barely glances at the crowds. He shrugs. "This is nothing. It's tiny compared to the bigger cons. The San Diego convention is practically a city of its own, or so I've heard."

"Small?!" Emily shouts. "There's gotta be five hundred people here."

Oscar chuckles. "Yes. This is very small." He pulls out his

checklist again. "First things first. We need a designated meeting spot so we can find each other after we get ready."

"Meeting spot?" Emily asks. "What are we, kindergarteners in a mall?"

"I don't think you understand how overwhelming a convention can be." Oscar waves his hands toward the sea of anime and video game characters pushing toward the entrance. "We need to make sure we stay together so everyone can get the full effect of our team's costumes."

Emily huffs. "Okay! Okay! Take a chill pill."

Oscar's eyes look like they're about to pop out of his head, so I step in.

"How about Emily and I go to the bathroom to get ready? We'll meet you both at the giant inflatable Pikachu statue in forty-five minutes."

Emily turns to admire the statue where it peeks out from the giant convention center windows. "Huh, how about that."

Gerrit takes off toward it as he pulls his phone back out of his pocket.

Oscar is starting to look a little green.

"Nod if you understand me, Oscar."

He nods.

"And try to take some deep, meditative breaths while we're gone."

He nods again.

When we enter the convention center, I realize Oscar may have been right about the whole not-getting-lost thing. I had no idea there were enough geek subcultures to fill an entire convention center with booths ranging from comic books to celebrity meet and greets to steampunk clubs. It's like a whole underground world I didn't even know existed.

Emily pokes my arm, then points to a sign indicating where the bathrooms are. When we enter, we nearly walk straight into an entire group of Marvel characters. Near the mirrors, two women are adjusting their Mario Bros. mustaches. Next to them, there's a gorgeous elf dressed entirely in leaves. She's applying skin glue to her synthetic pointed ears. There's even a group of tiny bionic children with exposed gears and top hats. The air in this room is electrified with excitement.

This is not the Cosplay Babes scene I had anticipated. As I look around this bathroom, I don't see a single Heidi Klum lookalike dressed as a sexy Catwoman. Instead, there's a brown girl dressed as Wonder Woman who has the most badass guns I've ever seen in my life. And I don't mean the foam kind hanging in Oscar's basement. Her arm muscles are fierce! She could kick anyone's ass. This is a *real* version of Wonder Woman that I didn't even know I've been missing. She represents a female superhero who is strong, not just sexy. I am aaaalll about this. What the hell is wrong with the internet if it keeps this sort of artistry hidden in a convention center bathroom like it's the shady underbelly of cosplay? Only in this backward version of the world, the underground is full of real, identifiable people.

Here are the *real* humans of cosplay. Reflecting in the bathroom mirror are black and brown women who've turned traditionally white video game characters completely upside down, claiming them as their own. A big girl in a short Lolita gown adjusts the most elaborate headdress I've ever seen. A conservative seamstress added more fabric to the neckline of her favorite superhero costume and—get this—it looks even better than the original.

And you can tell by the way she's beaming that she actually feels comfortable wearing it in public!

I am in awe. These are the artists that make my jaw drop, not the supermodels on the internet.

It takes me a full ten seconds to realize I'm frozen, staring at the scene. When I look at Emily, her mouth is hanging open.

"Well, we're in deep now," I say.

She turns to me. "When we leave, do you think we'll be able to wash off the geek contamination?"

My throat gives a little involuntary cough from the hairspray saturating the air. "Maybe not."

A small girl in a dinosaur costume stares at me. She points at my eyes. I remember the red sparkles on my lids and do a few slow blinks for her. She grins and runs toward a woman dressed as a *Jurassic Park* ranger.

We muscle toward an open space at the mirror. I pull out my bag of supplies and start lining up hairpins and makeup along the edge of a sink.

"How much magic do you have in there, Mary Poppins?" Emily picks up a tube of lipstick. "Oooo. Pretty!"

I tussle her short dark hair, then run some mousse through it, trying to give her that devil-may-care look that Han Solo pulls off so well. When she's good to go, I hide in a stall to start my transformation. I feel very much like Superman locked in a phone booth. My heart pounds as I use makeup wipes to remove all my glitter and glam. No one has seen me without my goth makeup in years. I feel vulnerable. Exposed. It's like I've left my identity behind.

I fully expect to be humiliated when I step out of the stall in my Leia costume, but, instead, I get appreciative nods. Okay. I guess this is the place where it's socially acceptable to let my freak flag fly. These geeks are starting to warm my cold, dark heart.

"You look awesome!" Emily reaches out to touch the draped folds in my long white dress. "If I didn't know you'd spent the last two weeks driving yourself crazy at a sewing machine, I'd swear you bought this."

I mentally cringe at the casual use of the word "crazy," but I don't mention it. That's my own shit I gotta deal with. The impulse to check my phone for a message from Reigna_NYC is red hot right now. I squash it down. I am *not* going to obsessively check my inbox all day.

Emily holds foam donuts on either side of my head so I can twist my long hair around them. Bobby pins secure everything in place. When I'm done, I have to give myself a pat on the back because Emily and I look exactly like Han Solo and Princess Leia.

"We're so badass," Emily says.

And I have to agree. Who knew dressing up in costume after the sixth grade could be so much fun? I mean, I guess some people would think I do this every day, being goth and all, but that's my identity. It's literally who I am. This is different. It's like trying on someone else's skin for a while, as creepy as that sounds.

After I add a bit of highlighter, mascara, and some lip color, we're ready. We take a few photos in the bathroom mirror before we go so I can quickly post them on Insta.

"What the hell," Emily says, holding her phone inches in front of her face. "Why didn't you tell me you're practically Insta famous?" She's scrolling through my pics. "I had no idea you have a cult following."

"I don't have a cult following," I say. Underneath my Leia dress, I'm wearing leggings. I tuck the ankles into my black boots.

"Um, you're some goth celebrity and you have devoted followers. Would you rather I call them your coven?"

I shrug. On my phone, I see she's followed me. No one has ever spoken to me about my Insta profile before, at least not in person. This feels a little like a *Twilight Zone* episode where my online life and my real life merge. It's kinda weird while also being surprisingly awesome at the same time.

We find C-3PO Gerrit and R2-D2 Oscar by the Pikachu, like we said we would. Gerrit's long arms and chest are now encased in metallic gold foam, like sleek hockey padding. His leg pieces are only attached at the hips. Straps dangle around his ankles to be firmly attached later. A C-3PO head rests on the ground by his feet. I have to admit, it looks legit.

Oscar is pacing, wheeling around his R2-D2 shell on its rickety dolly. Sweat is forming at his temples. He doesn't even notice us until we step directly into his path. He gives me a double take.

"Oh, Jess. I didn't even recognize you."

Is he blushing?

"You look . . ."

He's definitely blushing.

Next to me, Emily grins like a shark that smells blood.

Gerrit glances up from his video game momentarily. "What he means to say is you look hot."

"What?" Oscar sputters. "I didn't . . . I wouldn't say it like . . ." The little man bun on top of his head quivers as he fumbles.

Han Solo Emily circles him. "You think she's pretty," she teases in a singsong voice.

Oscar stammers as he reaches for his checklist again. "Guys, can we just focus? Please?"

"I don't know, can we?" Emily leans toward him, wiggling her eyebrows. She really does make a perfect Han Solo.

Oscar glares at her, his doe eyes turned murderous. He crosses something off his checklist. "We need to drop all our extra stuff back in the car. Then we need our foam weapons to get approved by security to make sure we're not sneaking any real blasters inside the hall. Then we have to walk the perimeter together and slowly spiral our way to the center so everyone at the Fest can see our costumes. Then we need to check in for the competition at least one hour before the start time . . ."

And so it begins.

CHAPTER 11

NEVER TELL ME THE ODDS!
HAN SOLO, *STAR WARS: EPISODE V, THE EMPIRE STRIKES BACK*

By the time we follow Oscar around the Fan Fest perimeter, check in for the competition, and find our places backstage, we're all more than a little stressed out.

Tension is high for all the groups who signed up for the show. In the dimly lit backstage waiting area, several teams practice choreography they've prepared for their bit. A limber Mortal Kombat fighter does backflips to attack an imaginary villain. I feel like I'm in waaaay over my head.

"So, um, what do we do now?" Emily asks. She ducks out of the way as a Super Family jogs down the hallway in spandex. "Were we supposed to work out for this or something?" A few feet away, a green Hulk is literally doing one-handed push-ups.

"No, some people just get really into their characters," Oscar says, although his voice sounds less than confident. A group of ladies in 1980s workout gear are doing stretches. One of them has black veins drawn up her limbs. There's a puppet monster of some kind attached to her neck.

My stomach starts to turn in this weird fantasy realm I've found myself in. Something tells me it isn't from the smell of sweat that permeates the air. What's the difference between the Hulk hulking out and my mother acting like she's a member of royalty? Taking the costume off at the end of the day? I suddenly feel very awkward in my Princess Leia outfit. I know this isn't real; therefore, it's fine for me to be doing this. Right?

"Jess."

I turn to see everyone looking at me, even Gerrit.

"What?" I shake my head to clear out the psychoanalytic thoughts building up along the walls of my skull. Now is not the time to play Freud.

"We were just going over the game plan," Oscar says. "We need to act out a scene when we get onstage. Something super short, just so everyone gets who we're supposed to be."

"I don't think they're going to have that problem," Emily says. She taps R2-D2's protruding camera eyeball. His shell is open so Oscar can climb in and scoot himself across the stage on the dolly's wheels.

He ignores her. "I was thinking we just go in and do a little battle scene. Like we're escaping the Death Star or something."

"Um, I've only seen this movie once," I point out. "I didn't, like, study it or anything."

"That's okay," he says, waving off my concerns. "It's not super complicated."

"I have a bad feeling about this . . ." Emily says.

Gerrit actually laughs.

"What?" she asks.

He glances up from his video game. "You do realize that's ac-tually a line in, like, every Star Wars movie?"

"Um . . ." Emily pauses. "Of course I knew that."

Gerrit raises one eyebrow and stares at her for three long seconds. "Liar." He returns to his video game.

Oscar starts giving orders again. "Gerrit, put the video game away and buckle up your leg casing."

"But they don't move at the knees. I can hardly walk."

"It doesn't matter." Oscar waves his protests away. "C-3PO more hobbles around anyway. It'll look realistic."

I watch as the other competitors conduct practice runs. They dance, they do backflips, they reenact memorized scenes, and they march with clearly choreographed precision.

Under my breath, I echo Emily's sentiment. "I have a bad feeling about this too."

Gerrit pokes his head around the curtain to spy on the team practicing some sort of fantasy scene. He comes back looking mildly gray. He side-eyes Oscar.

"Are you sure about this?"

"It's going to be fine. Just put your helmet on," Oscar instructs. "You're making me nervous."

"You *should* be nervous," Emily says as a trio of anime characters walk by, giving each other high fives. "It makes you perform better." She starts hopping from one foot to the next, holding her fake blaster at different angles like she's practicing for an audition as the world's most agile gunslinger.

Oscar's breathing is speeding up. Something's off. While Gerrit and Emily get into character, he takes a few steps away and braces himself against the wall.

"Hey," I say, walking toward him. "You okay?"

His eyes are closed like he's concentrating. He's taking slow, deep breaths.

I eyeball him as several monstrous-looking Skeksis shuffle by, their bulky, pillow-stuffed robes dragging on the floor behind them. One is holding a giant purple crystal dangling from a chain like it's an incense ball from the middle ages. The Skeksis' decrepit bird-like faces show seriously impressive craftsmanship. Oscar should be geeking out about them, but he doesn't even notice. That's a bad sign.

"Seriously, you don't look so good," I say.

He waves a hand. "It's fine. I'm fine. Just trying to head off a looming panic attack."

His baby-smooth skin is shiny with sweat.

Uh-oh. "Is there anything I can do?"

"Just don't tell me to calm down." He looks at me sideways. "I hate it when people tell me that. I have an anxiety disorder. Obviously, I'd calm down if that were an option."

I hold up my hands in surrender.

He leans the back of his head against the wall, his breathing speeding up like he's running a marathon. How do you stop a panic attack? Without thinking, I reach out and slap his face.

"Ow!" He holds a palm up to his cherubic cheek, his eyes accusatory.

"Oh, hell!" I cover my mouth in horror. In my own brewing hysteria, I reacted without thinking. "I'm sorry. I didn't know what to do. I thought maybe . . ."

"That only works in the movies!"

"I'm sorry!"

Goddess, we're both unraveling fast.

"Okay," I say to us both. "It's okay. We can do this." I have no idea where my chill went. Probably sucked up by the Skeksis' dark crystal. Damned Skeksis.

Oscar closes his eyes. "Please don't let me ruin everything," he whispers more to himself than to me. I have no idea how to help, so I end up hovering awkwardly like a mother hen.

He turns his head toward me. "Don't worry," he says, like I'm the one who needs comforting. "Anxiety has held me back all my life. I'm not going to let it take this from me. I am out of my house. I am doing something new. So far, that's a huge success." There's a glint of determination in his eyes, like he's conducting a serious *Prince of Moons* battle inside his own head. There's courage there, behind the fear.

That tiny glimpse into his soul fills me with admiration.

"Just, talk to me," Oscar says. "Distract me from the . . ." He waves a hand around his head.

"Did you know one of Edgar Allan Poe's most infamous protagonists had anxiety? In 'The Tell-Tale Heart.'"

"Really?"

"Yeah!"

His interest lights a tiny spark of hope in me. Maybe I'm on the right track now.

"I mean, he ended up being a psychotic murderer, but . . ."

"So, that's not helping." He hangs his head between his knees while he takes slow, steady breaths.

"Ew. You're absolutely right." Goddess, I can be so awkward sometimes. "That was a shitty thing to tell you." I nod emphatically.

What should I say? Aside from my mom and now Oscar, I can't even think of a single person that I know of who struggles with mental health. Only, that can't possibly be true. If 450 million people in the world have some sort of mental health condition, then I must know dozens of them. It's like a giant secret that no one talks about. This suddenly strikes me as strange.

"Have you ever noticed how no one really ever talks about mental illness?" I ask. "At least not in any useful ways."

Oscar nods his head, but his breathing isn't getting any better.

I suck at this. How can a girl with mental illness in her family be so damn terrible at talking about mental illness?

Looking at his pale, sweaty face, I know if there ever was a time for real talk, this would be it.

"So, you should know something." I take a deep breath. "My biomom has schizophrenia. So, I kind of get it."

He lifts his head to look at me. "Really?"

"Yeah." My throat feels like there's something large in it. I've never spoken about my biomom to anyone. *Ever.*

"I had no idea," he says. His breathing is starting to return to normal even though his coloring is still freakishly gray.

"No one does," I say. "Maybe don't mention it to anyone, okay?"

"Your secret's safe with me." He slides down to the floor with an exhausted sigh.

Guilt and fear course through my veins, like a toxic cocktail.

"I'm not even sure why I don't talk about it," I say. "I'm not ashamed of her or anything. I just . . ." What? I don't even understand what I'm feeling.

"People will judge her," Oscar says. "And you by default." He puts his hands on his chest to feel his heart. Hopefully the beats are returning to normal now. "Trust me, I know what I'm talking about. I'm the school reject for a reason, and it's not just because I love *Prince of Moons.*"

"It feels shitty to say that's true," I whisper.

What kind of daughter hides her own mother? I know I shouldn't care what people think. That's not the kind of person I want to be. But I can't change the way the world treats people like her. Or people like me by association.

"It's not your fault," he says. "The world wants us to be ashamed of ourselves for not being perfect. But I don't believe anyone *is* perfect. We all walk around with secrets."

Secrets are the story of my life.

"I think you're right," I say as a pixie skips by, trailing pink ribbons behind her. "I wish we lived in a world where we didn't have to feel ashamed for being who we are. Or for needing help."

It's an impossible situation to be in. How do you change the entire world?

Out on the stage, I hear the MC do mic checks. He makes some goofy comment about Thor's hammer. The backstage handlers touch their earpieces and snicker at some secret joke only they can hear.

Goose bumps tickle my arm. This is real. We're going to do this.

There's a gentle rumbling on the ground. It takes me a few seconds to realize it's from footsteps. Lots of them. They've opened the doors to let the audience into the auditorium.

Next to me, Oscar takes another deep breath. "I can't tell you how hard it is to hold myself together sometimes." He wipes the sweat from his forehead with his sleeve. "Most people just say I'm being a baby when I get like this. Like I could feel differently if I really wanted to. I *do* want to."

"Is that why you've decided to start competing now, after so many years of making this stuff?" I nudge the R2-D2 trash can with my toe.

"Partly." He nods. "I'm just so tired of feeling trapped in my own head. I don't want to live feeling anxious all the time. It's exhausting." He leans his head against the wall behind him and closes his eyes. "I can't imagine what having schizophrenia must be like for your mom."

"It's done a lot of damage in her life."

"It must have been hard for you too."

I shrug. That's not something I'm ready to talk about yet.

"Thanks," Oscar says. "For talking to me. I think I can do this now." He stands, his legs still looking a little shaky.

"Anytime," I say. I'm surprised to discover I really mean it.

When we rejoin the group, I feel like something between us has shifted a little. Secrets were shared. That's not a responsibility I hold lightly. I hope Oscar feels the same way.

When Emily sees us, she puts her hands on her hips. "Seriously, what do we do when they call our names?" she asks. "Wave like beauty queens?"

"Just run around and pretend to shoot things." Oscar does a few stretches, preparing to climb into his rolling R2-D2 costume.

"Some of us don't even have blasters," Gerrit points out.

"Just act nervous. Like C-3PO always does." Oscar crouches into his R2-D2 and closes the lid. "We can do this!" he calls from inside. His voice sounds weirdly hollow, kind of like you'd expect from someone who willingly encased himself inside a decorated garbage can.

A man with a clipboard approaches me. "Are you ready? You're on deck."

"Um," I say.

It feels like the floor has just dropped out from underneath us.

"Go!" The guy waves us into the line. We shuffle into place.

Before it's our turn, the other teams run onstage in bursts of energy. They twirl, shout, sing, and fight. Their costumes swirl around them or glint under the bright stage lights.

We more trickle onstage like a leaky faucet.

All except Emily, of course, who performs a somersault and attacks the audience with her natural-born Han Solo charisma.

Gerrit limps around due to his limited limb mobility. He looks less like a droid and more like a toddler with poop in his pants. Oscar wheels his R2-D2 trash can with his hands, moving forward in short bursts. As for me, well, I sort of just plod forward with a fake smile plastered across my sweaty face.

We look nothing like an action scene from *Star Wars*. More like Luke Skywalker's fever dream.

"Jess!" Emily hisses at me. "Stop fake smiling, you're supposed to be Princess Leia, not the Queen of England." She grabs my arm and twirls me around, then dips me backward in a swarthy Han-Solo-saves-the-day-and-wins-the-princess move.

I scowl and push her away.

"Now you've got it!" She grins.

The crowd is clapping politely, while we ping-pong around the stage in an erratic fashion. Then I notice Oscar. He's scooting his R2-D2 trash can dangerously close to the edge of the stage.

"C-3PO!" I call to Gerrit, who's the closest person to Oscar. I point, hoping it looks like an intentional save. Do droids save each other in *Star Wars*? They do today. This is all part of the planned skit, folks.

I can't see Gerrit's face through his gold mask, but he's spotted the problem. He lurches forward to grab the smaller droid, but his limbs are too stiff. He topples over, banging into Oscar in the process. R2-D2's wheels push forward. In seemingly slow motion, I watch as they both fall off the stage in a heap of fake droid parts.

CHAPTER 12

... AS FOR PROGRESS, IT WAS AT ONE TIME QUITE A NUISANCE, BUT IT
NEVER PROGRESSED.
EDGAR ALLAN POE, "SOME WORDS WITH A MUMMY"

The van is silent on the drive home. Even Gerrit put away his phone in favor of staring out the window. Oscar taps a pencil on his notebook as he thinks in the front passenger seat. Some of his hair has come loose from his man bun, giving him a wild-professor look.

"So"—Oscar clears his throat—"we learned a few things."

No one takes him up on the bait.

"For one thing, no more rolling around in trash cans." He jots that down in his insufferable notebook. "I need to actually be able to see where I'm going to control the droid." He rubs his shoulder where he landed on it. "Or, maybe no more droids." He nods to himself. "Yeah, definitely no more droids." He jots that down too.

Silence.

I can see him looking at me through the passenger seat's broken makeup mirror, which hangs open no matter how many times we tried to close it. I shift and stare at the passing farmland between Kalamazoo and Detroit. Oscar is not going to get any affirming eye contact from me.

"Emily rocked it," he adds cheerfully.

"Obviously," she says without her usual enthusiasm. She turns on the blinker and makes a turn with a little too much verve.

Oscar continues. "And leg joints are super important for mobility, even when portraying a stiff character."

I look back at Gerrit. He's still holding the ice pack the medic gave him for his knee. It's mostly melted now.

"Jess, your costumes were on point. I really think we could've placed maybe third if we'd just practiced the skit a little more."

"Or at all," Emily mumbles.

"Fair point," Oscar concedes. "Now we know for next time. Finish the costumes early, then spend at least a week choreographing an act." He jots these notes down as he says them. "No ... impromptu ... anything."

"What makes you so sure there's going to be a next time?" Emily asks.

"Oh, come on." Oscar looks at her incredulously. "Don't poop out on me now, just because we had a bad first run."

"No one's 'pooping out.'" Emily's voice rises in pitch a tiny bit. "Did you consider that maybe we're just crap cosplayers?"

"We'll learn!"

"You mean, *you'll* learn," Emily points out. "As you said, I already rocked it."

"Which means we should keep going."

"I'm just not confident you guys can make me look good."

"My leg hurts," Gerrit adds from the back seat, for good measure.

Oscar turns around in the front passenger seat. "I really don't need to hear a pessimistic attitude from you too, Gerrit."

"I'm just saying." Gerrit shrugs, then winces. "Video games are much less dangerous."

"Well, live a little." Oscar turns back around to face the front. "Besides, your mom won't let you quit, we both know that."

"All I said was my leg hurts."

"You'll survive."

"HE FELL OFF A STAGE!" Emily yells.

"SO DID I!" Oscar is seriously starting to lose his cool, which isn't a good look for him. His eyes are all squirrely in the mirror, and he keeps fidgeting with his stupid notebook.

I'm not really in the market to look foolish. I have a badass online reputation to keep up. But if I'm being honest, as humiliating as this disaster was, our costumes really did kick ass. And, excluding the public fiasco of the competition, I had a lot of fun throughout this whole process.

My phone buzzes. I try to drown out the bickering while I check my Insta messages.

Reigna_NYC: "That white gown makes you look just like your grandmother."

My grandmother. For some reason, I never even stopped to consider that somewhere out in the world, my mother has a family. *I* have a family. I might have grandparents or cousins or any number of *real* family members. What if they're looking for my biomom? Do they even know that I exist? I need to find out. I need to meet my biomom in person. This cosplay team has got to pull it together or we'll have no shot at getting to World Cosplay Expo in New York City.

"Enough!" I yell.

The bickering goes silent. Oscar gapes at me through the makeup mirror.

"No one is quitting," I say. "We just need to work a lot harder. To make it to New York, we need to get better."

Oscar smiles at me like I've just promised to read all seven Prince of Moons books.

"I have a plan," Oscar says.

Emily and Gerrit groan.

Emily drops me off late. She parks the van in the dark driveway for a few moments and waits until I get the door unlocked, to make sure I get in okay. It's a really nice gesture. After I wave to her, Emily reverses the van back onto the street to deliver Gerrit to wherever he lives.

I close the front door quietly. The house is dark except for the kitchen light. It's on. As soon as the front door latches, I hear Barbra.

"Jess, is that you?"

Dang. She's usually in bed by 9:00, the unofficial Old Lady Bedtime. Why did she stay up?

"Yeah," I say. "Sorry it's so late. It took a little longer than I expected."

"Would you come here a minute?"

Crap. Thankfully I took my Leia hair donuts out in the car.

"One second," I say as I dash upstairs to my room to take off the Leia dress. In a flash, I toss the bundle of clothes under the bed. I'm just wearing the tank top and leggings that I had on underneath. Do I look suspicious? I feel suspicious. It's like I'm hiding some horrible secret. As if I have a second life as an ax murderer, not a geeky cosplay competitor.

"Deep breaths," I whisper. "Compose yourself."

When I go back down to the kitchen, Barbra is sitting at the table, drinking coffee and reading a book about meditation.

"Isn't it a little late for coffee?" I say by way of avoiding the subject at hand.

"It's decaf."

"Oh." Gross. "Why drink coffee at all then?"

"I used to drink regular coffee all day long." She sets her boring book aside. "Now, just decaf. Honestly, it's more of a comfort thing at this point." She looks down at her cup sadly.

"Even in the morning?"

"Yep."

"But the coffee you make for me is definitely caffeinated," I point out.

"I make a pot for you after mine. I figure you don't have to sacrifice just because I can't drink so much caffeine anymore."

It must be an old person thing.

"Thanks." I didn't realize she was going out of her way to make coffee just for me in the mornings.

"I do it because I care." She smiles at me tiredly.

Guilt racks my insides. The kitchen feels extra small tonight with the windows dark. It's usually so warm and welcoming in the daytime, even with its scratched countertops and paint-chipped cabinets.

"You know, you didn't have to wait up for me." I turn the tea-kettle on to avoid her gaze. "It's way past your bedtime. And I have a key."

"I know. I just wanted to make sure you got home safe."

What, no lecture? No tirade about how irresponsible I am? That's the normal foster parent MO. Threats. Punishments. Disappointment. Mistrust.

"How was your school thing?" she asks, taking another sip of her coffee.

Guess I can't keep avoiding the elephant in the room.

"It was good." I sift through the tea cupboard. How have I never realized that almost everything in here is decaf?

"You look different," she says. "Did you change your look for school?"

It takes me a moment to remember I'm not wearing my goth makeup.

"Oh, yeah." I select a citrusy zinger tea, tear open the package, and put it in a mug decorated with cats. "You know, some people don't like the goth makeup. Didn't want it to affect our . . . grade."

Goddess, I almost said "score." Keep it together, Jess!

Barbra gives me a long look. Maybe there's a lecture coming after all. I brace myself.

She runs her hands over the edges of her meditation book. "I hope you don't feel like you need to change who you are, just to suit what other people think you ought to be."

I blink. Seriously? Since when do adults actually encourage me to be myself?

"You know," I laugh. "Most foster parents do everything they can to get me to take the makeup off."

She shrugs. "That's their problem. You should make a way for yourself in this world by being who you truly are. It never works when people force change for the sake of convention." She sips her gross decaf coffee.

"Right." Why does she have to be so great? Something in me wants to sit down at the table with her and tell her everything: Cosplay. Biomom. Oscar.

Just as I make a move toward her with mug in hand, my phone

buzzes in my back pocket, ruining the shiny illusion. I take it out. There are several waiting messages, one from my biomom.

Barbra watches me as I waver between phone and table. Biomom and Barbra. What am I doing? I know the foster care rules. Don't get attached. Don't let fosters fool you into being too candid with them. Don't get duped into believing they care. They'll still send you away the second they get tired of your bullshit. Blood relatives, now those are forever. Those are the relationships you're supposed to put all your effort into cultivating. At least, that's how it always looks from the outside.

Barbra is great, but I've been waiting to rekindle this relationship with my biomom for nine years. I can't compromise that by telling Barbra what's been going on. The social workers will get involved. They'll tell me to stop all unsupervised contact and insist on reading every word we've shared. They'd ruin every chance I have of fixing this relationship that broke when I was a kid.

"I gotta go," I say. I hold up my phone. "We already have more work to do for the next project."

Barbra's kind smile doesn't waver, though her eyes grow sad.

"You do whatever you need to do." She picks her book up from the table and opens it to the last page she read. "Let me know if you need anything. I'd love to help."

"Thanks."

I take the stairs two at a time. When my bedroom door is closed, I open Insta. The pics I posted from the con have hundreds of likes already.

FairyMagica: "Ahhh! I'm so glad you're branching out into costuming. That's soooo cool."

MarsGirl33: "How did you do that hair?!? You rock the space princess look."

Darkness449: "It's weird to see your face in a dramatically different makeup style. You're so versatile!"

My eyes drift to the DMs. Right below where my biomom said I look like my grandmother, there's another message.

Reigna_NYC: "We should travel to France so you can meet your grandmother soon. You need to be introduced to your family. It's long overdue."

France? Why would my biological family be in Europe? My thumbs hover over the comment button. If I can get a name from my biomom, then maybe I could reach out to my grandparents myself.

GothQueen_13: "Thank you for saying I look like my grandmother. That means a lot to me. I'd love to meet her. Can you tell me who she is?"

I don't expect a response straight away, but I get one.

Reigna_NYC: "Your grandmother is from a long line of European nobles. Your grandfather is Belgian. He died when I was a child."

Her response hits me with an unanticipated rage. Is this real or is she having an episode? Before I type a response, I take a few deep, calming breaths. She didn't say "royalty." Who knows, maybe this information is true. I remind myself that if this is a delusion, it's not her fault.

My stomach turns.

GothQueen_13: "If you're from Europe, why have I always lived in the US? I've seen my birth certificate. I was born in Grand Rapids, Michigan. I'm having trouble understanding what happened."

Reigna_NYC: "My real parents gave me to another family to keep me safe. Like I did for you. I was adopted. We need to meet our real family in France."

My mouth starts to taste metallic. Yep, there's a real chance I might throw up.

I've read enough about schizophrenia to know delusions of adoption are very common. Victims begin to believe that terrible, unspeakable things have happened to them or that they are special in some way. Logically, I know this. That doesn't keep my heart from tearing to pieces. I just can't tell if this is real or not. The doubt makes me feel so guilty.

> **GothQueen_13:** "Please, can you tell me who your adoptive parents are?"
>
> **Reigna_NYC:** "No. They're evil people. I won't let them get anywhere near you."

I lean down, my head between my legs. There is a possibility that this is true. But, then again, it could be a delusion. Diseases of the mind have endless victims. They destroy more than those whose brains are affected.

If I have any shot in hell of finding my family, I need to be honest with my biomom. My fingers type slowly, as if they're fighting my decision.

> **GothQueen_13:** "The thing is, I can't tell if you're having a delusion or not. Please, I need to know the name of another family member. It's not that I don't trust you, it's just that I need to know who my people are."

I hit send, then run to the bathroom to throw up. When I get back, my biomom hasn't messaged me back.

On Monday, she still doesn't respond.

On Tuesday, Oscar brings me a book he found about costume design. But I get nothing from my biomom.

On Wednesday, I attempt damage control by sending her

another message. "I'm sorry. I didn't mean to upset you. Please, will you talk to me?"

Thursday passes without a word. "Please?" I say again.

On Friday, I give up.

I've ruined everything.

CHAPTER 13

EVEN IN THE GRAVE ALL IS NOT LOST.
EDGAR ALLAN POE, "THE PIT AND THE PENDULUM"

That Saturday, Oscar drags us to a sprawling state park west of the city. After we pile out of the minivan, he opens the rear door with the excitement of a magician revealing an illusion. A collection of foam weapons, capes, and all sorts of geek nonsense practically spill out onto the pavement. There're a curiously high number of vehicles pulling into the parking lot, which makes me suspicious.

"You're going to beat us to death in a park?" Emily asks, tapping a spiked baton-looking thing. "Please don't tell me I abandoned learning advanced Python just to be murdered in the forest. That's the opposite of SSDGM. Karen Kilgariff and Georgia Hardstark would be very disappointed in me."

"You planned to do what with a snake?" Oscar squints at her.

Emily groans. "Python isn't a snake, you dork. It's a programming language. Keep up! I thought you were a nerd."

"And I thought you were doing this so you can get into a school that will *teach you* how to code," he grumbles.

She looks at him like he's a fool. "And, pray tell, which top school would accept me if I don't already know the basic programming languages?"

"I could teach you Python," Gerrit says without looking up from his Nintendo Switch.

Emily appraises Gerrit with an obvious newfound respect.

Oscar starts handing out weapons. Emily gets a giant bow that can hold multiple foam-tipped arrows, which are all painted violently bright shades of pink, blue, and green. As Oscar hands them over, he lowers his eyebrows at her.

"Do NOT lose these arrows, Emily. I mean it. Each one took me six hours to craft."

She's already testing it out, shooting Oscar's precious fluorescent arrows across the parking lot. He winces as they bounce off the pavement. Luckily they don't land too far away.

Gerrit has to put his Switch into his back pocket to grab the spiky mace with fake buttons all over the handle. He doesn't look too impressed. He's more hesitant, unsure of whatever it is Oscar has dragged us into this time.

Gerrit jabs at the buttons.

Oscar rolls his eyes. "Obviously you can't ignite a *fake* lightning mace. I might be an expert craftsman, but we don't live in the Adalasian Galaxy." Under his breath he whispers, "Unfortunately."

Oscar ties a belt with a sheath around his waist. It pinches a little at his love handles. He slides a huge gilded sword into the belt and taps it lovingly with his palm.

To me, he holds out a bejeweled staff with delicate silver vines that secure a purple crystal ball at one end. He hands it over gingerly, with both hands, like he's a serf bequeathing his prized possession to his overlord.

Behind us, a family gets out of an SUV. They're all dressed up in medieval armor decorated with space geek details. The littlest boy has a cape painted with a solar system on it.

"Oh no . . ." I say.

"There's a con in the park?" Emily scratches her shin with an arrow.

"Nope. Today, we're going LARPing."

"Come again?" I ask.

"LARPing," Oscar says. "It stands for Live Action Role Play. Today, people from all over East Michigan are meeting to reenact the famous Moonlight Moraine battle scene from *Prince of Moons*." He tucks his dark hair behind his ears nervously. He must have anticipated that this was going to be a hard sell.

"We haven't read that book," I point out.

Oscar hands us each copied pages. "This is definitely against copyright, but it's an emergency. We got here early so you can all take a few minutes to read up. Really, all you need to know is the Inhabitable Planets Union are fighting King Gregory the Mad for control of the Adalasian Galaxy. Emily, you're playing an elf with a moon-magic bow. Gerrit, your mace means you're sort of a human-orc hybrid. Brutal force is your specialty. You use lightning to enhance your weapons."

"Sweet." Gerrit bobs his head appreciatively.

"And Jess, you're playing a spinoff of the infamous space rebel, Queen of Thieves, only not really because the main characters are nominated way ahead of time. We're going to play with the army for the Union. I just figured you'd like to be a dark sorceress character."

I give him a slight bow of thanks.

"We're all on the same team. So, read up. When the game starts, we'll stick together and take back the Adalasian Galaxy for the Inhabitable Planets!" He says this with enthusiasm, like he was hoping we'd cheer. Gerrit just scratches his scalp with his pokey mace thing.

Emily looks skeptical. "How exactly is this going to make us kick-ass cosplayers? We didn't even make a full costume."

"That's okay!" Oscar assures us. "Today, we're learning how to act as different characters. Feel the tension, live the fantasy, that sort of thing."

I'm really uncomfortable with the whole live-the-fantasy angle here, but I squash it down. I'm not my biomom. I know the difference between reality and delusion. It just feels like a more delicate dance to navigate than most people realize.

"So," I ask, "why didn't you just give us these to read earlier this week?"

Oscar gives me a Wise Old Man look. "If I told you I wanted you to read a chapter from *Prince of Moons*, would you have done it?"

"Nope," Gerrit says.

"If I had told you I was going to force you all to act out a scene from *Prince of Moons*, would you have even shown up?"

"Hell no!" Emily says.

Oscar nods. Enough said, I guess.

We break to read the illegally photocopied chapter of *Prince of Moons*. I cringe with every sentence.

"*The Mage of Pentacles hovers over his fallen foe, jowls trembling in anticipation of his first kill.*"

Shiver.

"*Prince Cantor sweeps the delicate Raven Flora up onto his pure white mare, sealing her rescue with a kiss.*"

Barf.

Why does Oscar like this stuff? I sneak a look over at him where he happily parries at nothing with his giant sword, his longish hair flying wildly around his head. I guess we all have our own weird factor.

Once we're all on the same page—ha!—Oscar opens a box containing the rest of our costumes. He reaches in and throws long, baggy T-shirts at Gerrit and Emily.

Emily holds hers up. "What the hell is this?"

"Your tunic," Oscar says as he tosses her a length of rope. "Put it on, then tie this around your waist. Your clothes ruin the illusion."

She looks down at her jeans and patterned button-down, then shrugs. Gerrit puts his on without complaint. Its brown color makes him look like some kind of monk.

"Perfect," Oscar says.

He tries to hand Gerrit an additional cape.

"Nah, I'm good." He drags his lightning mace into the shade, then takes out his Switch.

"What about me?" I ask.

"You're already cool and dark enough to pull off a space sorceress all on your own."

I look down at my tattered black skirt and snakeskin patterned tights. Truth.

"But," he adds. "You're welcome to borrow some *accoutrements.*" He says this last word in a fancy accent, like a lord or something.

As dorky as it is, this feels like a compliment coming from Oscar, so I try to hide my pride by digging through the boxes. I toss out slippers, lengths of cord, and some sort of pelt. I shiver as I set it aside. I hope it's not made from a real animal.

"How did all these nerds even find out about this event?" I ask.

"The *Prince of Moons* fan page."

"Of course there's a fan page," Emily mumbles under her breath as she snags an ornate helmet out of the van's cargo area.

"Did you see the license plates on some of those cars?" I ask.

"Illinois, Indiana, Pennsylvania, Wyoming . . . can you believe people drive thirteen-plus hours to get here for this?"

"Yeah," Oscar says. "I can."

I'm a jerk. There's a fancy pair of metallic fingerless mittens. I put them on, admiring their badass-ness. I could totally wear these to school with my black pleather jacket. I waggle my fingers at Emily. "Look at my cool glove things."

Emily shakes her head sadly, then retreats to the shade with Gerrit.

"They're gauntlets," Oscar says. "In the Prince of Moons universe they'd be magnetic so you could hold on to the sides of spaceships." He looks a little more cheered now that I'm making an effort. As I rummage, I pick up a deep-purple cape.

I look toward Emily. She's over by the tree, still shaking her head at me. It's too late. Oscar has already seen the fabric in my hand. He tries to hide it, but there's glee in his giant childlike eyes. Pure, hope-filled glee. I bite my lip and decide to swallow my dignity. I put the cape over my shoulders.

Across the parking lot, I see Emily put her head in her hands.

As if I've magically granted him permission to be his joyous self again, Oscar digs excitedly through the boxes. He pulls out a forest-green cape to match mine. He adds a helmet on top of his head. Then, hesitantly, he holds out a delicate-looking silver circle. It takes me a moment to realize he's giving it to me. I hold it in my hands, trying to figure out what it is. Is it a necklace? A headband?

"It's the star circlet," Oscar says, as if he's read my mind. "You don't have to wear it if you don't want to, but, you know."

"I know what?"

"It's just pretty." His face is growing red. "You'd look pretty."

I raise one eyebrow at him.

"I mean, you always do! It would just be a little more . . ."

Thank Goddess Emily isn't watching this. She'd never stop teasing him.

"Sure," I say, placing it over my head. It lies just over my eyebrows, its thin swirls decorating my forehead. "And thanks."

Oscar hides his embarrassment by loading all the discarded costume items back into the back of the van. I take a few pics for Insta and upload them under the heading "Me, in all my goth queen glory."

Somewhere deeper into the park, a horn sounds.

We all look to Oscar.

His tone is grave, yet excited. "It's time to battle."

CHAPTER 14

WHAT'S A LITTLE GALAXY WHEN I COULD RULE THE ENTIRE UNIVERSE?
KING GREGORY, *PRINCE OF MOONS*

Prince of Moons geeks of every shape and size merge toward a central field. Emily, Gerrit, and I follow Oscar, our self-appointed liege lord for the day.

"Now, remember," Oscar instructs, "the main rule is once you're hit, you're down for the rest of the battle. Don't really hurt anyone, Emily."

"Why are you targeting me?" She gives him an affronted look.

"Because you're arguably the most violent one of the group."

"Touché." She smiles proudly.

Gerrit squints across the field. "The people in gray are the bad guys, right?"

"Right. They're the King's Army."

"So hit them with our foam thingies?" Emily holds up her bow and arrows. "And try to survive to the end of the game?"

"You got it."

An evil glint appears in her eyes. "You were right to fear me, milord."

Gerrit takes a few wary steps away from her.

All around us, LARPers are dressed in all the shades of the rainbow. Across the field, the opposing army faces us wearing varieties of gray and black.

This is supposed to be a game, but the fierceness in everyone's eyes is starting to make me nervous. They do know this isn't real, right?

Next to me a warrior wielding a large stick grinds it into the ground in anticipation as he stares across the field. His friend, a mage wearing a blue robe with gold trimming, is waving his arms around them both with his eyes closed.

"Hey," I ask. "What's that for?"

The mage opens one eye and looks at me without stopping his hands. "Protection spell. Want some?"

"Er, I'm good," I say. "Thanks."

Oscar is standing on his tippy-toes, looking into the distance. "Okay," he tells us. "It looks like the royal negotiations are failing, just like in the chapter you guys read. We're about to start fighting any minute. Wait for the war horns . . ."

Everyone around us grows silent. It's creepy. Anticipation prickles in the air like an electric current. The eerie quiet doesn't last long. The second a horn sounds, everyone begins shouting.

"And remember to stay in character!" Oscar yells. Emily is already running forward with a team of orcs, her weapon raised high into the air.

Gerrit is being swept forward too, but he looks a little less enthused about it. In a matter of seconds, he disappears into a crowd of mythical creatures.

The wave of people creates instant chaos. I do my best to stay close to Oscar, because I don't know what the hell I'm doing. In this fantastical universe, he's become my life raft.

We both jump out of the way as a gray-clad baddie in an electric wheelchair speeds directly toward us from across the lawn. I turn back to gape and see that her chair has spikes on the wheels like a gladiator's chariot. Spikes! I really hope they're made of foam.

Oscar unsheathes his sword and whaps at an oncoming horde of small children dressed in black. Their little faces are cracked with painted red lightning bolts across milk white skin. They giggle with maniacal laughter as they maneuver around the lumbering adults in costume, making an easy getaway.

"Why do those children look so evil?" I yell over the cacophony of battle cries.

"They're dark sprites from the asteroid belt," Oscar hollers back. "Stay the hell away from those little buttheads."

Note taken. I jump out of the way of an oncoming foam ax. A woman dressed in black, with horns glued to her forehead, screeches as she swings it at me again. I yelp and duck out of the way, covering my head.

"What are you doing?" Oscar asks me as he bops a small child on the shoulder. The child gleefully screeches like a banshee and runs away, keeping his arm dangling at his side like it's useless now. "Stay in character! You're supposed to be a fearless Queen of Thieves, remember?"

I dodge another attack.

"I don't feel very queenly at the moment," I say.

"Use your weapon!" Oscar yells at me as he battles another oncoming horde of evil asteroid sprites.

Oh yeah, the staff.

I whip it up and to the left, smacking the horned lady in the leg.

I'm shocked to realize how good that felt. Apparently, when wielding fake weapons upon a crowd of mythical creatures, I become consumed with a ferocious energy. I kind of like it.

The horned lady comes at me again, this time hopping on her

one good leg. "You humans destroyed my planet," she yells. "You will pay!"

I dodge and roll in a very action-hero move on my part. I could get used to this.

The horned lady loses balance. She topples over onto a pile of slain gray warriors. They all let out an "oof!" as she lands.

A demon-looking creature with a fox tail sees her in a moment of weakness and stabs her in the chest for me. I nod at the fox man in thanks. He takes off running, in search of another gray baddie. The horned woman lets out a wail, then gurgles, succumbing to a very theater major–style death. She lies still, atop the warriors.

"Can't. Breathe," someone on the bottom of the pile whispers. The dead warriors and the horned lady gently roll off him, then remain motionless in the mud.

"Jess!" Oscar calls my name. His voice sounds far away.

I see him several yards off, battling some dark-leather-wearing warriors who are pushing him farther and farther into the surrounding forest.

"I need an assist!" he yells as he dodges a foam mace.

I come running, my staff held high. Now, let's be clear, I don't run. Ever. The very thought of running usually makes my stomach turn. That's how much I hate it. But right now I'm not Jess. I'm the Queen of Thieves and something in me yearns for battle and speed. I dash across the field, giving a gray knight a good whap on the back of the knees as I go. He jumps into the air, then sprawls out on the ground, a little too gleefully for someone who has just died.

I take out the last of Oscar's sprites while I'm at it.

Oscar pants, his hands on his knees. "Thanks."

I attempt to twirl my staff but drop it. Smooth.

The grin on Oscar's face is almost as big as the first time he showed me his sword collection. "It's fun, right?" he asks. There are those dimples again.

I shrug, keeping cool. "I suppose I could get used to playing the Queen of Thieves."

His dark eyes literally sparkle.

I point my staff at him. "Don't you dare start gushing about *Prince of Moons* right now, Oscar. We're supposed to stay in character, remember?"

He wipes dirt off his hands onto his green cloak, trying to hide his obvious delight.

"But," I add. "Should you choose to leave a pile of fantasy books on my front step one afternoon, I wouldn't be opposed to reading them."

Oscar's clenching his jaw shut to keep from squealing in excitement.

"Don't ruin it."

He coughs and looks back out over the battlefield.

"Now let's go kill some gray dudes, or whatever they're called."

I take off into the trees, where a fierce battle is taking place. I stab a spaceman in the ribs, maneuver around a clump of intergalactic fairies throwing invisible spells at each other, whap a dragon-alien-looking thing, and jump away from some more of those damnable asteroid sprites. How are there so many of them? They dart in between battling foes and throw mud at a centaur wearing metallic boots. One little scoundrel even rolls between the legs of a very tall two-headed warrior. He shakes his mace at them as they scurry away.

Then I see it, a mass of gray charging right toward us.

Oscar appears by my side. "Run!" he says.

We dart deeper into the trees, then duck behind a group of

scraggly bushes. There's already someone hiding there, nestled deep into the branches.

"Gerrit?" I say, astonished.

He's legit lounging, his Nintendo Switch in hand. His thumbs are beating at the controls vigorously.

"'Sup," he says without looking up.

I gape at him. "You little sneak."

He shrugs.

Oscar shakes his head sadly as the oncoming army runs past us. "That's not very orc-like behavior, even for a human hybrid."

Gerrit pauses his game to look at Oscar. "Actually, according to the *Prince of Moons* wiki, humans are cowards and cheats. So, really, by hiding until the worst of the battle is over, I'm just exhibiting some of my basest character traits."

I blink at him.

"I did a little research before the battle started."

"No kidding." I glance at Oscar.

He actually looks proud. "Okay, then. We'll leave you to it."

Gerrit unpauses his game.

A passing sprite crawls through the bushes, spots Gerrit, and jabs him quickly with a foam dagger.

"Ow," Gerrit deadpans.

The demon spawn turns toward me.

I hold up my magical staff. "Don't even think about it, fiend."

She giggles and scurries away.

Gerrit shrugs. "Guess I'm out."

Oscar sighs, then turns to me. "Shall we?"

When I peek around the bushes, I see most of the battle has moved back toward the field again.

"We shall."

As we walk toward the action, we pass the bodies of slain *Prince of Moons* geeks. Some are whispering and giggling in the dirt. Here and there, a few hobbled creatures poke at the dead with sticks, then hold out their hands for goodies.

"Hobgoblins from the planet Ohair," Oscar explains. "They rob the dead."

"And some people LARP as those characters?"

"To each their own."

"Gross." I give one a good smack in the legs with my stick—I mean magical staff—for good measure. The hobgoblin makes a big show of falling to the ground. He then drags his body through the mud with his arms, still poking the dead and taking whatever treasures they have in their pockets along the way.

Weird. Morbid. Kind of awesome.

I admire the hobgoblin's industrious spirit. Maybe next time I'll join their squad.

What am I thinking? Next time? Who am I becoming?

Oscar and I crouch behind a tree at the field's edge. There are several small groups battling it out a few yards away. Half a dozen short, skinny gray warriors with braces run past us in a frenzy. Emily is hot on their furry tails. She's yelling ferociously, her bow aimed directly at them. Behind her, a dainty elf maiden prances, throwing fake spells at the retreating army. Emily gives her a grateful, roguish grin. She's covered in dirt, head to toe. She's never looked more alive than now, when she's chasing down a group of terrified middle-schoolers dressed in fake battle armor.

"Okay, we've made it to the final phase of the Battle of Moonlight Moraine," Oscar says, excitedly. His round cheeks are flushed with exhilaration, instead of his usual bashfulness. "I never thought we'd make it this far!"

"Have ye so little faith in us?" I ask, one hand against my heart to show my affront.

He rolls his eyes at me.

"It looks like we're right on schedule." He points to the farthest end of the field, where a group, including the true Queen of Thieves, is battling out a highly choreographed scene. Their metallic armor glints in the sunlight as their capes flutter about with their dance-like sword moves. It's really very beautiful, but I'm not sure if I'm willing to inflate Oscar's head more by telling him that. I get it now. Being a geek is fun. But I'm still a little goth queen at heart.

"What's your character, exactly?" I ask. "You never did say."

He doesn't look at me, as his ears start to glow pink. "Sir Valorian," he says.

"Who's that?"

Oscar shrugs. "Just a knight."

By the way he refuses to look at me, I suspect Sir Valorian is more than a normal knight. I don't press the issue.

"So, now what?" I ask, but before he can respond, someone roars behind me. I spin around to find a giant troll with rock armor. He's swinging a hammer made of fake boulders. Oscar and I roll out of the way, in separate directions, as the hammer hits the ground where we were once crouching.

The rock troll turns to attack me, swinging his clumsy hammer. I reach for my staff, only to realize I dropped it by the tree when I ducked. I scoot backward, out of the troll's reach, as he swings again and again. I don't have time to stand up and run, or dash for my weapon. The rock troll lifts his hammer high over his head, a grin of anticipation spreading across his filthy face. I cringe, awaiting the final blow. It doesn't come.

The rock troll lets out a wail and spins around, revealing

Oscar—I mean, Sir Valorian—behind him with his sword pointed at the troll's backside. Sir Valorian jabs him again in the ribs as the rock troll falls. Sir Valorian jumps over the slain creature, then holds out a confident hand toward me. The sun halos behind his long hair giving him an otherworldly aura as his cape flaps majestically in the breeze.

I take his outstretched hand, stunned. What happened to the bumbling, awkward, blushing Oscar that I know so well? The chivalrous hero in front of me must have stepped right out of a fantasy novel. This is a side of Oscar that I've never seen before. Or is this who he's truly been all along? Maybe I just never saw it.

Sir Valorian helps me to my feet. He stands proudly over his victim.

"Thanks," I say.

He whips his cape out behind him and bows. "Anything for you, milady."

I don't even tease him this time. If there ever were an environment where he could play out his Sir Valorian fantasy, this would be it.

At the end of the battle, Emily finds us. She's arm in arm with the dainty elf maiden. When Emily spots us, the elf maiden kisses her on the cheek, then skips away to find her teammates.

Maybe I'm mistaken, but there appears to be a marked spring in Emily's step as she approaches us.

"Glad to see you didn't lose all my arrows," Oscar says, noting the full quiver strapped to her back.

Emily acts insulted. "I would never lose your precious pokey things, Oscar!"

She jabs him with one a few times, then hands the lot over.

"Did you survive to the end of the battle?" I ask her.

"Nah." She looks out to where the elf maiden is giggling with her friends. "The double-crossing minx turned on me in the end. Stabbed me when I let my guard down." She doesn't seem too disappointed about this as she stares across the field with a goofy smile on her face.

She turns back to us. "I have a new cosplay rule to add to our list. We need to do a fight scene for our next skit."

"We tried one last time," Oscar reminds her.

"Yes, but you all stunk at it. Now we're warmed up."

Oscar scratches his chin. "I think we can manage that."

"What's our next theme then?" I ask.

"Scream queens." He gives me a devilish grin. Or at least, as devilish as angelic Oscar can possibly pull off.

Emily screws up her face. "Does not compute."

Oscar explains. "You know how old horror films always have one survivor in the end, usually a woman? That's a scream queen."

"Since when do horror movies count as geek?" I ask.

Oscar actually scoffs. "Since, like, forever. Ever seen *The Creature from the Black Lagoon*? How about the original *Nosferatu* or *Frankenstein*?"

My eyes must betray my skepticism. This sounds too good to be true.

"The geek universe is a multifaceted diamond, Jess. Embrace it."

I shrug. If Oscar, the geekiest guy I've ever met, says we can do a horror theme, then horror we shall do.

Emily turns to me. "Does that count for your 'royalty' rule?"

"Actually," I say, thinking of all the gore makeup effects I could try out, "it's perfect."

Only problem? I haven't actually seen many *super* old horror films. I'm more of a 2000s and newer paranormal thriller kinda gal. Give me *The Conjuring*, *The Witch*, *The Others*, or *The Skeleton Key*. Or any scary movie that starts with the word "the," apparently. Is there a witch or a ghost? If yes, then I'm all in. Scream queens are waaaay before my time.

So I ask, "Which scream queen exactly?"

"I vote Jess picks." Oscar says this like he's gifting me the best present of all time.

A tiny thrill flutters in my heart. This. Could. Be. Epic.

Something in the back of my mind tells me Oscar put a lot of thought into this idea. It's pretty obvious that this theme choice was made specifically for me, considering it's definitely more aligned with my personal interests than his. Dear Goddess, are those fluttering moths in my stomach? They'd better not be.

Emily shrugs. "'Kay. Cool." She looks around at the slowly emptying field. "Where's that vagabond, Gerrit?"

I point back toward the trees. "Hiding in the bushes."

Emily takes a foam dagger out from where it's tucked into her belt. Where on earth did she get that?

"I'll go fetch him. Meet you at the van!" she yells behind her as she runs off.

Oscar and I start walking back toward the parking lot.

All around us grinning LARPers are chatting in groups, muddy and sweaty. The energy is markedly different than it was before the battle. Now everyone is laughing, slapping each other on the helmet or chest bumping breastplates. It's like everyone needed an hour to let the weird out so they could go back to normal life with all its boring complications. In some ways living in a fantasy sounds very appealing. My heart seizes in my chest as I think this and remember my mother.

No, it's not appealing to live in a fantasy, I remind myself. *Never think that again.*

I need to get away from this line of thought before it brings me down. Before it ruins every good thing about this day. It frustrates me that I can't even have fun without dark thoughts clouding my experience.

"What does the Queen of Thieves steal anyway?" I ask Oscar.

He digs the toe of his boot into the dirt. "Hearts."

I tilt my head at him. "I didn't take her for the romantic type."

"No, like literal hearts. She collects them in jars."

"Oh. Badass."

"Thought you'd like that."

All around us the fantastical creatures are making dinner plans and crawling into their vehicles for departure. I'm surprised to realize I'm sort of sad it's all over.

"So, that was a pretty cool rescue back there, Sir Valorian," I say, punching him lightly in the arm.

He blushes; the old Oscar is back.

"Did you have fun?" he asks. His shoulders are stiff like he's bracing himself for whatever negative response he's expecting me to give him.

"Actually," I say. "I really did." And I'm as surprised as anyone else to realize that's 100 percent true. Maybe deep down this goth queen is also a geek goddess. This might have been the most fun I've had in a really, really long time.

"I think I get it now," I say.

"This exercise was instructive for cosplay competitions then?" he asks.

"Definitely. The costumes are important, but we have to bring the characters to life if we really want to win this thing."

And winning this thing is everything, I don't say.

Oscar stops walking.

I turn back toward him.

"I really think we can do this," he says. There's a look of determination in his eyes, a flash of Sir Valorian that he keeps hidden most of the time.

My legs still tingle with the thrill of running through the battlefields. My arms feel strong with the staff clutched in one hand. And then there's an odd fluttering in my chest at the memory of a rock troll and a certain knight named Valorian.

Yikes, I'm not ready for that particular confrontation.

"We're going to make it to New York," I say instead. I touch the delicate silver star circlet at my temple. "Let's kick some cosplay ass."

CHAPTER 15

I EAT HUMAN ORGANS FOR SUPPER.
WITH A GLASS OF MERLOT, OF COURSE.
QUEEN OF THIEVES, *PRINCE OF MOONS*

After school on Monday, there's an extra dose of excitement in my step as I walk my combat boot–clad feet through the front door of Barbra's house. In anticipation of our next con, I made a pit stop at the public library to check out every major scream queen Blu-ray the librarians could find for me. One librarian, who happened to have pink hair and tattoos, seriously hooked me up. My arms cradle a veritable treasure trove of horror history.

As I push the front door closed with my hip, the chain I'd attached to my faux-leather miniskirt gets caught on the door handle. When I fumble to release my clothing, the giant pile of DVDs spills from my arms and crashes to the floor.

"You okay?" I hear Barbra call from another room.

Crap. I try to scoop them up again before she sees, but I'm too late. In seconds, she's kneeling down in her baggy meditation class sweats to help me. She pauses when she realizes what I've dropped.

"What's this?" she says, squinting at the cover of *Friday the 13th*.

"It's nothing," I say hurriedly. "You can go to your class." I reach under the foyer table to snatch up *Swamp Thing*. "It's just research."

Barbra picks up *Rosemary's Baby*. "Are you writing a paper on old horror films?"

"Something like that."

She holds *Rosemary's Baby* up with a look of pure excitement. "This was my favorite movie for an entire decade!"

I sit back on my haunches to study her. There's a real possibility she's messing with me.

"Are you sure you're not confusing it with something else?" I ask as I take the movie from her hand and read the back.

"It's one of the best films ever made," she insists. "It has a baby-sacrificing cult that worships the devil." She smiles fondly at it. "I think you'll like it."

I just stare at her, unable to calculate how this middle-aged normie knows so much about satanic-cult films.

She reaches out to grab the original *Halloween* DVD. She sighs and holds it to her chest. "Oh my god! I haven't seen this in ages!"

What the hell is going on?

She looks up at me. "Do you need to watch these for your research? Could I please watch them with you?"

My brain is buzzing with this strange new information about Barbra.

"Um, sure," I say.

She literally squeals like she's lost thirty years off her age. "How about Friday night? We can do an all-nighter. I'll get the supplies."

"Supplies?"

She drops the movie to her lap and stares at me wide-eyed. "Don't tell me you've never done an all-nighter before?"

I mean, I have. Alone. Not with any friends or anything. Definitely not with my foster parents.

"I guess not like this?" I say.

If it's possible, Barbra grows even more excited. "This is going to be so much fun. You're going to love these." She gestures toward my pile of DVDs. "They'll change your life."

I stare at her as I try to readjust everything I thought I knew about my foster mom. Her bulky sweaters and old lady loafers gave me no hint—none at all!—that we might have something in common. I'm not sure how to process this information yet.

When I slam my locker closed before class the next morning, I nearly punch the face that's three feet away from mine.

"Holy Hell, Oscar." My hand clutches at my chest. "You're lucky I don't have one of those space daggers. I have a tendency to attack first, then ask questions later."

Oscar takes a giant step back, holding up his hands to indicate he's not a threat.

"Sorry! Or, not sorry. I mean . . ." He stumbles over yet another apology. "Um, noted."

I pull the strap of my satchel higher up my shoulder. "Just tell me why you're here and we'll call it even."

"Right!" His ears glow pink as he sifts through his giant freshman-style backpack. "Have you picked out a scream queen yet?"

"No. Still working on it." My stomach twists at the idea of my impending movie night with Barbra.

"I have something for you," he says.

One of my perfectly shaped eyebrows arches without my explicit permission. "What do you mean?"

"Like, I got this thing." He's still shuffling through his bag. "Like a thank you . . . thing." His blush is out of control.

"You mean, like a present?" Goddess, I hate presents. They

always come with some sort of obligatory, unspoken request. Like a gift card that's laced with psychological arsenic.

Oscar finds what he's looking for in his bag. He pulls out a thin, square item, then holds it toward me without making eye contact. Whatever it is, he's wrapped it in black tissue paper and tied it with a red ribbon.

He shrugs. "It's just a little thing. To say thanks. For being cool about our first big fail and convincing the team to keep going."

"We haven't even won anything yet," I protest.

"That's okay!" He smiles genuinely. "We're still doing a ridiculously good job for newbies."

When I don't reach for the gift, he pushes it closer to me. "I wanted to show you how much I appreciate you. And . . ." He looks away. "For what you said before our first competition. When I kind of freaked out backstage. It was really nice."

"Nice? I'm not nice," I say. "And you don't have to pay me back for talking to you or anything."

"I know," he says as he looks back at me, his eyes earnest. "I wanted to." He pushes the flat square toward me again.

I hesitate. "I didn't get you anything."

"That's fine. I wasn't expecting you to."

I reach out to take the present, then pause awkwardly for a few seconds, not sure what to do now. "Did you want me to open it in front of you?"

Please don't ask me to open it now, I pray silently to the Goddess. I hate fake smiling when people are watching for your reaction.

"No, that's okay." His ears redden again. "Just, whenever." The halls are thinning out as people run to their next class. "I gotta go anyways."

My hand feels hot, like he's given me a live wire instead of a thin, lightweight square. I open my satchel and put the mystery present inside.

"See you this weekend," he says brightly, his Oscar dimples on full display. "I'm looking forward to scream queens."

He scurries down the hallway with his giant backpack, like a turtle late for work. My satchel feels like it's on fire with this secret thing inside. Really, I can't be expected to go to class with this mystery on my hands. I duck into the bathroom to get out of the hallway. It smells like bleach in here but it's blessedly quiet. I kick open all the stall doors to make sure I'm actually alone. The bell rings. That means I have at least a solid fifteen minutes before anyone leaves class to interrupt me in here.

My hand fishes around my bag until I feel the slick tissue paper. I pull it out and set the package on the sink. Why, oh why, did Oscar have to make things weird? What should I say when I see him next? Am I supposed to get him something in return now? If I don't, will things get weirder and weirder between us until we have to break up the group? Why does Oscar have to be so Goddess-damned sweet all the time? It's unnerving.

I poke the red ribbon with my finger.

"Well, here goes nothing," I mumble to myself as I untie the bow.

After I tear off the paper, I stand there, confused. It's a CD. Who even burns CDs anymore? That's, like, ancient tech now. At least he didn't spend much money on this surprise gift.

When I turn the CD case over, a man with a mullet and a rainbow-colored lightning bolt painted across his face greets me. It's David Bowie. The album name reads *Aladdin Sane*. Oscar used a blue ballpoint pen to write "And other songs."

"Why the hell . . ." What possessed Oscar to think '70s music would appeal to a goth queen?

I crack open the cover and a small notecard falls out into the sink. It's a little damp when I pick it up, but the scratchy handwriting isn't affected.

Jess,

I wanted to thank you for talking me down from my panic attack at the con. Also, I'm really honored that you told me about your mom. I didn't know how to bring this up, so I thought I could show you how much I appreciate you with this CD. Bowie has better skill with words than I do. His music explores his own complicated emotions about his family's battle with mental illness. Several of his family members were institutionalized for schizophrenia. Now I see how most of these songs are terribly depressing. Maybe we can make our own, more inspiring art to make up for it. For now, I just want to say thanks.

—Oscar

My hands tremble as I read the note. While something inside of me says this could be perceived as an extremely insensitive gift, it's not, because in many ways Oscar gets it. I'm growing so tired of hiding this side of me. Knowing there's one person out there who feels the way I do makes this gift feel less like an insult and more like a mini-liberation. I'm allowed to feel. I'm allowed to say this crap with my mom is a mess. It's fucked up. And it's just a little bit validating to know that I'm not the only one in the world who has ever felt this way.

The bathroom door creaks when I push it open. Instead of going to class, I veer toward the computer lab. No one notices me when I snag a station near the entrance and plug my headphones into an aging desktop. The CD drive whines when I put my new Bowie CD into its tray. As the strange sound of the 1970s drifts through my headphones, I listen.

The first song, "All the Madmen," has an eerie feeling to it before chirruping recorders add an oddly upbeat note. A synthesizer joins in, giving the music a confusing sound, like I'm not quite sure where this song is going. This certainly isn't the predictable music of today's pop. It's delirium in music form, and it makes me uneasy. When I pay attention to Bowie's lyrics, it's clear that was intentional. He sings about his friends who were sent away to be locked up in cold, dark asylums.

With a quick Google search, I see Oscar was right. Bowie did have a family history of schizophrenia. Several aunts and his half-brother were sent to asylums. His brother died by suicide, a terrifying but all-too-common reality for people diagnosed with the same illness that my mother has.

In middle school, there were nights when I couldn't sleep because of nightmares where my mother would take her own life. I'd lie in bed, paralyzed with anxiety because I couldn't stop her while I was locked up in foster homes. It was a relief when my social worker assured me my biomom had been sent to a hospital to keep her from hurting herself. And from hurting others, she implied.

Bowie continues singing through my headphones. His lyrics suggest that he doubts his own sanity. He sings that he can't relate to the normal, sane population. At least he can feel content around other people with mental illness.

It's suddenly hard to believe that I've lived this long without knowing another human being who understands what this is like. I wonder if Bowie felt the same conflicted emotions that I do.

I jump as the printer next to my workstation roars to life. I'd nearly forgotten where I was. A guy wearing a stupid graphic tee walks up and grabs his printout. He pauses to give me a curious glance, no doubt because I'm not in his class and therefore not supposed to be in here. I cock my head to the side and give him a dark smile that dares him to tell on me. He walks away, hands up in surrender.

My own hands reach for my phone in my satchel. Almost instinctively, I open Insta. Still no word from my biomom.

A lighting flash of pain ricochets through my skull. So, I guess the stress headaches are back along with the old nightmares. It's like I'm regressing into the terrifying childhood that I worked so hard to leave behind.

A new song begins on the CD: "Aladdin Sane." The title cleverly plays with the phrase "a lad insane." Bowie sings into my ears, asking who will love the mentally ill.

Honestly, I'm not really sure.

CHAPTER 16

YOU CALL IT HOPE—THAT FIRE OF FIRE!
IT IS BUT AGONY OF DESIRE.
EDGAR ALLAN POE, "TAMERLANE"

Friday night rolls around much quicker than I expected it to. All week, Barbra has been bringing up our impending all-nighter, like I should be just as excited as she is. And I guess I am, in a way. Mostly I'm nervous. Based on my personal experience, foster parent expectations for fun are rarely met. Still, I can't really back out now, especially since Oscar and the team are waiting for me to make a decision about which scream queen will reign supreme. We have to get started on costumes if we're going to be ready for the next con in two weeks' time.

From my bedroom window, I watch as Barbra pulls up in her rusty car after her late-afternoon yoga class. She's usually super chill after those sessions, but today she jumps out of the car with a huge grin plastered across her face. She opens the back seat door and loads her arms with bulging reusable grocery bags. I walk downstairs to open the front door for her.

"Are you excited?" She beams.

"Sure," I say, taking one of the bags from her overladen arms. When I open it to peek inside, I see popcorn, M&M's, peanut butter, and celery. "Um, this is an unusual grocery selection."

Barbra shakes her head vigorously as she puts her bags onto

the kitchen counter. "You've never experienced a true all-nighter. We're going all-out."

"And that includes celery?" I ask, waving the green sticks in the air.

"One of my favorite movie snacks when I was a kid." She digs into her bags to unpack them. "Celery and peanut butter with M&M's on top."

"Isn't it supposed to be raisins?"

She puts one hand on her hip. "You absolutely *do not* eat healthy food during a movie all-nighter, Jess. That's rule number one."

"Okay, okay." I hold up my hands in resignation. "You're the maestro. Teach me your ways."

"Catch," she says as she tosses me her phone. "Call Jimmy's Pizza. We're going to need a large, extra cheese with whatever toppings you want." She begins washing the celery and arranging it on a plate. "And jalapeño poppers."

"You got it."

Once the pizza is delivered and all the snacks are prepared, I stand in awe. I swear this is the least healthy spread I've ever seen Barbra prepare. Usually she aims for food that's at least somewhat good for her.

"You've turned into a rebel," I say, as I open the pizza box. We had to bring extra chairs into the living room to act as tables for the ridiculous array of snacks.

"This is fuel," she says. "It's a necessity to get us through the night." She reaches into the cooler she's placed alongside the sofa and tosses me a Faygo, Detroit's pop of choice. It's Rock & Rye flavored.

"By the way," Barbra says as she grabs a giant slice of mushroom pizza. "I've noticed you've been listening to a lot of David Bowie."

My shoulders stiffen. Of course she can hear my music in this tiny house. I'd still like to think my bedroom is more private than it is. I'm slipping on my foster kid rules. I'll have to amend that by investing in some better headphones, if we ever win cosplay money.

"If you like these old movies, you should really watch *Labyrinth*. Bowie's in it. And in some very tight pants."

I snort Rock & Rye up my nose.

"The '80s was a golden era for the fantastical," she adds matter-of-factly.

"I'll keep that in mind." I wipe my stinging nose on a napkin and sift through the DVDs. "What should we watch first?"

Barbra ponders our choices, then points to *Halloween*.

"Let's start with my teenage crush." She settles into a corner of the couch. "You're going to adore Jamie Lee Curtis. She's the ultimate scream queen."

My head turns to look at Barbra as she loads the DVD into the player. Barbra knows about scream queens? What rabbit hole have I fallen into?

Two films in, I'm surprised by how much I love these movies. The ridiculous screaming, the fake gore, the strength of the women who survive against all odds. And I'm even more astounded by how much fun I'm having with Barbra.

And yes, I am hyperaware that the bad guys in these films are mentally ill. This is a long tradition in which my own life has become wrapped up. These movies include an entirely different kind of terror for me because I can sympathize with both the monster and the heroine. That doesn't mean I can't separate people like my mother from fictional characters like Michael Myers. I'm lucky enough to know how to separate fact from fiction. I'll have to untangle these complicated themes later, when I have time to parse them apart and really think about why people like my mother have become public enemy number one.

I'm beginning to understand that these types of films are at least partially responsible for the stigma that I feel about mental illness, but that doesn't mean I'm not allowed to love them for the ancient history that they are. I can be critical of something and still love it. That's the beauty of art. It's a mirror that reflects our society back at us. If we critique it, we can slowly change the reflection we see.

"Okay," Barbra says as the credits roll at the end of *Psycho*. "I didn't tell you this at the beginning of the movie because I wanted to watch your face while I blow your mind."

"Um, okay."

"You've now been introduced to Janet Leigh, the actress in *Psycho*."

"I sure have." I open a new bag of M&M's.

"That was Jamie Lee Curtis's mom."

"No!" I spill M&M's all over my lap in astonishment.

"Yes! Spooky acting runs in their family."

"That's a family legacy I could get on board with," I say, truly surprised. "Good reveal." I pretend tip my imaginary hat toward Barbra.

She gives me a bow. "I've learned a few things about dramatic timing from those gals."

"I guess so," I say, as I pick all the M&M's out of the crevices of the couch.

There are a few moments of silence as Barbra considers our

next movie choices. It's getting close to midnight, but we still have hours left if we're going to complete this all-nighter. Barbra has had a constant supply of caffeinated coffee brewing in the kitchen for me. I'm committed.

From behind me, I hear Barbra say, "I think it's time."

"For?" I ask. I blow some lint off a piece of candy and pop it into my mouth.

"The masterpiece," she says with gravitas.

I turn to raise an eyebrow at her. "That being?"

She picks up *A Nightmare on Elm Street* with gentle hands, like it's treasure. "This is the greatest horror movie ever made."

I scoff. "It can't be. We just witnessed the magic of Jamie Lee Curtis."

"And yet, you haven't met Heather Langenkamp as Nancy Thompson." She nods at me solemnly. "You're never going to sleep again." She slides the disc into the DVD player with so much glee, I have to laugh a little.

Twenty minutes later, I'm so wrapped up in Freddy Krueger's mission to murder the teenagers of Springwood, Ohio, that it takes me a long time to realize I'm hearing some kind of echo in the dialogue. I look around the room, confused, only to see Barbra's face stage-lit from the glow of the TV, her eyes glued to the screen as she says every single line along with the cast. I watch her for several minutes. She does not miss a beat. I reach for the remote and pause the movie.

Barbra looks up as if shaken out of a daze. "What happened?"

I lean forward. "Do you seriously know every single line in this movie?"

She grins sheepishly. "Sorry, that must be annoying. I'm so used to watching movies alone. I forgot I do that. I'll stop."

I lean back in my chair, astounded. "You're a geek."

She laughs. "I guess that's one word for it."

"No, seriously, how have I never known you like old horror movies?"

She shrugs. "Guess it never came up."

Something deep inside of me is yelling, *Tell her! She'll understand!* But I don't. No one, especially not fosters, will think competing as fantastical characters is normal teenaged behavior. And I'm not about to ruin the tentative peace we have going on in this house. I've ruined too many foster family situations to risk it. Still, maybe Barbra doesn't need to know the *whole* truth.

"Oh no," she says as she drops her head into her hands. "Am I embarrassing you? Have I become the foster parent you can't tell your friends about?"

A laugh bubbles out of me. "No." I pick up the remote. "Strangely, I think it's actually kind of cool."

She picks up a celery stick covered with candy and points at me with it. "'Cool' is definitely not a word people usually associate with me." She crunches the weird snack, smiling to herself.

"Maybe," I say. "Though it turns out being a geek is actually in vogue right now."

She gives me a skeptical look.

"Seriously!"

I am dying to tell her about the cosplay team, even though I don't fully understand why. Maybe it's just because I'm starting to like her. Not as a foster, necessarily. More as a person. I'll never like fosters. That's just a fact. You can't care for someone who you hardly know, who's being paid by the government to keep you housed and fed. But Barbra is, I don't know, different. As corny as that sounds.

"So, there's this thing I do sometimes," I say, choosing my words carefully. "With my friends, Emily, Oscar, and Gerrit."

"Something geeky yet cool, I presume?" she asks.

"You could say that. At least, some people think so. There are definitely still a lot of people who would think we're weirdos." I avoid her eyes while I think of how to tell her about cosplay *without* telling her about competitions that lead to biomom reunions in New York City.

"Well," Barbra laughs. "I'd like to see someone try to give you a swirly. I'm sure you'd kick their butts." She gives me a serious look. "Some people might think you're weird, but I think you're an impressive young lady."

I scoff. "An 'impressive young lady'? You sound like you're from another century."

She shrugs, taking another bite out of her celery stick. "Well, if you'd like me to be vulgar about it, you're a badass B who doesn't take crap from anybody. You're a survivor. And I admire you for it."

My face feels like it's heating up. Since when do fosters think I'm impressive? I'm usually the bane of their existence.

"Thanks," I mumble, taking a sip from my pop can.

"So, what's this nerdy-but-cool thing you do with your friends?" she asks.

I shrug. "It's nothing big. We just create different looks from popular science fiction and fantasy books or movies. Then we post our photos on Insta. People seem to like it."

"What do you mean by 'looks'?"

"Like, we pretend to be different characters. I usually do our hair and makeup so we look like them, then we pose as if we're in the movie."

Barbra surprises me by laughing. I flinch. Maybe telling her even this much was a mistake.

"That sounds like so much fun!" she says.

I eye her skeptically. "You don't think I'm ridiculous?"

"What? No!" she insists. "I wish I had thought to do something like that when I was a kid. What movies have you done?"

My shoulders are still tense while I try to figure out if I believe her or not. "*Star Wars*, for one."

"Who did you pretend to be?"

"Leia. Emily was Han Solo. Oscar made droid costumes so he and Gerrit could be R2-D2 and C-3PO."

Barbra's eyes are shining with amusement. "Did you wear the cinnamon bun hair?"

I nod.

"Could I see?"

Part of me thinks I've gone too far. This is where she figures everything out. I select my favorite group shot of us, one where you can't see the chaos of the con in the background. I hand over my phone and hold my breath.

Barbra holds it up to her face and lets out a sigh. "You kids are so creative." She looks up at me. "And talented." She hands the phone back to me. "Don't ever let that go."

I take the phone back and stuff it into my hoodie pocket. My heart is beating like a jackhammer. I've never willingly told a foster anything about my personal life. Ever. Only time will tell if this was a terrible impulse to follow or not.

Flustered, I pick up the remote and push play. The DVD picks up right where we left off, with Nancy running from Freddy Krueger in her nightmare. It's difficult to pretend not to notice the glow of happiness that spreads out from where Barbra is sitting. Her smile is more comfortable and genuine than any other foster I've seen. Maybe this can work between us after all.

As the movie plays on, I learn to appreciate all the cheesy 1980s horror effects. I also start to see why Barbra loves this movie so much. Yes, it's a story about a monster who chases teenagers so he can brutally murder them one by one. Yes, it's over-the-top dramatic with problematic themes. And yes, it's a story of a maniac with unstoppable cruelty laced with homicidal creativity.

But.

It's also a story about surviving trauma. It's a story about madness and all the complex ways society treats people labeled with that word. It's about being chased down by an invisible monster that no one else can see. I am Nancy Thompson. I can't help but wonder if maybe Barbra is too, in her own way.

Also, it's a story about baby Johnny Depp getting sucked into a mattress and turned into a violent, spewing pile of gore. I am 100 percent into that.

So, which scream queen will reign supreme? When I look at the pure joy on Barbra's face, I know in my heart that there's no other choice.

Look out cosplayers, Nancy Thompson and Freddy Krueger are going to wear the crown this time.

We're gonna need fake blood.

A lot of it.

CHAPTER 17

Deep in the depths of the basement Costume Lair, my phone burns in my back pocket with a message from my biomom.

> **Reigna_NYC:** "Can I have your address? I want to send you something."

It's been weeks since I last heard from her. She didn't even mention the grandparent fiasco. Or the fact that I didn't trust her. It's like nothing happened. While I'm glad she finally responded to me, it's a little unnerving that she completely skipped over our last conversation. Not to mention the fact that she left me freaking out for so long. Her mini-disappearing act only reinforces my need to get to New York in May. She could disappear forever if I wait too long to find her.

My hands run over the mousy brown wig that's propped on top of a mannequin's head that I've secured to the worktable with tape. Somehow, I need to turn this cheap hairpiece into a fabulous perm. We're doing *A Nightmare on Elm Street*, but we're going big. Like, literally. Nancy Thompson's hair is spectacularly curly.

I pick up a strand of the wig's hair and wrap it around the hot curling iron. I'm not used to curls since my goth aesthetic typically includes straight hair or braids. These little guys are proving to be much wilier than I expected. Nice curly wigs are expensive, so

I thought I'd buy a cheap one and style it myself. Suffice it to say it's not going so well. So far, half of the mannequin's head looks like a glorious rat's nest.

The next competition is in two weeks. We've already blocked our skit. Still, it's going to be a genuine scramble to get everything done on time. I really don't have the mental or emotional energy to deal with my biomom's request right now, on top of everything else.

You're thinking, what's the big deal, right? My biomom just asked for my mailing address. What's so stressful about that? If that's your initial reaction, you're obviously not a foster kid.

Foster Care Pro-tip number seven: Never, EVER give your bioparents your foster address. Social workers drill that into your head from the moment you enter the system. It's a real threat. Bioparents have been known to show up unannounced for un-authorized visits, send death threats to foster parents, kidnap kids, etc....

Right now, I'm not sure I believe my biomom's motives for asking for my personal information. What on earth could she want to send to me? I feel like total shit for being suspicious of her—again!—but this only reinforces the idea that I don't actu-ally know this woman. We're related by blood, but I have no idea who my biomom is.

The wig hair gets tangled in the curling iron, and the sickening smell of burning hair meets my nose.

"Goddess damn it all," I mumble under my breath. I tug the curling iron a little too forcefully, knocking the mannequin head clear off the table. "What fresh hell . . ." I grab the wig to save it from the filthy carpet and manage to smack my own hand with the burning hot iron in the process. "Arg!"

I throw everything back onto the table and pull the plug out from the wall in what I am ashamed to admit is a bit of a hissy fit.

Across the room, Oscar pushes his goggles up to his forehead. They left pink indentations in his cheeks.

"So, how are things?" he asks innocently.

I stick my burned finger in my mouth. Clearly, I'm not in the right emotional state for this.

His steps sound light as he walks across the carpet in bare feet. He picks up the severed-looking mannequin head, brushes it off, and sets it on the table. Then he sits on the floor next to me.

"At the risk of being too nosy," he says hesitantly, "is life going okay with the foster situation?"

Am I that obvious? Yes, I tell myself. I just threw a mini temper tantrum over a wig. I couldn't be more obvious if I tried.

"Barbra is fine."

"I couldn't help noticing how much time you spend here in the dungeon."

"We have a ton of work to do," I snap.

"I know," he says. "I just want to make sure you're, you know, good over there."

"I'm good." Even I can tell my voice doesn't sound convincing.

"At the risk of pissing you off, can I ask you a personal question?" He picks at the dried splatter of craft glue that's stuck in the carpet.

I eye him. "That depends. Why?"

"I dunno." He shrugs. "I'd like to understand you a little better. Get to know you." He blushes.

No one ever asks me personal questions. I assume it's because I'm far too creepy. Like, maybe they think I'll bite them. And maybe I would. Besides, once people dip their toes into the personal waters with me, they tend to regret it. My foster care status always pops up. Then people feel awkward and wish they'd never asked. It's like I'm toxic. No one seems to have immunity to me, except Oscar, oddly enough. He already knows I'm a foster. And, thus far, he's treated me . . . I don't know. Normal.

"If this is too weird or rude or anything, feel free to push me into a locker again sometime," he adds hurriedly.

Despite my shitty mood, I laugh. Somehow this geeky guy's awkwardness has grown from supremely annoying to goofy. Dare I say cute?

"If you're going to ask me a question, ask it already," I say.

"So." He clears his throat. "I think by now you understand that I'm being totally honest when I say I like your goth look." He waits, watching to see if I'll strike like a cobra.

I don't. "Go on."

"Great." His shoulders relax a bit. "I was just wondering how the goth thing started. Was it a movie you saw? Or do you like a goth from one of your other schools?" His face grows redder.

I squint at him. "Are you asking me if I'm crushing on some mysterious goth?"

Oscar holds up his hands defensively. "It's a perfectly honest question."

I doubt that, but it still makes me smile. When I look at Oscar, little moths threaten to flutter about in my stomach. Bad, moths.

"No," I say. "There's no one else in one of my past schools, goth or otherwise."

He looks relieved. I decide not to pester him about it.

"So, why the dark exterior, then?"

"If I'm being completely honest, it was Edgar Allan Poe."

"The writer from, like, olden times?" Oscar glances toward his bookshelf even though it's covered end to end with fantasy and sci-fi novels, not Victorian macabre poetry.

"Yeah." I reach over and grab the wig to analyze the mess I made. "I discovered him when I was going through a rough time in middle school. He had a big influence on me. Not just because of his spooky short stories and poems. But, him. As a human being."

Oscar reaches up toward the table and starts feeling around for something as he talks. "How did he influence you as a person if he's been dead for, what, a century?"

"Over one hundred seventy years."

He whistles and hands me the mannequin head.

"Thanks." I set the wig on top and start picking apart the curls that have already matted together.

"That's . . ." He looks at me with worried eyes. "You mean to tell me you see ghosts? Because that's totally believable coming from you with your mysterious vibe and all."

I nudge his shoulder with my toe. "I can't see ghosts. But I kinda wish I could."

"Back to my original question."

I hesitate. "Why do you want to know?"

He looks bashful. "You're interesting."

Yeah, those are definitely moths I'm feeling in my stomach. I take a deep breath. "Poe was the first famous person I learned about who was a foster kid, like me."

Oscar's eyes go wide. "Really? I didn't know that about him." He tucks his hair behind one ear and leans closer.

"Yeah, I did a paper about him for literature class and it, I don't know, blew my mind. When you're a foster kid, you kinda get used to feeling like you're worthless and you'll never do anything good in your life. You get depressed by all the statistics."

"What statistics?"

I reach for a comb and start styling the ugly half-curled wig. "Like how foster kids grow up to have higher rates of alcohol and drug addiction. They often live below the poverty level and most don't end up going to college. They're more likely to develop mental illnesses or commit suicide than other populations. They have a higher rate of PTSD than the military. Did you know that?"

Oscar shakes his head.

"Don't look at me like that," I snap.

His eyes go wide. "Like what?"

"Like you're pitying me. I hate that."

"I'm not pitying you. I'm just . . . impressed. You're really impressive."

I shake my head. "No, Poe was impressive. He was the first foster care survivor that I learned about who *did* something with his life. Yes, he struggled with addiction and likely had a mental illness of some kind. He dropped out of college. His foster family disinherited him. He got into debt. He did all the things people expect from foster kids like us. But he made a difference in the world, despite all of that. He wrote poetry that people still talk about today. He matters. People with mental illnesses matter. Foster kids matter."

Oscar nods his head. "Yeah, they do."

A tingling feeling runs down the length of my spine. "So, if Poe could matter. So could I."

Oscar looks straight into my eyes. "Jess, you do matter. Very much."

I look away from Oscar to set the mannequin on the table.

"Anyway," I say, avoiding his flattery. "Poe showed me that your life can be totally messed up, but you can still create art. I can still influence the world around me. I really needed to hear that in middle school, when I felt lower than low. It gave me a sense of agency. I'd been in and out of foster homes, no one wanted or loved me, nothing I did was ever good enough to make a family want to keep me. Now I don't let the statistics, or the bad foster parents, or the bullies get under my skin. I've turned my skin into my art."

I frame my face with my hands. I'm wearing purple, shimmering lipstick. There's a tiny skull sticker just below my right eye, like a morbid beauty mark.

"This is how I show the world that I may come from a dark place, like Poe, but each and every day, I put my best face forward. Poetry isn't my thing, but my kind of art might be just as important to someone else. At least, that's what the Instagram followers lead me to believe."

"I think that's really cool," he says. "Thank you for telling me."

"It's my life." I shrug. "I guess it's just nice to have someone who I can identify with. Even if he has been dead for over a hundred seventy years."

Oscar laughs, his dimples flashing. "Well, I guess I know who you'd want to talk to if you could have a conversation with anyone from history."

"Poe. One hundred percent."

Oscar picks at the carpet again. "You know, maybe I can relate to him a little bit too."

I raise an eyebrow. "Really?" How could cherubic Oscar relate to the patron saint of goths?

"Yeah. I know what it's like to not belong." He looks away, his usual bashfulness creeping back in. "You know how I live with my abuela?"

I nod.

"Well, my mom was Mexican American, like me and my abuela. But my dad isn't a citizen." He clears his throat. Now it's his turn to feel vulnerable with personal confessions. "So, my mom died when I was a kid. Not long after, my dad was deported back to Mexico."

My hands cover my mouth. "I'm so sorry, Oscar. I had no idea."

"It's okay." Then he starts over. "No, actually, it was really awful, but it was a long time ago. We only get to see each other over video chat now. It's not like he left intentionally, but he's still gone. I guess I'm having a hard time adjusting to that. I feel like I don't really know him."

Goddess, I know that feeling. I don't know my mother because she got lost in her own mind. He doesn't know his father because he's trapped in another country. These are borders of madness and state. Both of us are made orphans by walls.

"I'm just so glad to have my abuela in my life. She really saved me."

His eyes shine with emotion. It makes me just a tiny bit jealous to see that he has such a special relationship with his grandmother.

"How often do you get to talk to him?" I ask.

"I try to call him every Sunday. But, honestly, the older I get, the less I feel we have to talk about." He's picking at the carpet again.

"What do you mean?" I ask. "You have so much going on right now with your designs and cosplay competitions." I threaten to poke him in the shoulder with the comb. "I know for a fact that you could talk hours and hours about *Prince of Moons*."

"We don't talk about that stuff."

"Why not?"

"It's . . . different in Mexico. If my dad knew I was playing dress-up, he'd be really mad."

"You told me yourself, it's not just dress-up."

"Yeah, but he'll never see it any other way." He shrugs. "In Mexico, guys don't mess around with costumes or makeup or fantasy. I know you've noticed how the other guys at school treat me. It's like that, times a million."

"And your dad won't love it simply because you do?"

"No. He's . . ." Oscar pauses. "He'd be humiliated. I'm his only son. I need to make him proud. That's kinda why I'm trying so hard to turn this into a legitimate business. To prove to him that it's not just a game. It's a real art form. It could even be profitable someday. Maybe then he'll be able to appreciate me for who I am." He shakes his head. "But not yet."

"Have you tried to talk to him?"

Oscar rubs his hand along the back of his neck. "Not about this, but when I tried . . . about my anxiety disorder . . ." He folds his hands roughly in his lap. "Well, he didn't exactly understand. He thought maybe I was making it up or, I dunno, being a coward."

"Oscar, I'm so sorry."

"It's hard, getting people to believe in an invisible illness. If they can't see it or feel it, they can't really grasp how paralyzing it is."

I bite my lip and nod. Goddess do I know how damaging a hidden illness can be.

"I know you get that," he says, giving me a shy smile. "This is how my brain works. I need to learn how to work with it rather than fight against an immovable wall and torture myself over it. That's no way to live. Every day I feel sick and anxious and afraid, yet I find ways to get out of the house to do the things I love. I understand those goals might be different from person to person, but every moment I'm not hating myself for the way my brain works is a giant success for me."

I swallow hard. I've never had a real, raw conversation with anyone about mental illness before. Suddenly all those years with my biomom yo-yoing between sickness and health make a little more sense. How do you vanquish a demon that's a part of your own brain chemistry?

"I do get it," I say. "I mean, not really. I have no idea what your life has been like, but I understand why you haven't told your dad about cosplay."

"Thanks."

"And for the record," I say, "you've convinced me, and I'm a really tough sell. You'll be able to convince your dad someday. In the meantime, if you need me to beat up any of the assholes at school, you know where to find me."

He laughs. "Well, you *are* pretty scary."

Oscar's business plans give me an idea, something that might help with my current biomom problem.

"Oscar, have you thought about starting your branding now?"

He stands up and stretches. "What do you mean?"

"Like, you're going to need business cards to hand out at competitions, a maker's blog, and . . ." Here I go, being sneaky Jess again. "A PO box."

"A PO box? Why would I need that?"

"I was just thinking." Scramble, scramble, scramble . . . "We need a place to send business mail. I'll need to order a new wig and supplies for upcoming competitions. It would be best to have an official work mailing address for stuff like that, right?"

Oscar rubs his chin. "Yeah, I guess you're right. It takes a long time to build an empire. Might as well start early with the simple things."

He walks back over to his workbench. "When were you planning to order, um, hair and stuff?"

"Soon," I say. I'm such a manipulative jerk.

"Right. Well." He picks up his Dremel tool. "I'll ask Abuela if we can get a PO box tomorrow. I'm not eighteen, so I think I'll need her to sign off on it. I'll text you the official address once it's all in order." He grins. "Good thinking, Jess."

The feeling of treachery haunts me for the rest of the day.

CHAPTER 18

So I don't feel like a total liar, I do order a new wig online. I've sworn off curling irons.

"Hey, Jess!" Someone calls my name at school three days before our next convention.

I close my locker to see Oscar a few yards away, a huge backpack slung over his shoulder. I blow bubbles with my gum as he jogs down the hall. Halfway to me, he fumbles with his worn copy of *Prince of Moons*. It falls to the ground with a slap. Oscar holds up one finger toward me in a "just a second" motion.

When he reaches down to grab the book, a chem nerd kicks it across the floor. Oscar chases after it, but a jock gets there first. He swipes the book through an open classroom door.

"Goal!" the jock yells.

Oscar's visibly sweating, but there's a forced smile plastered across his face.

"Ha, Ha. Very funny, you guys."

He jogs into the classroom to retrieve *Prince of Moons*. The book zooms back out, to a peal of laughter. Oscar runs back into the hall, his hair a mess. Someone else makes a move to kick the book again, but I stomp on his foot with my combat boot.

"Gah, you scary bitch!"

I stare at him, unblinking.

He backs away, shaking his head. "Psycho," I hear him whisper to his buddies. They all give me angry looks as they walk away.

Oscar picks up the book, brushing away the dirt on his jeans.

"Whew!" He smiles good-naturedly. "Got my workout in for the day."

I blow another gum bubble. "Mhm."

"Got something for you," Oscar says, shrugging off his backpack. "These were the first packages delivered to our new PO box." He's beaming. "It feels so official."

He hands over two cardboard boxes, one clearly from a wig shop in LA called Luscious Locks. The other is smaller and less flashy. The return address says it's from New York, New York. I nearly choke on my gum.

Oscar looks at the box with concern. "This is something you ordered, right?"

I nod enthusiastically. "Yeah, sorry. I wasn't expecting it to get here so fast. Sorry."

He narrows his eyes at me. "Now who's over-apologizing?"

"Ha!" My laugh sounds forced. Nervous.

He stuffs his *Prince of Moons* book into his now-empty backpack. "So, how've you been liking the book?"

My hands are tingling. Literally, one of the last people to touch this box was my biomom. I'm sure of it. It's like I can feel her energy through the cardboard.

"Helloo? Jess?"

"What?" I redirect my focus to Oscar.

"*Prince of Moons.* Do you like it so far?"

"Yeah, it's great," I lie. I haven't even read the first page since he left the brand-new copy on my doorstep after the LARP.

"Fantastic." He holds out the hem of his baggy T-shirt so I can see the design he's wearing today. A knight with shining armor battles a troll alongside a woman. She's wearing a black gown and wielding an ornate staff that glows purple with magic.

"The Queen of Thieves," I say. I'd recognize her anywhere now.

What is this life I now live where I'd recognize some fantastical book character sooner than I'd recognize my own flesh-and-blood mother? I have to open the box. It's like a burning need inside of me. It's a magic entirely separate from the Prince of Moons universe.

"And that's Sir Valorian." Oscar points. "I found this woman online who makes custom *Prince of Moons* designs and I figured, what the heck."

He chats happily while I toss the wig box into my locker. I dig my hand into the depths of my satchel to fish out my house keys.

"I thought you'd like it," he says. "When I saw her store online, I had to ask her to make a design to commemorate our great battle with the rock troll." His voice grows distant while I work.

When I find my keys, I stab one of them into the tape along the box seam. A few good rips and the box reveals its secrets to me. Tucked inside a nest of crumpled up newspapers is a tiny box tied with twine. A little notecard reads: "For my beautiful princess. Love, Mom."

My mom.

"So, if you want, I could totally order one in your size. Now that she has the design, it would be no big deal to . . ."

My hands shake as I untie the twine and lift the lid. Inside the box is an oval brooch depicting a crown made of entwined silver and gold. It's not expensive, probably made out of some kind of painted plastic, but it feels precious in my hands. My fingers caress it, yearning for a connection to the woman who sent it. My mother.

"Jess?"

I close the box and stuff it into my satchel. "What?"

"You seem upset."

"I'm not upset."

"Was that pin not what you expected?"

I don't know what I expected.

"No. Yes. It's fine." I shake my head to clear it.

"What's it for?"

"What do you mean?"

"Is it for scream queens? I don't remember there being a pin in the movie."

"There isn't," I say. "Nancy's costume just seemed a little too . . ."

"Simple?"

"Yeah, simple." I force a laugh. "I thought maybe I could attach something more . . . sparkly. Some '80s flair or something."

"A little maker's personal touch." He smiles. "The judges like that kind of thing. Each designer should have their own mark, a little splash of their personality in their work. All great artists have one."

"Exactly," I say. Can he tell how fast my heart is racing?

"It's pretty." He points his chin toward the box hidden in my bag. "And the crown suits you, especially given the royalty rule you have."

I nod, but if I don't get out of this hallway I might just hyperventilate. I need to find a quiet corner somewhere so I can process this in private.

"Look, Oscar, I gotta go."

"Oh, okay." He swallows, deflating a little in front of my eyes.

"Cool shirt," I say distractedly as I turn to leave.

The brooch practically burns through my satchel. It's a reminder of all that's at stake.

CHAPTER 19

IT'S ALL MAKE-BELIEVE.
LAURIE STRODE, *HALLOWEEN*

When I walk down Oscar's basement stairs on Friday night before Sunday's competition, he flashes me a wicked grin. He swipes the air with his newly crafted Freddy claws.

"Spooky." I nod in approval.

He holds them out like he's admiring a manicure. "All they need is a little roughing up. I'll add a few more dings and oxidization marks with paint. They can't look too pretty." He brings the long, metallic-looking nails close to his eyeballs to get a better look.

I cringe. I know the blades are made of foam, but eyeballs and sharp objects—even fake ones—should never be in close proximity.

Oscar is too distracted to notice my discomfort. He brings his gloves back to the workbench for further inspection while I grab a seat near his laptop. For this scene, we're going to rely heavily on surprise elements. Gerrit offered to make a *Nightmare on Elm Street* soundtrack mix that's nothing short of a masterpiece. We'll have two minutes to make an impression. Music will certainly help.

Even though I know we're going to rock the Cleveland Fanpalooza, I'm nervous. This will be the first competition that will take me outside of Michigan, which is certainly not allowed without prior approval under foster care rules. Barbra definitely can't know about the competitions now. There's no way square, goody-two-shoes Barbra would let me drive to Ohio and back without getting the social workers involved.

Thank the demons below, our scream queen theme isn't super heavy in the sewing department, because we're short on time. This job calls for upcycling. I spent all last weekend scouring every thrift store in the greater Detroit area.

For my Nancy Thompson look, I located old lady khaki pants with pleats at the hips and a collared long-sleeved button-down blouse. And, of course, the iconic pink sweater vest. Emily is more than happy to be Tina, the best-friend-turned-first-victim. All she needs to wear is a long white button-down. Gerrit's Freddy look is a little more complicated. It took several thrift trips to locate a floppy hat and Christmas sweater with red and green stripes.

Oscar will be Glen, Nancy's boyfriend and debut role for teenaged Johnny Depp. I ignored Emily's smirk when she first saw our role assignments. I have to consult the internet to find a white-and-blue football jersey with the number ten, but I guess you can't find everything at Goodwill exactly when you need it. Oscar takes one for the team and okays my plan to cut the shirt into a crop top, like what Johnny Depp wore in the film. The '80s was a very strange era for fashion.

All that's left is to perfect my gore technique.

Oscar is going to be my guinea pig, though he doesn't know it yet.

After I open the Google file where I dumped all my maker's notes, I take ingredients out of my satchel. I fight the urge to laugh, evil scientist–style.

"I need warm water and a beaker," I announce.

Oscar looks up at me. "A beaker?"

"What?" I ask. "You don't have one?"

"What do you think this is, a laboratory?" he calls to me on his way upstairs to retrieve my items.

"And measuring spoons!" I yell.

There's an audible sigh at the top of the stairs, so I know he heard me.

A few minutes later, he returns with a tray laden with everything we need. I hear Abuela at the top of the stairs, speaking quickly in Spanish.

"No, Abuelita, no vamos a cocinar con esto."

She follows him down the stairs, speaking animatedly. She shoots me a wide grin when she sees me sitting at a workstation. I wave.

Oscar sets the tray down on the table. It's covered in bowls of different sizes, mixing spoons, and a measuring cup full of water.

"Abuela wants to know if you're hungry."

I know better than to say no.

"Always." I give her an appreciative smile. She practically skips back upstairs to make us some food.

"You know she's going to return with a six-course meal now."

I reach for the biggest bowl and pour one cup of warm water into it. "It's a good thing I love to eat."

Oscar picks up one of the ingredients I brought with me. It's a bag filled with white powder. He reads the label, "Guar gum? What the heck is guar gum?"

"Not entirely sure," I admit as I take it from his hands. After measuring half a teaspoon of the stuff, I sprinkle it into the water. I grab the spoon and start mixing vigorously until it turns into a goopy, pale slime. An evil grin spreads across my face.

"You're not trying to poison me, right?" Oscar asks.

A laugh bubbles out of me. "I dunno, am I?" I don't break eye contact with him as I drop several violently green drops of food coloring into the bowl.

He sniffs. "Sometimes I'm just not sure about you, Jess."

This pleases me. "Just, maybe don't eat the slime, okay?"

"Deal."

When I'm done mixing the goo, we're left with a revolting green semisolid sludge. For a final effect, I mix some long-grain rice into it.

"What's that supposed to be?"

"Maggots to spill out of Gerrit's flesh." Mixed with the slime, it's actually quite convincing.

"Delightful."

Next, I take out layers of burnt skin that I made with liquid latex, then painted to match Gerrit's exact skin color.

"Oh my god, that's disgusting."

"We'll use spirit gum to stick these all over Gerrit's face to give him that charred Freddy look. But these are much too stiff to use for our pustule effect."

"Spirit gum?" Oscar raises an eyebrow. "Is that a pseudonym for witchcraft?"

I roll my eyes. "It's a real thing. I promise. Professional makeup artists use it to glue prosthetics to skin."

He continues to watch me skeptically.

"Also not poison," I promise.

He nods in acceptance.

I pick up several different strips of skin, holding them in the air. "Now I need a victim to let me test out methods of creating a skin pocket that I can fill with slime, so when Gerrit rips it open onstage, it'll ooze our lovely green concoction."

"I assume I'm the willing victim?"

I bat my long spider-leg eyelashes at him. "Please."

The door at the top of the stairs creeks open. Abuela appears with a second tray filled with snacks for us, including her homemade tortillas and guacamole.

Abuela sets down the tray and watches me, expectantly. I take a giant scoop of her homemade guacamole and nearly die from deliciousness. "Gracias," I tell her in my terrible American-accented Spanish accent. She pats my arm lovingly.

"Muchas gracias, Abuelita." Oscar kisses his tiny grandmother on the cheek. She is so pleased it warms even my cold, dead heart.

Once she leaves, we get straight back to business.

Oscar sits down across the table from me and hands me his arm. "Do your worst."

After about an hour of experimenting, Oscar displays several gooey green flesh wounds that rip open when prompted.

"I gotta hand it to myself," I say proudly. "I'm kind of amazing."

"Evil genius," he says, holding out both of his slime-pustule-covered arms.

Oscar and I poke at the lumps of latex flesh and watch green goo squish out. This is more fun than it should be.

Oscar's hair has grown so long over the last couple of months, I suddenly notice. A few strands are stuck on his eyelashes. Without thinking, I reach out to tuck the hair behind his ear for him. When I realize what I'm doing, he's looking at me with those intense dark eyes.

I clear my throat and start collecting the dirty spoons and bowls, piling them on the tray. There's a beat of awkwardness before Oscar saves me.

"Where did you learn how to make this stuff?" he asks as he pokes some rice maggots.

"I tried about a dozen different slime recipes from the interwebs," I say. I take a bottle of spirit gum remover out of my bag. "This one has the best color and consistency for what we're looking for."

"Your kitchen must have been a mess. What did your foster mom say?"

"Nothing," I admit. "It was all cleaned up before she got home."

He gives me an odd look.

"What?" I ask, defensive.

"You still haven't told her about this, have you?"

This irritates me. "Have you told your dad yet?" I snipe, regretting it as soon as it comes out.

His face falls slightly. "No."

There're a few moments of silence as I focus on removing a used fake-skin pocket from Oscar's arm.

"Sorry," I whisper. "I shouldn't have brought up your dad. That wasn't fair. Not to mention none of my business."

"It's okay," he says. Of course good-natured Oscar wouldn't take offense. He always forgives me for my every infraction.

He smushes a blob of fluorescent green goo, then holds up his finger, where tiny rice maggots cling. "That is truly disgusting." He makes a face mixed with revulsion and delight.

"I am a mad scientist," I say, with a mild self-deprecating tone.

"I wish you wouldn't say that."

"Say what?"

"'Mad.' You drop the word like it's harmless, but we both know it isn't."

I shrug.

"Do you maybe want to talk about it?"

"Not really."

"Okay."

This intimacy is starting to make my skin prickle, and not from fake maggots. This is dangerous. I need to be more careful around Oscar. As much as I refuse to admit it, I know deep down that I'm starting to really like this guy. And that's *not* a good thing.

Foster Care Pro-tip number eight: Never become emotionally involved with anyone. Ever. You'll have to leave them eventually. That will hurt. A lot.

Maybe if I were a normal girl with a normal life, this thing that's starting to ignite between us would be the highlight of my junior year. But my life is more complicated than that. *I'm* more complicated than that.

Avoiding Oscar's eyes, I wipe the messy table with paper towels. There's green slime everywhere. I pick out the salvageable pieces of latex skin to reuse on Gerrit's face for the competition.

Oscar watches me for a few moments. "Can I take you somewhere?" he asks.

My arm freezes, midwipe, with slimy paper towel in hand. "Now?"

"No." He shakes his head. "Tomorrow morning. Early."

"How early?"

"Four a.m."

A bark of laughter escapes my chest. "Riiiight."

"Seriously," he says. "I promise you'll like it."

I put one hand on my hip and try to figure out if he's serious or not. "What in all of Detroit could possibly require a four-a.m. departure time, besides the airport?"

"It's a secret."

The air between us is slowly starting to defrost again. The awkward darkness dissolving away like magic.

"You'd better bring me coffee," I say.

Oscar's smile could melt the polar ice caps on the Prince of Moons' home planet.

CHAPTER 20

IT'S ONLY A DREAM.
NANCY THOMPSON, *A NIGHTMARE ON ELM STREET*

It's still completely dark outside as I sit on the front step Saturday morning, shivering in the predawn chill. Summer can't get here soon enough. At 4:00 a.m., right on the dot, I see Abuela's van turn the corner on our street. I stand up to meet Oscar in the driveway. When I jump into the front passenger seat, I notice Oscar has the heat on full blast, thank the Goddess.

I give him my well-practiced death stare. "It's very early, Oscar."

He just smiles and hands me a steaming cup of coffee. "Good morning," he says cheerfully. His hair is sideswept today in a very Harry Styles sort of way.

I growl but take the coffee from his hands.

We drive about an hour outside of the city. I have no idea where we're headed. When Oscar pulls up next to locked wrought iron gates, I slowly turn toward him, confusion making my newly caffeinated brain whirl.

"Why are we parked outside of a dark cemetery at five o'clock in the morning?"

"Because it's the creepiest, most beautiful place in all of East Michigan." He unbuckles his seat belt, walks around the front of the car, and opens my door for me. So chivalrous.

The cool air greets me again. I frown at Oscar.

"But it's cooold," I whine.

He opens the back door, takes out a blanket, and wraps it around my shoulders.

"There. Better?"

I nod and get out of the car.

Oscar grabs a bag, then locks all the doors. He starts walking toward the dark cemetery, but I'm still frozen in place trying to figure out what on earth is going on.

Oscar looks back toward me. "Well, come on, Goth Queen. I'd have thought this place would feel like a second home to you."

"Excuse me," I say, stomping toward him. "I love cemeteries, especially hilly, tree-filled beauties like this one. I'm just not accustomed to breaking the law by entering them before daybreak."

Oscar shrugs. "Well, then, I guess you'll miss the big surprise."

I start walking. "Fine, lead the way."

When we pass the ornate, wrought iron gates, Oscar moves quietly through the graveyard like a ghost. He uses his phone flashlight to navigate down the twisty paths. It's obvious he knows his way around this place in the dark. The graves are black masses without the light from his phone, so I keep close, not wanting to trip over any roots or headstones.

We make our way toward a particularly forested area, atop a hill. Here Oscar stops. He opens his backpack and lays another blanket on the ground next to a giant willow tree. When he sits, he pats the ground beside him. I drop to the ground, pulling my blanket tighter around myself to protect me from the crispness of the air around us. From inside his bag, Oscar pulls out a thermos of hot coffee. He takes my cup from me and refills it. The steam rises up into the air.

"Bless you," I say, cradling the mug close to my face.

As if on cue, the lighting around us starts to change. It's so gradual at first that I hardly notice it. The statues and mausoleums begin to take definite shapes in the darkness, their granite luminescent in the light of dawn. The draping willow blows in the breeze. Its long tendril-like branches reach out toward us, distinct from the blackness that once engulfed them. Birds begin to chirp. It's as if the entire world is changing before our eyes, waiting for the sky to turn from black to a deep, royal blue.

"Look that way," Oscar whispers, trying not to break the spell.

I follow the direction he's pointing. There, between a break in the trees, is the horizon. It slowly opens up to reveal a pale light. We watch it change from blue to a bright pink almost too fluorescent to stare at. I look in amazement as the cemetery becomes alight in the fire of dawn. The flowers, bushes, and marble angels face the sun as if to worship its glow. This sunrise is the single most beautiful thing I have ever seen in my entire life.

Oscar and I sip our coffee while the world comes alive around us. I know that no matter what my future brings, I will never forget this morning—or this boy—for the rest of my life.

When the sun is fully risen, I awake from the spell of serenity it enshrouded me in. I look around as if dazed. A squirrel scurries up a nearby oak tree while a rabbit chews on some early clover blossoms. There are birds hopping through the dewy grass, searching for worms. There's a nudge on my arm as Oscar hands me a doughnut. I munch on it happily before tossing a few crumbs to a nearby robin.

That's when I see it. The gravestone behind us reads:

Gloria Martinez

Beloved daughter and mother

October 14, 1982–April 26, 2010

A deep sadness fills my heart as I realize who this is.

Oscar notices me looking. "I hope you don't mind," he says. "I wanted to introduce you to my mom."

I look back to him, my eyes a little wet.

"Of course I don't mind." I reach out and grab his hand. It's slightly calloused from years of working with crafting tools.

"I really think she would have liked you," Oscar says, still staring at the golden horizon. "This was her favorite place."

"Really?" Somehow, I never imagined cherubic Oscar with a mother who loved cemeteries.

"She used to bring me here when I was little," he says. "We'd plant flowers by all the graves that appeared forgotten." He reaches out to wipe a small speck of moss from the top of a nearby stone. "She thought this was the most peaceful place on earth."

"Is that why you wanted to bring me here?" I ask.

"Part of it. I wanted to share this with you because it's special to me." He pauses. "And you're special to me."

I swallow hard. The moths inside of me flutter about like they're caught in a storm.

"I don't know why," he says, "but I felt like my mom wanted me to bring you here too. To share this place with you. I think she thought it might give you some peace."

Despite the warming morning air, I take my hand from Oscar's to pull the blanket tighter around my shoulders.

"Thank you," I whisper. I don't know what else to say.

Dew has soaked through the blanket we're sitting on. I don't mind. The feeling of dampness keeps me grounded. Which is necessary right now because my heart is trying to fly away.

"Do you ever get jealous of other people?" Oscar asks. "Like, how Emily has two parents who are frickin' awesome?"

"Sometimes," I admit. "But I realized a long time ago that it's pointless. I'll never have what other people have. I try not to let it hold me down."

Oscar lets out a deep breath. "I'm embarrassed to admit it, but sometimes I get really mad at Gerrit. His family isn't perfect, of course. His dad is always at some base somewhere in the world, but they clearly love each other. And his mom might be a bit . . . much . . . but she adores Gerrit." He shrugs. "It's hard sometimes, to know how he takes that for granted." His eyes dart to his mom's gravestone.

"I'm learning so much about you this morning." I take a sip of my coffee, feeling the warmth spread throughout my core. "I never knew you had a negative bone in your body."

"Yeah," he says, smiling sadly. "I don't really. I just get a little jealous sometimes. I wish I had what people like Gerrit and Emily have. And I might be a little jealous of you too."

"Me?" I turn to squint at him. "I'm the poster child for *not* having what other kids have."

"Not because of your family situation." He shakes his head. "Because of your confidence. I wish I had that. I've always been the awkward kid. The weirdo that everyone makes fun of. I wish I had your ability to brush it off instead of crumbling."

"That took many years of practice."

"I know. Maybe someday I'll be as awesome as you." He grins and tosses a tiny stick at me. "Until then, I'll envy your badass-ness."

I laugh as we both look back to the horizon. My mind and my heart are at war. It's impossible to deny that I really like Oscar, but I can't encourage this. Because I have one more haunting secret. One that terrifies me more than anything in this world.

"Do you ever wonder what you inherited from your mom?" I ask.

Oscar looks back at her grave marker. "Sometimes," he says. "I'm lucky that I have my abuela to tell me about her. And my dad, even though we don't really talk about sentimental things. But once he told me something that I'll never forget." Oscar smiles at the memory. "We were on Skype. I think I was twelve. There were a bunch of kids picking on a girl because her family couldn't afford to pay for her lunch at school. You know how mean sixth graders can be."

I nod. "I've always been the new kid, remember?" I ask.

His eyes grow intense. "I wish I knew you back then," he says. "I would have protected you."

"Like Sir Valorian?" I ask.

"No," he says. "Like me."

I look away, back toward the rising sun.

"What happened?" I ask, feeling uncomfortable under his attention.

He picks up a nearby twig and twirls it in his hands. "It's the only time I got so mad I hit a guy."

I'm so shocked that I turn back toward him, my mouth gaping open. "You hit someone?"

Oscar blushes. "Right in the nose. I'm not proud of it."

"You should be." I nod at him in approval. "Oscar Martinez punched a jerk in the nose." I laugh. "I never could have guessed it."

"Yeah, well," he says, poking his stick into the ground. "As you can imagine, I got in a lot of trouble. Abuela made me call my dad, to confess. I expected him to be mad but . . ." He pauses for a while. When he speaks again, his tone is different. It's lower, almost sad.

"He said I was like my mom. Brave and kind. He said that's exactly what she would have done."

We let the silence hang between us for a long while. The wind rustles the trees as small drips of dew fall from the branches, landing on us where we sit in the grass.

"I wish I knew the good things I inherited from my mom," I say.

"I'm sure there are many." Oscar bumps his shoulder into mine. "You are pretty great."

"Oh, I know that," I say with my characteristic confident tone, though it sounds a bit off. "The thing is, I only know one thing I got from my mom. And it terrifies me."

He raises an eyebrow at me.

I take a sip of coffee for strength.

"Schizophrenia is genetic."

Saying these words out loud makes my core solidify, like someone poured concrete all over my insides. The vulnerability of these sentences instinctively makes me wary, like a flinch before a punch.

"You mean you could develop it?" Oscar asks, his face void of emotion.

I nod.

This knowledge has hung over my head for years, like the grim reaper. If my biomom has it, that means there's a chance that I have the gene too. It would be unfair to invite Oscar into this world. More than anyone, I know the damage this can cause. The only way to protect the people I care about is to stay away.

"My biggest fear is that I will go crazy."

"Don't say that." He shakes his head like I've just cursed.

"It's a real possibility for me," I say. "Have you ever thought of the phrase 'psychotic break'? It's the moment when your mind severs from reality. When you instantly turn into an irreversibly broken thing." I close my eyes to block the sight of the schizophrenia gene monster where he lurks in the back of my mind. "We're all so fragile, like eggs. I'm terrified of breaking. Sometimes you can't be put back together again."

"You don't know that you'll end up like her."

"That's just it, Oscar," I say. "You need to understand. The statistics show it's more likely to happen to me than anyone else. Not just because I'm genetically inclined to inherit the disease from my mom, but also because I've experienced key environmental conditions for it. Stress and trauma are major triggers for schizophrenic breaks."

He shakes his head slowly, his hair falling into his face. The color has drained away from his cheeks. He's looking at me with worried eyes.

"Foster care is like this demonic ghost that never lets you go," I explain. "You don't just get to leave once you turn eighteen. It's not like I magically become normal once I'm out of the system. Being a foster kid follows you around for the rest of your life, haunting you. You never stop *being* a foster kid. You never get to leave that trauma behind for good. It becomes a part of you, like your DNA."

Oscar thinks pensively for a few moments before he looks at me again. "Do you think Poe was forever a foster kid?"

"Definitely," I say. "I think Poe was haunted by it. I think I am too."

Oscar tosses away his stick. I can't help noticing his hands are shaking.

"Even if you do develop a mental illness," he says, "you don't have to end up like Poe or your mom. You can get help, like I did for anxiety." Oscar makes a frustrated sound. "I mean, I know my disorder and your mom's schizophrenia are two entirely different things. But you can learn tools for living a happy life, even with a mental illness. Thousands of people do. It's not a death sentence."

I close my eyes. The sun is so warm on my skin I could almost forget I'm sitting in a cemetery, discussing my fate. When I take a deep breath, I can smell the scent of the world waking up, even amid the death that surrounds us.

"Maybe," is what I say.

I wish that were true, is what I feel.

When Oscar puts his arm around my shoulder, all I want to do is lean into him. I want to feel the warmth of his body on this chilly morning and know that I am safe. That we are safe together. I want to allow this relationship to blossom, but I'm frozen. It's not fair to him.

They say every girl fears growing up to become her mother, but not every girl has to stare the schizophrenia gene monster in the face when she looks into the mirror every morning. I wouldn't want to hurt *anyone* the way my biomom hurt me when she got sick. When she fell apart and left me broken and alone. I couldn't bear it if I did that to Oscar. That possibility is always there, whispering at me from the shadows of my mind.

My mother's fate could ultimately become my own.

CHAPTER 21

WHY ARE YOU SCREAMING? I HAVEN'T EVEN CAUGHT YOU YET.
FREDDY KRUEGER, *A NIGHTMARE ON ELM STREET*

When we get to the Cleveland Fanpalooza parking lot on Sunday, my jaw literally drops. The sidewalk is littered with *The Witcher* characters, *Bob's Burgers* families, and *Game of Thrones* lookalikes. There's even a couple dressed as Colonel Sanders and a giant chicken. I'm not sure how that fits into this geeky scene, but I'll roll with it.

Now it's easy to see why Oscar insisted the event in Kalamazoo was small. This time we feel more prepared with our top-secret, kick-ass skit, even though the number of competitors makes me a little worried.

"We got this," Oscar says as we walk toward the convention center entrance. Though the sweat glistening near his hairline suggests he might be a little less confident than he's willing to admit.

At the street corner, I watch as a public bus pulls up to drop off a dozen or so fae creatures, bespectacled steampunk enthusiasts, and video game characters. Someone in a full-size Iron Man suit squeezes through the narrow doorway while the bus driver watches in bewilderment. I wonder what it must be like to drive superheroes around the streets of Cleveland. It's going to be a very interesting day for him.

One thing I can't help to think about is how, only a few weeks ago, I had no idea this entire community existed. Never in my life would I have guessed there was a place where bros can dress up as Trojan warriors alongside science nerds wearing lab coats and green body paint. It's like cosplay is the greatest unifier. It's a fantasy realm where everyone can let their weird out, no matter what that weird may be. There's no need to hide who you really are when you're standing in line next to groups of gender-bending Disney characters and couples dressed as *Alien vs. Predator*.

We're not as early as Oscar would have liked since it was a three-hour drive here and, of course, we hit massive construction traffic along every major highway surrounding Lake Erie.

"I told you a dozen times we should have left last night," Emily grumbles under her breath as she and Gerrit drag a futon mattress through the line for our super-secret skit.

She knows I couldn't leave last night. It would've invited Barbra to ask too many questions, so I had to disclose my foster care status to Emily. It's easier to leave a note on the table while Barbra's at her morning yoga class, rather than explain that I'm crossing state lines for a cosplay competition thing I've been working on secretly for weeks.

We arrived at Fanpalooza in full costume this time, so we don't need to make the long trip back through the parking lot to deposit our stuff, which is good considering the amount of security here. Cosplayers are required to send all swords, staffs, throwing stars, etc. through the prop station so security can verify they're not real weapons.

Luckily, I'm not carrying much, just a small makeup bag tucked into my bra beneath my baggy pink sweater vest. When I fish out the bag and toss it on the table, the security officer gives me a strange look.

"What?" I ask. "Carrying things in my hands would ruin the aesthetic."

She nods, waving me through. It's not worth taking the time to explain to her why I need all the teeny bags of fake blood, glue, and latex skin. It took me three hours to organize all this last night. We'll need to apply our gore effects right before the competition starts for optimum effect. We don't want to give the other competitors a clue as to what our skit will be.

"Let's make the rounds," Oscar says after we tuck the mattress backstage for safekeeping. He eyeballs a merchant booth filled with multicolored dice, like precious gems for RPG fanatics.

I fluff my enormous permed wig and readjust the brooch my biomom gave to me, which I'd pinned to a hair tie at the back of my head like a gaudy clip. My hands keep reaching up to touch it for good luck. In a weird way, it makes me feel like my mother is here. Even though this situation we're in is extremely messed up, I still want her with me.

Oscar leads the way in his crop top football jersey. His hair is teased up in an '80s film heartthrob bouffant, and enormous metallic headphones are slung around his neck. He looks more ridiculous now than in any cape or suit of armor, but I have to admit, it's not a bad look for him. When he puts on a costume, his entire demeanor changes. He becomes braver, more confident—more like his Sir Valorian alter ego.

Behind us, Emily imitates Tina Gray with her jumpy skittishness. She keeps looking over her shoulder nervously as Freddy/Gerrit clicks his long knife fingers together with menacing glee. All around them, people are starting to notice the little show they're putting on in the middle of the crowd. A group of comic book characters take out their phones to film while Emily hides behind a life-size cutout of the *Stranger Things* cast, then ducks behind a group of distracted LOTR characters. Gerrit hams it up, walking after her with the long strides of a nightmarish villain.

Oscar and I pause to watch as our creations take on lives of their own. Our little cosplay babies are growing up. When they pose for a selfie, Emily side-eyes Gerrit nervously while he makes a peace sign with his knives for the camera. They have fully become the characters of *A Nightmare on Elm Street*, far beyond just their costumes. The crowd adores them.

Pride swells inside of me. I made an entire mask of false burned skin that perfectly matches Gerrit's skin tone. Oscar handcrafted that glove out of leather and foam to make it look like real knives. Goddess dammit, we did a fantastic job. After the fifth group asks Gerrit and Emily to stop for photos, Oscar holds up his hand for me to give him a sneaky high five. So far, this con is going a million times better than our first attempt. Oscar was right to force us to try it again.

While the Gerrit/Emily duo are performing their magic, I take a minute to dash across the convention hall to use the bathroom. After washing my hands and fluffing my enormous hair in the mirror, I head back out into the mass of fantastical characters come to life.

That's when I see it: the most gorgeous red dress I have ever witnessed in my life.

The woman glides through the exhibition hall like a larger-than-life muse, her skirts swirling around her feet and her sleeves billowing out like red smoke. The dress has a golden belt and she's wearing her long blond hair unbound, giving her a dramatic silhouette. She's holding the hand of a man wearing all black, with a black mask covering his eyes. They're cosplaying *The Princess*

Bride. The romantic beauty of the pair is enough to melt even my cold, undead heart.

I'm not the only one who's noticed the costumed couple. Nearby, two anime characters scoff.

"Since when is Westley Indian and Princess Buttercup fat?"

From the way she bites her lip and turns her face away, I know Buttercup has heard them. Westley grips her hand tighter and leans in to whisper in her ear. They stand tall again. Westley's eyes are defiant, but Buttercup's are shining with what I know is embarrassment. She shouldn't be embarrassed—she's a goddess!

As the couple walks away, I see red. And it's not from Buttercup's dress.

"Are you frickin' kidding me?" I say, turning to the anime characters.

They startle and stare at me wide-eyed.

"Is that seriously the first thing you see about those artists?"

The anime girl with a stiff, fluorescent blue wig takes a step back, like I'm a threat. Good.

"How do you *not see* the masterful draping of that red fabric? Or the impeccably matched black hues in that man's costume? That sort of perfection does not come easily. Anyone who's spent time at a sewing machine could see that!"

I look them up and down with disgust. Nothing they're wearing is homemade. Their baggy screen-printed shirts even have square creases from the packaging they bought them in.

"Well," I say, considering their head-to-toe store-bought ensemble. "Maybe you wouldn't recognize a great craftsperson when you see one."

"You're a bitch," the second anime character says.

"Yes," I say flatly. "And you're a bigot."

He grabs his friend's arm and they scurry away.

Behind me, someone slow claps.

"Well, that was the best thing I've seen since the con of 2009."

I turn around to see a guy dressed as Lord Varys, from *Game of Thrones.*

"That year, there was a brawl between dueling Doctors. They toppled over a TARDIS."

"What?"

"I heard them too," Lord Varys says, pointing his chin to the retreating anime characters. "I wish I could say that sort of rudeness doesn't happen all the time, but . . ." He grimaces.

"That's . . . disappointing," I say. It's more than disappointing. It's crushing. I remember my first foray into the depths of cosplay web browsing, with all the overtly sexualized female characters and the trolls who made fun of every woman who didn't look like a supermodel. I know I'm big, I'm beautiful, and I'm allowed to take up space in the geek universe. And everywhere else for that matter. But does the rest of the world agree?

A woman wearing a brightly colored aloha shirt joins Varys. She's holding a fake margarita glass complete with salted rim. Thanks to Oscar's geek tutorials, I recognize her long, pointed hat and the Triforce necklace around her neck.

"Are you from the Legend of Zelda games?" I ask.

She beams. "I'm Link on vacation! He works so hard saving Zelda that I figured he deserved a trip to paradise." She takes a fake swig from her plastic cocktail for effect.

Breaking canon looks fun, but something tells me Oscar would never allow us to put a tropical swing on one of his beloved fantasy characters. Maybe I could convince him to try it sometime. Bribery might be in order.

"Based on that magnificent spectacle, I bet you'd be interested in joining our club for body-positive cosplayers." Varys hands me a tiny business card. When I squint down at it, I see it advertises a social media group called Midwest Body Positive Cosplay Coalition.

"Your costume is wicked," Vacation Vibes Link says. "I hope you're entering the competition. We need more competitors with diverse body types. I *see* you. And you rock." She grabs my shoulders and stares directly into my eyes meaningfully.

"Er, thanks," I say. "That's really nice." After ten straight seconds, she still hasn't unglued her irises from my eyeballs. Or blinked, for that matter. My alarm bells are ringing.

Varys senses my discomfort, or maybe he's used to intervening when Vacation Vibes Link gets a little too intense. He steps forward, bringing with him the smell of jasmine. Why the hell don't I ever smell that magical?

He gently removes Vacation Vibes Link's hands from my shoulders. "It can be super hard to get recognition in the fan world when you have a different body type or skin color than the characters you're portraying. Online forums are still biased toward white people with movie star bodies. Jerks still verbally harass us all the time when we 'don't look right for the character.' And few people ask to take photos of our hand-sewn masterpieces." He runs his fingers over his elegantly embroidered robe.

Vacation Vibes Link shakes her head. "We're on a mission to change that."

"This is great," I say, pocketing their business card. "I'll consider the group."

Before they leave, Vacation Vibes Link holds up her margarita glass and whoops. "We'll cheer for you at the competition!"

Once I find Gerrit, Emily, and Oscar again, we sign in at the main theater for the cosplay competition. The air back here smells of hot glue, paint, and sweat, like a gymnasium decorated for prom.

"Which category?" a lady with a clipboard asks. She snaps her gum.

"Apprentice." Oscar gives her a charming Johnny Depp smile.

She gives us an upward glance. "You know we have a teen category too."

"Yes, ma'am."

"There are fewer teen competitors," she says. "You might have a better shot at winning something if you compete within your age group."

"Teens win a smaller prize."

She shrugs, then hands us our passes. "You're number twenty-three. Good luck."

I lean in to whisper so the lady can't hear me. "Oscar, how many categories are there?"

He whispers back, "Four." Then leads us away from the sign-in table. "There's Teen for the, well, teens. Apprentice for the noobs like us who haven't competed much before. Then there's Journeymen, for people who've been doing this for a few years now. And, lastly, there's the Master Crafters for the serious cosplayers who win awards all over the world." There's a tone of reverence in his voice as he says this. "They're who we all want to be. They're the artists who make a living out of cosplay by traveling for competitions and owning businesses where they sell their pieces."

"Whew." Emily whistles. "Professional geeks."

"How come there weren't multiple categories last time?" I ask.

"Last time, there were hardly enough competitors for one group," Oscar points out. "Kalamazoo was small potatoes. These are the big leagues. There are too many talented craftspeople to have a single category here."

Gerrit looks down at the pass. "We're number twenty-three though. That sounds like a lot of competition." He scratches his striped ribs with a faux metal claw.

"Oh, it is." Oscar nods. "And it will be challenging, but the general categories have a bigger payoff, more exposure, and—most importantly—they're the path to the championship in New York." Despite Oscar's confident strategy, he gulps. The sweat in his brow is more pronounced now. Yeah, he's definitely worried.

When we find a good spot to wait backstage, I pull the bag of gore out of my bra.

"Holy Batman, Jess." Emily looks at me with awe. "It's like you have secret weapons stashed in your underwear."

"I do." I grin as I pop open a tube of lipstick and reapply Pink Sunset to my smile.

"Me too." Emily unstraps the hair products that were strapped to her thigh, then tosses them at me. When she looks down at her costume, her face twists in horror.

"Ack, Gerrit! You got yarn bits all over me!" When I squint up at her, I see that Gerrit's red-and-green sweater shed all over her from the multitude of selfies they'd been taking.

I dig around for the tiny roll of duct tape that I'd tucked into my makeup bag, then rip off a strip for her. Good goths always keep emergency lint removal handy. You learn a trick or two when your entire wardrobe is black.

Emily throws the tape at Gerrit. "De-lint me, you cretin. This is your doing." She holds her arms out as Gerrit begrudgingly uses the tape to unstick the red-and-green lint from her costume.

"Are you ready for your blood bag?" I ask Oscar.

He pulls up his crop top. "Do your worst."

I slap a plastic bag of gore onto his chest and tear off another piece of tape, wincing in advance for how we're going to need to rip this off later. He's definitely going to lose some skin from this.

"Hey!" Emily calls to us. "Gerrit and I are gonna go get the mattress ready for the skit." She points to a guy wearing a headset who nods for them to hurry up. Oscar gives them a thumbs-up.

I sift through my stash of beauty products until I find the comb and tiny bottle of mousse. "We need to do something about your hair, you'll get kicked out of the '80s if you go onstage with that deflated mess."

Oscar chuckles and sits on the floor so I can get a better angle. He winces as I tug a comb through his hair, which is already stiff with product from this morning.

"So, this is what happens when people get too close to Nancy Thompson." He winces again. "Pulled hair and the promise of a bloody death."

"Love is a dangerous thing," I say. With a few tiny dots of mousse, I mess his hair with my fingers.

He's looking up at my face.

I pick up the comb and focus on teasing his hair into a poof again.

"Are you okay?" he asks.

"I just . . ." What? I wish my biomom were here, even though I don't really know her? I'm haunted by the looming threat of schizophrenia that runs through my veins? I'm worried that we won't win a spot at the World Cosplay Expo in New York and I'll never get to see my biomom? Nothing I could say right now could possibly make him understand how this feels. And I don't *want* to feel like this. Especially not right now. Not when I'm supposed to be crusading for cosplay glory.

Not when I'm with Oscar.

"It's nothing." I shake my head. "Just nerves." Our disastrous last completion plays through my head on repeat.

"We're going to do great." He smiles at me, holding my gaze a little longer than necessary.

"We're all set," Gerrit interrupts.

I take a giant step away from Oscar. "Good," I say. My voice sounds weird.

Emily crosses her arms at her chest and gives me a sly grin.

Whatever, we weren't doing anything wrong.

Oscar stands up. "Who's next?"

"Me." Emily pushes past Gerrit to get her blood bag for the performance. "Ahem." She gives Oscar a pointed look.

"Oh, sorry." He blushes and walks away, dragging Gerrit behind him.

She unbuttons the top of her shirt so I can reach in to attach her allotment of fake blood. I can feel Emily's smile before I see it.

"I'm not trying to feel you up," I say, rolling my eyes.

She continues grinning.

"You're unnerving, you know that?" I button the front of her shirt back together.

"I wasn't complaining."

"Then why are you looking at me like that, you weirdo?" I crouch to the ground to start cleaning up the mess of random gore and makeup items.

"You and Oscar looked pretty intimate over here."

She slides down to the floor to sit next to me.

"It's nothing," I say. "I was just giving him some flesh wounds."

"Mhm. And I'm just imagining the expression of utter devotion on his face whenever he looks at you."

I shrug. "Then that's on him. Not me."

"So, you're telling me you didn't like the feel of his baby-soft flesh under your fingers while you caressed his belly just now?" She raises an eyebrow at me. "You're blushing."

"I am not!"

"You soooo are blushing, which is an unexpected thing to see in a normally ghostly pale goth girl."

"You're just trying to pick a fight."

"Usually, that would be accurate." She nods. "But right now, I'm just truth telling."

I roll my eyes.

"Ever thought about how you and Oscar are portraying a romantic couple?" Emily puts one elbow on her knee so she can face me better.

I groan at her implication.

"You love that squishy nerd, don't you?"

"I don't believe in love," I say.

Emily rolls her eyes. "Why the hell not? Love is the best."

"Coming from someone who finds a new girlfriend everywhere we go?"

"Don't pin this on me, just because I'm a sexy girl magnet. We're talking about you right now."

"Goddess help me," I mumble as I rub my temples.

"Why don't you believe in love?"

I ignore her.

She smacks my arm. "I'm serious!"

"Uh, fine." I turn toward her. "Because Edgar Allan Poe was engaged to a woman who left him to marry another man."

She shrugs. "That sucks, but everyone goes through one bad breakup."

"They reunited decades later and became engaged again."

"Awww! Old people love."

"No, not *aww*." I shake my head vigorously. "Poe died, literally days before the wedding. They never got to be together. After all of that."

Emily stares at me, open-mouthed. "That's a terrible story."

"That's reality," I say. "Poe is the King of Macabre for a reason. He wrote from life. Life is macabre."

I turn back to watch the other competitors walk onstage to perform, one by one. We must be getting close to our time slot now.

Emily pouts her bottom lip. "Remind me not to ask you to give a speech at my wedding someday."

"Noted." This subject is making me feel a little too squirrelly inside. I toss our makeup hoard into a dark corner to retrieve it after our skit.

Oscar steps up behind us. "Let's get in line," he says, waving toward the stage. "It's almost our turn."

"Whoo!" Emily pumps her fists in the air like a prizefighter. "Ready for some action?" She lightly punches Gerrit in the chest.

"I'd rather be playing video games," he says. It's hard to tell with all the fake skin, but his face might look a little gray.

Emily starts jumping from foot to foot, getting amped up for the stage.

"Cheer up." Her charismatic grin looks positively evil in the dark backstage lighting. "You're about to murder us all, in front of a live audience."

CHAPTER 22

WE STAND UPON THE BRINK OF A PRECIPICE.
EDGAR ALLAN POE, "THE IMP OF THE PERVERSE"

We are the last team to perform. The pressure steadily rises while we watch one team after another fight robots and evil emperors. Our costumes aren't nearly as elaborate as some of the other teams, but I'm surprisingly not worried. I know our skit is solid gold. We got this.

When the stage lights go out, we set our super-secret prop mattress onstage in the dark, then hide behind the curtain again. Gerrit's *A Nightmare on Elm Street* mix begins to play over the speakers as the lights come back on. The audience cheers with recognition. We let the eerie sounds play for several seconds, to lure the crowd into a feeling of unease. Then we begin.

Emily runs onstage, screaming, fighting to get an invisible monster off of her. She scratches at the buttons on her shirt. Several pop open to reveal the bloody claw marks I molded across her chest this morning with latex and paint. Just like we practiced, she secretly scratches open the blood bag I tucked inside minutes ago. As she struggles, she smears it all over her face and arms. Her now bloody button-down shirt swirls around her like a morbid gown as she struggles. She's a mess. She's a terror.

She's perfect.

Then out comes Gerrit as Freddy. Someone in the audience

screams. He lunges for Emily in an expertly executed attack. Our blocking is perfection. The two fight in three-quarter speed, like in a dream.

Oscar squeezes my shoulder just before our cue. Onstage, Emily falls to the ground. We run out from behind the curtains to face Freddy.

Out in the audience someone roars with the ferocity of a soccer mom on her third wine cooler.

"GET HIM, NANCY!"

It could only be Vacation Vibes Link.

Onstage, there's a standoff. Gerrit lifts his shirt to expose the secret fake-skin pocket we've glued to his ribs with spirit gum. He tears at his side with his metallic claws. A maniacal grin spreads across his face as our disgusting green goo spills out, flopping to the floor like a living thing. The audience reacts just as I'd hoped. They're disgusted, and loving it.

While Gerrit chases me, Oscar yawns and stretches, his belly button on full display in his '80s sports crop top. He curls up on the mattress we've placed there—possibly the most ridiculous prop item in cosplay history. With dramatic flair, Oscar places his oversized headphones over his ears to sleep. The audience laughs. Then, while Gerrit is attacking me, Oscar begins to struggle on the mattress, kicking and flailing like he's fighting his invisible foe. He tears open his own hidden gore bag and smears it all over the bed. The white sheets are thrust into the air to expose the shiny, blood-red, tattered ones we've secretly hidden underneath. As Oscar flails, he covers himself in the red and disappears from view as he tucks himself into the hole we cut out of the middle of the mattress. Someone in the audience cheers. Baby Johnny Depp has been swallowed by his own bed, just like in the movie.

Gerrit flashes his clawed gloves at me with a wild grin. Who knew this guy could be so damn creepy? He runs toward me, but I trip him. I tackle him on the ground but he gets away. He comes at me again and freezes for my scream queen finale.

I am Nancy. I know what it's like to be chased by demons that no one else can see. I feel the stares and the judgments of people who think I'm not worth listening to or taking seriously. I am suffocated in my own helplessness. I'm paralyzed with the very real fear that I live with every day, that I have my own invisible monster that constantly chases after me.

The second our music ends in a crashing crescendo, Freddy grabs me.

I scream.

It is a glorious cathartic release.

Silence surrounds us. Slowly, the applause trickles through the haze. The emotional roller coaster of the last minute has winded us all, cosplay team and audience. Finally, the cheers grow thunderous, like the pounding of my heart.

All of my limbs are shaking when Emily takes my hand and we run offstage. Her skin is sticky with fake blood. When I look up at her, there are red smears all over her face but she's laughing. She's a mess of gore as she bounces around with her leftover adrenaline. Even Gerrit is smiling like a goon, making his false, burned skin look even creepier.

Oscar must sense the strange energy radiating off of me. His eyes grow concerned.

"Are you okay?" he asks, his voice low and intimate against the raucous background.

A smile finally blooms across my lips. I am breathless when I say, "Yes. I'm more than alright." I reach my arms around his neck and hold him close. My eyes are closed, so I can block out the rest of the world. "Thank you for making me do this," I whisper.

I know he can hear me because he hugs me back. For a moment, he isn't goofy Oscar with his fake sword collection and his *Prince of Moons* obsession. He's Sir Valorian the Wonderful. The knight who is so brave and kind, he can only be from a science-fiction novel.

Or, maybe, they are one and the same.

A hushed silence falls over all of us when the MC walks onstage with the judges' scores in hand. He does some time-wasting banter with a giant robot from some Pixar movie before he gets the ball rolling.

"First, we have a few special mention categories," he says. "These competitors don't qualify for the final competition in New York. However, the judges feel these teams have a lot to give to the cosplay community in the future because of their stage presence and costume designs. Would the following teams please come onstage to accept the Most Anticipated award?" To my left, Emily is clinging to Gerrit for dear life, her eyes wide with hope.

"The Singing Sirens," the MC yells.

The team of mermaids scream and hop onstage, trying to stay balanced in their rainbow-colored tails.

"Congratulations," the MC says to them as they hold each other and cry.

"Red Dead Toy Story!"

A large group of cowboys run out, the spurs on their boots clinging on the hardwood floors. Each one has a stick pony. It's a combination of serious video game–inspired artistry with a cute childhood animation spin.

They accept their award as one of them yells, "There's a snake in my boot!" The audience laughs.

"And last, but not least," the MC says, "*A Nightmare on Elm Street*!"

Emily literally screams as she throws her arms around Gerrit's neck. I'm in shock, rooted to the ground.

I can't wait to tell Barbra, I think. Whoa. That's a very weird, unexpected reaction, which I promptly push out of my mind. I can't share this with her. She may be cool, but she's still a foster.

I glance toward Oscar for a cue about how I'm supposed to feel. This means we didn't make the top three, so should I be upset we're not invited to the World Cosplay Expo yet? We *have* to get to New York in May. So much depends on it. Worry prickles at my insides, but when I see Oscar's face alight with pride, I realize he wasn't sure if we'd win anything at all. His eyes have a mix of shock and delight. We're doing better than he expected. I decide not to worry too much yet.

"Come on!" I grin at him. We follow our teammates out onto the stage.

"Great stage presence," the MC says. "And you, sir"—he points at Gerrit—"are a terrifyingly good Freddy." He holds out the certificate of achievement. Gerrit shakes his head and points to Oscar with his claws.

"Congratulations," the MC says as Oscar takes the award in his trembling hands.

His eyes tear up. "Thank you," he says, his voice thick with emotion.

When we run offstage, Oscar's still staring at the award like he's not sure if it's real.

"We killed it!" Emily yells.

"You mean, I killed it," Gerrit laughs.

"Yes! You killed it!" She grabs his spiky hands while jumping up and down. "And your music was a frickin' fantastic idea! We should go pro!"

Oscar is laughing along with them, but I'm still trembling. I feel fragile, like a newborn. I've put all of my emotion into this skit. It wasn't just a performance for me. It felt very real. All I can think in this moment is how much I wish Barbra were here to see it.

With reverence, I take the framed certificate from Oscar's hands. "I think this will look quite nice in the Costume Lair." I turn the award this way and that, admiring the fancy calligraphy.

"Do we really need to keep calling it that?" he asks with a tired smile.

"Would you prefer Kink Dungeon?"

Gerrit snorts.

Emily jumps in. "We're going to need an entire table to display this puppy. With a fancy tablecloth. Maybe some candles. And some gold. Like it's an altar to us!"

"It'll go right beside the award we're going to get at the next con." Oscar has his scheming face on again. "Next time, we're going to qualify for the World Cosplay Expo."

"Or die trying," Emily adds with her characteristic dramatic flair.

"And if we don't?" Gerrit asks.

"Then we try again," Oscar says, unperturbed. "And again."

"And again?" Emily asks.

"And again," Gerrit groans with unmasked dread.

I don't say anything. My relationship with my biomom depends on us making it to New York in May. We have to qualify, and soon. I can't wait another year to keep trying.

Emily jumps on Gerrit's back. "Giddyap, nightmare creature! I think we deserve french fries."

"I guess I'm hungry," Gerrit agrees as he jogs toward the exit with Emily whooping behind him.

Emily looks back toward us. "The last one to the van has to buy chocolate shakes!"

Oscar chases after them, holding his award up in the air like it's the greatest thing he's ever held.

Like I said, I don't do running. So I walk at a leisurely pace as I post one of our selfies on Insta. I look so weird in the brown hair and normcore outfit. It's like I'm an entirely different person.

I scroll through the comments from this morning's Nancy Thompson reveal.

> **SkullChic:** "Good luck, Goth Queen!"
>
> **BioHazard23:** "Whaaat? Are you a time traveler now? #80sSoCute"
>
> **Finntastic:** "Never have I ever thought a perm looked so good."

After I finish scrolling to the end of my comments, a little nugget of disappointment tinges my mood. There's nothing from Reigna_NYC. Her lack of response makes me afraid that she's on the streets somewhere, in the middle of a psychotic episode like she was when I was a kid. As soon as the thought registers, I feel guilt bite my insides. She's better now. She's taking her meds and seeing doctors. It's time I start trusting my own mother and stop being so paranoid.

The schizophrenia gene monster grumbles inside me again, making the back of my neck prickle. I can't fix my biomom from here, but french fries with my teammates should fix me.

At least for now.

CHAPTER 23

WE TREMBLE WITH THE VIOLENCE OF THE CONFLICT WITHIN US,—OF THE DEFINITE WITH THE INDEFINITE—OF THE SUBSTANCE WITH THE SHADOW.
EDGAR ALLAN POE, "THE IMP OF THE PERVERSE"

The second I step off the school bus and into the spring morning air, I know there's trouble brewing. While I'm used to nervous side-glances and open hostility, that's not what I see in the faces around me this morning. It's something more sinister.

As I walk through the crowded halls, a bizarre hush peppered with snickers follows me around. Groups of girls grab each other's arms and whisper with cruel excitement. Their eyes are brimming over with glee. A band nerd laughs at me with a snort.

Oh Goddess, what is it now?

After I grab my chemistry book from my locker, I spot something out of the corner of my eye. Taped to the wall is a photo of Oscar and me in our scream queen costumes. My hand instinctively reaches out to tear it from the bricks. In the photo, my curly '80s hair and pink sweater vest look ridiculous out of context. My lack of goth makeup renders me almost unrecognizable. Oscar's cherubic face, on the other hand, is very identifiable. His football jersey crop top exposes his soft belly for all our high school tormentors to see. I know this photo. We took it after our big win. This is one of my Insta uploads. You can see my Insta handle and the subject line I wrote: "Me as the badass '80s Scream Queen Heather Langenkamp, with a guy dressed as Johnny Depp from *A Nightmare on Elm Street.*"

We look so happy in this photo, but these posters are intended to fill us with shame. Someone decided to turn our pride into something dirty, like a poison.

My chest fills with dread. Oh no.

Above our faces someone wrote in Sharpie: "Recognize these nerds?"

When I look down that hall, I see there are dozens of posters. These stupid pictures are everywhere. I run to the next one to tear it down, not caring that the printer paper slices into the soft skin between my thumb and forefinger. The sting matches my growing rage. The Sharpie marks on this poster read: "Secret lovebirds of Detroit River High." Another has a halo around our heads. A fourth says: "Off hours, our resident geek and goth live in a fantasy world."

How did these twerps find my Insta account? Who would take the time to print photos just to torment us? When I look around the halls, I can see in the eyes of my peers that it could have been anyone. This is one of the awful truths about high school. Kids will do anything for a laugh, especially at the expense of someone else.

While everyone stares at me, I make a decision. I shrug and toss the posters up into the air, then walk away as they float gracefully to the ground.

Someone behind me says the word "crazy." It makes my skin prickle, but I ignore it. At this point in my life I'm growing used to this particular flavor of ridicule. This is just one more insignificant jab. I shake it off and remind myself that I'm much too badass to let this bother me.

Unfortunately, when I see Oscar, I realize he isn't.

He's standing very still, his face inside his locker. By the movement of his shoulders, I can see he's breathing heavily. When I walk closer, the glint of sweat at his temples shines like a warning. His eyes are closed as if he's trying to focus on being somewhere, anywhere, else. He's fighting with his anxiety.

Brent Tyler, Detroit River High's hockey golden boy, pounds on the locker next to Oscar and he jumps. The jerk is positively dripping with joyful cruelty.

"You're delusional if you think you can dress up like Johnny Depp," he says with a smile. "For one thing, he isn't chubby. And for another, he isn't Mexican."

"Hey, Brent," I yell, "want to learn what it's like to be punched in the face by a girl?"

The asshole makes kissy noises in Oscar's ear while staring at me.

I give him a double barrel of birds.

He glides away from Oscar like he's untouchable, because he is. In the universe of Detroit River High, he who picks on the little guy reigns supreme.

I hate this shit.

"Are you okay?" I ask as Oscar closes his locker.

When he sees me, he straightens his shoulders.

"I'm fine." He hugs a pile of books close to his chest like they're armor.

"I take it you saw the posters."

"They're hard to miss," he says.

Someone bumps into Oscar's shoulder, causing him to drop everything in his arms. His holy book, *Prince of Moons*, lies open on the ground. I bend down to help him pick it up. When I hand it to him, I notice he tucks it between two other books, as if to hide it.

"Hey," I say. "Seriously, don't let the nitwits get to you."

"I'm not," he says, his voice tight.

"You are. I'm not ignorant. I saw you hide your book."

"I just don't want to give them more reasons to mess with me," he says as he stands up. His eyes flick around the hallway at the faces that sneer at us from every angle. "I'm protecting myself."

"No," I say, irritation flashing. "You're hiding yourself."

A girl down the hall yells, "Where's your crown, beauty queens?"

"It's scream queen," Oscar mumbles under his breath.

"There!" My voice is rising. "You did it again."

"Did what?" he snaps. He bristles like an irritated cat.

"You didn't stick up for yourself," I insist. "You just lie there and take it, like you're broken. This is why they mess with you so much. You make yourself an easy target."

"That's why I'm trying to be invisible!" he snaps. His cheeks are red and not from blushing this time. "Like in your Insta post. I'm just 'a guy.' I don't really exist as an individual who matters."

"What are you talking about?"

"Nothing." He tries to walk around me.

Someone calls out, "Hey, Oscar, nice belly shirt!"

He doesn't acknowledge him.

"What are you doing?" I ask. "Say something back!" I wave my arm wildly in the direction of the latest comment.

"I'm ignoring him," Oscar mumbles.

My fingers clench at my sides in frustration, midnight-black nails glinting in the light like a threat. "You're embarrassing your-self!" I say through gritted teeth.

"Oh really," he says as he spins to look at me. "Or am I embar-rassing *you*?"

"What?" I ask, incredulous. "I didn't say that."

"You didn't have to."

His eyes look so disappointed in me that I actually flinch back. I stand, stunned and silent.

How could he accuse me of such a thing? I've spent every moment of my spare time with him, working on his pet cosplay project. But even as I think that, an annoying thought worms its way to the front of my mind: *You* are *embarrassed.*

Oscar pauses in front of me, waiting for a response.

It's just his damnable *Prince of Moons* obsession, that's all. Not him. I like Oscar. I just can't be associated with the weird parts of him. He's not that ridiculous Sir Valorian character, no matter how many foam swords he crafts. He needs to be stronger in *this* realm, not some fake planet stuck in some medieval dimension. He has to learn to stand up for himself, like I had to do. He can't pretend his way out of reality. Life isn't all about slaying intergalactic dragons and saving spacesuit-wearing damsels in distress.

The bell rings.

Oscar nods at me slowly. "I gotta go," he says.

I don't say a single thing to stop him.

My nerves feel prickly all day, like I could ignite at any moment.

The stress nightmares will be in full swing tonight. My voice will be gone. Everyone I love will leave. And I will be utterly alone. Maybe it's time to take a page from Edgar Allan Poe's life and welcome the darkness of it all. Perhaps, if this cosplay gig doesn't work out, I could try my hand at writing macabre poetry as a coping mechanism.

At the end of the school day I ride the bus home surrounded by the usual cloud of chaos as guys throw paper footballs at each other across the aisle while small groups gossip and giggle. I'm hyperaware that I have absolutely nothing in common with these normal people. Teens who worry about sports, prom, and pop quizzes feel about as foreign to me as a Martian would feel to them. Still, it's grown more difficult to block out the whispers carrying my name. Especially now that it's caused a serious rift in my relationship with Oscar.

I put my mental blinders on and scroll through Insta. At least these internet friends aren't cruel. They don't look at my goth or cosplay photos and see a freak worthy of tormenting. In the world of Insta, I can block a troll quicker than they can type "freak." In the physical realm, I have to find ways to live with real ghouls breathing down my neck on the daily. Too bad blocking functions don't work on Detroit River High jocks IRL.

Along the top of my screen my DM indicator flashes. I know who the message is from before I click on it.

Reigna_NYC: "You should sew yourself a gown for when we go home. Our subjects will expect us to greet them formally for the royal homecoming. There might be a soiree thrown in our honor."

Oh no. No. No. No.

My hands shake. This is the last thing I needed to see today. She's gotta be off the meds. Was she ever on them in the first place, or was that a lie to get me to trust her? For half a second I consider telling my social worker. Maybe she could get in contact with someone in New York who could check on Reigna? But no. That would mean admitting I've been talking to my biomom in secret for months without authorization. It would blow my opportunity to go to New York and see her myself without social workers shadowing me the whole time.

I stuff my phone back into my satchel when the bus rolls to a stop at the corner of Barbra's street. Ignoring the eyes that bore into my back like poisoned daggers, I throw my bag over my shoulder and get up to leave. A paper football hits my arm, so I pirouette to flash the entire bus a glorious smile framed by black lipstick and two middle fingers. As expected, the chorus erupts with whispers of "crazy," "weirdo," and "psycho." The bus driver rolls his eyes at my antics, like usual.

When the bus door closes behind me, the silence of the street hits me like an embrace. The spring breeze blows through the skinny sidewalk trees with their baby leaves popping forth from tiny buds. Spring is supposed to be a time of rebirth and new beginnings. It doesn't extend to me. I very much feel the drag of the past holding me down like rusty chains.

As I walk up the street, I snatch up stray candy wrappers and disposable cups from the side of the road, then stuff them into trash bins. I can't clean up all of Detroit, but I can at least try to make my tiny corner of the world a little less messy. Shouldn't that logic apply to my personal life too?

The more I think about New York, the more I realize getting there is only the first of many obstacles to overcome. I want to help my biomom, even though I'm not sure how. All the experts say I'd need to be honest with her, not reinforce the delusion. We can't exist together in this realm of make-believe. The truth is, I'm scared to do that. She might block me out again. She might spiral deeper into her illness.

I sit on Barbra's front stoop with my phone in my hand. How do you talk to someone in the midst of a psychotic break? All I can think to say is the truth. No lies, not to my real family.

My thumbs text my answer.

> **GothQueen_13:** "I need to be honest with you. I know we're not royalty. And that's okay with me. I'm fine being a regular person as long as I get to be one with my real mom."

Three little dots appear, like she's typing a response. She must be signed in to Insta.

The dots disappear. A small feeling of disappointment makes a hole in my chest. Will she just pretend I never said that, like when I confronted her about my biological family?

The dots reappear. A few seconds later, there's a response.

> **Reigna_NYC:** "I don't know what they've been telling you, but you ARE a princess. We ARE from royal stock. We need to go back home so I can prove this to you."

The disappointment inside of me starts to simmer into irritation. She can't really believe this. Somewhere deep inside, she must know this isn't possible.

> **GothQueen_13:** "No. It's not true. There's no evidence to back this up. Mom, I know you're sick. I want to help you get better. I can't do that if we can't be real with each other."

> **Reigna_NYC:** "You want to talk about evidence? How about the fact that I had to give you up to keep you safe from THEM."

I bite my lip and squeeze my eyes shut. Speaking with the insane is making me doubt my own sanity. How do I know my worldview is correct, when my own mother believes her reality with such an overwhelming conviction? Is there some truth in what she says? Or none?

No. I can't allow myself to fall victim to that mind game.

> **GothQueen_13:** "Mom, there is no all-evil 'them.' I know this must be difficult to hear. You gave me up to keep me safe from yourself."

I regret this choice of words the second I hit send. Logically, I know I'm too worked up to have this conversation right now. Maybe I should close my phone and wait until I'm feeling less hostile. Less hurt. This day has been filled with one gut punch after another. I really should discuss this with a cooler head, but I don't.

A pair of mothers walks by, pushing a stroller. The moms coo at their newborn like he's the best thing in the world. Their little family is so carefree and in love, it radiates off them like an aura. I'm jealous of the familial comfort they share. I wonder if my own mother ever looked at me like that. Or was she always this paranoid?

When she doesn't respond, I continue.

GothQueen_13: "The last time I saw you, you had a psychotic break. The police found me after you left. They told me you were sent to a psychiatric hospital. It wasn't the first time either, Mom. This is my evidence."

Reigna_NYC: "That? That isn't evidence. It was a setup! They took me away and locked me up in the wrong hospital. All I had was food poisoning. They wanted to steal my inheritance."

GothQueen_13: "All anyone wants is for you to get healthy again. You have schizophrenia, Mom. You need to take care of yourself. You need to see doctors and take your medicine. Please, if not for yourself, then do it for me."

Reigna_NYC: "I AM NOT SICK!"

My chest caves in, leaving me feeling broken. The sting is real, even though no physical blow has been cast.

GothQueen_13: "You are. You were sent to the correct hospital. You needed help with your mental illness. That's nothing to be ashamed of. We all need help sometimes."

Reigna_NYC: "They wanted to take you away."

The simmer inside of me has transformed into a rolling boil.

How can she think I'm stupid enough to believe her lies? I'm not a child who accepts everything she's told anymore. I faced the nightmare of foster care and survived. I'm not easy to fool.

The spring air brushes my hair from my face, like the earth itself knows I need comfort. If I could close my eyes and exist inside the wind forever, I would. I'd dissolve into nature and never need to make another difficult decision again. Breezes don't worry about maternal loyalties or brokenhearted boys. They don't care if you're sick or lonely. They don't require choices that hurt or abandon people they care about.

> **GothQueen_13:** "They did take me away, but only because you never got better. You didn't even try to follow their rules so I could live with you again. Do you know what it's like to be a seven-year-old, waiting for her mother to come back day after day? I went home to my foster parents, convinced I'd find you waiting. BUT YOU DIDN'T EVEN TRY TO GET BETTER FOR ME! It took me years to accept that. Years of waiting. Years of watching the front door. Years of racing to the mailbox, hoping for a letter. I will never understand why you didn't work harder to get better. Why you didn't even try to get me back."

There's a humming in my ears. That lightning spark of an impending stress headache pinches at my temples. The schizophrenia gene monster scratches at the back of my skull, reminding me that I'm looking into a mirror. My mother is showing me my true inheritance.

"I will not cry," I whisper to myself. "I will not cry. I am stronger than that."

My phone buzzes.

> **Reigna_NYC:** "I'd have thought you're too old for tantrums. You can speak with me again when you're ready to face your true destiny. Being a princess is an enormous responsibility. Right

now, you're acting like a spoiled child. Let me know when you're ready to be a grown-up."

I throw my phone down and cry like the silly baby my biomom still thinks I am.

CHAPTER 24

POE GRAPPLED WITH THE DARKER SIDE OF MANKIND, WITH THE DEMONS
THAT RESIDE WITHIN US: OUR MIND, A CRUMBLING EDIFICE, SINKING
SLOWLY IN A SWAMP OF DECADENCE AND MADNESS.
GUILLERMO DEL TORO, INTRODUCTION TO *THE RAVEN: TALES AND POEMS*
BY EDGAR ALLAN POE

When Barbra comes home a little after 5:00, she knocks on my bedroom door.

"You home?" she calls through the wood.

"Mhm," I mumble weakly.

I've been lying on the bed for over an hour, staring at the ceiling, focusing on breathing. Air is a funny thing. You never really notice it until you're so stressed out you forget to breathe. It's like I have to be conscious of it now or else I'll hold my breath until I feel my chest burning. My entire body is falling apart, just like my life.

"Want some dinner?" Barbra calls through the door. "I thought I'd make sesame tofu and brown rice. I found a new recipe in *Vegetarian Times* that looks interesting."

"I'm not really hungry," I say.

There's a long pause.

"Are you okay?" Her tone has changed from upbeat to concerned. "You don't sound too good."

"Eh."

"Can I come in?"

"Sure."

The door creaks as she pushes it open. I haven't changed out of my school clothes. I'm still wearing my constricting pirate tights with skull and crossbones all down the legs. Even my boots are dangling from my feet where they hang off the edge of the bed. It's all I can do to turn my head to look at her.

"I'm not feeling great," I say by way of explanation.

Barbra takes a few steps into the room to examine my face. "Are you sick?"

"No. It's just . . ." I sigh. I don't have the words to articulate the chaos inside of me. There's no logical way to explain what it feels like to know you have a parent out there in the world, beyond reach. I'm physically here, but I'm lost at the same time. "It's been one hell of a day. That's all."

Barbra sits next to me on the bed. "A bad day can wipe you out as surely as the flu, in my experience."

No kidding. I don't respond.

"I think I know what you need."

I raise an eyebrow at her.

"You need some friends and some good, old-fashioned soul food. That's the best way I know of to fix heartache."

"I don't know," I say.

"Why don't you see if one of your friends wants to come over for a bit? I'm ordering out. I'll call you when the food's here." She stands up, pats my knee, and leaves the room.

Despite my lethargy, I can see the sense in having a distraction right now. I haven't invited anyone over to a foster's house since I was in elementary school. There were too many instances when it went sour. After a while, it seemed better not to have friends over at all.

Barbra doesn't seem like all the other fosters though. So, since there are only two people at Detroit River High who know about my foster care status—and one of them hates me right now—I pick up my phone to text Emily.

> Hi. Do you have plans tonight?

She responds right away.

> Oh, you know, just the usual. Playing God of War until 1:00 a.m. which is about the time my eyes feel like they're ready to pop out of my head from staring at the TV screen for six hours straight. Unless . . .

> Unless?

> Unless you have a better idea?!

> Any chance you'd wanna come over?

> Sure! Would 7:00 work?

> See you then.

She sends a smiling poo emoji for confirmation.

Despite my emotional exhaustion, I can't help but smile a little. Then I go back to lying prone.

Forty-five minutes later, the food delivery guy rings the doorbell. I listen as Barbra answers it. She doesn't even need to tell me what she ordered, because the smell drifts up the stairs. Barbecue. I'm both interested and confused. I haven't had barbecue in years, not since I became a vegetarian. But damn, my stomach is betraying me. It rumbles.

With great effort, I push myself up into a sitting position. Even my arms feel weak. My legs tremble underneath me when I walk downstairs. It's really weird that emotional exhaustion can take such a physical toll.

When I enter the kitchen, Barbra is setting takeout containers on the table.

"Want to get plates and such?"

I move toward the cabinets. "Do I smell meat?"

Barbra turns to me with hands on hips. "I would never do that to you, Jess." She grins widely. "It's veggie barbecue! Slows has some of the best vegetarian-friendly soul food I've ever had. You're going to love it."

After two servings of mac and cheese, cornbread, potato salad, and shredded jackfruit in BBQ sauce—which has a frighteningly similar texture to pulled pork—I am about as stuffed as I've ever felt in my life. And, remarkably, less depressed. Guess Barbra knows a thing or two about healing the soul. Or, at least, she knows how to give it a break once in a while.

"I thought you weren't hungry?" Barbra asks with a wink.

"Well, it looks like my soul needed to feed."

She chuckles. "Do you want to talk about it?"

"The food?" I joke.

"Well, I suppose we could talk about food all day." She nibbles on a piece of jackfruit slathered in delicious sauce. "But I meant your terrible day."

I stuff another piece of sweet cornbread into my mouth to buy me some time. It's impossible to tell her about the fight I had with my biomom without exposing that major secret. Still, maybe there's a way to bend the truth about my fight with Oscar.

"So, you know my friend Oscar?" I say hesitantly.

She nods. "The one who does the movie makeup with you."

"Yeah," I confirm, avoiding her eyes. "We got into a really big fight today. Like, really big. I'm afraid we might not be able to bounce back from that."

"How come?" She stands up and pours herself a mug of decaf coffee. She settles back into her chair, like she's anticipating a long chat.

"Um, it's hard to explain." I poke my fork into what's left of my rapidly solidifying mac and cheese. "There's some really awful people at school who've targeted us for . . . the makeup thing."

"Ah, the bullies." She shakes her head morosely. "Unfortunately, that hasn't changed about high school since I was there. Actually"— she pauses to think—"I'm not sure it ever does change. Bullies seem to live forever."

"I've dealt with them all my life," I say. "I've learned how to keep them from hurting me. But Oscar, he's just so—I don't know— fragile. It frustrates me."

She nods, encouraging me to continue.

"I haven't had many friends," I admit. "Actually, the last real friend I had was probably in the sixth grade. It ended pretty badly."

"What happened then?" she asks.

"Uh, well." I bite my lip. "That was about the time I discovered Edgar Allan Poe. I was reading all his short stories and poetry. My friend—Christina—said I was turning creepy. She didn't want to be around me anymore. It kind of culminated in a massive fight where she told our entire class that I was a weird foster kid who was probably crazy."

Barbra cringes. "Yikes. That's rough."

"It wasn't a good year for me." As I say it, my stomach tightens up, bracing itself for the pain of that memory. That was the first time my classmates called me "psycho." It seems I never shook the name, though I did shake that feeling of utter betrayal. I learned to be tougher. To care less.

"If I remember correctly," Barbra says, "sixth grade isn't a good year for anyone, though yours sounds particularly rough. I'm sorry about that."

I shrug. "That's life as a foster kid."

Barbra takes a long, slow sip of her coffee as I use my fork to smash my cornbread crumbs into ever-smaller pieces.

Barbra breaks the silence. "Many people would say some nonsense like: 'If she wasn't your friend when you discovered your most authentic self, then she was never your friend in the first place.'" She scrunches up her nose. "I think that's hogwash. That's just something we say to people to make them feel better about themselves."

My fork pauses in the middle of massacring my cornbread. "You think I deserved it?"

"No." She shakes her head. "I think some people are in our lives only for a season, to teach us things about ourselves. It doesn't mean the time you had together wasn't important. It just means people grow. They change. They make mistakes. Often times it means they grow apart." Barbra looks down at her hands, clenching them around her coffee mug. "And I'm sorry to say you'll probably have more Christinas in your life. Cherish the good times you have, but don't let old wounds hold you back from making new friends in the future either." She gives me a pointed look.

"I kinda tried to break that habit this year."

"I can tell." She gives me a small smile. "You've made several friends since you moved here. That's really great."

"Then, today, the thing with Oscar happened." My mouth

suddenly tastes sour, like I'm just now realizing the bullies weren't the only problem. I hurt Oscar too. "I think I might have screwed it all up. Made it worse."

Barbra gives me an understanding look. "Maybe you can find a way to make up. That's one of the many life lessons you get to learn." She ticks them off on her fingers. "How to apologize. How to admit when you've made a mistake. How to fix things. How to make compromises. How to know when to walk away."

"Or maybe Oscar is my new Christina." I set down my fork, feeling sick for real now. Or maybe I'm *his* Christina.

"Unfortunately." She winces. "There have been many Christinas in my life too. I'm not the same person I was when I was a teenager." She chuckles. "Heck, I'm not the same person I was six months ago. That's probably a good thing."

"I don't know." I shrug. "You seem like a decent person. I can't imagine you've hurt anyone."

Her face grows sad, remembering some hidden wrong. "We all have to hurt people sometimes, Jess. That's life as a living, breathing human. Most of the time it's unintentional. None of us is perfect. We all make mistakes." She looks out the darkened window. I follow her gaze, but all that we can see is our own reflections shining back at us from the kitchen's overhead lights.

She turns back to me. "That's not to say I don't regret hurting people in my life, but I'm trying to be glad for what they taught me. I had a lot to learn. About the world and about myself."

It strikes me suddenly that I've never heard of Barbra's friends. As happy as she is, she seems to be a bit of a loner.

"Do you have friends now?" I ask, without realizing how much of a jab it could be.

She smiles at me, unperturbed by my rude question.

"Well, I guess I have you. Though you're right, that's not enough." She points her fork at me. "I need to work on that."

The doorbell rings.

I get up to answer it. When I open the door, Emily's standing there wearing a hot-pink button-up and a yellow bow tie.

"Friend!" she practically yells. "Never in my life would I have expected you to invite me over for girl time. I'd hug you, I'm so excited, but I'm afraid you might punch me for it." She pushes the strap of her backpack farther up her skinny shoulder.

"Um, thanks," I say, then open the door wider so she can come in.

I lead her into the kitchen, where Barbra is peacefully sipping her gross fake coffee.

"Barbra, this is my friend Emily. Emily, this is my foster mom, Barbra."

Emily is all charm. She holds out a hand for Barbra to shake. It's clear she's mastered more than a few parental meetings. She's a pro.

Barbra shakes her hand, clearly pleased. "It's so nice to meet you! Jess showed me your *Star Wars* movie poster. I loved it. You make an excellent Han Solo."

"Uh . . ." Her eyes dart to me where I'm nodding my head emphatically behind Barbra. "Thanks!" she says cheerily.

Barbra motions toward the feast of Slows BBQ on the table. "Would you like to bring some cornbread or something upstairs with you?"

"No thanks," Emily says, patting her tiny belly. "I just had dinner with my parents."

"Okay then, go have fun," Barbra says as she stands up from the table.

I pause, feeling like I should at least help her clean up from dinner before I abandon her.

Barbra senses my hesitation. She waves her hand in a shooing motion. "Go on, I can take care of this."

"Thanks," I say as I practically push Emily out of the kitchen.

On the way upstairs to my bedroom, I whisper to Emily. "I showed her a pic, but she doesn't know about the competitions. She thinks we make fake movie posters for fun."

"I mean, that *does* sound like fun." Emily has that faraway look on her face, like she's been struck by a brilliant idea and she's allowing it to wash over her. "We could do *Stranger Things* sometime and Oscar could make one of those creepy-gross monster things." She makes a dramatic gagging sound, but looks excited about the idea nonetheless.

At the top of the stairs I turn around to look at her. "What? No, we already have a hobby. Remember? We don't need another one right now."

"I'm just saying, Barbra might be onto something with this."

I shake my head and close the bedroom door behind us.

"Sheesh," Emily says as she looks around at my bare walls. "You like it sparse, huh?" She drops her backpack on the floor by the bed.

I shrug and turn on some Rasputina to avoid eye contact. Late '90s cello-rock music streams through my phone speakers. "I've only lived here for three months."

"Yeah, but don't you decorate the hell out of your room the second you move in? It's called nesting."

"Nah, it's too much work, especially if you expect to move every few months." I freeze, realizing I've just said one of those things about foster care that make normal people feel terribly uncomfortable. I watch her for a reaction, but, like Oscar, she surprises me.

"Touché." She nods to me, like I've won a battle. Oscar's weirdness is really rubbing off on all of us.

"So," she says. "Let me tell you what I envisioned for you. First off, black walls or at the very least dark gray. Like grave dirt, only less dusty." She waves her arms around like a celebrity interior decorator, indicating toward things that need to change about the space. "Black curtains to block out the sunlight, because, well, you *do* like a good vampire aesthetic. And, for sure, a giant canopy bed with gauzy drapey things akin to spiderwebs or maybe a *Phantom of the Opera*-esque Victorian . . ." Emily silences midword, which is remarkably uncharacteristic of her.

I whirl around, half expecting to see a murderer hiding in the closet.

She raises one finger to point to the pile of books on my dresser. *Prince of Moons* shines in all its metallic raised-letter-cover glory.

"What. The hell. Is that?"

I shrug like it's no big deal. "Oscar gave it to me a while ago. I'm a slow reader. And by that, I mean I haven't touched it since."

Emily shudders and turns her back to the book as if to block the tome from her vision. She leaps up onto the bed.

"Sooo?" she asks, her face expectant.

"So, what?" I feel awkward, standing here with another person in my room. How am I supposed to entertain my guest? Isn't that what you do when you invite someone over? Keep them occupied? I should have thought about that before I sent the damn invite text.

"So, why are you only now inviting me over?" she asks. "I kinda thought you didn't like people."

"I like you," I say a little too defensively.

"Well, duh." She rolls her eyes. "Everybody likes me. I'm

awesome. That's not the point." She runs her hand through her short hair like a wannabe Justin Bieber. "Was it those stupid posters?"

I crawl up onto the bed too. "Yes. And no. It's been a rough day."

She rubs her hands together like she's plotting. "Well then, what should we do to make you feel better for our first girls' night? Should we curse someone?"

A guffaw escapes my chest. "No, you little monster." I can't help laughing at the direction her mind goes.

"You know, everyone thinks you're capable of magic because you look so scary." Emily says this with so much awe, I take no disrespect.

"Well, I am pretty magical."

"Do you think a fake magic spell will get me into my number one coding program?" She scratches her cheek. "Or maybe we should figure out how to do a real one?"

I roll my eyes. "I think we should leave the magic to the real witches. Wouldn't want to accidentally open a portal to hell or anything. Besides"—I bump her with my shoulder—"something tells me all the work you've been doing will speak for itself."

Emily sighs dramatically. "If you say so . . . I just *really* want to get in. I need to be massively impressive to video game design companies after graduation so I can change the business from the inside, you know? I need them to take me seriously if I'm going to be a force for diversity in gaming."

"You already are massively impressive. No matter what coding program you go to, they're going to have no idea what they got themselves into with you."

Emily flops down onto the pillows. "Geek world domination is so stressful."

"Sounds like it."

She leans over the edge of the bed to grab her backpack. She pulls out a laptop and scoots closer to me. "Wanna help me test the game I've been coding? It's an RPG with a goth queen character. You're gonna love it. The goth queen has superpowers like moth minions and spiderweb nets."

"You made a game?!"

"A simple one, but yeah."

I shake my head in wonder. "How long did it take you?"

"Around a thousand five hundred hours." She shrugs. "I'm sending it in with my coding school applications."

"A thousand five hundred hours?" I blanch. "When did you have time to sleep or eat?"

"To the first, I didn't." She sticks out her tongue. "Except when my mom was testing or editing the code I wrote. To the second, my dad supplied me with a steady stream of food while I worked." She rubs her belly. "He makes excellent dumplings, which are great for eating one handed while typing."

"So, your parents are cool with the coding dream then?"

"Totally." She nods. "Though, to be honest, I could've chosen to be a trapeze artist and they still would have been my personal cheerleaders. They're kinda great like that."

The jealous pit of fire that's been burning in my chest flares.

She hands over the laptop.

After several levels of tripping jocks and scaring preps, I finally find Dracula's coffin in the dungeon of the high school. The game prompts me to choose between smashing it with an ax or crawling inside for a cold cuddle. Of course, I opt for cuddles.

"Bold move," Emily says. "I'd expect the murderous option from you."

In spite of how terrible this day has been, the clenching pain in my chest is slowly easing. It looks like I've made a real friend in Emily. This is a surprising—though not entirely unwelcome—turn of events for this goth queen.

CHAPTER 25

Five days later, I still haven't heard from Oscar. No brainstorming for the next con, no jokes about intergalactic domination, no texted suggestions for geek universes left unexplored, nothing. It's time to be the bigger person and apologize. The situation with the posters wasn't my fault, but I definitely didn't help by shaming him for his reaction.

I ring his doorbell on Saturday morning, with presents in tow. Abuela opens the door. She greets me with a wide smile, but there's something a little off about it.

"Is everything okay?" I ask. "I was hoping to see Oscar."

She nods emphatically, grabs my arms, and pulls me into the house. She's speaking Spanish in a hushed tone, and all the while her eyes keep darting to the closed door of the basement.

"Is he downstairs?" I ask.

She nods, makes an exaggerated frown, and huffs.

"He's depressed?"

She gives me a giant grandmotherly hug. I can feel her worry on my shoulders, like the Duke of Dark Matter's black cloak of oppression. When she pulls away, her eyes are wet. She pushes me toward the basement door, then rushes off to the kitchen. Pots start to bang around while I take a few deep breaths for courage. Here goes nothing.

I open the basement door and descend into the depths, feeling very much like a cave goblin on the planet Do'hran. It's oddly dark down here. The only light seems to be coming from a lamp at one of the worktables. Oscar's hunched over something, with a pair of magnifying goggles strapped around his head.

"Abuelita, gracias, but I told you I'm not hungry," Oscar says without turning away from his work.

I clear my throat. "Me neither, surprisingly."

Oscar freezes, then spins around in his chair. He pulls his goggles up to look at me.

"Sorry," he says. "Thought you were Abuela."

"No need to be sorry."

He nods, probably remembering how many times I've given him crap for apologizing. I kinda feel like an ass about it now. Oscar looks a little rough. His hair is a bit greasy and his shoulders are slumped like they used to be when I first met him.

"So," I say in a terrible attempt to break the ice. "I have something for you." I hold up the box I've carried all the way from home.

He raises an eyebrow at me. "Like a present?"

"An 'I'm Sorry' present, perhaps?" I say holding it out toward him.

He eyes me, skeptically. "*A*, I thought you hate presents. And *b*, is this your attempt at an apology?"

Sheesh, I don't like Moody Oscar very much. All the more reason to get the cherubic variety back.

"I never said I hate presents," I stammer.

"Again, didn't have to."

"AND," I say, continuing on. "No, that wasn't me apologizing.

This is me apologizing." I walk toward him and kneel like a medieval knight. "My liege, wouldth thou find it in thy gracious heart to forgive this lowly peasant for my multitude of evil deeds?"

A tiny smirk pulls at the side his lips. "That was terrible."

"Well," I say, as I sit back on my haunches. "It shouldn't be. I learned from the best." I give him my sauciest grin. "And that's just the first part of the apology." I open the box and hand him the first book in the Prince of Moons series.

He takes it in his hand, with a quizzical look on his face. "You're gifting me with my own duplicate copy of *Price of Moons*?"

"Yes."

"I don't get it."

"I felt like a jerk for the way I spoke to you on Monday. So I spent all of Tuesday afternoon reading your book. And Wednesday. And Thursday. And Friday. And Saturday. And until about three a.m. this morning."

Oscar lets out a low whistle. "That's a lot of nerd reading for one goth queen."

"Thank you for appreciating my sacrifice and dedication," I say with a flip of my long black hair. "But you should know it wasn't all drudgery."

"No?"

"I maybe actually kinda enjoyed it just a smidgen of a little bit."

"So who's your favorite character then?"

"The Queen of Thieves, of course."

"I could have predicted that. Oh, wait." Oscar puts one finger to his chin and pretends to remember something. "I did."

"But wait, there's more!" I say with my showiest daytime television game show host voice. I hand him a rectangular box.

When Oscar takes it, I hold my breath while he opens the lid.

Inside, there are about one hundred business cards. I cut and illustrated several myself, then duplicated the lot at the Copy Shop downtown. He holds one up and analyzes it through his magnifying goggles.

It reads:

The Costume Lair

Custom Cosplay by Oscar Martinez

SirValorian123@gmail.com

"I thought that, once we make it to the big leagues, you might want something to hand out to potential clients."

"You forgot your name," he says.

I shake my head. "Nah, this has always been your dream. I'm just along for the ride."

Oscar visibly swallows hard. "Why did you make these for me?"

"Because, you're going to need them. Like I just said?"

"No, I mean . . ." He runs his hands through his hair and spins his chair back to his workbench. After a long breath, he gets up and walks to another table. His hands move over some chain mail in progress. "I mean, why did you, Jess, go out of your way to make me such a thoughtful gift?"

"Well, geez," I laugh lightheartedly. "Don't jump up and down in excitement or anything."

He looks at me. "I'm being serious."

"This is a very serious gift," I say. "I expect great things from you, young Skywalker."

Instead of laughing, he shakes his head.

"Sometimes." He pauses like he's fighting the words that want to come out and replacing them with others that sound more palatable. "Sometimes, I can't tell if you like me or not."

His face looks a little spooky in the shadowy light.

"What do you mean? Of course I like you, we're teammates."

"I think you know what I mean," he says. "Sometimes I can't tell if you like me as . . . more."

No one is more astonished than I am to see that he isn't blushing. But I sure as hell am. Suddenly I'm glad for the dim basement lighting.

"And then other times," he continues, "like earlier this week. You make me feel like an annoying complication in your life. Like I'm a humiliating younger brother or something."

Guilt floods my veins. "Oscar, about the other day . . ."

He holds up his hands. "No, I'm not fishing for more apology. I'm just confused."

Silence envelops us both. In this moment Oscar feels so far away. I know it's my fault. Isn't this what I wanted? To keep him at arm's length? Yes, I remind myself. This is how it has to be.

"I don't like you like that." My voice comes out soft, like I know I'm delivering bad news. What Oscar can't know is it's not just bad news for him. It is for me too.

He sniffs. "Is it because I'm too embarrassing?"

"No," I say hurriedly. "It's just, we're too different. It would never work out. Trust me on that."

Oscar nods his head and plucks at the chain mail on the workbench in front of him. "Okay."

"Okay?"

"If all we are is business partners, then okay. I can live with that." The determination in his eyes tells me it won't be easy.

I stand up and hold out my hand. "Business partners."

He takes a few slow steps toward me, looks me in the eyes, and shakes my hand formally. "Business partners."

I pull my hand away quickly, trying to stem the flow of warmth that his touch gives mine. Oscar turns back to his workbench.

This is good, I tell myself. We're on the right track, finally.

I clear my throat. "So, I was thinking," I say. I walk toward one of the many *Prince of Moons* suits of armor that Oscar has made over the years. "You've put an awful lot of work into these. It would be a shame if we never used them."

Oscar is so still I think for a moment that he wasn't listening.

"Did you hear me?" I ask.

"Mhm."

"What do you think?"

"Of what?" he asks, his back still to me.

"Of doing *Prince of Moons* for the next con."

He turns back toward me, his face twisted in confusion. "Are you messing with me?"

"No!"

"Is this another apology present?"

"No," I say. "I just thought, since you were nice enough to suggest scream queens for me, we should do something that represents your interests this time."

I wait several long moments for his reply. Finally, I see the spark of the old Oscar shine brightly in his eyes.

"Emily and Gerrit are going to hate it."

We both grin conspiratorially.

"Let's get to work."

CHAPTER 26

WHAT MISSION IS GREATER THAN HAVING
ADVENTURES AND SEARCHING FOR LOVE?
SIR VALORIAN, *PRINCE OF MOONS*

I lace my thread through the needle of the sewing machine Mrs. Heavers let me borrow. She was so tickled when she saw my Princess Leia costume that she told me I could keep the machine until the end of the semester. We keep it in the Costume Lair, since I don't really want Barbra to know too much about my costume-making hobby. The clunk and whirr of the ancient sewing machine would definitely spark more questions. It's important that I can control the amount of information she knows about what exactly I'm dressing up for.

"Goddess damn it all!" I yell as my fabric bunches up under the needle for the sixth time today. The ancient technological beast definitely has its quirks. While it *is* better than hand sewing, it's older than I am and ten times as cranky.

Emily whistles low from where she's sitting at her laptop, working on her coding school applications. Gerrit lounges on the couch in the back of the Lair, his thumbs tapping over the screen of his cell phone in what sounds like a nonstop one-note tune. His skinny jean-clad legs hang over the armrest where he's kicked off his immaculately white sneakers.

"You need a newer machine," Oscar says from his corner of the dungeon. He's wearing his magnification goggles as he adds tiny paint details to the sword hilt he's making for Emily's costume.

"Duh," I say under my breath. Like I don't know that. This machine isn't great with delicate, slippery fabric.

I cut away the knotted thread and start again. It tangles within seconds.

"Gaaahhh!" I tear the fabric out of the machine, bunch it up, and throw it on the ground. It lies there like a deflated animal carcass.

Emily grins at me devilishly from across the room.

"Are you just going to loiter here all day or are you maybe interested in helping for once?"

"Loitering." She refocuses on her laptop.

I mumble under my breath. "Good for nothing teammates."

Gerrit titters in the back of the room. It's an unexpectedly cheerful sound from a normally silent guy. I lower my eyes at him, but I can't tell if he's laughing at me or something on his phone.

I stand up to retrieve the newly crumpled fabric. Now I need to re-iron it or it will never sew nicely. Well done, self. Well done. I plug in the iron and do a few yoga stretches while I wait for it to heat up. Barbra is starting to rub off on me in the weirdest ways. When the iron is sizzling, I use the steam function to tidy up my fabric. I never realized how much work—also frustration, swearing, and literal pain—goes into making a luxurious gown. But I shall overcome.

I sit back at my sewing machine and realign my seams. With a press of the foot pedal, I'm off and running again.

Above the whirr of the machine, I hear Gerrit titter in his nook again. My eyes flicker over to the couch for just a moment, but I can't get distracted midstitch again. Focus, focus, focus. I need perfectly straight seams if I'm going to couture the hell out of the Queen of Thieves.

He snickers again. Out of the corner of my eye, I see Emily slowly turn to look at him before returning to her laptop. Seconds later, he does it again. What has gotten into that guy?

I pause my machine to watch as Emily slowly leaves her workstation, sliding out of it like she's made of Jell-O. She tiptoes behind where Gerrit lounges on the couch, his entire focus on the screen of his phone. Emily strains her neck forward to squint at his phone. She grins like a cat who's caught a juicy mouse. Then she snatches the phone out of his hands and holds it up over her head victoriously.

"Here ye! Hear ye!" she shouts as Gerrit scrambles up from the couch. "Let it be known to one and all that Gerrit has a girlfriend!"

"I'm going to murder you." Gerrit reaches for the phone, which honestly isn't such a stretch for him, considering he's a head taller than Emily.

She lets him have his phone back without fuss. "Who is she? Tell us all about her." She is beaming.

"That's none of your business, you little tyrant." He stuffs his phone into the pocket of his jeans and drops back onto the couch. He adjusts his NBA cap over his eyes.

"Aw, come on," Emily whines, sitting on the armrest of the sofa. "What's a little gossip among teammates?"

Gerrit removes his hat to squint up at her. "Knowing you? Disaster, probably."

"Oh psh!" Emily waves her hand, unfazed. "How'd you meet?" She gets comfortable, crossing her legs and resting her chin on her palm.

"Online."

"Ooooh, a dating app?"

"No, gaming forum."

"I love it." Emily slaps her hand on her knee. She turns to Oscar. "Did you know this scandalous information?"

Oscar, who had been watching the theatrics, shrugs and picks up a tube of superglue to continue working. "Maybe."

Emily feigns affront. "And you didn't tell me?" She looks toward where I sit at the sewing bench. I hold up my hands in surrender.

"I know nothing, Jon Snow."

Emily lowers her eyes momentarily, then turns back to Gerrit with a giant grin. "I need more deets. What's her name? Have you met IRL? Where's she from?"

"Why would I tell you anything?" He's back to hiding under the brim of his hat.

"Because we're friends and friends dish, so dish."

"Her name is Naomi. We have not met IRL. She lives in Chicago."

The joy on Emily's face is blindingly bright.

"CHICAGO?!"

"You've wounded my eardrums," Gerrit says with annoyance.

"Um, I don't know if you've realized this yet, but we just so happen to be going to Chicago. In three weeks. For the Fan Faire con. Ever heard of it?"

Gerrit doesn't respond.

"Gerrit," Emily says evenly. "Are you going to meet your ladylove at the con?"

He sinks deeper into the couch cushions.

"Yes!" Emily shouts. "The answer is: Yes, you are indeed going to meet your ladylove at the con in three weeks and you weren't even going to tell us about it."

"I can't imagine why not," Oscar mumbles from his workbench. I shoot him a conspiratorial smirk.

"Does your mom know about this mystery girlfriend?"

"Hell no, my mom doesn't know!" Gerrit says, removing his hat to show Emily his horrified face.

"Why the heck not?" Emily asks, like it's the most normal thing in the world to spill all of your most personal details to your parents.

"She'd never shut up about it." Gerrit run his hands over his face. "She'd constantly ask me questions, want to know about her, and act like it's a big deal."

"Like, in a bad way?"

"No, not bad, just . . ." He lets out an irritated sigh. "Like overly excited. She thinks I don't have a 'normal' enough life because I spend a lot of time online. She doesn't understand that I have friends. I have a life; it just doesn't look like the one she had when she was a teenager." He takes his phone back out of his pocket and checks the screen for a text from Naomi. "I swear sometimes I think I'm adopted."

My heart pounds erratically in my chest. Across the room, I catch Oscar's eye. He mouths a subtle "Sorry."

Honestly, I'm tired of people saying stuff like that flippantly.

"I'm pretty sure your mom doesn't deserve *that*," I say before I can stop myself. "You don't need to be such an ass." My face is burning.

Everyone turns to look at me in shock.

"Excuse me?" Gerrit sits up straight.

"You have a mom who loves you. Yet you treat her like she's nothing. Like you wish she wasn't around." My rage makes my voice sound hollow in my ears.

"You don't know anything about my family."

"You have one. That's all I need to know to see that you're being a jerk."

Gerrit gives me an incredulous look. "What the hell is your problem?"

Emily bites her lip, knowing full well what "my problem" is.

I clench my eyes closed to keep from seeing the worry on her face.

"Um, Jess," Oscar says from behind me. "Do you maybe want to go take a walk with me? Cool off a little?"

I shake my head. "No."

"I don't know what I did to make you so frickin' mad," Gerrit says. "But I have a feeling it's something to do with you. Not me."

As furious as I am, he has a point. I sit down and put my face in my hands for a few seconds. *Breathe*, Jess. *Breathe.*

Everyone is silent. I can feel them staring at me, waiting for an explanation for my outburst. I suppose, if I'm going to keep working with them through the convention season, I'm going to have to come clean with Gerrit. He's the only person in this room who doesn't know. I can't stay the secret foster kid forever.

I sit up and stare at the wall over Gerrit's head. It's too hard to say these words while looking directly at him.

"Before you make jokes about adoption in front of me, you should probably know that I'm in foster care." I wipe my now-clammy hands on my black jeans.

Gerrit sits back into the couch cushions, his anger dissolving instantly. "Oh, man, I'm sorry. You're right, that was too far. I'm an idiot."

I shake my head, willing my heart to stop beating so fast.

"You're not an idiot. It's a common thing people say. It's just not cool around me. Okay?"

He rubs his head, looking sheepish. "No. You're right. I need to check myself. I had no idea."

I pick at the loose fibers that have collected on my black sweater from the fabric I'm sewing. "That's because I don't usually talk about it. People have weird reactions sometimes. And don't any of you go pitying me or anything!" I point my blood-red manicured finger at each of them in turn. "I just figured, if we're spending so much time together, you should probably know that."

"You mean, because we're *friends*?" Emily singsongs and waggles her eyebrows at me. I toss a spool of thread at her. She ducks behind her laptop, then peeks above the screen to make sure I don't have more ammo.

"You being in foster care doesn't change anything in the Lair," she says. "You're still our creepy possibly-a-vampire teammate."

A laugh bubbles out of me, helping to ease the tension in my chest. "Gee, thanks."

"How long have you been in, you know, foster care?" Gerrit asks. While I usually get squirrely around questions like this, for some reason this feels okay. I trust them, I realize with surprise.

"Since I was seven."

"How come you're new at Detroit River High? Were you with another family before now?"

"More like I was with a lot of other families before Barbra," I say. "Some for a few months, some for a few weeks. Plus several stints in the city's group homes. I've been around."

"Now I feel like even more of a dick," Gerrit says. "I really am sorry, Jess."

It strikes me that this is the longest conversation I've ever had with Gerrit. I look around the room at my three teammates and I feel, I don't know. Warm inside. Comfortable. This isn't something I'm used to.

"Thanks," I say. Maybe this is what it's like to have People. Friends who listen and maybe actually care about what I say. A girl could get used to this.

After a bit of chitchat, I get back to work on my sewing. Emily types away at her applications while Oscar turns on his trusty Dremel tool. Across the room in Gerrit's corner, I hear the faint music of a new video game. From upstairs, the mouthwatering smell of Abuela's cooking infiltrates the Lair, making my stomach grumble.

My phone buzzes on the workbench. My foot slips off the pedal of the sewing machine as an Insta indicator lights up on the screen. I finish sewing the seam in my hands, lift the foot of the sewing machine, and cut the thread before I pick up my phone with trembling fingers. My heart is racing.

> **Reigna_NYC:** "I am so sorry, Jess. Please forgive me. I went back to my doctor and started taking my medicine again. I'm working on getting better. I promise."

I want to believe her. I want to trust that she is working hard to get better because I want, more than anything, to see my biomom. We may never have a supportive relationship like Emily has with her parents, or a complicated one like Oscar has with his dad. Or even a strained one like Gerrit has with his mom. But I want a relationship that's more than the occasional social media message.

We have to make it to New York.

CHAPTER 27

IN THE STRANGE ANOMALY OF MY EXISTENCE,
FEELINGS, WITH ME, *HAD NEVER BEEN* OF THE HEART,
AND MY PASSIONS *ALWAYS WERE* OF THE MIND.
EDGAR ALLAN POE, "BERENICE"

It's going to be a five-hour drive to get to the Fan Faire in Chicago. This time, there's no leaving early in the morning. I have to sneak out the night before.

Barbra chats cheerfully as we eat veggie curry with brown rice for dinner. I'm terribly distracted. Whenever I pick up my fork, the tips of my fingers ache from all the pinning I had to do to make my gown in time. And it's not just my fingers that paid the toll for the competition. My back hurts from hunching over the machine, but it's worth it. The costumes look fantastic. I decided to call it Space Couture.

"You okay?" Barbra asks.

I ignore my bruised fingertips and take a large bite of tofu. "Mhm," I mumble as I chew.

She sits back in her chair. "You sure? You've seemed a little, I don't know, off lately."

I swallow the lump of health food in my mouth. "It's just this schoolwork is really getting to me," I say by way of excuse.

She sets down her fork and taps the floral tablecloth with her fingers. "When I was in school, we never had this many group projects," she says with a worried tone in her voice. "Do you want me to talk to your teachers about it? See if there's any way we could lighten your load a little?"

"No!" I yell before I can remember my cool. I clear my throat. "I mean, I don't want my teachers to think I can't handle it. Everyone else has the same amount of work. I'll be fine."

She looks at me for a long moment. "Okay, but I hope you know you can come to me with anything." She looks down at her plate. "You've had to change schools so many times, it's really okay if you need a little help."

The understanding in her voice touches me. No foster has ever acknowledged the fact that I've had additional challenges in school because I'm never in the same class long enough to catch up to the rest of the kids, let alone excel.

"Thanks," I say. Guilt colors my heart in every shade of betrayal.

I know I can't tell Barbra about the competition. It's not just that I'm afraid she'll think I'm strange. By now I know she's just as weird as I am, in her own way. But if I tell her about the competitions, she'll learn I'm going to Chicago—and trying to go to the big con in New York. If she knows that, she'll be obligated to tell my social workers. If the social workers find out that I already left the state without authorization for Fanpalooza in Cleveland, things could go very badly. Barbra could lose her license to foster kids, and I'm starting to realize how great she really is at this, even if I am resisting her at every corner.

I get up from the table to start cleaning the kitchen.

Barbra rarely goes to bed later than 9:00. I sit in my room, waiting. At 9:30 I creep down the hall to listen outside her bedroom. Her soft snores reach my ears from behind the door. It's time to text Emily.

Okay, I'm ready.

My fingers shake as I tap my phone's screen.

As quietly as I can, I gather up my costume and makeup supplies. Just as I'm about to close my bedroom door, I decide to take an extra precaution. I mess up the bed, stuffing pillows under the covers so it looks like I'm sleeping under them. Usually I don't crawl out of my room until well after Barbra leaves for yoga class in the morning, but I don't want to raise any suspicions just in case she peeks in.

In the dark I make my way out the front door, then run down the block to the end of the street. We didn't want the van's headlights to wake Barbra up, so I asked the team to meet me a few houses down.

When I open the van's sliding back door, I dump all my bags on the floor but take care to hang my gown up on a hook. I put way too much blood, sweat, and tears into this costume to rumple it before we even make it to Chicago Fan Faire.

Gerrit's face is alight in the glow of his Nintendo Switch.

"'Sup," he says without looking away from the tiny screen in his hands. His thumbs are pounding on the controller at a speed my eyes can hardly follow in the darkness.

"Hello, friends, how's everyone doing tonight?" I ask as I settle in. My nerves are making me sound like Mr. Rogers. It's weird.

Emily squints at me through the rearview mirror. "Sucky," she says.

"Oh, uh, why?" I ask.

"Finished my coding school applications."

"Shouldn't that be a good thing?"

"She's just nervous," Oscar says, without looking at me.

Emily grunts. "I hate waiting."

I bite my glossy lip, unsure what the best response should be. Cheer up, I'm sure you'll do great? Worst case scenario, you try again next year? Both are liable to get me punched in the face.

"Close the door," Emily growls. "We have an intergalactic geek competition to dominate."

The five-hour drive is quieter than usual. There aren't many cars on the road, thankfully. The long, dark highways are mildly unnerving at this hour. When we pass the Michigan border, I try to swallow the trepidation that rises in me. I crossed the border for the last competition and we made it back just fine. It's only for twenty-four hours or so. I'll text Barbra this evening to tell her I'm sleeping over at Emily's house. Her parents are out of town, so there's no one to blow our cover if Barbra calls there. We have a plan.

Emily takes over the music selection since she's driving. We listen to everything from K-pop to death metal, but no one complains. She quietly sips from a can of energy drink to keep her wits about her. No one sleeps.

When we reach the outskirts of Chicago, the bright city lights reflect off the low hanging clouds in the distance. It's nearly 3:30 a.m., since we had to make several bathroom breaks along the way thanks to the ridiculous amount of caffeinated beverages we all drank throughout the ride. We pull into the last rest stop before Chicago so we can sleep for a few hours in the parking lot.

Oscar locks the car doors as we all roll our seats back to try to get as comfortable as possible. Emily throws a sweatshirt over her head to block the orange streetlights. I gaze out the window while everyone settles in to sleep. We're not the only vehicle parked here, not by a long shot. There are semitrucks, tiny eco-friendly cars, and more than a few minivans like ours. One is crammed full of boxes and garbage bags filled with clothes smashed up against the windows. I truly hope they're moving, not living in there.

A memory floats down over me like a quiet dream. My mother and I, sleeping in our car at rest stops much like this one. We'd been evicted from yet another apartment. This didn't bother me as a small child. It was all I'd ever known. Each time we had to leave a place, I saw it as one big adventure after another. I never knew where we'd end up next. Atlantic City? Yonkers? Indianapolis?

Now that I'm older, I look at these cars and wonder where they're going, who they're leaving, and why. Why did my mother move us from place to place so often? Was it her illness? I was too young to understand the signs back then. Now that I'm older I'll be able to see them more clearly. I can help keep my mom on the right track. We may be broken, but we're still family. We'll be reunited soon.

My hand reaches for the brooch in my pocket. I've taken to carrying it around like a good luck charm. It reminds me why I'm doing all of this.

Gerrit mumbles something in his sleep. In the reflection of the van window I see his hands twitch like he's playing a video game, even in his dreams. I roll to the side and catch a glimpse of Oscar in the rearview mirror. He looks so peaceful with his eyes closed and his chin tucked into his chest. A strange feeling rolls over me like I've missed out on something that could have been truly great.

Sleep is clearly not going to happen for me, but I can't sit here and stare at Oscar like a creep. I grab the car keys as quietly as I can, then slip outside, locking the car behind me.

The night is quiet except for the occasional sound of tires on the highway. I walk into the blaring brightness of the rest stop building. There's a gentle hum of electricity in here. The lights flicker, directing my attention to a decrepit vending machine. Like a beacon, it calls to me. A midnight snack might be just the thing to calm my overactive mind.

Luckily, I have a few crumpled dollar bills in my pocket. I feed one into the machine's greedy mouth. This night's dis-ease calls for chocolate. A Twix bar sings my name. The buttons beep as I make my choice, then I'm greeted with the whirring sound of the metal spirals twisting. Just before the Twix falls into the bin below, it freezes, stuck.

"You damnable machine!" I yell at the inanimate object. I pound my fists into the Plexiglas to no avail. My legs give in to hopelessness as I slide to the filthy floor, looking longingly at my chocolate where it dangles. So close, yet so far.

"My candy," I whisper sadly to myself.

The rest stop door opens.

"Well, isn't this a pathetic sight." Emily's voice greets me.

I turn around and squint up at her. Her head is haloed by the bug-filled overhead lights.

She pulls out her wallet, then graciously puts another dollar into the vending machine. A second later, not one, but two Twixes fall into the bin below.

"You might be an angel," I say to her as I fish out our prizes. I hand one to her.

"Let's sit on a less disgusting surface." She indicates toward a bench.

Caressing my candy bar, I follow her.

"Okay, spill the beans," she says once we've started munching on our chocolate.

"The demon machine ate my dollar."

"Not that," she says. "What happened between you and Oscar? Did you two kiss or something?"

"What? No." I focus all my attention on my food, ignoring the prying eyes. Hell, she's like one of those octu'urak creatures in *Prince of Moons* that can use their eyeballs to delve into the secrets of your mind.

She lowers her eyes at me. "For the last five hours, neither of you has spoken a word to each other. Oscar has made a concerted effort to not even glance at you through the broken makeup mirror. Unlike every other road trip we've taken in that spaceship of his, I might add."

"It's nothing."

"Well, if you two aren't embarrassed about making out, then it's gotta be a fight."

"We're not in a fight."

She raises an eyebrow at me.

"And we didn't make out either," I say defensively. "Why are you so nosy?"

"Because it's part of my nature." She bites into her Twix. "Besides, I'm finally coming to love this weird ragtag geek team we have going on here. I don't want to see it ruined by some lovers' spat."

"We're not lovers."

"And I'm not Emily Foo. I'm the Prince of Moons, himself."

I roll my eyes.

"Listen," she says with an earnestness that takes me off guard. "I'm not trying to give you a hard time. I just want to know if there's anything I can do."

"Thanks, but we're fine."

She nods. "Maybe you are, but I've known Oscar a long time.

And he is most definitely not fine. He's lost that sweet puppy dog look of his."

My voice betrays me. "I'm sorry if that's my fault."

"I'm not saying it's anybody's fault." She crumples up her candy wrapper and tosses it into the bin across the way. It bounces off the rim, so she gets up to throw it away properly. "I'm just saying I care."

I don't know how to respond, so I focus on chewing very slowly.

She waits for me to say something. I don't.

"You know he's in love with you, right?"

A crumb finds its way into my windpipe and I cough.

Emily's eyes bore into my soul. "I think you love him too, but you're too scared to admit it."

"You don't know anything about it."

"Believe me, Jess, I know a lot about love. Have you seen the number of women who have fallen at my adorable little feet? I'm not new to this."

Despite myself, I smile a little.

"Look, I don't need to know the specifics. Just be gentle with him. Okay?"

"I'll do my best."

"That's all any of us can do." She watches me closely while I nom my candy.

I groan. "What? I can see thoughts swirling around your diabolical mind."

"There's something up with you too. You've lost something." She waves her hand in front of my face. "Your oomph."

"My what?"

"Your oomph. Your ish. That thing that makes you you." She pats my head gently. "You've deflated."

I slouch a little farther on the bench. "Maybe you're right."

My hard-earned confidence seems to be elusive these days. But, really, who am I to walk around acting like I'm amazing when I'm the poster child for broken kids? I'm breaking hearts and spouting lies left and right. I'm kinda trash.

"My confidence has crumbled a bit lately," I admit.

"I loved your confidence."

"So did I," I admit. "It just doesn't feel like I deserve to feel good about myself anymore."

"Psh!" she scoffs. "Of course you do. You're amazing, flaws and all. You deserve everything." She boops my nose. "You deserve the moon and the stars and anything else your little black heart desires, because you're worth it. The places we come from, the mistakes we make—none of that defines who we are inside." She punches my shoulder hard.

"Ow." I stare at her accusingly.

"You better be listening to me, Jess, because I'm giving you a real-life lesson here."

"I'm listening!"

"All that stuff is filigree and lace. It dresses you up, but it's not who you are. You're someone special. You deserve to love yourself. You got that?"

"Okay, okay."

"Want me to write it down for you so you remember it? Maybe tattoo it across your forehead?"

"I really don't think that will be necessary."

"Good." She stands up and yawns. "Bedtime?" she asks.

"Bedtime." I hold out the car keys. Emily leads the way.

It's a long night, but I do eventually fall asleep. Around 8:00 a.m., we all crawl back out of the van to stretch.

"Oh god," Gerrit grumbles. "My legs. I can't feel my legs." He wobbles to the grass to lie flat on the ground.

"You know," Emily says, her voice scratchy from sleep. "That's where drivers let their dogs pee."

He doesn't make any indication that he's heard her.

Emily and I take our costumes into the restroom to get ready for the competition. It takes considerable effort to ignore the curious glances of the road-weary travelers who walk in, not expecting to encounter intergalactic royalty applying fake eyelashes in the filthy mirror.

When I'm done, I step back to admire myself. I never would've thought I'd be happy to dress up as a *Prince of Moons* character, but when I see my reflection, I'm ridiculously proud. The long, black gown is split open at the front to reveal black faux-leather leggings and high kick-ass boots. The bodice is midnight black with a dramatic, scooped neckline and sleeves detailed with tiny embroidered stars. My mother's brooch is pinned delicately to the belt around my waist. It's a personal touch that's not exactly canon, yet somehow brings the whole creation together. I look like the Queen of Thieves, ready to steal the very night from your sky. Not to mention, take over the entire intergalactic kingdom. I'm good on that too.

Emily lets out a low whistle. "I would not mess with you if I were truly that dastardly Prince of Moons."

She holds her armored jacket out for my approval. The added filigree and shoulder pads make her look very regal indeed. She pats the electric sword at her hip fondly.

I smile. "Good. Because, seeing as we're rivals for the throne, I'd kick your cute little butt out of orbit."

She snickers. "Ugh, listen to us. Two little geeks on their way to the nerd ball."

When we meet Gerrit back at the van, he's wearing a suit of armor that appears to be made out of some sort of otherworldly element that glows with a faint fluorescent hue. His face looks a little pale, but not from the costume.

"Are you going to barf?" Emily asks him.

"No," he says, his voice hoarse.

I pat his shoulder pads. "Nervous to meet Naomi?"

He nods and turns to climb into the van.

"Oh no you don't." Emily grabs the neck of his armor and hauls him out again.

"What are you nervous about?" I ask.

He shrugs, his eyes darting toward Emily.

"Seriously." I point my thumb at Emily. "Ignore her. It's her job to torture you."

"That is true," she agrees.

"What, specifically, makes you worried?" I ask again, turning him so he can't see Emily's evil glee.

"We've never seen each other in person before."

I consider this with an air of gravitas. "You're a good-lookin' guy in a kick-ass costume. What's not to like?"

"What if she thinks I'm boring in person?"

"How can a dude in a fluorescent suit of armor be boring?"

"What if I choke up and can't think of anything to talk about? What if she decides I'm too weird?"

I try to hide my smile behind a mask of composure. Poor Gerrit, struck down by puppy love. Emily starts to say something, but I shoot her an eyeful of don't-you-dare.

"First"—I hold up my pointer finger—"you met in a gamer

chat. If all else fails, talk about video games. And second"—I hold up another finger—"she's attending a con. I'd bet my best liquid eyeliner that she's going to be weird too. It's a match made in heaven."

Gerrit swallows hard and nods, but his face doesn't look any less gray. He makes a slow move to climb back into the van and Emily doesn't stop him.

Oscar joins us, dressed as his tried-and-true Sir Valorian character. Only this time, he has an ornate suit of armor that looks so realistic I keep expecting it to clank when he walks. I'm more than a little saddened to notice that Oscar hardly even looks at me. I remind myself over and over again on the drive to the convention center that this is what I wanted. I did this. And it *is* a good thing.

But if I need to remind myself of this fact, does that mean it's not truly a fact?

CHAPTER 28

MISERY IS MANIFOLD.
EDGAR ALLAN POE, "BERENICE"

This convention center is the biggest one yet. Thousands of people stream in through security at the front entrance. An entire family dressed as *Bob's Burgers* characters chug from their water bottles once they find out they can't bring liquids inside. A security guard analyzes a broom from someone dressed as Kiki from *Kiki's Delivery Service*. I'll probably never get tired of seeing fantasy characters doing normal human things like eating french fries from a concession stand or waiting in long lines for free swag.

Gerrit cracks up when he spots a cosplayer dressed as Geralt of Rivia. Her wheelchair has a name tag that says "Roach." Geralt and Gerrit fist-bump over the joke.

"I don't get it," I say.

Emily pats my arm softly. "That's okay, Jess. It's a Witcher gamer thing."

Geralt hands us a flyer that says her name is Jay Justice and she promotes visibility for POC, queer, and disabled cosplayers. I'm surprised by how excited I am about this. I'll have to connect her to Varys and Vacation Vibes Link once I get back to Detroit.

We pass posters for the different panels attendees can listen to throughout the day:

10:00: Steampunk, What Is It? (Theater A)

10:00: How to Run D&D (Theater C)

10:30: Fantasy Writing and World Building (Theater B)

10:30: Meet the Cast of *Jurassic Park* (Yard D)

11:00: Nerdy People of Color (Theater A)

11:00: How to Make Puppets Like the Masters (Theater C)

The list goes on and on. At the very bottom is the whole reason we're here.

6:00: Cosplay Champion Qualifiers (Mainstage)

My throat feels thick with fear. I swallow it down. With the feigned courage of a born ruler, I lift my chin, throw back my shoulders, and lead my teammates onto the convention show floor to exhibit our creations. Emily was the natural choice for the charismatic, elegant Prince of Moons. She has fully inhabited her character. She looks down her nose at everyone we pass, but I spot her give a sly wink to a cute Super Girl.

Gerrit's costume, as usual, gets a lot of attention. It took me an hour and a half to finish his makeup in the van. His skin is rugged, complete with bruises and gaping wounds along his square, false jawline. The intense makeup is probably a good thing. It covers up his sickly nervous-over-a-girl coloring.

"Gerrit, stop sweating!" Emily fans his face. "You're going to ruin your costume."

"Can't," he chokes out.

"You'll be fine," she says with a surprising amount of compassion. "You're dressed as the best-looking rogue at the con. Show a little poise."

Oscar puts Emily on the task of handing out business cards to any interested parties, since she's so good at talking to strangers. She takes to the assignment with verve, but I can't help noticing how our Sir Valorian seems a little deflated. Oscar isn't bossing us around like normal. He's hanging out along the sidelines, staring idly at the wares sold at the booths. His hands run over original art posters and plastic-encased comic books for sale. He doesn't look at me all morning, not even once. When I spot him staring at tiny figurines of *Prince of Moons* characters, an ache fills my chest. He grimaces at the miniature Sir Valorian on a white mechanical steed, then flicks him over before walking away.

Gerrit keeps checking his phone. His eyes dart around the convention floor like a small animal that's scented a predator.

"Dude," Emily says. "Chill."

"She's here," he whispers.

"Where?" Emily perks up, her head whipping around in every direction, looking for his mysterious internet girlfriend.

"Not *here* here. She texted that she's in the game wing."

Emily grabs Gerrit and Oscar by the arm to abruptly steer us in that direction. "How will we know when we've found her? Did she tell you what she looks like?"

Oscar removes Emily's death grip from his elbow. "This isn't 1822, Emily, they've video chatted before."

Gerrit doesn't respond. He's turning his phone over and over in his hand, like it's a fidget toy. I take it away, gently.

"Just breathe," I say.

We wander around the game wing, where people are testing unreleased video games, buying fan art of their favorite characters, and talking to sales reps. I have no idea who to look for, but it becomes obvious we've found her when Gerrit halts midstep. Oscar, Emily, and I visually scour the area looking for any would-be Naomi in our midst. Then I see a dark-skinned girl in a black bodysuit with a cape. She has pale contacts in her eyes and is wearing a long white wig. Her fingers are working a video game controller like a pro, her eyes hyperfocused on the screen, where a tiny dragon hops over multicolored jewels in a cave of dripping lava.

"Is that Storm from X-Men?" I ask.

Emily sighs proudly. "No. That's Naomi."

Gerrit gulps.

"Go talk to her." Oscar nudges him with his elbow.

"I don't think I can." Gerrit does an about face to run in the other direction. It takes all three of us to hold him back.

"Enough with the dramatics," Emily says, swiping her mussed hair away from her face. "That's supposed to be my role. You're the cool collected one, remember?"

Oscar throws an arm around Gerrit's shoulders. "Excuse us for a moment, would you?" he says to me and Emily.

He leads Gerrit a few yards away, where they turn their backs to us. Emily strains on her tiptoes to listen in, but I hold her back. Gerrit bends his head down low to listen as Oscar whispers, his eyebrows pulled together in a look of intensity. They both nod. Oscar claps Gerrit on the shoulder, then juts his chin in Naomi's direction. She's completed the level she was playing and is now digging into a tiny black fanny pack. She pulls out a phone and checks the screen.

Oscar returns to us, alone.

"What did you say to him?" I ask Oscar.

"I told him he'll forever regret it if he doesn't at least try to talk to the girl of his dreams." His eyes flicker toward me momentarily.

"Psh," Emily scoffs. "You lie."

Oscar kicks the toe of his boot into the flooring a few times. "And I promised to tell him where the most powerful sword is hidden in this game we've been playing online."

I can't help laughing.

He shrugs. "I found it on accident once and vowed to never tell a soul. I thought, if there's ever a reason to break a vow, it should be in the name of love."

Emily rolls her eyes.

We watch as Gerrit approaches Naomi. Her face lights up with joy at the sight of him. She throws her arms around his shoulders in a hug, which Gerrit awkwardly returns with stiff limbs. We can't hear what Naomi says, but she's clearly asking him a question. He nods. She asks him another. There's panic in his eyes as he looks toward us.

"Talk. About. Video. Games," Emily mouths.

Oscar gives him two thumbs-up.

Finally, Gerrit's talking and Naomi's responding excitedly.

"Oh, they're laughing!" Emily grabs my hand. She sniffs.

"Okay, okay," I say. "Let's give them some privacy."

"Are you sure we should leave him alone?" Emily asks, glancing back at them. "What if he needs help?"

"He's a big boy," Oscar says. "He can take care of himself. We'll all meet up later." Without even looking at me, Oscar turns around and wanders into the crowd.

Since the competition isn't until this evening, Emily and I kill time by sitting in on some of the panels. We watch a costume makeup tutorial given by the amazing Lucky Grim, listen to a presentation called Why Diversity Matters in Cosplay, and take notes while the Calico Queen discusses her couture Elphaba costume and gives tips for how to be a thrifty sewist.

"Do you think Gerrit's okay with Naomi?" Emily whispers to me every twenty minutes. She strains her neck, trying to find Gerrit in the crowd.

I stop responding after the fourth time.

We mingle, admiring draping prowess, expert tailoring, and all the creative spins on characters that are represented at this con. I'm thrilled by all the attention my Queen of Thieves gown gets. Cosplay enthusiasts run their fingers over my painstaking embroidery and ask to see the seams I've sewn.

I freeze in the middle of the crowded exhibit hall when there's a roar of cheers from a nearby group. Emily and I push our way through gamer dudes to find a giant video wall displaying two dancing animated characters wielding weapons of ridiculous proportions. When my eyes drift to the gaming tournament setup below the screen, I have to do a double take. Sitting in a throne-like gaming chair, chill as ever, is Gerrit, his face wounds glistening with fake gore under the spotlight. In the seat next to him is Naomi.

Gerrit and Naomi battle onscreen, their bodies moving with intensity as they pound on their game controllers. The crowd screams as their characters high kick, throw lightning, and dodge punches. Finally, the female character lands a throat chop that sends the muscle bro flying into a brick wall. The screen flashes "KO!"

Gerrit laughs through his defeat, then takes a sip from a refillable mug of soda that's branded with a video game company name. An announcer hands Naomi a winner's hoodie emblazoned with the con's logo and poses for a photo with her. Before the competitors walk offstage, the announcer shakes Gerrit's hand. All around them gamers are going bananas about their sweet skills.

Emily pushes people out of the way and stomps right up to Gerrit.

He has to freeze midstep to avoid colliding into her.

"What?" he asks as he hands his mug of soda to an adoring fanboy who freaks out about it. "You know I like gaming."

"Excuse me," Emily says. "You never said you were a video game wizard or anything."

He shrugs.

Naomi walks up behind him and slings her hoodie prize over his armored shoulder.

"You must be Naomi," I say. "You're pretty badass. We like badass."

"Thanks." She smiles genuinely and looks at Gerrit.

"Oh," he says. "Sorry. Naomi, this is Emily and Jess."

"Your teammates?" She smiles genuinely. "That explains the costumes. You look awesome."

Emily's eyes actually glisten. "He told you about us?"

"Of course," Naomi says. "He said Jess is the ridiculously talented designer and you are the star of the group."

Emily's lower lip trembles, and she throws her arms around Gerrit's middle in a bear hug.

"Oof!" He nearly stumbles backward. "I also told her you're a weirdo, you weirdo. Get off of me."

"You actually love us!" Emily squeezes his ribs harder, then hugs Naomi. "I'm so glad he found you."

Emily grabs their arms and proceeds to drag the couple toward another tournament sign-up line. "Let's make some prize money."

For the next two hours, I watch as Emily coerces Naomi and Gerrit into defeating reigning champs on video games ranging from team first-person shooters to partner puzzle RPGs. I have no idea where Oscar is, and I have to admit it's a little weird to be exploring the con without him.

When it comes time to register for the competition, we leave Naomi and meet Oscar near the stage area to get our assigned number. As usual, backstage is a dark mass of excitement mixed with the panic of artists who are so nervous they're in danger of wetting themselves. Someone is sobbing because the glue on her EVA foam mega sword failed. Her weapon lies on the ground in pieces, where she weeps like she's mourning the death of a dear friend.

Oscar finds a dark corner and sits on the ground with his eyes closed. It's clear that he's fighting his anxiety, but this time I think it's best that I leave him alone. There's a terrifying rendition of Bioshock's Big Sister looming over him. I consider asking her to move, but think better of it. Oscar can stick up for himself.

All around us people are affixing tiny hats with long pins, centering tails on backsides, creating clouds of hairspray to cement elaborate hairstyles, practicing blocking with outlandish foam weaponry, and panicking. Lots of panicking. A trio of horror-video game characters walk by practicing their twitching and jerking leg movements. They're all wearing hospital gowns. It takes me a few moments to realize they're pretending to be monsters from an asylum. I fight back the urge to trip one of them.

Once we hear the MC greet the audience from the stage, an eerie hush falls over us all. Competitors watch silently as, one by one, our numbers are called. Oscar, Emily, Gerrit, and I march forward, on deck.

Oscar looks around to all of us, feeling the need to impart an uplifting speech as our captain.

"There's a saying in *Prince of Moons*," he whispers. "'The road to intergalactic domination is blocked with asteroids. But all you need to do is . . .'"

"'Blow those feckers up,'" I finish.

Gerrit gives me a startled look.

I shrug. "I read the book."

"When, exactly?" Emily asks.

"Recently."

She gives me a knowing look. "I see."

"Hey, focus." Oscar brings our attention back. "We already know we're good. We need to be *great* to get to New York. We can do this. Let's get onstage with the energy of a supernova blast and take the prize."

"Yeah!" Emily cheers a little too enthusiastically.

"Shhh!" I say.

Gerrit knocks her on the shoulder.

"Sorry," she whispers. "I'll contain my supernova until our music starts."

We wait.

The second Gerrit's custom *Prince of Moons* soundtrack begins with laser blast sound effects, Emily runs onstage. She searches the crowd with one hand above her eyes like a sea captain searching the horizon. Gerrit lumbers over, his evil villain persona in full swing. The two mime making a deal. Kill me, the Queen of Thieves, and the outer colonies can keep their measly solar system. The Prince of Moons will let them live in peace when he wins his rightful throne back from the Mad King.

I run onstage now, my whip flashing before me. Gerrit and I engage in a battle, made all the more dramatic by my whirling skirt and well-practiced high-kicks. The Prince of Moons must not win domination over the universe. I—the evil, heart-thieving witch from the far reaches of the Adalasian Galaxy—must stop the monarchy and bring back self-rule. I'm an unlikely hero wrapped in the fancy dress of an intergalactic rogue who collects her enemies' organs in decorative jars.

But, oh no! I lose my whip. Gerrit kicks it aside. I tumble to the ground. He grabs my hands, holding them behind my back as he raises his mace above me. I brace myself for the final blow.

That's when Oscar appears. I turn to look at him like we've practiced a million times. Only now, under the stage lights, he's glorious. It doesn't matter that he's shorter, darker, and rounder than the book depicts his character. Oscar's Sir Valorian has an aura of confidence, power, and strength the likes of which I've never seen a cosplayer possess. When he looks straight into my eyes, I see something else: passion. He burns with it as he runs toward where Gerrit has a dangerous mace poised above my head. Sir Valorian unsheathes his sword in a flash, knocking Gerrit's mace aside. He stabs the self-proclaimed King of the Outer Colonies, and Gerrit lets out a well-practiced gurgle before falling to the ground.

Oscar pretends to untie my hands. His arms are stronger than they look as he lifts me to my feet. Next, Emily runs onstage again, ready to fight us both in a duel to the death. Oscar doesn't turn to face her like we practiced. He stares into my eyes for one long moment, breaking our rehearsed blocking. He puts one arm around my waist. I know what's coming next before he moves. I lean in completely, caught up in the fire in his eyes and the pounding of my own heart. Oscar dips me backward, one of my legs lifting into the air like a dancer's.

He kisses me.

The stage, the audience, the lights ... everything melts away. It is Sir Valorian kissing the Queen of Thieves. It is Oscar kissing me. And I know in this moment that it's not the Queen of Thieves who's stolen a heart this time. It's Oscar who has stolen mine.

CHAPTER 29

"We're going to the World Cosplay Expo! We're going to the World Cosplay Expo!" Emily can't stop yelling. Even two hours into our drive home, she keeps remembering our third-place win, thus beginning another round of joyful squealing. She's too hyped up to drive, so Oscar is behind the wheel.

We've all had ridiculously silly grins plastered across our faces ever since we left Chicago.

"Um, we know," Gerrit says from the middle of a Nintendo Switch battle in the back seat. He's grinning too, even if he is preoccupied.

Our third-place trophy sits in the front between Oscar and Emily, shining in all its glory. Every time we hit a red light, Oscar's hand reaches out to touch it as if he's still not convinced it's real.

I posted our winners' selfie on Insta only two hours ago. My phone is blowing up with congratulations. This time I made sure to tag everyone in the pic, even Naomi, who joined us in the celebrations. We're all equal winners in this intergalactic battlefield. In the photo, we all have our arms around each other, our faces squished in close so we fit into the screen. Naomi is planting a kiss on Gerrit's bruised cheek as he smiles bashfully. Emily is pointing wildly at the trophy. My face is very flushed, but Oscar's surprisingly isn't. His eyes aren't even on the camera. They're on me.

I didn't really have time to respond to the impromptu kiss onstage. The audience went wild for it. When Oscar let me go, I was so dazed I missed the first two steps of our practiced fight with Emily, but no one seemed to notice. Emily grinned mischievously at me through it all, looking all the more like the conniving Prince of Moons.

My phone buzzes in my pocket. I pull it out to see Barbra has finally answered my text about sleeping over at Emily's.

"Okay. Be safe. Have fun." I try not to feel like a total liar, since I *am* going to Emily's once we get back to Detroit. That's just not the only place I've been all day. This is for the best, I remind myself.

We drive along I-90, flirting with the Indiana-Michigan border, as a light rain starts to fall.

Suddenly, the van swerves. A rumbling noise fills me with dread.

Oscar gets the car back under control, but it's obvious we need to pull over on the side of the highway. My heart hammers in my chest.

"Please no please no please no," I repeat. Goddess above, I will do anything, *anything*, for this not to be happening right now.

Oscar steps out into the rain to take a look at our front right wheel. Through the van windows, I watch as his frown deepens.

A groan escapes me before he even walks back around to the driver's seat.

He closes the car door after he climbs back in out of the rain. His wet hair is plastered to the side of his face.

"It's a flat," he confirms.

"Got a spare?" Gerrit asks. "I can fix a flat, no problem. My dad taught me."

Oscar fidgets a bit. "Er, no."

"What?" Emily yells. "You drove us through three states without thinking to pack a spare tire?"

"I forgot about that possibility," Oscar defends himself. "It's not as though I've taken many long-distance trips."

"It's common car sense, Oscar." Emily looks furious.

"It's not his fault," I say. "He didn't know this would happen."

Oscar's face flushes, but he doesn't look back at me.

Emily crosses her arms. "Great."

"We might have another problem," Oscar says tentatively. "We're still in Indiana." He looks into the rearview mirror to catch my eye. The full weight of this makes my breath catches in my throat.

"Oh no," I whisper.

"So, what does this all mean, exactly?" Gerrit asks.

"It means I'm in serious trouble if we don't get this van back to Michigan before Barbra finds out." I slide down my seat and cover my face with my hands.

"Let's just think for a minute." Emily holds up her hand for silence. "There must be someone we can call who can help. My parents are out of town, so they're no use."

"My abuela can't come get us. We're in her van," Oscar points out.

"Obviously, I can't call Barbra," I say. "She doesn't know I left the city, let alone the state."

We all turn around to look at Gerrit.

He feels our eyes on him. He pauses his game to look up.

"What?"

Emily gives him her best puppy-eyed stare. "Help us, Obi-Wan Kenobi, you're our only hope."

He groans. "Noooo. I'm not calling my mom."

"Why not?" Oscar asks. "I thought your mom wanted you to go on this trip? She pressured you to join the team in the first place."

"Because." He squirms in his seat while he thinks of how to explain the problem. "She's going to get all motherly and stuff. This is the exact sort of situation she wanted me to get into. She'll call it a 'real-world learning experience.'"

"And that's bad how?" I ask.

"You don't know my mother."

Emily crawls into the back seat with about as much grace as a baby elephant. She thrusts her phone out toward Gerrit. She gives him a long, meaning-filled look.

Finally, Gerrit sighs. "Fine."

He ignores Emily as he takes his own phone out of his pocket. "I'm seriously going to regret this."

We listen as the phone rings. Gerrit closes his eyes like he's in terrible pain while he holds it up to his ear. It's past ten o'clock; hopefully she's still awake.

Gerrit's phone stops ringing. "Hello?" he asks.

"Gerrit, baby!" a cheerful voice sounds on the other end. "How did it go? Did you have fun? Did you all win anything?"

"Yeah," he says, unenthusiastic. "Third place."

His mom positively screams on the other end. Gerrit pulls the phone away from his ear and gives Emily a murderous look.

"I knew you'd do great, honey. I'm so proud of you for doing this!"

"Well, you kinda forced me," he grumbles.

She ignores his retort. "And you've made friends!"

"I already had friends, Mom."

"Oh, I know your online buddies are real people too, but these are kids you get to hang out with outside of video games. I'm so happy for you!"

"Thanks," he deadpans.

"You kids get to go to New York City now! Oh my goodness, you're going to love it. Did I ever tell you I spent a few weeks there in college?"

"Mom," Gerrit tries to interject.

"I know several great spots where you can eat for cheap. As long as they still exist, of course. It *has* been nearly twenty years. Oh my god, it's been twenty years! You're making your mom feel old, Gerrit."

"Mom, I need to tell you something." His tone is clipped. He's starting to lose his cool.

"We'll definitely have to book you kids a spot on the Statue of Liberty ferry. And of course you can't miss Central Park. I wonder if they still do those carriage rides?"

"Mom!" Gerrit yells into the phone.

"Gerrit, there's no need to shout. I can hear you."

"Mom, I have to tell you something."

Her tone does a 180 turnabout. "What is it? Did something happen? Is everyone alright?" Her voice sounds mildly panicked. The complete opposite of the cheerful chatterbox that had existed mere seconds before.

"Mom, we're fine. It's just the car. Someone forgot to bring a spare."

Oscar visibly shrinks in the front seat.

"So," Gerrit says. "We're not sure what to do."

The relief in her voice is palpable. "Well, why didn't you say so, honey?"

Gerrit grits his teeth. "That's what I'm doing right now."

"I'll just call your Uncle John. He has a truck with a hitch and a two-wheel dolly trailer. We can tow your van home. I'll just pop on over to his house and borrow it."

"Couldn't he just come and get us instead?"

"Excuse you, Gerrit. We don't need to inconvenience him. I'm your mother. It's my job to help you out of sticky situations. Besides, I'd love to meet your friends."

Gerrit closes his eyes in irritation.

"I'll see you kids in a little bit!" Her cheerful tone is back.

"Thank you, Mom."

"You're welcome, Booboo."

Gerrit's neck disappears as he slumps down into his seat. He hangs up his phone.

"Well, that went well," Emily says lightheartedly. "Don't you think so, Booboo?"

Gerrit pulls his hat over his eyes. "I hate you all."

We wait in relative silence. I must have fallen asleep, because I wake up to a horn honking behind our van. When I look at the clock, it's a little after 1:00 a.m. A petite, dark-skinned woman jumps out of the front of the truck, waving.

Luckily it's stopped raining, so we all clamber out of the car to meet her. The second she sees Gerrit dragging his feet, she gives him a giant kiss on the cheek, leaving an imprint of her berry-colored lipstick behind.

"Hello, Gerrit's friends!" She looks around at us, one hand on her hip. Her clothes are very fashionable. No wonder Gerrit is always meticulously dressed even though he's never struck me as particularly interested in clothes. Or anything besides video games and Naomi, for that matter.

Cici makes the rounds, introducing herself to each of us in turn. She puts her hands on her heart when she greets me. "Jess, dear. I saw photos of the costumes you've sewed. And the makeup! You are a truly talented young lady."

"Oh, um," I stammer, not expecting praise in the midst of our midnight disaster. "Thank you, ma'am." She rubs my shoulder, perhaps sensing that I'm not exactly a hugger. Especially not with people I hardly know.

"Okay," Cici says as she turns her attention to the van. "Gerrit, would you get the tools out of Uncle John's truck? We have a bit of work to do."

Twenty minutes later, Abuela's van is attached to a trailer behind the truck. Cici, despite her tailored clothes and small frame, is as much a pro with cars as any greasy coverall-wearing mechanic.

Cici inspects her work with a smile. She takes a few pictures with her phone. "So I can send them to your dad. I like to keep him up to date with everything that's going on at home. It's hard on him, being deployed for so long."

"You're going to tell him?" Gerrit asks.

"Of course! He's your daddy. He'll be happy to know you crawled out of your video game cave long enough to get into a little trouble." She winks at him.

In spite of himself, Gerrit actually smiles a little.

He climbs into the front passenger seat while Oscar gets into the back. Emily practically pushes me in next to him, either not willing to sit sandwiched in between us, or purposely making sure my thighs and shoulders are squished up against Oscar's. I try to protest. By rights, as someone half my size, she should sit in the middle. But she uses all her small person muscles to push me into the truck. How do tiny people always have an inordinate amount of strength?

I feel mildly feverish during the drive back to Detroit. For two and a half hours I try to channel my psychic powers to shrink my body in on itself so there's less of me touching Oscar. Considering he isn't a skinny human either, it's impossible. Thankfully, he doesn't seem to mind being squished. He stares out the window for the entire trip, avoiding my gaze.

"Gerrit was such a smart kid growing up." Cici chats happily from the driver's seat. She's so small she has to adjust the seat up as high as it can go in order to see over the steering wheel. "His dad and I decided to homeschool him. Sometimes I wonder if he missed out on all the normal kid things because of it. I'm just so pleased he has a friend group now."

"Mom, they know. They heard you the last fifteen times you said that."

"I'm just saying, if you had gone to public school, you might be a different person. Maybe you'd play fewer video games and go out more."

"I like video games. Besides, it's my job."

"Oh, I know. You have a good gig testing new games."

"I code apps too."

"It's just such an isolating career."

Career? I give Emily a look. She's staring at Gerrit like he's grown a third arm.

"Excuse me, Miss Cici," Emily interrupts.

"Yes, dear?"

"What do you mean 'career'?"

"Didn't Gerrit tell you?" Cici gives her son a look. "He graduated from high school early. He's spent the last two years competing at gaming professionally, and now he tests games for the big companies. He uses the money to fund his own coding projects."

"Mom, that's none of their business."

"Honey, these are your friends. Don't you tell them anything about yourself?"

"I'm a private person."

Emily interrupts their bickering. "I just assumed you were in the middle of a gap year before college."

"No." Cici shakes her head. "We don't believe college is for everyone. Gerrit already taught himself how to code, so he doesn't need to jump hoops in college for a degree. He's always known what he wanted to do. And he's doing it." Cici glances at her son proudly.

Emily leans forward to look around me toward Oscar. "Hey, did you know this already? Our man of mystery is a tech genius?"

Oscar nods his head but doesn't look away from the window.

"My son is very smart," Cici says with a loving tone. She reaches one hand across the front seat to rub Gerrit's head.

Emily gives Gerrit an appraising look.

"Whew!" She whistles. "Video games got you a career *and* a girlfriend? I am seriously impressed."

Cici's foot slips off the accelerator. "A girlfriend?"

Gerrit turns around slowly to give Emily an icy glare.

"You have a girlfriend?" Cici's voice is thick with emotion.

"Jeez, Mom, it's not a big deal."

"This is a huge deal!" she says. "You're so grown-up."

"Please don't start happy crying. You're embarrassing me."

"I just . . ." Cici sniffs. "Want to know everything about her."

"Can we please just talk about it later?" he asks.

Cici coughs a little. "Okay, sweetie."

After a moment of silence, Gerrit reaches out and puts his hand on his mom's arm. "Her name is Naomi."

His mom pats his hand lovingly.

Cici continues chatting about this and that all the way back to Detroit. Once we pull onto more familiar streets, she glances into the rearview mirror to look at us.

"Okay, who do we drop off first?"

"How about me?" Emily asks. "Jess is staying at my place tonight."

Cici shakes her head authoritatively. "No, ma'am. I'm bringing each of you to your respective homes. I need to talk to your parents so they know everything's okay."

"Oh, you really don't need to do that," I say, dread making my voice sound thick. "It's fine, really. No one is worried about me." The cramped truck is beginning to feel extremely warm. I shift uncomfortably, but there's not much space to move.

Cici glances at me in the mirror again. "Well, they should be! Didn't you tell your parents you were stranded in Indiana in the middle of the night?"

"No. It's complicated."

"Honey, I can handle complicated. What's the problem?"

I look to Emily for backup.

"Jess already made plans to sleep at my place tonight," Emily explains. "She didn't want to worry anyone by calling home."

Cici's eyes flicker in the mirror back and forth between Emily and me. "I see. So, what I'm reading from this is that your parents don't know you drove all the way to Chicago and back." Gone is the cheerful, motherly Cici. She eyes us suspiciously.

"Mom, it's okay," Gerrit says. "Like she said, Jess's situation is complicated."

"No, it's not okay. Parents generally want to know where their children are, Gerrit."

"I'm a foster kid," I blurt out.

Cici is silent for a long moment. "And you don't think your foster parents want to know where you are?"

"It's not that," I scramble. There's no way out of this but the truth. "My foster mom doesn't know I do cosplay competitions. She can't know. I'm not technically allowed to leave Michigan without permission from the state."

Silence.

My palms are starting to sweat.

Cici lets out a low whistle and looks to her son. "Well, I did tell you to get out of the house and into a little trouble like most kids do. But this wasn't exactly what I had in mind."

Cici pulls the truck over onto the side of the road. We all sit in silence for a few moments while she thinks, her lips pursed thoughtfully. Eventually she unbuckles her seat belt and turns around to look at me.

"Jess, does your foster mother hurt you?"

"What?" I ask, shocked. "No. She's not like that. She's . . ." I think of the right word, something to clear the look of growing protectiveness on Cici's face. "Great."

"Great?" Cici asks slowly.

"Yes."

Cici looks into my eyes like she's trying to find out if I'm lying to her or not. "So, if you tell your foster mom that you made a mistake, she's not going to hit you or physically punish you in any way?"

Horror crosses my face. Barbra would never. She's not that kind of person. Of course everyone hears the terrible stories about abusive foster parents who beat their kids or worse. I can't allow Cici to suspect Barbra of anything so awful. Suddenly, this situation I've found myself in isn't just about me. Barbra's reputation is at stake.

"I promise you, Cici," I say with as much conviction as I can. "Barbra is a good person. I just didn't want to get her caught up in this. And I really wanted to compete with the team. Barbra would never hurt me in any way."

Cici turns back to the front. My heart is beating so fast the sound of it fills my ears.

"Okay," Cici says finally.

I let out a slow, relieved breath.

"Here's the deal. I'm bringing you home, but I'm going to speak with your foster mother. I don't want anything to threaten this team either. You're clearly an integral part of it." She glances toward Gerrit.

"Thank you, Mom."

She nods. "And I need you to promise me something, Jess." She looks at me through the rearview mirror again. "If you ever feel unsafe or threatened at this foster home or any other, I want you to come find me. Okay?" There's a fierce protectiveness in her voice that's foreign to me.

I nod my head.

"You deserve to be safe and happy," she says. She gives me a sad smile.

"Thank you," I whisper.

No adult has ever offered to help me like that before. I wonder how many times I could have used an ally like Cici in the past. Too many to count.

It's clear there's no changing Cici's mind. All of my deceptions are going to come out. The thought fills me with shame. Barbra is going to find out I've been sneaking around all semester. What will the social workers do when she tells them I've crossed the state border without permission, not just once, but twice? How will I reunite with my biomom if they forbid me from competing in the competition in New York? Worst of all, how will Barbra feel when she discovers I've been lying to her all this time?

I sit on the saggy couch while Cici and Barbra talk in the dining room. Cici's voice carries through the dark house as she tells Barbra about what happened tonight. How our van got a flat tire and she towed us all back to Detroit from Indiana. How I wasn't sleeping over at Emily's tonight or working on a school project yesterday.

For Cici's part, she does her best to convince Barbra that the cosplay competitions are a good thing. I feel even worse when she tells Barbra about how talented she thinks I am. She urges Barbra to give me permission to continue on to the finals in New York, with all the proper permissions from the state this time, of course.

Barbra listens silently through it all.

I glance at my phone. It's half past 5:00 a.m. When Cici and I arrived twenty minutes ago, we'd startled Barbra out of sleep. A rude awakening, if there ever was one. If all had gone to plan, Barbra would've woken up about now to get ready for her early morning yoga session. She'd have no reason to doubt me or feel betrayed.

I don't fully understand the relationship Barbra and I had before this. All I know is that now it will be forever changed. A deep tremor of fear rushes through me as I realize Barbra could very well send me back. I've been dumped in group homes for much less than this. I wouldn't even blame her if she gave me up. This time I'd probably deserve it.

When I hear two sets of feet leave the kitchen, I sit up straighter. Cici pauses in front of me on her way out.

"Good night, Jess," she says. "I hope to see you again soon."

Barbra locks the front door behind her when she leaves. We wait in silence as we listen to Cici get back into the truck and drive away.

The silence is torture. Barbra isn't looking at me as she leans against the front door in her robe.

I can't stand the silence anymore.

"I'm sorry," I whisper.

Barbra looks at me. Her eyes are red rimmed and not from lack of sleep. A pang of remorse slams into me like a semitruck.

She clears her throat. "I just don't understand," she says.

"I know. I shouldn't have lied."

Barbra holds up a tired hand. "I gave you every opportunity to be honest with me. I thought we trusted each other." She sniffs. "I thought we had a good thing going here."

My heart aches because I did too, but I went ahead and ruined everything.

Barbra slowly ascends the stairs. I listen as she makes her way back to her room. The latch of her door echoes throughout the house like a single-note death march.

CHAPTER 30

MYSTERIES FORCE A MAN TO THINK, AND SO INJURE HIS HEALTH.
EDGAR ALLAN POE, "NEVER BET THE DEVIL IN YOUR HEAD"

Despite the fact that my world is crumbling all around me, I still have to get ready for school two hours later. I dress in black leggings and an oversized hoodie with Edgar Allan Poe's face on it because I just don't have the emotional energy to do anything more elaborate today. When I tiptoe out of my bedroom, Barbra's door is firmly closed, causing another wave of shame to flood my chest.

Downstairs in the kitchen there's no indication that Barbra has come down here yet this morning. She didn't even leave to go to yoga at 6:00 a.m. This has literally never happened in the four months that I've lived here. Instead of filling the pot with caffeinated coffee for myself, I add decaf grounds to the filter and leave it for whenever she comes out of her room. Maybe Barbra just needs some time alone to figure out how we can fix our relationship. At least, that's what I hope she's doing, instead of planning how to get rid of me as fast as possible.

This is my fault.

The only sound in the house is the hum of the refrigerator. I can't stand it. Before I even have my black ballet Converse fully tied, I'm out the front door. From a distance I can hear the bus lumbering down the street. I have to run to catch it just in time. The driver sighs but says nothing when I jump in just as the doors are closing. It takes about two seconds for me to realize I'm going to *really* miss my morning thermos of coffee. This will be a long, exhausting day.

At school, it's like nothing happened. Somehow the rest of the world isn't falling apart around everyone else's shoulders. I try to catch Oscar's attention in Spanish class, to no avail. His eyes are rimmed with red and his hair is a disaster. It doesn't look like he slept last night either.

While Ms. Eva's busy writing verb conjugations on the white-board I tear out a piece of paper from my notebook, ball it up, and throw it at Oscar. It bounces off his shoulder. He rearranges himself in his chair but doesn't look in my direction. That little buttmunch is deliberately ignoring me. I tear out another sheet of paper and scribble, "What is your problem?" I toss it lightly so it lands on his desk. He wipes it off with a gentle flick of his hand.

Why is everyone punishing me?

When the bell rings, I scurry up from my desk. I have to push a few nerds out of the way to beat Oscar to the door before he can escape.

"Why are you refusing to look at me?"

"I'm not," he says, without looking up. He steps around me.

"You are," I say, following him down the hall. "And you ignored my note."

"I was trying to pay attention."

"You already know Spanish."

"What do you want from me, Jess?" He finally looks up. There's hurt on his face. Do I have the magic touch of pain or something? Everyone I come into contact with seems to regret it.

"I just wanted to talk about the finals."

"Are we still doing that?" he asks. "I kind of figured the gig is up."

"Says who?"

"Didn't Barbra ground you or something?" He shrugs his giant backpack up his shoulder, nearly dropping the books in his arms.

"Not yet."

The tension in his face relaxes a little. I realize he'd been bracing for me to tell him it was all over, that his dream had come to a crashing halt. Not yet, Oscar. Not if I can help it.

"Okay," he says, nodding more to himself than me. "Okay, we could still do this. Maybe."

"I'll do everything within my power."

Behind us, Ms. Eva is collecting worksheets from our desks. She gives me a disappointed look from afar when she sees mine is empty. I pretend I don't see her.

Oscar leans up against the doorframe, eyeing me. "Did you get in serious trouble last night?"

I shrug. "I guess, but I'm not sure. Barbra still hasn't really spoken to me."

"Do you think it would help if Abuela talks to her?"

"In Spanish?"

It's Oscar's turn to shrug. "I don't know. I'm just thinking out loud."

"No." I shake my head to clear it a little. "I'm the one who needs to talk to her. To apologize."

"Well," Oscar says. "It's a good thing you're so darn good at apologizing."

I have to smile a little at this. "Thanks."

People are starting to file into the Spanish classroom for next period. We slowly make our way down the hall toward the math wing.

"So, what look should we do for the World Cosplay Expo?" His voice is lighter now, less terse than it was moments ago.

"Why are you asking me?" I pause at my locker so I can swap out my Spanish book. Unlike Oscar, I don't carry everything on my back like a snail. "Don't you want to be the one to choose our grand finale?"

He shakes his head. "You've proven to have great instincts about these things. I think this one should be up to you. Besides," he says, moving his *Prince of Moons* book to the top of the pile in his hands, "we already won a trophy with my ultimate theme. We'll never beat that. I'm up for anything."

The responsibility feels fragile in my care, like a delicate crystal egg that might contain anything from a dragon to an intergalactic rebel force. I do not want to disappoint Oscar, not after all we've been through thus far. This choice must be made carefully.

"Alright." I take a deep, grounding breath.

The crowd is thinning around us, so we head in our separate directions.

"If I survive the night," I call out to him as I run down the hall toward geometry, "I'll have a new battle plan for you in the morning."

At home that afternoon I pause on the front step, swallowing hard. My hands tremble where they're frozen on the doorknob. When I go inside, I hope Barbra is back to her cheerful self, freshly returned from meditation class or reiki or whatever new age shenanigans she's up to today. With any luck, she'll be whistling to herself as she puts some vegetarian delight in the oven. Realistically the more likely scenario is that I'll find social workers inside waiting to take me away again.

I channel Sir Valorian, the only fictional character I can think of who's brave and true. He would face the consequences for his actions with his head held high. He would apologize. So will I.

When I open the door, the house is silent. Barbra must still be out. Instead of going upstairs to my room like I usually do, I set my bag down on the kitchen table. My eyes catch sight of the coffeepot. It's empty and clean. I hope the coffee I made for Barbra made her day just a tiny bit better after the night I put her through. I boil some water and open Barbra's tea cupboard. A multitude of flavors stare back at me, from tulsi lavender to ginger honey. In the end I settle on a simple lemon zinger. I set the hot mug on the table and take my books out of my satchel so I can get a head start on my homework.

Without Barbra here, chatting cheerfully or bouncing around in the kitchen, it's much too quiet. Thankfully, I'd downloaded all the Bowie songs from Oscar's CD onto my phone. I connect it to Bluetooth speakers, then settle about solving math equations while Bowie sings about star men and rebels.

It must be two hours before my pencil freezes at the sound of a key in the front door. Barbra enters the house to Bowie's unusual voice singing on repeat. When she finds me in the kitchen she pauses, taking in my books and empty teacup.

"Here's the thing," she says with no preamble. "I don't know where we went wrong. But from here on out I want us to do things right." Her voice isn't angry. It's more tired. She tosses her car keys into the little dish on the counter.

"I called your social worker," she says.

My breath catches in my throat.

She takes off her lumpy sweater, revealing her sweaty yoga clothes underneath. I vaguely wonder if she signed up for a late class so she could work off her anger at me.

"I asked for official permission for you to travel to the competition in New York."

A weight lifts off my chest, but it leaves a hollow pit in its place. "Did they ask about the other competitions?"

"Yes."

"How much trouble am I in?"

"None. For now." She gives me a leveling look that's not very characteristic for her. "I told them I chaperoned you and forgot to get permission to take you out of state."

My eyes grow wide in astonishment. "You lied for me?"

"Better me than you."

"What did they do to you?"

She waves a hand. "Just an administrative slap on the wrist. I promised to never let it happen again. Please don't make me a liar a second time."

I nod, fully knowing that I'm going to put her in an entirely different predicament when we get to New York. When I reunite with my biomom without the state's permission.

"I just wish you had told me the whole truth," she whispers, weariness composing a note of betrayal in her voice.

"I know," I say. "I'm sorry."

"Can I see the other pictures?"

Tears threaten to sting my eyes. "Yes." I pull out my phone to open Insta. "You can see them all."

She smiles as she swipes through them, laughing outright at

our *Prince of Moons* selfie. She pauses on my scream queens photo. "I wish I had been there to see this."

I don't tell her that I'd wished the same thing.

She sets the phone down. "I got something for you today." She stands up from her chair, walks out of the kitchen, and returns with a large box.

My hands reach up to cover my mouth. A photo of the Singer Stylist 7258 sewing machine is printed onto the box's surface. Its immaculate LCD screen for 100 computerized stitch designs stares at me. My fingers itch to touch the box as if to be certain I'm not dreaming.

I glance up at Barbra, not sure what to do. "Aren't you supposed to be punishing me, not giving me gifts?"

She chuckles. "Maybe. But I figured if you spent the last few months making all of your costumes, you must be pretty serious about this cosplay team. I want to help you succeed, no matter what you set your mind to. I want you to know that you can trust me to help you."

She shouldn't have spent her money on this for me. New York might make her regret it. Maybe Barbra and I could be happy together. Foster mother and foster daughter. We could be a family. But deep down, I know that can't happen while my heart is still stuck on my biomom. I need closure.

"Thank you," I whisper as I bite back the tightness in my throat. "Would you like to help me pick our next theme?"

Barbra's eyes grow wet instantly. "Yes. I really would."

"Okay," I say. "There are just a few rules. First, we need four characters, one for each of the team members. And Emily refuses to be anything overtly girly, so that's something to consider. Also,"

I pause, deciding she doesn't need to know that this rule was exclusively my doing. "It must include characters of royalty."

"Royalty? Like kings and queens?"

"Or princes and duchesses."

She nods, thinking. We listen to the music for several long seconds.

Over the speakers Bowie asks if there is life on Mars.

Barbra's eyes grow wide. Excitement pulses through the room as she gets up to grab my phone. "Would you unlock this? I have a song to play for you."

I enter my passcode, realizing I don't even know what kind of music Barbra listens to. This could be very interesting. But instead of some strange honkytonk or show tune mix, a familiar voice sings an unfamiliar tune: David Bowie's "Magic Dance."

"I know the perfect theme." Barbra grins at me.

Relief spreads through me. "What is it?"

"*Labyrinth.*"

I do a quick Google search when she passes my phone back to me. What I see is a world filled with fantastical creatures, an eerie masquerade with noblemen in dark masks, and—best of all—a creepy goblin king portrayed by David Bowie himself. What seals the deal is a girl dressed in an ethereal gown of white, silver, and gold. Sarah is forced to leave the normal world behind so she can save her family from the Goblin King. She is a human princess of fae. She navigates the labyrinth to rescue someone she loves from the seductive forces of a fantasy underworld.

Sarah is like me, the would-be princess of a realm no one could possibly believe or understand.

CHAPTER 31

I MOVE THE STARS FOR NO ONE.
JARETH, *LABYRINTH*

When I flip down the makeup mirror on the passenger side of Barbra's car, my bloodshot eyes stare back at me. There's also a matching pair of under-eye bags to boot. Glorious. These stress nightmares have culminated in a serious lack of sleep. I wonder if Barbra can tell how off I feel. Based on the happy humming sounds coming from the driver's seat, I suspect not. Edgar Allan Poe would have understood this festering brain of mine.

Barbra has taken to helping our cosplay team with verve. She spent the past three weeks choreographing a spooky ballroom dance number for our *Labyrinth* masquerade skit. That's in addition to about six major rhinestone hunts throughout the greater Detroit area while I sat in the Costume Lair sewing away on my new Singer machine. We could not have pulled this off without her.

We've practiced our dance what feels like a million times already, but today is the first time we'll practice in full costume. For weeks I've been cutting fabric, sewing, and tailoring our *Labyrinth* pieces. They are the most gorgeous collection I've made yet. This set is so good we've decided to take promotional photos for the website Gerrit and Emily are designing for the Costume Lair.

Lucky for us, Cici works events at the Whitney, Detroit's fanciest mansion-turned-bar. Emily's dad offered to take the photos for us. It feels extremely weird to have so many parents involved in our team now, but no one else seems to mind. I chalk it up to me not being used to adults taking an interest in anything I do.

When Barbra drives her rusty Ford Taurus wagon up in front of the stone mansion, my jaw quite literally drops.

"It looks like a castle," Barbra says, peering up through the dirty windshield.

There's a knot of anxiety in my stomach. "Is Cici sure we're allowed in there?"

Barbra chuckles. "Yes, Jess. They'll let the likes of us inside. At least for today." She smirks at me.

I stick out my tongue and unbuckle my seat belt.

"They don't technically open until this evening," Barbra says as she grabs her keys from the ignition. "So there's probably no one else there right now."

My masquerade gown is so voluminous it takes up the entire back seat of the car. I have to wrestle with sequins and tulle to squeeze it out from the car door. Barbra locks up, then meets me at the front walkway, where we both stare up at the windows glittering in the morning light. This place is usually bustling with weddings, engagement parties, and other fancy occasions, and it's easy to see why. I feel like I've stepped off the Detroit sidewalk and onto the film set of a nineteenth-century television drama.

Barbra nudges me with her shoulder. She's brimming with excitement.

I let her lead the way up the front steps. She's carrying my wig, which took me six hours to arrange into the dark, voluminous locks with rhinestones that Sarah wears in the movie. The second we step up to the front doors, they open to reveal the most beautiful space I have ever seen. The inner foyer has a wood-carved archway, which would be impressive enough if the floor wasn't designed with tiny tiles arranged in artistic patterns. Beyond that there's a room with walls covered in tapestries, multiple marble fireplaces, and stained-glass windows depicting scenes with angels and musicians. The foyer walls are wood paneled, the molding carved with ornate loops and swirls. When I look up, the ceiling is gilded and lined with twinkling chandeliers. Right in the middle of the foyer is a grand staircase with polished wood railings topping iron wrought into swooping floral designs.

I close my eyes and reopen them again just to make sure I'm not imagining this. When I glance at Barbra, she is open-mouthed staring at everything in awe. From the look of her, she's never been in here before either. I hear high heels clicking on the tile to our left. Cici emerges out of a doorway. She waves at us.

"Jess, Barbra, welcome!" Her smile is brighter than the polished lamps on the mantelpiece above the second, enormous fireplace. "Everyone else is already here. They're getting ready upstairs. I prepared dressing rooms for you. Please, follow me."

My legs wobble underneath me as I follow Cici up the grand staircase, too terrified to touch anything. I spot Barbra running the tips of her fingers over the polished wood banisters as we ascend, a look of wonder on her face. When we reach the second floor, marble busts of gorgeous ladies, a sleek piano, and flickering candelabras greet us.

Cici leads the way through a wooden door marked Ladies. Of course even the bathrooms are decorated with plush cushioned seats and giant mirrors worthy of a queen's boudoir.

"Jess!"

I snap out of my daze to see Emily, grinning. "Isn't this place amazing?"

Barbra turns to Cici. "We really can't thank you enough for allowing us to shoot their promo photos here."

Cici waves her hand as if shooing away a fly. "Oh, please. It's the least I can do for these kids. They've worked so hard. I'm just happy I can help." She looks down at her watch. "Emily, I'm going to go meet your father in Mrs. Whitney's sitting room. Would you all join us there as soon as you're ready?"

We nod as she disappears back through the doorway like a fairy godmother that just finished turning a grungy foster girl into a royal princess. I half expect to see a pumpkin carriage waiting for me.

Emily's fully dressed in the costume I made for her. Half of it is a long-sleeved, mauve gown with spiderwebs trickling down over her hips. The other half consists of black skintight pants, a billowy white shirt, and spiked knee-high boots, so she can act as two different characters in our dance scene. Since she insisted on having a weapon if we were going to force her into ballroom dancing, Oscar made her a sword hilt that glitters silver. Her wig is also custom-made. I cut and dyed it myself. Half of it has a long, lavender braid that's tied up with ribbon. The other is silver white, teased and held in a mad style with spider clips. It's goth and glamour all mixed into one.

Emily feels our admiring eyes. She poses to the right, holding up a gold mask with tear drop crystals cascading down with invisible wire. Then she pivots left and holds up a black mask with silver horns placed at each side of the grimacing papier-mâché goblin face. Oscar's masks are both frightening and beautiful at the same time.

Barbra applauds. "You look amazing! This is all going to come together so well with the music and choreography."

"So," Emily says with a huge grin on her face. "I have news."

"Oh?" I ask as I take my makeup supplies out of my bag. They look so professional all lined up on the marble countertop together. It makes me feel like I'm a real makeup artist.

"I got into my top coding bootcamp!" she squeals. "Full scholarship!"

"Hell yeah, you did!" I yell, and pump my fist into the air.

We both jump up and down, giggling like children. I'm so ridiculously proud of her. My smart, fearless, badass friend.

"When do you go?" I ask.

"It's a three-month program. I'll go over the summer and be back in time for senior year."

"Then what's next?" I ask.

"Then I apply to the best video game design programs in the frickin' world. I'm unstoppable!"

As I stand there, positively overflowing with pride, I realize that she is. Nothing can stop Emily.

Barbra helps me wiggle into my dress with its numerous layers of white and silver fabric. The corseted bodice is covered in glittering gold sequins. Its sweetheart neckline is enhanced with my bio-mom's brooch, affixed at my solar plexus, where my anxiety hums low, warning me to breathe deep. Emily pins my wig into place, adjusting the crystal headpiece where it's needed. I add costume chandelier earrings just before touching up my simple makeup.

Sarah is supposed to be an innocent girl caught in the web of the evil Goblin King. I need to look cherubic. Pink lips, blush, mascara, and a light smoky-purple eye shadow will be enough to give me a doe-eyed look. For Emily, I add white shadow and gold eyeliner to one eye and a heavy midnight black to the other. While neither of us look like the Hollywood actors from *Labyrinth*, it hardly matters. We own these characters. Big or small, we deserve to feel this good in costume. It makes me think of Vacation Vibes Link and Lord Varys. They would definitely approve.

As Emily and I stand in the light streaming in through the windows, it feels like we've entered a parallel dimension. In this world we live as queens and ghouls in a mansion from another century. It's not too far off from what my own mother believed.

"Are you ready?" Barbra asks us as she spritzes one last layer of hairspray to our heads.

I nod, ignoring the inexplicable terror in my gut. Out of the corner of my eye, I can almost see the schizophrenia gene monster watching me from the shadows.

Barbra leads the way across the landing toward a room where we can hear voices. Emily skips ahead as usual, but I pause when I catch sight of myself in the mirror above a fireplace mantel. In the chandelier's glow, the silver rhinestones in my hair glitter like diamonds. Light streams in through the stained-glass window on the staircase, haloing me in multifaceted colors. I am a creature from another realm. In this moment, I look like royalty. I feel dangerously close to what my mother tells me I truly am.

My heart races and my hands prickle with sweat. It has taken me far too long to fully appreciate that I am playing with fire. I know this isn't real, but I can see how easy it would be to live in this illusion forever. How a small change in my brain chemistry could make me believe this is my life. I turn decidedly away from my deceptive reflection.

I push open the door to Mrs. Whitney's sitting room and gasp. The space is layered from floor to ceiling in white gauzy material sheer enough to let in the morning light from the many windows. On tables draped with fabric, there are piles of mother-of-pearl oyster shells and crystal vases filled with large white feathers. The chandeliers are dripping with strings of pearlescent beads.

I look to Cici, stunned beyond words.

She gives me a knowing smile. "It looks good, right?"

"Good?!" Emily asks. "How about magical?"

Cici laughs. "We host so many weddings in this venue, we had a lot of decorations in the storeroom to work with."

I wander throughout the space touching the silky material with wonder. In one corner of the room there's a gilded clock that beckons to me. Its face reads quarter past ten, but I've seen the movie; I know this clock means time is running out for Sarah. My fingers tingle as I push the time back just a little.

Behind me, Cici lets out a sound of delight. I turn to see Gerrit give her a sheepish grin. His costume is also split in half, but that's where his and Emily's similarities end. One half is a sage-green tailored suit with long tails and white puffy sleeves. He has watch chains dangling from a multitude of pockets. His other side has a silver vest over a black, ruffled shirt. His pants are tucked into high boots like Emily's, but they're painted gold and swirled with intricate silver decals. Instead of a wig, Gerrit has a headband. From one side of his head sprout antlers, while the other is dripping with strings of black beads like hair that stop short of his shoulders.

He holds up his two masks for everyone's approval. One resembles a beige ogre with a brown mouth and sharp teeth. The other mask has a long, plague doctor-esque beak with black feathers sprouting from the top. Oscar's creativity never ceases to amaze me.

That's when Oscar walks into the room. The light from the chandeliers bounces off the blue rhinestones attached to his sharp midnight-blue suit jacket. His shoulder pads and white ruffled shirt give his top half added bulk to sculpt his silhouette, with sharp angles that peter in toward his waist. His pants are black pleather, and his boots sport a pointed heel. On his head, Oscar's wearing the choppy rock star wig I cut and styled for him. He applied glitter to his cheekbones, and white eye shadow to his lids, and used eyeliner to draw his eyebrows at a sharp, upturned angle, just like I showed him. In his hand, he holds a shiny black mask with long, twisted horns that end in sharp points. Feminine and masculine styles are rolled into one complex character, just like David Bowie.

There's no hint of Oscar's nervous anxiety as he walks into the room. He looks taller, more elegant, and oddly alluring—just like the Goblin King.

Emily's dad wastes no time ushering all four of us into the middle of the room. He adjusts several professional-looking lights and reflectors.

"I think the best thing will be for you to perform your skit," he says from the floor where he's squatting, camera in hand. "I'll shoot a bunch of photos while you dance, then we can get a few posed shots afterward. Sound good?"

"You're the boss," Emily chirps. She bounces up and down on her toes.

Barbra pulls a Bluetooth speaker out from a tote bag and connects her phone to it. "The music's ready whenever you are."

I feel like I'm going to faint. We've practiced this skit dozens of times already; there's no reason for my heart to be pounding so much. Dizziness makes the room feel even more surreal, with the lights bouncing off so many surfaces after streaming in through the gauzy draping. I take several deep breaths. I can do this.

Oscar and I walk to separate corners of the room as Gerrit and Emily take their places in the center. They hold their masks in different hands, one up to their face, with the other held behind their back. They face each other close but not touching. The room stills. Then a tinkling, romantic melody breaks the silence. Goblin King Bowie sings about finding a deep, sad love within Sarah's eyes. The music lulls and captivates me in a mysterious, drowsy sort of way.

At center stage, Gerrit and Emily spin around each other. As their different angles face forward, they switch their masks with exact precision, giving the illusion of several dancers swirling on a dance floor. Couples flicker in and out of view in the tall mirrors behind them. The sound of the camera clicking fades away as if we've all stepped through the veil into the world of the Labyrinth, leaving everyone we know behind.

The sound of my blood rushes in my ears as I move toward them. I am searching for the elusive Goblin King. Oscar hovers around the perimeter, his eyes watching me intensely. Every time I step near him, Gerrit and Emily swoop in to block him from my view and the Goblin King disappears.

Bowie's voice permeates the room as he promises to be there for his love, even as the world falls down around them. My heart squeezes in my chest and I feel momentarily breathless.

I spin and come face-to-face with a stranger in a dark mask. We dance with our hands held up but our palms not touching. There's an energy vibrating between our fingertips, electrifying me. I look into the eyes behind the mask, Oscar's eyes.

Bowie tells us that we may have been strangers until now, but we aren't anymore. When I look at Oscar, I see how far he would go to be with me—to the end of the universe and beyond. Bowie sings that our love can be found in the stars. As the world glimmers around me, draped in gauzy silver and white, it's as if the stars have come down to meet us for this dance. To show us how true Bowie's lyrics are.

My breath catches in my throat. Gerrit swoops in and steals me away just as the stranger lowers his mask to reveal he's the Goblin King. I am passed between Gerrit and Emily, spinning around in disorienting circles. I search for the Goblin King, but he is always just out of my sight. There's a feeling of intoxication in the dance. The upside-down has been turned right-side up. I've lost all control over my movements as I'm passed from one fantastical creature to another.

I'm lost.

Then the crowd breaks. I see the black mask again. He walks slowly toward me while the other creatures dance. He lowers his mask to reveal smoldering eyes that beckon me to accept a world where I can live like this forever. The Goblin King takes my hand, turning me. My dress swirls out around me like a glittering snowflake. I find myself oddly relieved when I finish spinning and he's still there, waiting for me. Our hands touch. The fire between us burns my fingertips.

The world is falling down around us, but I am most certainly falling in love.

Everything fades away except for Oscar's eyes and the warmth of his hands on mine. But even in the Labyrinth the spell must end eventually. We all know how this story ends. Sarah doesn't choose the Goblin King. She rejects his world of fantasy, to go back home with her real family. As Bowie's voice fades away and the song ends, that is the choice I must make too. I can never let myself fall into a fantasy world. I've seen how much pain that causes.

No one ever said it was easy to find your way through a labyrinth.

CHAPTER 32

YOU HAVE NO POWER OVER ME.
SARAH, *LABYRINTH*

New York City is bustling in every way I dreamed it would. Women in power suits talk on cell phones as they push their way through crowds of tourists with cameras flashing. The lights turn night into day, making the club-going twentysomethings squint as they stumble blearily toward hot dog stands after one cocktail too many. Religious men with brimstone posters shout from atop milk crates while they hand out fliers with dogma printed alongside images of sinners seeking salvation. It is a mix of beautiful chaos poised on the brink of terrifying madness.

Yesterday Cici and Barbra took turns driving the van as the rest of us sat in the back, trying to avoid squishing wigs or crumpling costumes. Cici insisted on coming because she wants to film the competition for Gerrit's dad overseas. Barbra had no choice since she has to serve as my chaperone during my first authorized out-of-state journey. Even if this trip hadn't been mandatory for her, I have a feeling she would've come anyway.

Throughout the entire drive to New York, my black jeans pocket weighed heavy with the return address Reigna wrote on the package she mailed to me months ago. She had no way of knowing she sent me two gifts that day, the brooch and her address.

I silently brainstorm plans for sneaking out to find Reigna after the competition. Back when I thought it would just be Gerrit, Emily, and Oscar, I'd planned to evaporate into the nighttime crowds like a mist in the sun. Now, with two chaperones, that seems impossible. Every plan I come up with falls apart at the slightest pressure. Barbra and Cici have obviously been talking. One of them follows me everywhere I go.

Worry eats my insides all morning as we dress in our costumes and take the subway to the convention center. No one on the train even bats an eye at four teenagers dressed for a masquerade ball, but Cici and Barbra think it's marvelous. They take dozens of photos of us holding on to the sticky train handlebars while passengers squish us from every angle.

By now, Oscar, Emily, Gerrit, and I have seen enough of these fan conventions to know what we're in for, but for Cici and Barbra, it's all brand-new. The second we arrive, our chaperones turn into giggling girls, their eyes alight with excitement. Barbra openly gawks at a giant Transformers Bumblebee costume as we file into the line to go through security.

"Now I wish we had dressed up too," Barbra says to Cici. She looks down at the cat sweater she's wearing from our bonding Goodwill trip.

"Notes for next year," Cici agrees. "I'm going to force the kids to make a costume for me."

"Oh god," Gerrit mumbles. He runs his hand over his face.

Oscar's face falls minutely, but then his smile returns. That jealousy is infectious though. It hurts, how much I wish my biomom were here for me the way Cici is here for Gerrit.

My phone buzzes from somewhere in the folds of my dress. It takes me several seconds to find the pocket I sewed underneath all the tulle—because, yes, I frickin' sewed a pocket into this magnificent dress. What woman doesn't want pockets in her gown?

My screen flashes with a new Insta message.

> **Reigna_NYC:** "Your masquerade pictures took my breath away. I am so proud of the talented young woman you have become. I wish I could see you."

My eyes dart around to make sure no one else saw the message, but my teammates are distracted by our chaperones, who are laughing hysterically as they pose with the Tarzan in line behind us. Gerrit averts his eyes in embarrassment while Emily takes one picture after another, a ridiculous grin plastered across her face.

I hurriedly type back. "What if you could?"

Barely ten seconds pass before I get a response.

> **Reigna_NYC:** "Wouldn't that be wonderful? We'd dress up and have tea in the garden. It would be lovely."
>
> **GothQueen_13:** "I mean that literally. I'm in New York. I want to meet you."
>
> **Reigna_NYC:** "I'll fix up the best guest room for you."

My eyes sting with tears of longing. I don't want to wait until tonight to see her. This competition is a huge deal for me. This is the culmination of months of hard work. More than anything, I want to share it with my real mother. I want to make her proud of me.

My eyes wander back to Barbra where she's laughing with Cici as they pose like Charlie's Angels with Emily. Sadness pokes at my chest, preventing me from breathing properly. If I've learned anything from the Prince of Moons books, it's that fulfilling your destiny requires bravery.

The competition doesn't start for five hours. There's plenty of time to sneak away, find my biomom, and bring her back to watch us perform. Barbra might not even need to know I left the con before the competition. How long could it possibly take to travel uptown and back?

I tuck my phone back into its hiding place just as Oscar turns to me, his cheeks pink.

"Parents can be super weird."

After weeks of hardly speaking, I'm a little startled to discover he's addressing me. I intend to make a sound of agreement but a nervous laugh comes out instead.

"You okay?" he asks, looking at me sidelong. While I'm glad he isn't ignoring me anymore, his attention isn't exactly helping my escape plotting at the moment.

"Yeah," I say. "Just nervous about the competition."

Oscar gives me a confident smile with dimples. "Surprisingly, I'm not . . ." He pauses.

"What?"

"I should have told you sooner," he says guiltily. "I Zoomed with my dad last weekend. I told him everything. Cosplay, the competitions, my dream of making this a business. All of it."

My eyes grow wide. "This is huge," I say, truly stunned. "What did he say?"

Oscar looks back over toward Cici and Barbra. "It went really well. Great even."

My chest swells with pride. "I know that wasn't easy," I say. "I'm really happy for you."

"He doesn't *totally* get it, of course," Oscar admits. "The dressing up bit is still weird for him. But he understands that it's something I love and that I'm good at it."

"*Really* good," I emphasize.

He chuckles. "Yeah. He started calling me his young

entrepreneur." The look on his face tells me a huge weight has been lifted off his shoulders. He's wanted his dad's approval for longer than I've known him.

"Thank you," he says.

I frown. "For what?"

"For helping me do this." He waves at his bedazzled costume. "And for helping me scrounge up the courage to talk to my dad."

I shrug off his words. "That was all you, Oscar."

"Maybe," he says. "But none of it would have happened without your influence." He's searching for my eyes, but I can't look back. I'm afraid he might see the secrets hidden there.

I decide to accept his thanks though I really don't think I deserve it after all of my treachery. Later today I'm going to have my own confrontation with my parent. I can only hope mine goes as well as his did.

Oscar is looking at me with concern. "Still nervous?" He takes my hand and squeezes it. His skin is warm and comforting. Still, I gently pull my hand away. I have to.

"Maybe."

"Do you want me to give you another one of my famous team leader pep talks?"

"Thanks, I'm good." I force a smile back onto my face, but when I look into his eyes, it falters. There's genuine concern there. Not just one teammate looking out for another. He cares. About me.

And I can't deny how much I care about him too.

"Oscar," I say slowly. "Things have gotten a little ... off ... with us lately. I'm truly sorry about that."

Oscar's eyes grow soft. "Yeah. Me too."

Kind, sensitive Oscar. How did I mess this all up so badly? Maybe there's a way we could make a fresh start when this is all over. After New York, I could spend less time pushing him away and more time drawing him close. The moths inside of me flutter at the thought. After we go home to Detroit, I could learn to accept the joy—and dare I say love?—that is Oscar.

Just, not yet. I need to close the past with my biomom before I open up a future with Oscar.

"Do you think, when all of this is over, we could maybe start again?" I ask. My voice shakes, betraying my fear.

I can't read the expression on his face. It's wariness, pain, and hope all rolled up in one.

"Yeah," he says. "Maybe."

Emily runs up to us, her phone thrust out in front of her. "Oh my god, you guys have to see these pictures. Just think of the parental blackmailing opportunities!"

"Has anyone ever told you you're just a little bit evil?" Oscar asks her.

"Psh!" She waves him off as she zooms in on a photo starring Tarzan's pecs.

Gerrit leans toward us, groaning miserably. "I'm never going to be able to forget this humiliation."

Emily holds up her phone. "Definitely not. I'll make sure of it."

Gerrit sighs forlornly but doesn't protest.

Cici and Barbra turn back toward us, grinning widely.

"Why didn't you tell me these things were so much fun?" Cici asks. "Look at this photo!" She leans close so Gerrit can see her posing with her arms flexed alongside Tarzan's. "I'm sending it to Naomi." Her fingers dance over her phone screen.

"Wait." Gerrit blanches. "How do you have her number?"

Cici just winks in response.

We're nearly to the front of the security line now.

Oscar puts his leader hat on. "Okay, team. It's nearly time to make the rounds. We have four hours before we need to check in for the competition. Let's use this time wisely." He hands a stack of business cards to Cici. Then he gives Barbra fliers with our promo photos and new web address on them. "Since you're both officially a part of the group now, you have jobs to do," Oscar explains. "Every time someone takes a photo with us, give them a flyer so they don't forget our name. We need buzz for the Costume Lair. With any luck, we might have custom orders for next year's convention season."

"Such a boss!" Emily says admiringly.

He looks toward her, his eyebrows pinched together in focus. "Em, are you ready to dazzle the ladies?"

"Always." She smiles coquettishly.

"Good." He nods. "Gerrit, stick close to her so everyone can see your costumes work together. Jess." He turns to me.

I'm pulled out of my worried distraction by the sound of my name. When I look at Oscar, I see he's holding his elbow out toward me like a gentleman escorting his lady into a ball. I take his elbow gingerly, ignoring the warmth that floods my veins at the touch.

"Okay, team," Oscar says. "Let's work the dance floor."

We spend the next hour hustling like we've never hustled before. I take photos with *Addams Family* members, colorful chefs wielding burgers and pizzas from *Overcooked*, and so many *League of Legend* champions that it makes me wonder if everyone in the world plays this game except for me. Bob Ross asks me to draw on a canvas strapped to his back. Princess Peach poses next to me, our voluminous gowns taking up an entire aisle of the exhibit hall so people need to squeeze around us. So many people ask to take photos of us that I lose track of time. I feel surrounded, trapped.

"Jess!"

I whirl around to find Lord Varys and Vacation Vibes Link waving at me from a booth a few feet away. A sign over their heads displays "Midwest Body Positive Cosplay Coalition," and the table is covered with flyers and swag with their logo. These two are seriously taking over the geek universe.

Vacation Vibes Link and Varys are wearing the same tried and true costumes, but this time, Vacation Vibes Link has added a vibrant orange lei around her neck.

"What are you guys doing here?" I ask, astounded.

"We're promoting MBPCC!" Vacation Vibes Link hands me a sticker. It has a happy cartoon cat with a speech bubble that says: *I love myself for who I am right meow.*

"We make the cosplay circuit ever year," Varys explains. "It's our way of vacationing."

Vacation Vibes Link fluffs my poufy sleeves. "You look awesome! I expected you to perform in the same costume all the way to the finals, but you've outdone yourself. There's no way you're *not* getting a prize tonight."

"Seriously." Varys takes in my giant, sparkling gown. "We're going to post your team's photo on the Coalition's twitter ASAP. We're all rooting for you."

"You're an inspiration!" Vacation Vibes Link's face is so earnest it sends a pang of nerves ricocheting down my spine. There's so much riding on this competition, but for me it still feels hollow. I'm missing something important. No, not something—someone.

"Thank you," I say. I point back toward my team members where they're calling me for another photo op. "I gotta ..."

"Go! Go!" Vacation Vibes Link waves me away.

"Make us proud!" Varys calls.

After another thirty minutes of constant photos it becomes

apparent that there's no way I'm going to be able to sneak away in the middle of all of this. With my giant dress and shining accessories I don't blend in, not even here in a convention hall with thousands of cosplayers. The first real pangs of panic start to hit me. I need to slip away and bring Reigna back here in time for the competition. Looking around at these costumes, I can see that we have a very real shot at winning this thing. In my core, I feel that I *need* my biomom to be here to witness my crowning glory. It suddenly means everything to me.

My phone buzzes in my pocket just as the overhead speakers crackle.

Everyone stills.

"We have a special announcement," the voice above us says. "Jeff Goldblum has arrived for a surprise visit. He will be posing for photos in the *Jurassic Park* garden in five minutes. Everyone in line will get a chance to enter their name into a raffle to win a one-on-one dinner date with him tonight."

All around us people start screaming with excitement. Like a stampede, they begin running through the convention hall in the direction of the gardens. My opportunity couldn't be clearer. I'm instantly filled with a mixture of blessed fate and paralyzing fear.

This is it.

My choice burns inside of me: escape for my biological family or stay for the family I've found.

A surprising amount of guilt floods my chest in the moment I allow my instincts to take over. The entire reason I agreed to do this competition in the first place wasn't to win. It wasn't to make friends or perfect my sewing and makeup artistry. It was to find my biomom.

Like a fairytale princess, I choose to leave everything behind in exchange for the chance to get one thing back: my real family.

I hope Emily, Gerrit, and Oscar will forgive me for this. My eyes flicker toward Barbra. She's giggling while asking Cici if we should all put our names in to win a date with Jeff.

I will come back for you, I think.

I take two steps backward and allow myself to be carried away by the crowd.

CHAPTER 33

THINGS ARE NOT ALWAYS WHAT THEY SEEM IN THIS PLACE.
SO YOU CAN'T TAKE ANYTHING FOR GRANTED.
WORM, *LABYRINTH*

I pull my phone out of my dress pocket to check the address. This is definitely the right place, but the building isn't what I expected. It's a dingy mammoth of a thing, not a cute brownstone like I passed on my way uptown. It's not even a sleek apartment building near Central Park, like you see in all the movies.

Sweat drips down the back of my neck, dampening my dress. Goddess, I'm melting. It was stupid-warm in the subway tunnels and the late trains didn't help my nerves. My phone was buzzing nonstop with messages from Gerrit, Emily, and Barbra, so I turned it off. It's too distracting. I need to focus, find Reigna, and hurry back to the con.

When I walk up the front steps to try the door, it's locked. To my right there's a metallic speaker system with numbered buttons. My biomom didn't write a unit number on the return address, so I just start beeping buttons at random, hoping someone will buzz me in.

The speaker screeches before an irritated voice yells. "Knock it off!"

"Um, excuse me," I say to the inanimate object. "I'm looking for a woman named Reigna."

The speaker is silent. This irritates me, so I start pressing all the numbers again. I've come too far to let a cranky doorwoman keep me out.

"No visitors allowed," the speaker croaks.

"My mother lives here. I want to come in."

"Are you listening? No visitors."

"Come oooon," I say, changing my tone and playing up the lost-little-girl card. I'm not sure how well I pull it off in full *Labyrinth* masquerade regalia. Maybe my flowing gown could be misinter-preted as an eccentric prom dress? "I really want to see my mom."

"Ma'am, if you don't vacate the premises, you'll force me to call the police."

Outrage burns my insides. Screw the innocent little girl act. Maybe my curled and teased hairstyle works better on a toddler in the midst of a tantrum. I use my heeled white boots to high kick the door.

"They're on speed dial," the speaker says in warning.

"Okay! Okay!" I start to leave but then turn back to the speaker. "Could you at least tell me if I have the right building? Does a woman named Reigna live in any of your apartments?"

There's a long pause. I seriously wonder if the doorwoman is calling the police on me.

"I can't give out any information about residents."

"So she does live here?"

"I can neither confirm nor deny if certain individuals live or have ever lived in this facility."

"Well, screw you then!" I kick the door again, then turn to leave. I must be visibly fuming because a homeless man on the street stands up from the nest he's made on the sidewalk. He waves me over. Maybe he knows my biomom? I approach him.

"Hey, do you know what that place is? I think you might be lost."

"I'm looking for my mom, Reigna. Do you know her?"

He shakes his head sadly. "Sorry, baby girl, but no. Even if she does live there, they aren't allowed to tell people that."

New York City is the most infuriating place I've ever been to.

"Why the hell not?" I throw my arms up into the air in frustration.

"That's St. Dymphna Halfway House."

I pause. That doesn't sound like a normal apartment name. It's certainly nothing like the residential neighborhoods in Michigan with their dreamy titles like Pine Falls Community, Meadow Hills Estates, or Lake Serenity Apartments.

He must sense my confusion, so he clarifies. "As in, people live there if they need a little help getting back on their feet. Addicts, people released from the hospitals, you understand?"

I'm feeling a little light-headed now.

"You okay?" the man asks. He's wearing several layers of dirty coats and a red scarf, even though it must be seventy-five degrees out today.

"Yeah," I say, thinking fast. Clearly, I need to come up with a new plan. "If someone did live in the halfway house"—I wave my hand back toward the damnable building—"where else do you think I could expect to find them?"

The man smiles at me like I've finally asked the right question.

"Well, the library of course!"

"Oh."

"It's the most precious resource the city has to offer. You can use the computers to apply for jobs, check out books to read in the park, learn new skills." He checks things off on his fingers as he goes. "Attend events, stay warm in the winter, and dry when it rains."

By the way his eyes light up, I can tell he truly loves this place.

"Of course, why didn't I think of that?" I shake my head. It's not much, but it's a lead. "Thank you."

"If your momma does live in this neighborhood, she'd probably be at the branch around the corner." He indicates down the street to our left.

"You're a lifesaver."

"No problem." He tips his hat to me. "If you find her, tell her not to lose you again."

I start to head in the direction he pointed. "I will. Thank you!"

He calls after me, "And tell her to get you some new clothes!"

The library is easy to spot with its bookish posters and advertisements for upcoming reading programs. When I step in through the front doors, my nerves threaten to get the better of me. A large clock on the wall tells me I've already lost an hour of my precious time. Only two more to go before the competition. It's really time to hustle.

There are a lot of people here. How will I find my biomom in this maze of bookshelves?

I weave my way through the stacks. One little girl literally freezes midstep and stares at me, open-mouthed. A young couple ogles over maps in the travel books area but I don't see anyone who looks like my biomom. In the cooking section, I tiptoe around an older man who's sitting right on the floor, a giant stack of dinner party recipe books next to him. There are many people perusing the DVDs and CDs, but no one looks like Reigna.

On the third floor, my feet halt so abruptly it takes my brain several seconds to register why. In the middle of the reading room there's a woman bent over a table as she looks through a large photography book. My heart beats so heavily it's hard to breathe.

"That is my mother," I whisper to myself. The words feel

unfamiliar in my mouth, and I realize I haven't said them in a very long time. Thought them, yes. I've been thinking of her seemingly nonstop for nine years, yet I've never dared to say them out loud. My mother.

This is what I've been working toward.

My dress's corset suddenly feels much too tight as I take a few tentative steps forward. The open book on her table is a little clearer now. European castles nestle between mountains and valleys filled with wildflowers. The woman turns a page to reveal turrets with an ocean backdrop.

I take a moment to look at my mother. Like, really look at her. Her hair is stringy with grease as it hangs lose over her face. Her baggy T-shirt shows days-old sweat spots under her arms. The sneakers on her feet are gray with dirt, the heels worn down nearly to nothing. It shocks me to realize that I can smell her odor from where I stand. That's when I notice the dried urine stains trailing down the legs of her gray sweatpants.

My heart seizes in my chest. Pity and a confusing sense of fear battle inside of me. What happened to this woman? She's nothing like I remember her. She used to take immense pride in her appearance. She wore perfectly fitting dresses, fresh from the dry cleaner. Back then, she never left the house without bobby pins in her long hair and lipstick on her smile—even when she was in the midst of an episode.

When I was a child, she was a regal figure, like a queen who always looked the part. Now even her posture is off. She's slouched forward like gravity weighs her down. Still, underneath the years of decay I can see the woman who I loved. That's still the mom who read me books about fairies and mermaids. She's the woman who loved me enough to leave me when she became a danger to us both.

My biomom starts to wave her hands around her head. Her mouth is moving like she's talking to someone, but there's no one sitting next to her. My heart sinks. Oh, no.

She told me she was seeing doctors and taking medicine. I thought she was getting better, but this looks like she is much, much worse than I ever remember.

What am I doing here?

She sits back in her chair, nodding her head enthusiastically. I can't hear what she's mumbling.

I don't have time to think about what to do next because my biomom looks up. She freezes for several seconds as she takes me in. Her eyes drift from my elaborately curled hair, down to the silver embroidered hem of my gown. I wish I could see inside her mind. I wish I knew what to say.

Reigna's lips set into a firm line. "Good," she says. "You made it."

She waves her hands toward the chair across the table from her, indicating for me to sit down. Apparently whichever imaginary person she had been speaking with moments ago has vacated the seat. I take a few wobbly steps forward and sit, my voluminous skirts making it difficult to get situated. My eyes never leave her face. It's lined with stress. Her pupils jet from left to right as if she's looking for someone.

"Mom," I say in a hushed tone. "Do you know who I am?"

She looks back toward me. "Of course!" She says this as if I'm a naughty child, asking a ridiculous question. "You're my daughter, Her Royal Highness, Jessica, Princess of Denmark, France, and Scotland."

For now, elation fills my chest because she knows me, though I'm still deeply worried about the fancy title she's given me. Is there even a royal family in Scotland anymore?

"Is everything okay?" I ask slowly.

She doesn't say anything.

"I'm worried."

She sniffs.

"I went to your apartment, but they wouldn't let me in."

"What?" She cocks her head at me grimacing.

"The return address, from the gift you sent me." I point to the brooch pinned to my dress's sparkly bodice. It matches my elaborate costume perfectly with its regal design affixed to the delicate beaded fabric. "The front door lady doesn't like me much."

She doesn't appear to recognize the brooch. That stings a little.

Reigna waves her hand in disgust. "I don't live there anymore. They didn't understand."

"Understand what?" I ask.

"That we're special," she says, looking at me intently. "You and me. We both are." Her eyes dart to the bookshelves behind me again. I turn to look, but there's just an old woman poking through the romance paperbacks.

My mother leans close and whispers to me, "They're watching us."

"Who?" I ask in a normal tone of voice.

Her eyes grow wide in panic. "Shhh! The assassins."

There's a bad taste in my mouth. "I really don't think anyone is trying to assassinate us." Maybe she just needs someone she loves to convince her that some of the things she experiences aren't real. Maybe I can show her there's nothing to fear.

But when I look at her, I can tell I've lost her attention again. She's wringing her hands vigorously on top of the photography book. It's starting to crumple the pages. I pull the book out from under her hands and close it. Its title reads *Palaces of Medieval Europe*.

She sees me frowning at the book. "That was our family home for generations," she says. "Before we had to go into hiding. But we'll get it back."

I'm feeling extremely unprepared to challenge this, so I change the subject.

"Aren't you wondering why I'm here?"

"I know why you're here."

"You do?" My eyes grow wide. "Would you like to come?"

A surge of excitement fills me as I imagine my biomom sitting in the audience, watching my team compete. My eyes dart to the clock on the wall. There might still be time for us to go back. We could pick up some new clothes for her on the way to the convention center.

"Of course I'm coming," she scoffs. "What, you thought I'd let you go back to France without me?"

Confusion fills me. France? Did I say something on Insta that made her think the competition was in France?

"I don't think . . ."

She stands abruptly. "You should have told me it was today." Her face has grown dark with irritation. "There's so much I need to prepare." She waves her hands again, like she's shooing something or someone away from her. "None of that matters now. Once we have our inheritance, none of this will matter." She starts pacing with renewed energy.

I'm frozen in my seat. "I think you've misunderstood me. I'm here for the cosplay competition."

"The inheritance is in the Royal Bank, of course." She looks at me meaningfully. "You'll have to buy the tickets. Someone stole my purse." Her voice is growing louder with each new thought. A few people shoot nervous glances our way. A man at a nearby table packs up his things quickly.

"Mom, please sit down. I can explain everything."

"Sit down?" she yells at the suggestion. "They're WATCHING!" She spins around. Several people vacate our section of the library.

My neck is prickling. What do I do?

"Please, there aren't any assassins. They're staring because I'm dressed really strangely. Just . . ." What? Stop freaking out? Stop believing you're next in line to a royal throne? Stop being delusional? Stop humiliating me in public? Guilt eats me alive as I realize I am ashamed of my mother. I am embarrassed that she's yelling in the middle of a public library with urine stains all over her pants and madness in her eyes. I'm mortified that she's freaking out about assassins and royal inheritances that are so obviously not real.

I'm her child. I'm supposed to love her and take care of her. Who could fix her if not me? I thought this would be easy once we met. I thought I'd know exactly what to do, but I don't. Tears start to nip at the corners of my eyes.

"Mom! Calm down."

She whirls on me, staring silently. Her head turns to the side as she whispers to an invisible person next to her.

"My angel tells me you're not who you say you are."

"What?"

"You're not my Jessica. You're an imposter." Her face is growing red, her voice low. "You tried to trick me."

"No, I am Jess. It's really me." I hold up my hands, placating. "I drove all the way from Detroit to compete in the World Cosplay Expo. I came to find you. I . . ." Words catch in my throat. "I wanted you to see me perform."

Why am I turning into a crying baby? What happened to all my hard-earned confidence? This isn't me. I don't shrivel up when someone yells at me. I never get scared. What is it about my biomom that's turning me into a pile of mush?

She points a finger three inches away from my face. Her nails are crusted with dirt. "Prove it."

I'm totally and completely out of my depth.

"How?" How could I possibly prove I'm the daughter she remembers from nine years ago? Especially since I'm *not* her anymore. I've grown. I've changed.

She doesn't answer me. She spins around again, her eyes darting back to the bookshelves. Most of the people have left the area, fled to safer grounds. Part of me wants to do the same, but I can't leave my biomom in distress. I never imagined her delusions could be so powerful, so terrifying. She's not just confused. She's scared too.

I stand up from the chair and walk toward her slowly, my legs trembling beneath me.

"It's okay, shh."

It's not helping. She's ignoring me again. She's arguing with the invisible person. Her angel, she called it. More like a demon, if you ask me.

"Mom, would you please listen to me for a minute? I want to help you."

She keeps her back toward me. "You can't help." Her voice is alarmingly normal. This, more than anything, hurts me the most. My mother is in there somewhere, but she's lost. Unreachable.

Across the room a security guard enters from the stairway. He begins walking toward us at a fast pace.

"Ma'am," he says. "Is everything alright?"

He's looking at me. It's as if my mother's illness has made her both invisible and indescribably present at the same time.

"I'm fine," I say. My voice shakes.

My biomom starts to back away, her head shaking back and forth violently. "No, no, no, no . . ." She reaches for my arm. Her touch is electric. For years I longed for my mother's embrace, but not like this.

I keep my voice low, soothing. "Mom, please let go. You're hurting me."

"Get away!" she yells at the security officer. He reaches for his walkie and calls for backup.

"It's okay," I tell him. "We're leaving."

"I'm going to have to ask you to calm down," he says to my mother.

She's still gripping my arm, twisting it as she continues to back toward the elevators. "They're here for our inheritance. They're going to kill us!"

I can't tell if she's speaking to me or the angel in her mind.

"No one is going to hurt you, Reigna," the security guard says. "You know this. We've helped you before."

He knows her? The shock of this renders my mind fuzzy for a minute.

"Remember a couple weeks ago?" he says calmly. "How we had to ban you from the computer lab for a while because you got very upset? I really don't want to have to take away your library privileges." He gestures toward me slowly. "Let the girl go."

My mother is shaking. "No!" She looks to me with wide, terrified eyes. "They're going to lock me up again. Don't let them take me!"

"Reigna," the security guard says, "if you let me escort you out quietly, no one will take you anywhere. You'll just need to take a break from the library for a few days."

Several police officers arrive on the scene.

My mother sees them. "No!" She starts screaming, tears streaming down her face. "We're going to France! We're going to get our inheritance! We're in line for the royal throne!"

My Goddess, I wish it were true. I wish I weren't dressed as a ridiculous fantastical princess. I wish I were on my way to Paris with my biomom. I wish I had a million dollars to retrieve from a royal bank. I wish I had a palace in the country, far away from filthy New York City. Most of all, I wish my mother weren't sick.

The reality is I can't have any of that. All I can do is help my mother as best I can.

"I need you to listen to me," I say. "They're here to help you."

She jumps away from me like I've turned into sizzling iron fresh from a blacksmith's fire. She stares from me to the police as they inch closer.

"Liars," she hisses. She shoves a nearby chair. It topples to the ground between us.

Behind me, I hear the cops murmur among themselves about an escalation. Someone decides they need to take a different approach.

"Reigna," one of them says in a soothing voice. "We're going to bring you to someone who can help you calm down. Remember the doctors at Bellevue Hospital? They've helped you feel better plenty of times."

It hurts to hear that these people know more about my mother's life than I do.

"Assassins! Help!" My mother darts toward the elevators. The police catch up to her. She fights them like her life depends on it and maybe, in her mind, it does. I stand watching with my mouth open in horror while my mother flings herself to the ground, screaming about murderers and thieves.

I know mental illness can be passed down genetically from mother to child as a biological inheritance from hell. Logically, I've understood this for years. But still, this sight terrifies me so deeply it rattles in the depths of my bones.

"I'm royalty, you can't treat me like this!" She kicks as they cuff her hands behind her back. "Release me or I'll call the embassy!" She tries to bite a police officer's arm, but he evades her.

Outside I hear sirens. When I glance out the window an ambulance pulls up in front of the library.

The elevator dings. I realize I'm about to lose my mother again, just like I did when I was seven. Without meaning to, my feet run after her.

"Mom!" I yell.

The cops look at each other in surprise. One nods and steps back out of the elevator toward me.

"Where are you taking her?" I ask. "Is she under arrest?" There's a terrifying panic that tints my vision in shades of deep purple. It's the color of choking, suffocating death. Oddly, it's also the color of royalty.

"No," the cop insists. "She needs to get back on her medication. We're taking her to the hospital. She's going to be okay."

He's trying to ask me questions. What's my name? How old am I? Whose custody am I under? I'm not really listening.

"Isn't there anywhere else? She doesn't want to go to the hospital."

The police officer shakes his head at me sadly. "No, there

isn't. Not unless she can afford private medical accommodations, which . . ." His eyes dart to my mother in her stained pants.

No one with money would be living on the streets the way my mother has obviously been doing. It's so unfair. If only I were older. If only I had money. If my life were different, I could help her instead of standing here uselessly while she's taken to a hospital against her will. As usual, I'm helpless.

My mother's eyes glare at me. They're filled with hurt. She spits and it lands on the folds of my silver gown.

"You led them here," she says. "You've double-crossed me."

"No." My hands reach out, pleading for her to believe me. "I didn't. I wouldn't."

"You're a filthy traitor," she says. "I disown you."

She may as well have stabbed me with the Prince of Moons' own Claymore of Misery. Tears flood my eyes in earnest now. Spilling over my cheeks.

When I think about why I came here, I want to punch myself. What did I expect would happen if I found her? Did I want her to weep or apologize? To recognize all the pain she's caused me? In the crevices of my subconscious, the truth bares its ugly head. I desperately wanted her to acknowledge the truth—that she is sick. That she left me all alone. Obviously that wasn't going to happen. I hate myself for hoping. I feel childish for even wanting it.

When the elevator doors close, the look she gives me is one of utter betrayal. She called me a traitor. This is a label that I feel I deserve. Deep down, I must have known my fantasy of a happy reunion was a lost cause—a delusion of my own—but I still held on to it with white-knuckled fingers. I desperately wanted to believe that I could get my mom back.

Schizophrenia is a thieving bitch.

CHAPTER 34

TRAGEDY REQUIRES NO VILLAIN.
GUILLERMO DEL TORO, INTRODUCTION TO
THE RAVEN: TALES AND POEMS BY EDGAR ALLAN POE

Everyone stares at me as I stand on the sidewalk outside the library, watching EMS workers load my mother into the back of an ambulance. The cop who realized I'm a minor won't leave me the hell alone. He keeps asking me ridiculous questions.

Who is my father? Where are my other relations? Why am I here? Where's my home? Who should he call to come pick me up?

I don't know. I don't know. I don't know!

I don't know any of my real family. I don't know why I traveled all the way to New York under a childish fantasy. It seems ridiculously naïve now and impossible to explain. My true guardian is the State of Michigan. I never have a "home." Foster houses? Yes. Institutional living? Yes. Pit stops on my way to adulthood? Yes. Home? Never.

Now an EMS worker starts laying into me. Am I going with them to the hospital? Who should they contact for insurance purposes? Do I know my mother's medical history? When was her last psychotic episode? Who takes care of her when she's like this?

Who?

Where?

Why?!

"No," I whisper. "I don't know anything."

The world feels too raw, too real. I start walking away from the library's front entrance at a brisk pace.

"Where are you going, miss?" a police officer asks.

"Away."

"I can't leave you unsupervised right now," he says, hustling after me. "Not after all that."

"Then you'll have to follow me, won't you?"

"Please stop."

"Not happening."

I can hear his feet running on the pavement behind me.

My mind is in chaos. What was this entire mission for if not to find out who my real mother is? Who my family is? Who I am? Where I truly belong?

A grouchy New Yorker bumps into me, nearly knocking me down.

"Fuck you!" I yell after him.

He doesn't even look back. Only in New York City would a screaming fantastical princess in a glittering gown not even warrant a curious glance.

I keep walking. A blessedly cool breeze blows my dress around me. It starts to rain.

Over my shoulder, the cop says something into his walkie.

"Where are we going?" he asks me.

"Away."

"Can I have some specifics, please?"

I pull the hem of my gown up a few inches so it doesn't drag in the dog poop that seems to speckle the sidewalk every few feet. Maybe if it starts to rain a little harder it'll clean this damnable city. Wash away its filth and its decrepitude.

How can people live here? There's nowhere to escape the madness. Everywhere I look, I see masks of anguish on broken faces. The buildings seem to loom over you like brick blankets of oppression. There's poop everywhere. The hot garbage on the side of the road smells like ass. I'm starting to feel claustrophobic in this city with over eight million people.

"I just need air," I mumble to myself. "Why is there no clean air in this city? There's crap, mental hospitals, and police galore, but no frickin' clean air!"

I pull at the sparkling corset of my dress. Goddess, it's hard to breathe.

My voice must sound pathetic enough to warrant a helpful suggestion from my law-enforcing tail.

"You should turn left. Toward the river."

I turn left. Good behavior gets a reward, so I call out my name and my social worker's contact information. There's a fumbling sound as he scrambles to record it.

There will be hell to pay when I get back to Michigan. The state will probably send me back to another group home. They'll call me unmanageable, a problem teen, etc. . . . They'll tell Barbra she did the best she could given the circumstances. I'm just "one of those kids." I've heard that line spewed to a dozen foster parents already.

This just makes me feel worse. Barbra doesn't deserve any of this mess I've created. She deserves someone better, a kid who's nice. Barbra should help a foster kid who won't lie or sneak or take advantage of her, not a kid who's wrapped up in a cocoon of suffocating confusion and fear.

There's a pang in my chest as I realize I didn't just fail one mother today, I failed two.

When we reach the gray Hudson River, I drop onto a soggy

bench. I try to stanch the flow of tears without much success. This might just be the most New York City scene I could have ever imagined myself in. Here I am in all my cosplay glory, crying by the filthy river with a cop shadowing me. In the misty rain. If I didn't feel so miserable, I'd have to laugh at myself. I feel a lot more like a sobbing prom queen than a badass goth queen.

How could I have been so stupid? Why did I want a mother so badly? I'm a strong, independent woman who doesn't need anyone else. Yet here I am, like a disappointing cliché after her date left the dance with another girl. Pathetic.

Behind me, my police shadow says something into his walkie. A fuzzy response breaks through the gloom surrounding me. He calls over to me.

"You want to go inside? It's kinda wet out here."

"Leave me alone," I mumble. My gown is growing heavy in the rain. The puffy sleeves are wilting on my arms like dying flowers. I curl up into fetal position and nestle my head in my arms.

"Okay. Just let me know. Whenever."

The tried-and-true sobbing girl character wins again. Not to mention the added bonus of being a foster kid who just witnessed her biomom have a total mental breakdown.

Foster Care Pro-tip number nine: If you can use the pathetic foster kid label to your advantage, you may as well. There aren't many perks to this life, so get what you can.

I close my eyes and listen to the traffic as cars speed down the parkway.

After a few minutes I hear footsteps walking up behind my bench. Someone sits down next to me. The lack of raindrops hitting my exposed shoulders suggests they've covered me with an umbrella. I'm about to verbally bite their head off to scare them away until I see it's Barbra.

"How did you . . . ?" I can't even finish the sentence because a sob bubbles up into my throat. I can't speak.

I expect her to be furious with me, but all I see on her face is sadness. She doesn't try to rub my back or comfort me the way moms do on TV. I'm glad for that. I would completely fall apart if she touched me. As it is, I'm doing a terrible job of holding it together.

"The police called Michigan Social Services," she says. "Your social worker called me."

I'm property of the government; of course the cops would be able to look me up that quickly. A strange combination of irritation and gratitude combat inside of me. After spending the better part of the semester trying to keep Barbra at a distance, I'm surprised to find she's the only person I want to see right now—even if she is wearing that embarrassing cat sweater.

"I'm so sorry, Jess." Her voice tells me she means it.

The childish sobs start to spill out of me again. There goes all that remains of my composure. I'm exposed. Brokenhearted. A shell of a girl in a silver gown. Once again, I ask myself: How could I have been so stupid?

The brooch attached to my dress stabs my skin. I fumble to unpin it.

"What's that?" Barbra asks.

"A stupid, worthless brooch." It tears free from the fabric. "That woman said it was a family heirloom, but it's nothing but plastic trash." My arm makes a move to throw it into the river. Barbra stops me. She gently unfurls my fingers to take the brooch out of my hand.

"It might not be expensive, but it still has value."

"I don't want it anymore."

Barbra smiles down at it sadly. "Then I'll hold on to it for you. Just in case you change your mind someday." She tucks it into her pocket. "Your mother gave this to you. That in itself makes it priceless."

I'm not sure if my mother really did give that brooch to me or if it was her angel or some other hallucination. Either way, I'm not sure I'll ever want to look at it again. It's tainted now. Tarnished with broken dreams.

"I hate her." The words come out in a whisper. Even as I say them, I know they aren't true. This is the pain talking.

"What you saw was terrible, Jess, but that's not who she really is. You know that, right?"

Of course, I do, but what good is that knowledge when it can't save my mother? It can't bring her back from the depths of insanity or mend all the hurt that lingers in us both. To love my mother is to love an eternal stranger. It's to love the schizophrenia gene monster than haunts me every day of my life.

"She stopped seeing doctors," I argue. "She stopped taking her meds. What am I supposed to think? She gave up on herself. She gave up on me."

Barbra looks down at the ground. "I know she's hurt you, Jess, but it's not her fault."

I shake my head, ready for a counterattack. "I hate her."

"It may feel that way now," Barbra says. "But it's important to remember to have empathy for people like your mother. So few people do. She doesn't mean to be like this."

My hands are shaking with rage. "How can you defend her after seeing the chaos she's caused in my life?"

The damp air is growing chill now, causing goose bumps to prickle my skin. I tuck my feet up onto the bench and wrap my arms around my knees.

Barbra's eyes are pained. "Usually, it's the people we love the most who we hurt the worst. You're right that you need to protect yourself, but try to imagine what this condition has done to your mother, if you can."

Even through my rage, I can't ignore the slow deterioration of a woman I used to love. My mother tried her hardest to protect me from every threat, real or imagined. This disease changed her in so many ways. It's changed us both.

"Mental illness, especially one like schizophrenia, is terribly manipulative." Barbra stares out into the gray river as she speaks. Maybe she senses that I'm primed to lash out. Speaking to the world at large, instead of directly to me, lessens the blow minutely.

"Her own mind convinced her that she didn't need the medications. It told her that the doctors were trying to hurt her. She stopped doing the very things that helped her because she truly believed they were harmful. That's the danger of her illness. It tricks its victims into harming themselves and the people around them."

The scariest part about the schizophrenic monster is that it makes you believe you're not sick. How can you battle a monster you can't see? After all I've done this year to meet my biomom, something has become abundantly clear. This illness is not so much fatal as it is fatalistic. All schizophrenic roads seem to end in predetermined tragedy.

"It's terrifying," I say.

"It truly is."

The mother I remember is gone. What's left is the woman in the library with jumbled words and paranoid thoughts. We'll never have that maternal bond that I envy in so many other mothers and daughters. I'll never have a normal family. I thought I had accepted that a long time ago. This journey proved how deep my pit of denial has been.

"I'm never going to speak to her again."

Barbra's voice is gentle, though firm. "Please don't say that. Right now, you're in pain. It's understandable, but no one deserves to be abandoned. Not even your mother. You know more than anyone how much that hurts. Someday you'll heal. When that day comes, you can try again."

Maybe she's right, but I can't wonder about this "someday" when the pain is so acute today. Right now, I need to focus on self-preservation.

A hand-holding couple walks by along the river path in front of us. They smile as they step gingerly over puddles between fits of giggles. It shouldn't hurt to see happy people, but it does.

"I feel like I'm going crazy," I choke out as I pick at the sequins sewn to my skirt.

"You're not going crazy."

"How could you possibly know that?" I sit up straighter to look at her. "I might end up like her. I have that same poison inside of me."

Just the thought of possessing that hereditary threat inside of me makes my skin itch.

"Listen to me." Barbra grabs my hand. "Even if you *do* need help managing your mental health someday, it won't be the end of the world. It's nothing to feel ashamed of. Do you understand?" She looks me straight in my eyes to make sure I'm listening. "It wouldn't be your fault. Just like it isn't your mother's fault. What happened to her is tragic. You don't have to end up like that."

I pull my hand away. "Don't act as if you know what this is like."

"You're right." Barbra nods firmly. "I don't know what it's like to have a schizophrenic mother, but I do know what it's like to have a mental illness."

"What?" Suddenly it all comes together. The little pills she washes down with decaf coffee every morning. The healthy meals she started cooking. All the meditation and yoga classes. The fact that she doesn't drink alcohol or stay up late. I thought she was just a boring middle-aged weirdo. Now I realize these are all the actions of a person who works hard to take care of their mental health.

"I'm bipolar."

"Why didn't you tell me?"

Barbra leans back on the wet bench and takes a deep breath. "I don't tell most people because they have a terrible habit of judging me in unfair ways. That's a difficult battle most people with mental illness face, unfortunately."

It's true. I've felt the shame, embarrassment, and fear of judgment. After years of listening to people make jokes about mental illness or disempower each other by accusing them of being "crazy," I've learned to be ashamed of my mother. I've learned to be ashamed of myself.

Barbra continues, "That's not really why I didn't tell you though. I knew about your mother. Your social worker told me your backstory when I applied to be your foster mom. I didn't want you to be afraid that I'd stop taking my meds or seeing doctors like your mother did. I won't do that to you. I will always be here for you, Jess."

My hands reach for my head to cradle the ache that's building there.

"I'm scared." It's the first time I've admitted this out loud. I've embraced the darkness in life, all the while hiding from the one thing that truly terrifies me: my own mind.

Barbra puts one cat-sweater-clad arm over my shoulders.

I don't shrug her off.

"If you ever show signs of illness, we can handle it. We'll make it through this life one day at a time. There are so many resources available to help you take care of yourself, if you need them." She leans closer to me, peering into my eyes. "And I hope you'll always consider me to be one of your strongest allies."

I've never had anyone promise to be there for me, no matter what. My mother left, my father is a mystery, all my other foster families gave me up when life got hard, and I've never had real friends until this year. I'm not sure how to respond, so I just do what my instincts tell me. I lean into her shoulder and let her hug me.

She sniffles in response.

I look up at her. "Are you crying?"

"No," she says, obviously crying.

"You really are strange."

Barbra laughs. "I know. So are you."

"I know."

"Guess that makes us a good pair."

Who would've thought a cat-sweater-wearing Midwestern foster mom and a teenage goth-queen-turned-cosplay-geek could get along so well?

Fuzz from her sweater sticks to my lip gloss. I blow it away from my mouth.

"Just one question," I say. "Why are you wearing that ridiculous cat sweater?"

"We're in New York City." She shrugs. "Someone once told me this was fashionable."

"They lied."

"I know." She smiles. "I like it because it reminds me of someone who's important to me."

Together, we sit on the soggy bench, feeling not so alone anymore.

CHAPTER 35

LIFE IS PAIN, HIGHNESS. ANYONE WHO SAYS DIFFERENTLY
IS SELLING SOMETHING.
WESTLEY, *THE PRINCESS BRIDE*

My head feels woozy as we stare at the hotel room door, and it's not because the hallway smells like industrial carpet cleaner. I close my eyes and focus on my breathing to keep from fainting with fear.

"We have to go inside eventually," Barbra says, not unkindly.

"What if they hate me?" I whisper.

Barbra takes a moment to respond. "My advice is to allow them to feel however they need to feel. Just remember that it's not permanent. They might be angry with you, but they still care about you."

I'm not so sure they'll care about me after this huge betrayal. Whatever venom my teammates have in store for me, I deserve it. I lift the keycard to the door. The click of the lock booms in my ears like a death toll.

My ears buzz with the hum of my own heart pounding when I push open the door to our shared hotel room. I step in, smushing my layers of soggy skirts in through the doorframe. The TV is playing *The Princess Bride*, but no one is watching it. They're all looking at me.

They've swapped out their costumes for various versions of

lounge wear. Cici and Gerrit are sitting on one of the beds, leaning against the headboard. There's a bowl of popcorn between them. Gerrit seems to be frozen midchew with a handful of popcorn halfway to his mouth. Emily is staring at me wide-eyed from where she's stretched out on a cot on the other side of the room. And Oscar, the person I was most afraid to face, is leaning forward in a chair, his elbows resting on his knees. It's his eyes that send a lightning bolt of pain coursing through my chest. While I expected to see fury there, all I see is a terrifying blankness.

I know I need to apologize, but it's as if my voice has completely seized up with terror.

Emily jumps up from her cot and leaps across the room. I brace myself for a sucker punch. She throws her arms around my neck instead.

"You giant butthead!" she says. "We were so worried about you!"

Worried? I'd expected fury, uncontrollable rage, seething anger—really, any synonym for extremely pissed off. But worried? That, I had not expected.

Over the sound of her sniffles, I hear Westley arguing with Princess Buttercup on the TV.

"Life is pain, highness. Anyone who says differently is selling something."

So, so true.

Emily releases me. "When you just disappeared, we were afraid you were kidnapped by some weirdo superhero character or something." She looks me straight in the eyes. "Why didn't you tell us where you were going?" She smacks my arm.

Ah, there's the anger I'd been expecting, albeit a severely diluted version.

"I'm sorry," I choke out. "I didn't think you'd understand." My voice sounds hoarse from crying so much.

"Jess." Emily pinches the bridge of her nose like she's trying to channel the patience to speak with an obtuse toddler. "How many times do I need to tell you this? We're friends. I care about you. And I care about whatever the heck you care about. Whether it's freaky cosplay or finding your biomom. I would have helped! Hell, I would have distracted the parentals if that's what you needed!"

Behind me, Barbra clears her throat pointedly.

"I mean," Emily deflects. "No, I wouldn't have. I definitely would not have done that. No, ma'am." She whispers, "But you know I would have, right?"

"I do now," I say. "I should have trusted you. I'm sorry about that."

Emily takes a step back. "Well, I'm glad we've reached an understanding. Now I demand retribution."

"I expected nothing less." My stomach tightens as I brace myself. The damp corset of my dress itches like hell against my skin.

Emily holds up three fingers. "We'll go on no less than three thrift store shop-till-you-drop–style adventures. Then you have to sew an entirely new wardrobe for me based on whatever treasures we find."

I raise my eyebrows.

"I'm thinking something timeless." She puts a finger to her lips as she plots. "Like '80s power suits, suspenders, and other such finery that demand respect. I'm sure you can tailor those to fit me." She waves her hand around like it's no big task.

"I'll do my best."

Emily nods, satisfied.

"And I can't tell you how sorry I am that I threw the

competition." I look to Gerrit and Cici because I can't stand to face Oscar yet.

"You worked so hard to get here," I say to Gerrit. "We all did. I was extremely selfish in taking that opportunity away from you."

Cici's lips are pursed. She's clearly biting her tongue. Of course she'd be mad at me too since I took this opportunity away from her son.

"I mean, yeah." Gerrit shrugs. "We're all really disappointed, but I didn't do this to win anything. I still had a good time until, you know, you disappeared." He looks down at his hand and stuffs more popcorn into his mouth.

"Whew!" Emily says as she skips back over to her cot. "You should have heard him. I didn't know that kid knew so many colorful words."

"I'm over it," Gerrit says through a mouthful of popcorn.

The thing we're all dancing around here is the fact that we all knew how much winning meant to at least one team member, but Oscar still hasn't said anything. My voluminous skirts rustle as I finally turn to face him. He sits motionless in his chair, his hands covering his mouth as he stares at me.

Tears prickle at my eyes again when I look at him.

"Oscar," I start. "I don't expect you to forgive me. I just . . ." My voice breaks.

On the TV, Westley is rolling around on the floor of the Fire Swamp, battling a ROUS to save Princess Buttercup.

I swallow hard. "I'm so, so sorry."

He doesn't say anything. His dark rimmed eyes are unreadable.

Not knowing what else to do, I grab my duffel bag and escape into the bathroom to change out of this ridiculous costume. When I close the door behind me, no one speaks on the other side, though someone blessedly turns up the volume on *The Princess Bride*. Presumably, this is to give me some semblance of privacy. I cover my mouth with my hands and stifle a sob.

In the mirror, I get a good look at myself. Dear Goddess, I am a horror. My once beautifully styled hair is frizzy and damp from rain. My gown is deflated and gray along the bottom from dragging it through the city's street puddles. My face is completely unrecognizable. Mascara runs down my cheeks in rivers, my nose is red, and my eyes are swollen from crying. I look every bit as awful as I feel.

After washing every trace of makeup off my face, I change into my comfiest clothes. Black leggings and my oversized Poe hoodie make me feel a little more like myself, but no less despicable. I pull up the hood to hide behind, like it's a tiny shelter away from the world. The *Labyrinth* dress and wig hang over the shower rail to dry out.

After another deep breath, I emerge from the bathroom. Everyone keeps their eyes glued to the TV this time. On the screen, Inigo and Fezzik have brought a limp Westley to Miracle Max.

"He's dead," Inigo says.

"Woohoo, look who knows so much," Miracle Max responds. "Well, it just so happens that your friend here is only *mostly* dead. There's a big difference between mostly dead and all dead."

If only it were that easy to bring someone back from the brink. I can't sit here and watch TV with my teammates while they all try to pretend like everything is normal. If only Miracle Max were real, I'd buy a miracle of my own to get out of this mess.

I turn to Barbra. "Can I go sit at the pool?" I ask. "I just . . . need to think."

She nods, getting up. "I'll have to come with you, but I'll give you space."

We walk through the silent hotel hallways, avoiding any room service trays lying out on the floor. The flickering lights overhead make it feel like we're in some horror film.

Up on the roof deck, strings of hanging lights make the pool sparkle. In better weather, I imagine fancy cocktail parties happen up here on the regular. What I wouldn't give to wear a black evening dress and drink bubbly beverages with my friends without a care in the world.

Everything on the roof deck is soaked from the rain earlier, so no one else is up here. Barbra grabs a towel, wipes down one of the pool chairs, and sits down to read a book. She's doing her best to give me privacy, even when she has to watch my every move. Which, after my disappearing act, I totally understand. My social worker most definitely left her a long voice mail about keeping a better eye on me, proper chaperone duties, and blah, blah, blah. It's not Barbra's fault I'm a total screwup.

I make my way to the other side of the roof to lean up against the high wall. Beyond our hotel, New York City rooftops glitter. It's a new perspective of the city for me, one that's entirely different from ground level. Up here, you can see far over Manhattan. Lights from windows glow in the night and wind whistles through the tunnels made by tall buildings. Here and there, tiny rooftop gardens give this concrete monster a more human feel.

A clean breeze cools my face. The city even smells better at night.

Behind me, footsteps splash through puddles. I turn to see if Barbra has come to join me, but it isn't her. It's Oscar.

Shame floods my chest again, and my cheeks burn. My hands grip the railing along the wall, bracing myself for what's to come.

Oscar stands next to me and looks out over the city. Neither of us speaks for several minutes.

"You know." Oscar clears his throat. "Before I read *Prince of Moons*, *The Princess Bride* was my favorite book."

Okay, that's not at all what I was expecting him to say first.

"Is it like the movie?" I ask, not sure how else to respond.

"In some ways, yes. In bigger ways, no."

"Hm." I look sideways at him. "Care to elaborate?"

He nods, still looking out over the rain-soaked rooftops. "Its basic romantic principles are the same. It's a story of love, betrayal, and two people finding their way back together."

The moths in my heart flutter with hope.

"But the last page of the book turns everything on its head."

"No spoilers." I say, only half-jokingly.

He smiles weakly. "Suffice it to say, the couple doesn't make it."

The fluttering moths die in my chest.

"That might be a more realistic ending." He turns toward me, and I finally take a moment to look at Oscar. Like, *really* look at him. The damage I've done is written all over his face. His eyes are bloodshot and there are dark circles around them. Stress wrinkles crease between his eyebrows.

"Just, tell me why you did it." He swallows hard. "I need to know the truth."

My hands are trembling. "I guess, I felt that I had to give her a chance. No one ever does because she's sick, you know? No one believes her without making her prove herself all the time. I didn't want the complication of supervision or worried friends. I just wanted to see my biomom, like a normal kid might." I shake my head. "Maybe I was naïve. Or reckless."

"And now?" Oscar asks.

My throat tightens. What do I feel about her now? I haven't really had much time to think about it. This day has been such a whirlwind. Still, the second a thought enters my brain, the truth of it pours out of me.

"Now I feel like I've abandoned her. Like I've always felt she did to me." I rub my hands over my eyes to keep from crying as pain ricochets through my chest. It hurts to say it out loud. I've abandoned my mother when she needed me most.

"You didn't abandon her," Oscar says. "You can't take care of her on your own."

I close my eyes and wish the pain away. I've had boundaries all my life to protect me from the constant pain of foster care, but did I even think of making any for my biomom? I guess not.

"My abuela always says, you need to take care of yourself first, before you can take care of other people." He shrugs. "Just because things went bad this time, doesn't mean you can't try again in a few years, when you're ready and you feel safe."

I just nod. I'm not ready yet, but maybe someday. It's too much to digest tonight. Right now, I need to work on fixing the giant mess that I made with Oscar. He didn't deserve to be abandoned either. When I look at his profile, his mouth is tight without his characteristic smile.

Goddess, I really hurt him. And here he is, trying to comfort me. If our places were reversed, I don't think I'd be as forgiving.

"Oscar, I . . ."

He shakes his head. "You don't need to apologize again."

I swallow the words before they escape. All I want to do is tell him how sorry I am again and again, until this awful feeling of betrayal vacates my soul. I want him to know that I wish I could take it all back. I'd make different choices. I'd stop pushing him away all the time and quit lying to everyone. But you don't get do-overs in real life; that only happens in fantasy. I need to live with my decisions. And with their consequences.

"Here's the thing." He looks away from me again. "When you left, all of my dreams to impress my dad with a big win were ruined. Our chances at getting press to turn the Costume Lair into a real business flew out the window."

His words hit me square in the gut. I drink them all in. I earned them. Oscar needs to tell me the hard truths.

"But that wasn't the worst of it."

I brace myself.

"The worst thing was not knowing what happened to you or if you were safe." His voice cracks. He turns back toward me. Tears make his eyes glisten under the lantern lights. "And even worse than that was finding out that you left without telling me, because you didn't think I'd care."

He sniffles as his face grows blotchy.

"Because I care, Jess. So, so much. And it hurts to know that you still don't."

His shoulders shake as he begins crying in earnest. No one could ever say Oscar is a pretty crier, but the fact that he feels secure enough to cry in front of me might be the most beautiful thing I've ever seen in my cold, dark life.

I throw my arms around his shaking shoulders. "Oh, Oscar. I *do* care." Tears stream down my cheeks too. "I care more than I ever allowed myself to admit."

We hold on to each other as we both ugly cry. Tears and snot run down our faces and onto each other's shoulders, but neither of us lets go. Across the pool, I catch sight of Barbra. Her red-rimmed eyes peek over her book as she cries too, in secret.

When Oscar finally breaks away, he pulls a crumpled tissue out of his pocket and blows his nose noisily. He takes out another one and hands it to me. What a dorky move, to travel with tissues in your pocket. I love him for it.

When we both calm down and look back at each other, we start to laugh. Nervously at first, then uncontrollably.

"Oh, man, we're a mess," I say, finally.

He grabs my hand. His swollen eyes sparkle at me. "Maybe so, but some messes are really beautiful."

"Is that what you were trying to say about *The Princess Bride*?"

He shakes his head. "What I was trying to say is sometimes you have to change canon, because it's what the people truly want. I don't want a sad ending for us. We've both made mistakes."

"Some bigger than others," I say.

"And that's okay." He rubs his thumbs over my hands. "We can work through them together. Westley and Buttercup deserve to have a happy ending, and so do we. This doesn't have to be the end of our story. That is"—he pauses, unsure—"if you don't want it to be. I don't want to be presumptuous or anything . . ."

I throw my arms around him again and kiss him fiercely. Our faces are wet from tears and our noses are stuffy, making it hard to breathe. But, to me, it's the most romantic kiss in all of geekdom.

Beat that, Leia and Han Solo.

CHAPTER 36

THERE IS NO EXQUISITE BEAUTY . . .
WITHOUT SOME STRANGENESS IN THE PROPORTION.
EDGAR ALLAN POE, "LIGEIA"

Late summer sunlight envelops Oscar's ranch-style house in Detroit, but you wouldn't know it by the moody lighting in the Costume Lair. I'm concentrating on a particularly tricky seam that I've had to rip out twice already because I can't seem to sew straight lines today. The seam successfully sewed, I hold up the sheer green sleeve of what's going to become a plus-sized Poison Ivy costume. It's for one of our new customers who I met after joining the Midwest Body Positive Cosplay Coalition. Vacation Vibes Link was so geeked that I signed up, she sent our website to everyone in the group.

It turns out throwing the New York competition didn't mean throwing the whole cosplay business. Thanks to all the attention our team got on the convention floor throughout the competition season, we have more potential customers than we can handle. That's a good problem to have for a small business.

The Costume Lair now has a mission: inclusivity. We choose which projects to take on, and we prefer to work with traditionally underserved cosplayers of the world—we specialize in making fat girls look fabulous, creating genderbending LGBTQ+ friendly ensembles, and developing creative costumes for people with disabilities. Because everyone deserves to look and feel confident in a suit of armor or a kick-ass gown.

At the moment, it's just me and Oscar running the show, with help from Barbra and a constant supply of snacks from Abuela. We've already mapped out next season's looks for our team. Next year, we're focusing on video games. We each chose our own: Oscar wants to do *Zelda: Breath of the Wild* with its somewhat medieval-inspired weaponry, Emily insists on *Horizon Zero Dawn* for the badass female lead, Gerrit wants to do *Apex Legends* since he insists it's the ultimate battle royale, and I selected *Bloodborne* for its gothic aesthetic.

Right now, Emily is out of state at coding bootcamp. When she gets back, she's going to team up with Gerrit on his own video game app enterprise. She said it would look fantastic on her applications for video game design schools. Like she said, she's unstoppable.

Cosplay bloggers have been asking us if we plan to move the Costume Lair to New York or Los Angeles after high school, but no. Oscar and I want to foster a creative costuming community here in the Midwest. Besides, I've finally found my people— my real family—and I won't give them up so easily again.

I reach into my satchel and dig around for the new needles I bought at the sewing supply store yesterday. My biomom's brooch winks at me from where it's pinned firmly to the bag's canvas. It took me a few weeks to realize Barbra was right. I still want it, if only as a reminder of the woman my mother used to be. I haven't heard from Reigna_NYC since the library incident. That doesn't mean I want to forget about her entirely. She is still my biomom, after all. I'm not ready to make contact with her again, the wounds are still too fresh, but I like having a reminder of her.

Maybe someday, when I feel strong enough, I'll reach out to

find her again. Only this time, I know I won't have to do it alone. My support team will be there for me. No matter what happens.

I sip the last of my coffee from a dainty teacup with Edgar Allan Poe's worried face on it.

On the other side of the Lair, Oscar is happily heating up a piece of foam with a blow drier, molding it into submission. He's making one of his *Prince of Moons* swords, which are surprisingly popular with our online orders. We already saw four of them at the last LARP we attended.

Oscar turns off the blow drier and catches me looking at him.

"May I help you?" he asks, brushing his dark hair out of his eyes.

"I was just wondering what you're doing over there."

"Want to come see?"

I get up from my sewing station and walk to his workbench. It's covered in tiny metallic paints and half-finished costume items. One in particular catches my eye. It's a diadem, made of intertwining silver and gold pieces, with a sprinkling of stars at the center.

Oscar sees my interest. He picks it up and turns it to the side. Along the inside rim, I can see tiny words painted in delicate gold ink: "For my queen of the universe."

I look up at him, a smile spreading across my face.

"I made it for you," Oscar says, shyly.

He sets the diadem on my head. It's cheesy, not to mention unbelievably geeky, yet I can't get enough of it. Oscar brushes my long dark hair away from my face with one gentle hand while the other circles around my waist. I lean in as he presses his lips to mine.

It doesn't matter that we're in a stuffy work basement. My life is infinitely more beautiful with Oscar in it—kind, brave, forgiving Oscar with his *Prince of Moons* obsession and his unending cheerfulness. Who would have thought a goth queen could ever fall for a geek king? Before this year, I would have said it was inconceivable.

Knowing wonderful people like Barbra and Oscar, who talk openly about mental illness, has changed how I see my biomom—and how I see myself. My biomom is no less of a person because she is sick. She isn't less worthy of love or health care or a decent life because she has a disability. The world we live in wants us to believe that minds or bodies that look or work differently are somehow *less*, but that isn't true. And while I would give anything to have my mother healthy again, illness in itself is not a crime. It's nothing to be ashamed of.

Most importantly, it does not make *me* less worthy of love either.

There's a loud knock on the Lair door.

Oscar kisses the tip of my nose and breaks away from me.

"You can come down!" he calls up the stairs.

The door creaks open and we watch as old sneakers pad down the steps.

"Hello, friends," Barbra calls cheerfully. "I stopped by for a tea date with Abuela." She sets several small paper packets on a nearby workbench. "I also got some flower seeds at the nursery this morning. Thought you two might want some more."

"Thanks, Barbra," Oscar says. "Jess and I were just talking about visiting mom's grave later this week." He grins as he flips through the different seed packets. "Wildflower mix, bee-friendly blooms, butterfly habitat garden. These are perfect. We'll spread them around graves that are looking a little worse for wear, like Mamá used to do."

Cleaning up old gravestones at the local cemeteries has become a weekly tradition for Oscar and me. Since New York, I've learned we get to choose some of the things we inherit from our parents. I've even started taking yoga and meditation classes with Barbra. It's helped calm my worries over the schizophrenia gene monster.

Barbra sets a thermos of coffee on the table, winking at me.

"You're a saint," I say as I throw my arms around her for a giant hug. This is a new thing for me, hugs. I've never had an affectionate relationship with a foster parent before Barbra but somehow this isn't surprising to me. Barbra has taught me to break all the foster care rules I spent years making. And I love her for it.

She hugs me back. "Anything for my girl."

When we break away, Barbra sees the leafy bodice I've started sewing for the custom Poison Ivy dress.

She runs her fingertips over the tiny red flowers I've nestled among the ivy leaves. "So pretty," she says admiringly. She turns to Oscar. "Isn't my daughter so talented?"

Oscar visibly beams with pride. "She sure is."

Barbra heads back upstairs. She calls down to us as she closes the Costume Lair door. "Don't work too hard, you two."

"We won't," Oscar says, giving me a saucy wink.

I throw a bobbin at him.

He gives me a feigned affronted look.

"Oooh, you're going to pay for that." He grabs one of his foam battleaxes and rushes toward me.

I scurry away from him, giggling madly like a girl in love, because I guess that's what I am.

I've had many trials in my life, but they've all led me here to this odd basement filled with fantastical costumes and fake weaponry. They've led me to a home with a parent who may not be biologically related to me, but who cares about me nonetheless. They've led me to Oscar.

Sure, my life isn't perfect. I've learned that's the case for everyone. I may never know who my biological family members are or if they know I exist. I don't know if Reigna will ever get better or walk back into my life, asking to be my mother again. I don't know if I will ever succumb to the schizophrenia gene monster that still haunts me.

I'll never know a lot of things, but I do know one. I know, deep in my core, that my family is more than my biomom. It's the cosplay community. It's Oscar, Emily, and Gerrit. And it's absolutely, positively Barbra.

So, let this old goth queen turned geek goddess tell you one thing before she leaves this realm. Foster Care Pro-tip number ten: Someday you *will* find where you belong.

Just hold on, kid. It's going to be a wild, painful, beautiful ride.

ACKNOWLEDGMENTS

While this story is a work of fiction, it was inspired by many real experiences in my life. Some of the people I've met along the way deserve recognition and sincere thanks for helping me on this journey, including:

Dixie Harding Balcam, who was the first person to read my stories and the one who loved them most, until the very end. I miss you more and more every day.

All the mothers I've had in my life. Many were temporary, but they each taught me lessons that I'll never forget. Most importantly, Kimberly Harding, who showed me that the best mothers are sometimes the ones you find.

Job Cobb, my agent, who saw my foster care manuscripts and believed they deserved to be read.

All the social workers, CASA workers, group home staff, and foster parents who saw me as more than just another kid tossed into "the system." Particularly Sylvia Smith, who remained my exuberant cheerleader throughout my years post–foster care.

The boy from Somerville High School who cried on my shoulder after a panel when I spoke about having been a foster kid too. You reminded me why representation matters. I will never forget you.

Mari Kesselring and Meg Gaertner, my editors at Flux. I can still hardly believe you love my book as much as I do!

The glorious cosplayers at PAX East and Boston Fan Expo who were thrilled to talk about their costumes, makeup, and the (hopefully changing!) prejudices in the cosplay community: Jay Justice, Jennabelle Chelsey, Kaitlin Mott, John Mott, Ryan Mott, Meghan Corless, Jess Bolduc, and Lucky Grim.

My favorite Michigan ladies: Jackie Best, Irina Thompson, Jess Rosenberg, and Emily Reynolds. We've been through so much over the years, but I'm glad we had each other through it all.

Jordan Kincaid, the talented illustrator who created such beautiful artwork for this book's cover.

The entire team at Flux, who rallied behind this story and its message: Victoria Albacete, Emily Temple, Jackie Dever, and Taylor Kohn. Thank you!

Last, but never least, my wonderful family: Zack Zrull, who supported my dream of becoming a writer, even when I doubted myself. Our daughter, who patiently waited to arrive until there was a break in this book's editing schedule. And, of course, Mau Mau Kitten Cat, for all the snuggles when the writing journey got emotional.

ABOUT THE AUTHOR

Lindsay S. Zrull is a former foster teen and current book nerd. She graduated from the University of Michigan with a Master's degree in Library and Information Science and earned a second Master's degree in Creative Writing from Harvard Extension. *Goth Girl, Queen of the Universe* is her first novel. You can follow her on Twitter and Instagram @LSZrull.